Wabanaki Blues

Books by Melissa Tantaquidgeon Zobel

Wabanaki Blues

Wabanaki Blues

Melissa Tantaquidgeon Zobel

The Poisoned Pencil

An imprint of Poisoned Pen Press

The Poisoned Pencil
An imprint of Poisoned Pen Press
6962 E. First Ave., Ste. 103
Scottsdale, AZ 85251
www.thepoisonedpencil.com
info@thepoisonedpencil.com

Printed in the United States of America

This book is dedicated to my mother,
Mohegan Nonner/Nanu Jayne Grandchamp Fawcett,
who taught me to love and respect the northeast woodlands.

Acknowledgments

Thank You Michael White, Eugenia Kim, Da Chen, Karen Osborn, Nalini Jones, Porrachista Khapour, Randall Zobel, Mandy Suhr-Sytsma, Jacqui Cooper, Robert Rosenwald, Ellen Larson, The Mohegan Tribe, Richard & Jayne Fawcett, Brianna Seidel, Lisa Brooks, Bethany, Jeff, Cassie, Gabby & Emily Zobel, Elie Joubert, Madeline & David Sayet Kalbfuss, Rachel, Siobhan Senier,

The seasons are changing
around us...inside us.

From "Seasons" by Dawna Meader (Passamaquoddy),
Dawnland Voices

Part I

One

Mia Delaney Day

Some days you appreciate the dead; others, you don't dare think about them. Today's a bit of both. I push through the fist-dented double doors of Colt High, my guitar, Rosalita, bouncing against my back. The front hallway is a worn-out chessboard of cracked and broken floor tiles, set with students as game pieces. Diffuse light through the unwashed windows casts a sepia tone over their slack, wary faces, making them resemble old photographs. Most days, this is where you find them jockeying for position as kings, queens, and pawns. But today is the last day of school, the day we remember Mia Delaney, the senior who never made it out of here alive.

Cheer Captain Rasima Jones tries to lighten the mood, leading her bumblebee cheer squad in a practice routine at the center of the chessboard. Blond streaks whip through the girls' matching raven manes, inky bras peek out from beneath their lemon chiffon blouses, neon yellow laces stream over their flipping heads like electric snakes. The bumblebees leap, turn, and revolve in unison, all sticking their landings. Most people clap. I offer a caveman grunt.

One breathless bumblebee overhears me and pokes a finger into my cupcake-pink tee shirt. "What's this? Did they run out of black at the Goodwill?"

I tap my earbuds, pretending not to hear her insult. I'm not about to tell her that it was my grandmother who suggested I wear this shirt, or worse, that she's been dead for three years.

The cheerleader lunges and yanks out my earbuds. Her foot slips on a broken floor tile, sending her crashing onto another square that is already occupied by Rasima's foot. The queen bee screams. Her sympathetic hive swarms, buzzing about how this injury is all my fault.

I hustle away to homeroom, doubting my grandmother's tee shirt selection. She suggested I wear it because she knows I want Beetle to notice me today. Beetle is short for Barrington Dill, or B. Dill. He has butterscotch bangs, licorice eyes, a switchblade smirk, and he wears pastel polos that seem to make him glow. I have mudwood eyes, tree bark hair, and I usually wear black band tee shirts that turn me into my own shadow.

Now do you see the problem?

I zip around the corner that contains Colt High's sports trophy case and accidentally crash into a towering circle of basketball jocks. The circle parts to reveal Principal Millicent Dibble, holding up a third-place trophy. Her yellowed white suit matches her yellowed white hair. Everything about this woman carries a lifetime stain of nicotine.

She hands the trophy to the team's lofty center then points at my tee shirt. Her words rasp, like she once swallowed a cigarette that permanently lodged in her throat. "I see that your tasteless behavior is reflected in your tasteless attire."

Of course, she's overreacting. My shirt is fine. It's a tee shirt for The Dead Kittens band. The cupcake-pink front features a black line drawing of three dead cartoon kittens, lying on their backs, paws sticking straight up in the air, tongues flopping out of the sides of their mouths, and x's where their eyes should be. For years, I've worn graphically violent tee shirts for bands like Mama Cannibal and Kiss the Corpse. Dibble never said a thing. Now, on my final day of school forever, this woman reprimands me for wearing a pink cartoon kitten tee shirt, picked out by my grandmother. I tap my earbuds again, and exit speedily. Everybody is edgy and unpredictable today.

A student whispers "uh oh," and I glance over my shoulder. Principal Millicent Dibble is chasing me and rapidly closing in. I pick up the pace. My guitar, Rosalita, bounces hard against my back. I can't go any faster and risk a fatal encounter between her and some bully backpack. She is a classic Gibson acoustic made of golden curly Sitka spruce, inlaid with a letter "R" on the soundboard in shimmering mother-of-pearl. I think of her as my good luck charm because she was a gift from my grandfather, Grumps, and grandmother, Bilki, when I turned ten.

A finger hooks the collar of my tee shirt from behind, and my neck snaps back. Rosalita's luck has run out. Millicent Dibble's eyes glare at me like two wells drilled into the arctic ice. She yanks out my earbuds and flips through a school rulebook, its pages fluttering like the wings of countless fallen high school angels.

"School policy 14B prohibits the wearing of inappropriate tee shirts. You are in violation. Follow me."

I slump. "My shirt doesn't violate any rules. It isn't low-cut. It covers my stomach."

A freshman girl struts by with half her boobs spilling over the top of a shirt boasting the words "Any Time."

I toss a thumb in her direction and say, "Hello."

Millicent Dibble curls her gnarled finger, summoning me to follow. The clustered girls' soccer team snickers as we pass.

I know what these head-butts are thinking. *This girl got caught with drugs. All musicians do drugs.* Dibble halts at the entrance to the basement stairwell, where a handwritten cardboard sign says "Principal Dibble's Temporary Office" with an arrow that points straight down. A recent electrical fire in her regular office forced this relocation. Everything in this junk heap of a school is falling apart. She signals me to descend the stairs. How dare she force me into the basement, on today, of all days?

I take my first step down, and some kid behind me squeals. Over my head, the fluorescent lights strobe against the mortuary-gray cinderblock walls that connect to a ceiling laden with filmy cobwebs that a person less familiar with the dead might easily mistake for ghosts.

We reach the cement bottom. Dibble pushes a mop bucket and a canister of industrial-strength pesticide away from the entrance to the old janitor's closet. I wonder why the janitor has left his stuff out. She turns a rusty key in his closet door. My cheeks burn. This closet is her new office. Being sent to the school basement is bad enough. Being forced to enter this closet is too much. I freeze and scream inside, begging Bilki for help, begging the universe for help, because this janitor's closet is the spot where Mia Delaney died.

Everyone in Hartford, Connecticut, knows Mia's story. She disappeared nineteen years ago on the last day of her senior year at Colt High, after being seen taking off with her boyfriend on the back of his green-flamed Harley. But they didn't ride off happily into the sunset. The following September, the janitor discovered her starved shriveled body, locked inside his closet. The police never found her mysterious biker boyfriend. Urban legend has it that every year since then, one unlucky Colt High senior meets Mia's unhappy ghost on the last day of school. Some claim she is looking for a friend to keep her company in her hellish high school eternity. Others argue she's trying to bring her killer to justice. I won't be the one to settle that argument because I don't believe in ghosts. I know the dead are more than wispy spirits.

The door to the janitor's closet opens with an unearthly screech, revealing a space much larger than I expected. Millicent Dibble beckons me inside. I detect the scent of dead mouse. My stomach heaves. She drops into a metal folding chair behind a card-table desk. A picture frame lies atop the desk beside scattered paperwork. The walls are bare and the only window in the room is the size of a lunchbox. I lean on a cracked porcelain sink in the corner of this cramped space, as far away from her as possible. Two spectral yellow eyes gleam at me from beneath the card-table desk. I stop breathing. Maybe I was wrong about ghosts.

Dibble tilts her head under the table and calls, "Come here B.B."

Out strolls a potbellied cat with black and yellow fur patches and a zigzag grin. The creature tugs at Millicent Dibble's ankle like a kindergartener. She is a cat-mother, and I'm wearing a tee shirt for The Dead Kittens Band. Perfect. I was better off confronting Mia Delaney's ghost.

Millicent Dibble draws two fingers to her lips as though she wishes a cigarette were between them. "If you go home and change, right now, you can graduate without a mark on your school record. You need all the help you can get in today's job market. Are we agreed?"

I say nothing because I can't consider her offer seriously. It's a violation of my right to free expression as a musical artist. Water drips from the sink behind me. I imagine Mia, locked in this closet, hearing this same torturous dripping sound, day after day, knowing she had all the water in the world and nothing to eat. Millicent Dibble's hand fiddles with something small and rectangular in her crocheted handbag. Cigarettes. She's clearly dying to go outside for a smoke. She doesn't want a long argument. I can get out of this if I play my cards right.

"I believe in freedom of artistic expression," I say. "This is a band tee shirt." I point to the band members' names drawn on the upturned kitten paws on my cupcake-pink shirt. "Scratch plays guitar. Big Cat plays drums. Mew is the lead singer. Get it?"

Millicent Dibble doesn't respond. She lifts her cat and presses her fierce red lips to his zigzag mouth and nuzzles him. Her outdated lipstick smears across her face and the cat's snout, making it look like she and her kitty just munched down a family of field mice.

Her bottomless well eyes return to my chest. "Freedom does not belong to those who harm others. That is why we have jails. Your shirt condones violence against animals. Animals are innocents. People who hurt innocents are criminals. Criminals lose their freedom. Do you get that?"

What I get is that Millicent Dibble is a psycho cat-lover. I won't dignify her remarks with a reply. Her hefty black and gold feline flops off her lap onto the table and swats a paw at the picture frame on her desk, knocking it over. She doesn't move. I want to smack this cat for his brashness. But I worry this impulse may represent a genetic flaw, inherited from my Mohegan Indian grandfather, Grumps. He always keeps his pockets full of rocks, in case he sees a cat. He once explained this habit by saying, "Mohegan means 'Wolf People.' Wolves are dogs, so we hate cats. We can't help it. It's in our DNA." He claimed my mom escaped this tendency because her genes lean toward her mother, Bilki's, Abenaki Indian side, and all they care about are bears.

I'm thinking these thoughts when I hear Dibble's voice, like a faraway echo. "Mona, do you understand why your shirt is inappropriate?...Mona?"

Dibble tries to snap her poor rheumatoid fingers at me to hasten my response, but they fail to make a noise. Her cat lumbers over to lick her crooked hand and shoots poisonous yellow laser rays at me. I wish I had a rock in my pocket.

"I bet you wouldn't bother me if this tee shirt had a picture of dead dogs on it," I say.

A light flickers in her eyes, like a spark from a nearly dead fire. "WHAT! You must apologize to B.B.!" She pets her cat, protectively. "You can't seriously compare him to a dog. Everybody loves it when I bring him in on the last day of school. He's practically our school mascot."

Regardless of the creature's bumblebee coloring and not-so-subtle nickname, nobody at Colt High sees this cat as our bumblebee mascot. I conjure what I presume is a sensitive statement, minus an actual apology. "It's a good thing old B.B. won't need to remain our mascot for long—with our school slated for demolition and all."

Millicent Dibble gasps and caresses B.B., as if I've just punched him. "I'm contacting your parents."

She dials Mom's cell number and asks her and Dad to come here immediately because their daughter has violated a school rule. Dibble doesn't know it, but they won't be here for some time. Ever since Twain College laid off Mom from her professor job and reduced Dad to part-time status, they lounge around our apartment in their workout clothes until noon. They're definitely not dressed yet.

Millicent Dibble speaks smugly from behind her lipstick *schmear*. "Your mother is a volunteer at our local chapter of

PETA. Surely she will be able to convince you of the inappropriateness of your tee shirt, Mona *Lisa* LaPierre."

Mona *Lisa*! Now I have a *real* problem! Millicent Dibble knows my middle name. Nobody is supposed to know it. She better not write it on my diploma or call it out at graduation. I gave up that name in middle school because I'd had enough teasing about my famous Renaissance namesake. My parents officially removed it from my school record when I entered high school, or so they told me. You may feel inclined to laugh about my paranoia on this subject. DON'T. It's not funny. I have the last face on earth that anyone would want to paint, and I never, ever, smile. The only thing I have in common with Leonardo da Vinci's *Mona Lisa* masterpiece is that we both wear black—until today, that is.

I scratch my nails across the wall behind me and cut my index finger on a jagged piece of cinderblock. "How'd you find out my middle name?" I suck on my wounded finger.

Millicent Dibble faces me. Her eyes carry no light. "I know everything about you," she says. "I know you are an excellent blues musician, an average student, too mean to smile, and lousy at making friends."

She lowers her twisted hand to withdraw an oatmeal-colored ball of yarn from her crocheted handbag and tosses the ball to B.B. who claws at it and loses his balance, landing with a splat on the cement floor like an overfilled water balloon.

She lurches forward to prop him up. "You poor thing!"

I let a dry chuckle slip.

Her tone sharpens from a cigarette rasp to a razor's edge. "I will leave you down here for a few minutes to take stock of your careless attitude until your parents arrive—Mona *Lisa* LaPierre."

Hearing my middle name again makes me shiver. She strides out the door, one arm wrapped protectively around

B.B. The rusty door lock screeches to a close. Keys jangle. I lunge for the handle with my bleeding hand. The lock clicks shut before I can reach it. My hand lingers by that handle, vibrating. I'm stuck in the janitor's closet, and my parents won't be here until who knows when. My breathing speeds up. Getting locked in here is every Colt High teenager's worst nightmare. Last year, the girls' varsity basketball team locked three new players in this room for their hazing ritual and a petrified point guard suffered a minor stroke.

"Bilki, where are you?" I jingle the silver charm bracelet my grandmother gave me. It usually calls her right away.

But there's no reply.

I try her full name, "Bilkimizi!"

Still nothing.

I can't believe that didn't work. Speaking her name is the closest thing I know to an incantation. Bilkimizi means "maple tree" in the Abenaki language. Her Indian mother—my great-grandmother—gave it to her because she had a vision of a crimson autumn maple as she pushed her daughter out into the world. It was a perfectly prophetic vision and naming. Bilki grew up to paint New England fall landscape murals, in gorgeous shades of fox russet, golden flint corn, flaming crimson, and squash blossom. She finished each painting with a circular vortex of paint droplets, creating a focal point of swirling leaves that suggested a magical escape portal into another universe. I wish I could step through one of my grandmother's painted leaf portals, right now, and get the hell out of here.

The picture inside the toppled frame on Dibble's card-table desk catches my eye. It shows a much younger Dibble leaning against a classic Coupe de Ville in the arms of a hot guitarist in a stylish straw hat. It would appear that Millicent Dibble is a music lover. Perhaps this is a photo of Mr. Dibble, but I doubt it. I've never seen her wear a wedding ring.

Overhead, thunderous footsteps signal that the opening bell has rung. I imagine my fellow seniors, texting one another about where they'll hang out after school and party to celebrate surviving their last Mia Delaney Day, not to mention four years at Colt High. Meanwhile, I'm isolated on the last day of my senior year, maybe even forgotten, just like Mia. My thoughts roll downhill, dangerously close to the murky bottom. Mom's shrink warned me not to let this happen. "Keep your mind on the mountaintop or you'll wind up like your mom, at the base of the valley."

Everybody in America has some dumb theory about depression. Bilki says working on her murals was her way of fighting it. I imagine painting sloppy crimson graffiti on these walls with my bloody finger. I enjoy imagining that because I know Mom would hate it. She'd prefer these walls remain blank because she says blank colorless spaces help her think. She hates the woods because they're too cluttered. Some Mohegan and Abenaki Indian she is.

Mom inherited neither her family's artistry, nor their love of trees. She has nothing in common with Bilki. She calls her mother's fall foliage murals "inveigling," claiming they draw people in against their will. Granted, my ex-best friend Lizzy sprained her wrist trying to stick her hand through the mural Bilki painted on my bedroom wall. But Mom has no right to talk about inveigling people. With her beauty, she inveigles by simply walking into a room.

My heart races at the sight of a pile of messy dark curls on the floor by the sink. They say Mia had dark curly hair. I tell myself I'm seeing things and close my eyes. I refocus, and reopen them. Sure enough, it's only a dirty rag mop. I still don't like it. I edge as far away from it as possible and pretend to be somewhere happier—frying trout with Bilki in our kitchen, jamming with Lizzy at her brownstone next door, locking lips with Beetle on Rocky Neck Beach. Don't laugh at that last one. It could happen. He's a fanatic fledgling guitarist. You should see the expression on his face when he watches me play Rosalita. It's so beautiful that I almost forget the horrible things he did to me—like his Halloween Facebook posting that read, "Do you like horror?" next to a picture of a vampire, Frankenstein, and me. Beetle swore he was only mocking the Black Fang band tee shirt I was wearing with the salivating red-eyed dog on the front. But I'm not that gullible.

The day of that Halloween posting, I contemplated jumping off the roof of City Place, the tallest building in Hartford. I texted my ex-best friend Lizzy, "Wanna die, yeah, wanna die," borrowing a line from the Beatles' *Yer Blues*. She instantly wrote back, "take a sad song and make it better." You see, we text Beatles lyrics to one another when something powerful happens. We started doing it to make fun of Beetle's obsession with the Beatles, as his almost-namesake. Right after his toxic Halloween post about me, she showed up at my doorstep–bursting with her usual frizzled blond Cherry Coke cheerfulness–and shoved a lit cigarette and a flask of maple whiskey at me. The smoke burned my throat, but the whiskey was worse. It tasted like someone spilled Tabasco sauce on my pancakes. After the third big gulp, I didn't care about the taste.

The sad truth is I love Beetle and the Beatles, which Lizzy deemed peculiar. She said no respectable blues musician would obsess about a dumb-ass pretty boy and a fifty-year-old British rock band. But I don't care; I know what I like. Take The Dead Kittens. Their lead guitarist, Scratch, is the same age as me. After graduation, I want to go on tour with a band—not the lukewarm mess of a band that Lizzy and I cooked up—I mean a *real* band. Or, I might go solo with my blues act and head for St. Louis. I'm moving far away from here, that much I know.

I once told Bilki my ambitions, and she said, "So you want to be a musician? The creation of art and beauty is fraught with sacrifice. One day, you'll need to decide if you're willing to make the sacrifices necessary to achieve your goals or if those goals are a fantasy."

I'll admit me hooking up with Beetle is a fantasy. But me touring the world with my music is a certainty. It's only a matter of time. Trust me.

I play a couple lines of Louis Armstrong's "St. Louis Blues." *I got those St. Louis blues, just as blue as I can be. Oh, my man's got a heart like a rock cast in the sea...*

My face almost slips into a fluffy teen magazine cover grin at the thought of traveling west to the great city of St. Louis with Rosalita, when a shadow crosses my feet. It's Mia, for sure, and I doubt she'll be as friendly as my dead grandmother. I keep strumming in the hopes I can wish away my fate. But it's no use. They say Mia takes revenge on the naïve and vulnerable. And look at me: I'm a senior who's never been kissed, locked in a cinderblock basement cell playing a woebegone tune. I glue my eyes to Rosalita, hoping not to see anything that might be construed as the specter of a dead teenage girl. I don't dare look up—at first, anyway. But curiosity kicks in. I have to take a small peek. I raise my head and see...nothing. What I thought I saw must have been the shadow of some woman on the street, courtesy of the light streaming through the lunchbox-sized window overhead.

Imprisonment is making me crazy. I rush to the locked metal door and hammer my palms against it. My pounding sounds muffled and stuffy, like your hearing does after an airplane flight or inside a nightmare. I need to apply more force. I lift my foot to kick that door but pause when the lock starts to rattle and the door cracks open. I drop my leg. Crooked old fingers appear, winding around the door jam. Millicent Dibble reenters, her raunchy red lipstick neatly reapplied.

"I hope you've had enough time to reflect on your misguided clothing choice, Ms. LaPierre."

Footsteps thump down the stairs behind her. Mom appears and freezes in the doorway, her endless dark hair flowing past the narrow waistband of her yoga pants. She made it here in record time because she didn't bother to change. Fantastic. Mom stares at the dirty mop head in the corner of the room, precisely as I did. Like everyone else in town, she knows the legend of Mia Delaney, although she didn't grow up here. Mom moved to Connecticut from Hicksville, New Hampshire, to attend Yale University. Dad came from a similarly backwater town in French Canada. My parents met at a Yale conference called "Ancient Rituals in The Modern World." That was appropriate, as they both like outdated things. Dad had already been teaching at Twain College for a decade when they met. My guess is their connection landed Mom her job at Twain. Or, should I say, *former* job. I wonder if my parents liked each other back then. Now Dad finds every excuse to fly to remote parts of Russia on archaeological expeditions with his team of adoring graduate students. Mom never travels with him. She loves downtown Hartford and hates everything about everywhere else in New England, especially places that have too much fall foliage. She says it wears on her. What's up with that? She is a psychologist's dream. The only thing she doesn't complain about is our neighborhood on Manburn Street. She insists it has a good vibe—which is pretty funny. Our apartment building is a former cattle slaughterhouse wedged between a former funeral parlor and a former orphanage. My grandmother, Bilki, says places carry spirits, which suggests the sidewalks of my neighborhood creak under a heavy load.

Mom continues to zone out on the mop, her facial muscles limp, like she's correcting freshmen midterms. Clearly, this mop has triggered one of her depressions. They always begin like this. Some photo, or story, or random object elicits an unpleasant memory, and she goes on a mental vacation for days, forgetting all of her responsibilities. I should have reminded her to take her pills last night. On the bright side, whenever she freezes, she instantly transforms into a lovely Land O' Lakes American Indian butter girl.

Wait! I know what you're thinking and you're right. Calling my ex-professor mom a butter girl sounds like a sexist, racist stereotype. She would kill me for even thinking it. But I can't help it; it's true. That's the way she looks—minus the ridiculous butter girl outfit.

Dad's mildewed book, stale coffee scent enters the room ahead of him. Sweat drips from his weedy gray ponytail, and he wears only one argyle sock. After removing his fogged up glasses, he rolls his eyes backwards, way up into his head. He can't help doing this disturbing thing because he has a photographic memory. Faced with any tough situation, he focuses upward, searching the books in his brain for helpful information. Right now, he's probably researching advice on childrearing. I hope he is flipping through some friendly ancient guidebook like *Baby and Child Care* and not one of those nasty parenting texts like *Dare to Discipline*.

Dad's weird eye motions explain why freshman attendance in his Introduction to Archaeology classes has always sucked.

He does better with the upper level undergraduates, and his graduate classes are always packed. The more educated a student becomes, the more they think his eccentricities demonstrate brilliance. Now you see why I'm determined to go on tour with my music and skip college.

Millicent Dibble ignores Dad and addresses Mom. "Lila Elmwood, I realize Mona must have left home dressed in this vile shirt without your notice. I know how much you respect innocent animals. All of your people do."

Your people. Who says that to an Indian? Mom says nothing in response to Dibble's bigoted statement. She's still staring stupidly at the mop in the corner. I don't know much about the technical aspects of clinical depression, but personal experience suggests this is a bad sign. In the good old days before she lost her job teaching Native American history at Twain College, Mom would have rifled back at Dibble's remark with words hot enough to burn her ears off. I miss the old Mom with the Red Power picket signs. Down with Columbus Day! No More Native American Mascots! Save American Indian Burial Grounds! Now she is a mute, frozen butter girl, eyes fixed on a rag mop in the corner of a stuffy basement closet. Dad also stays silent, but for a different reason. His academic field of study is ancient Russian archaeology. Nothing in twenty-first-century America remotely interests him. That includes Mom and me. My parents share one true love, and it's their work. That's why it hit them so hard when Twain College made its cuts.

Millicent Dibble shakes her head at Mom, clearly vexed at her lack of response. She shouts, "Does the girl have a job lined up after graduation? Dr. Elmwood, your daughter needs discipline!"

My ears perk up at her mention of a job because this is a sore point. I *had* scored a great paid internship with the

Twain College music department. But the budget cuts that eliminated Mom's job also killed mine. I got the bad news last week. I expect Mom to explain this last-minute hitch in my employment plans. But she retains her lifeless butter girl pose. Millicent Dibble purses her lips, as if she pities me for having such an unstable mom.

"Dr. Elmwood!" she bellows, rattling Mom back into consciousness.

"Principal Dibble!" Mom barks back, abruptly coming to. "I agree that Mona needs a firmer hand! That is exactly what she is about to experience. This morning, Bryer and I accepted summer jobs on an archaeological field crew in Russia." Mom turns her back on me. "We will be working there for a month to investigate the site of an ancient bear sacrifice. We leave tomorrow."

My brain has trouble processing Mom's words. Surely she's speaking an alien language. What I think I heard can't be true. Or worse, what she said *is* true, which explains why she can't face me. Graduation is a week away. She can't possibly expect me to miss it. Never mind that it's inconceivable for my animal-loving mom to dig up bear bones and force me to spend a month doing that, too. This is the worst idea she's ever had. My guess is she's telling herself that working on her hubby's project will save her rocky marriage.

Millicent Dibble holds her hand to her ear in the universal symbol, asking Mom to speak up. She obviously thinks she misheard her. After all, what mother forces her child to miss their high school graduation? Admittedly, most teenage girls would have a friend's house to crash at if their parents decided to abruptly leave town. But my ex-best friend Lizzy moved to Toronto last year and my antisocial behavior since has backfired on me. I have no money and nowhere to go. Mom has no other choice but to drag me with her to Russia—something neither of us wants.

Mom lowers her voice making me strain to hear her. "Mona won't be coming with us. As she is still a minor, she will be leaving tomorrow for her grandfather's cabin in Indian Stream, New Hampshire, where she will be in firm hands."

My ears sting. My blood turns to ice. I thought missing graduation and digging up bear bones in Russia was the ultimate disaster. Now I know I was wrong. I will be spending the next month alone with my widowed grandfather, Grumps, somewhere in the New Hampshire wilderness. I've never visited his cabin. Until now, Mom insisted it was best for us to stay away. Now she's forcing me to live in a place she always avoided because of some stupid law that says I need some adult to look after me until I'm eighteen.

If Bilki was still alive, this might be tolerable. I loved my grandmother's annual Christmas visits to our home. We had so much in common. Sure Grumps came along, but we all tried to ignore him. Now, I'm spending a month alone with him! All this because of my unfortunate July birthday. Until then, I'm seventeen and a miserable minor. Summer birthdays suck!

Millicent Dibble reads my mind. The corners of her wrinkled red lips jolt upward in a wicked grin. "It's such a shame that Mona will miss her graduation. But I'm sure this experience will do her good. The least I can do is release her from school early today, so she has sufficient time to pack."

This is the final blow! Packing for the worst trip of my life is not my idea of a good way to celebrate the end of high school. Not that I planned to do anything new. I wanted to celebrate like I did junior year, when I jammed with Shankdaddy, the old blues man whose sweet music drew me to the other end of Manburn Street. I found him sitting on a worn-out stool on the metallic steps in front of Celine's fortune-telling parlor, beside a mangy cat. (What's up with me and cats?) His eyes whirled smoky gray, begging me to come closer. I sat beside him and admired his music, his chiseled cheekbones, and his lean muscles. His music hurt sweetly, like a caramel-coated toothache, and his cheekbones stood so high and mighty, you'd swear they'd been carved in granite. This man was ageless and omnipotent, like the God of Blues.

Once I started playing guitar with him, Celine stepped outside to listen, along with a few other curious neighbors. It must have sounded pretty damn good. After we finished jamming, I was shaking from the power of his mighty blues. I told Shankdaddy I was dropping out of school to hit the road and become a musician. He laughed cruelly, showing the raw pink tops of his gums beyond his big white teeth. He pressed his face into mine, challenging me, letting me know that he could always do me one gritty one better—whether it was bending notes on a guitar or bending the rules in life. Of course, I understood all that. I endured his test of will because he was the Master, a man who didn't just sing about hard times but conveyed them in a preternatural way. His music told me things about the universe that I'd have been better off not knowing—like how people who kill for love turn into ugly fiery angels that burn everything in their path, especially those who make beautiful music. When I didn't flinch at his tale, he decided I was worth a shiny pearl of gutbucket wisdom.

"Guitar Girl," he said, rising to the full extent of his impressive height. "What you don't understand is that you need to *become* the blues. You gotta let the blues fill you up so that every note hurts enough to make you double over and groan."

I reminisce about this amazing man while I trudge up the school basement stairs, trailing behind my parents. Knowing

I'm leaving Colt High for the last time, it occurs to me that while I can't be with Shankdaddy today, I can make him a promise. I swear in my heart that I'll play the kind of blues he admires, or die trying. Step one in the right direction is avoiding banishment to the musical desert of New Hampshire. Maybe I'll run away to Toronto, where Lizzy lives. There are plenty of hot blues venues there. Greyhound has cheap bus tickets. I might be able to sneak onto an Amtrak train. I've read that tribal IDs can work as passports for the Canadian border-crossing. I've got one of those, thanks to Mom putting me on the Mohegan tribal rolls. I've often wondered why I'm not on Bilki's Abenaki tribal rolls. Mom probably kept me off them to spite The Inveigler, even though she claims the United States Government forced her to pick a single tribe. Mohegans or Abenakis. Hatfields or McCoys. Crips or Bloods.

I hear Bilki whisper inside my head, "Go to New Hampshire. It will be fine because I'm watching over you."

Her words loosen my tightened muscles and allow me to exhale. Somehow, I believe her. When I was a kid, she would point to the constellations of The Hunter and The Great Bear and tell me how people turn into stars after they die. I know she's there, among those starry constellations. Whenever she speaks to me, I feel a connection to them.

I raise my head to the heavens and ask my starry grandmother to save me from my looming summer nightmare. Bilki doesn't respond exactly but I experience a woozy rush as we emerge onto the main floor of Colt High. Through the old-school sepia light, I spot a pretty girl smiling at me. She's wearing a retro Rush band tee shirt featuring a rabbit coming out of a hat. Her wide emerald eyes, heavy dark curls, and huge silver hoop earrings carved with the word "LOVE" across the center make her look more like a Rosalita than my guitar. Her shirt shows half her stomach, which is a clear violation of school policy 14 E. Her manicured fingernails flash electric blue as she scribbles something on the wall in front of us. Despite the fact that graffiti is a breach of every school rule on the planet, Dibble strolls by her without a word. It's ridiculous what pretty girls can get away with.

I dip Rosalita's neck at the girl, respectfully, because we know one another, sort of. We met last year when I was hanging around Celine's fortune-telling parlor with Shankdaddy. She and I never actually spoke. But she'd smiled at me that day, too, in a way that told me we were sharing the music at a deeper level, and pretty girls don't normally share intense moments with me.

The second period bell rings. Beetle spills out into the hallway, sporting a peach sherbet polo. I fast finger some delta blues on Rosalita, struggling to keep calm.

"Whoo-hoo, Mo-na! Nice tee shirt!" he calls, tossing back his butterscotch bangs and flashing his switchblade smirk.

I glance at Mom to see if she's catching this miracle moment. I want her to feel extra guilty about forcing me to leave town, just as the school's most popular guy decides to talk to me. But no. She's caught up in Millicent Dibble's rant about how the school board is too cheap to replace the faulty wiring in her upstairs office so she's stuck in the janitor's basement closet until they demolish our school in the fall.

I lift my head from my guitar and catch Beetle's licorice eyes focusing, not on my fingers, but on my tee shirt. My brain turns to strawberry slush.

"Hey, bad girl," he says, pointing at my chest. "I'm guessing this tee shirt earned you a ticket to our cat-loving principal's basement luxury suite. I didn't know you were a fellow Dead Kittens fan. I saw them perform in Stadt. It's my favorite city."

I keep playing in order not to scream. Beetle is acting like we're old friends. I can't believe he loves The Dead Kittens. I've never heard of Stadt. I have to get out of Hartford. There are so many great cities I need to see. If only I could take him with me.

He tugs my sleeve, "Did you see our resident ghost down there? It *is* the last day of school."

I don't understand how he can speak so casually about Mia Delaney. He sticks his hands in front of my face and wiggles his fingertips spookily. I remain mum.

"Mia Delaney was my dad's high school girlfriend, you know," he prods.

This remark irritates me because I know he's lying, like he's lied to me before. I slump, in the cool bluesy way Shankdaddy taught me, and say, "Everyone knows Mia left school on her last day with a guy on a Harley with green flames. Your dad doesn't strike me as the biker type."

"No." He moves in dangerously close. "But Mia was the type of girl who had more than one boyfriend. She was a bad girl." He winks.

"Right. I doubt that. Your story sounds like a tabloid headline: Bad and Beautiful Juliet Slain by Wicked Romeo." I clutch my chest. "They were young lovers so they had to die." I shoot him my muddiest glare. "It's a tired tale."

He smirks. "True enough. It is the cliché moral our parents tattoo to our souls: teenage sex always equals death."

I lift my mudwood eyes to meet his delicious licorice stare.

"Mona!" calls Mom, storming toward us, scowling at Beetle like she wants him to die. She must have been eavesdropping and heard the word "sex." If she were listening, it would be the first time she's tuned into one of my conversations in as long as I can remember.

Beetle's carrot-topped, perennially stoned best friend, Brick Rodman, ponies up and drags him away to class before I can ask Mom what her problem is. Beetle waves good-bye to me. I imagine I see a look of regret on his face. I never asked him where he's going to college. I want to ditch Mom and tell him that we should jam together sometime soon. But the truth is, I won't see Barrington Dill ever again. High school is over for me. Beetle is over for me.

Rasima's mom and dad trudge toward Millicent Dibble, arms wrapped around their limping daughter with the bag of ice tied to her foot. I can't afford to get dragged into a discussion about the cause of Rasima's injury, so I tell my parents I need to grab some stuff from my locker. From behind the metal door, I text Lizzy to cue her into the miracle that just happened between Beetle and me.

I write, "Help! I Need Somebody!"

"Let It Be," she replies.

Lizzy is right, of course. I need to settle down. Nothing really happened between Beetle and me. Nothing ever does. He likes to think of me as his artsy musical acquaintance. Everybody has one. Nobody dates them.

I head back to the main hallway and note with relief that the Jones family has departed. Naturally, Beetle is heading in the direction of the graffiti girl with the LOVE earrings. He is smirking worse than ever. It's easy to imagine what will happen next. The whole school knows the effect he has on women. Rasima said it best in our school blog, *The Weekly Stinger*, "Beetle's smirk is like a solid gold mirror with a crack in it: something that you must stare at, even though you know it will bring you years of bad luck." I don't agree with Rasima on much but she was dead-on about that one.

Beetle passes right by the graffiti girl and opens his arms to hug Dibble. What a suck up! He must be bucking for the Principal's Prize at graduation. I strain to listen to what he has to say to her.

"Thanks for everything, Principal Dibble." Beetle hugs her.

Dibble rasps, "I know you and some of your friends are headed to your family cottage on Lake Winnipesaukee for a few weeks after graduation. Enjoy yourselves." She sighs. "Oh, how I love New Hampshire."

The universe spins like I've fallen into a vortex in one of Bilki's murals. Beetle is going to New Hampshire. I'm going to New Hampshire. I've overheard tales, from girls with good hair, about endless summer parties there with boys who smell like cocoa butter. Up until now, that lake has been an imaginary place, never mind one I might visit. I live in the real world, where family discussions center on how to pay rent and utilities, not how much money to blow on long summer vacations. The kids in my neighborhood are lucky if their parents take them on an annual day trip to Mystic Seaport, Roger Williams Zoo, or Fenway Park. A month of lounging by some New Hampshire party lake is an unimaginable fantasy. Yet I'm on my way to that dreamland. Bilki must have a hand in this. This is one day when I truly appreciate both the living and the dead.

Overhead, the hallway lights flicker with a sparkling galactic majesty, offering all the possibilities of a glittering newborn universe. Through the hall windows, the summer sun beams down on me with the pure, glorious, healing white light of a loving cosmos. The hint of a first smile tugs at the left corner of my mouth. My heart is beating so hard that I swear it pumps life back into the dead kittens on my tee shirt. I glance down and see them dancing in a circle on my cupcake-pink chest.

From now on, I know things will be different. I lift the collar of my shirt and kiss it. I'll wash it on the gentle cycle. It's my new good luck charm.

Two

Light-years from Lake Winnipesaukee

Dad's famously mobile eyes sprint from me to the front door of our apartment. "I can't believe you're still in your room, wearing a towel. We can't miss our flight. This research trip is going to prove a link between ancient bear sacrifices, worldwide."

A monstrous bear claw necklace—from some creature that I hope to God lives where he's going—dangles from a leather rope around his wrinkled neck. I want to yank it off and tell him I'll take my bloody time because no one cares about his stupid bear rituals, his necklace looks ridiculous, and he lives in a delusional world of his own. Yet I say none of this. I'm still in shock from pulling up the Google map that says it's a three-and-a-half-hour drive from where I'll be staying in Indian Stream to where Beetle is vacationing on Lake Winnipesaukee. My Dead Kittens shirt now lies inside my bedroom trash can.

"Your daughter is nowhere near ready," Dad tells Mom, as he grabs two suitcases and storms toward the car.

Mom enters the room, smelling like fresh apples. She flops onto my "Meet the Beatles" comforter, wearing khaki shorts and a sky-blue blouse, knotted at the waist. Her hair dangles in a shiny braid. A red bandana wraps around her forehead in badass-Apache style, accentuating the two-inch scar on her left cheek. She looks like a Native American superhero. I loathe her.

"Are you here to gloat over my banishment from civilization?" I ask, slumping worse than usual.

"No matter what you may think, Mona, this trip isn't about me wishing you away." She peers out the door, eyes narrowed, as if she's staring down an invisible foe. "You need to spend some time with Grumps and your Abenaki relatives. There are important lessons they need to teach you."

"If these Abenaki relatives are so wonderful, then why did you desert them years ago?"

Mom trembles, probably from taking too many pills. "It's not what you think. There's so much I want to tell you about why you need to go north, about why I need to take this trip with your dad." She slaps her hand over her mouth and hurries out of my room.

This doesn't faze me because I'm accustomed to crazy behavior from my unbalanced Mom. In fact, seeing as how my parents are both crazy, I decide to give lunacy a go. I approach the mural Bilki painted on my wall depicting an autumn woods landscape. A vortex of colorful paint droplets swirls at the center. It looks like a real portal. Now would be the perfect time for me to discover that it's possible to step though it into another universe. I edge forward with my eyes shut, make a wish, drop my towel like Lady Godiva, and lift a leg. My knee whacks the wall, and it throbs like the time I tried out for soccer. My last-ditch escape plan has failed.

I make one final check of the contents of my duffel bag. I've packed the standard everyday travel junk plus a bunch of tee shirts too loud to wear in Hartford. I yank a caution tape yellow shirt over my head. It shows a picture of the amazing Etta James on the front, under the words "Rage to Survive." Mom hates yellow. I emerge from my room, triumphant.

"Yellow? Rage to Survive? Really, Mona." Mom swats at my tee shirt like it's a hornet. "Don't you dare start one of your downhill slides. Not today. Stay on the mountaintop," she says, quoting our shared shrink.

"Don't worry. I'm headed for the mountains today, whether I like it or not." I sneer as she grabs her laptop and heads out because I'm thinking of the rare Beatles butchered baby-dolls tee shirt I found on eBay last night. I wonder how she'd like to see me in that? Somehow, I've got to find the money to buy that shirt.

I focus on my silver charm bracelet from Bilki. This bracelet always comforts me. Bilki collected dozens of personal charms for it, including an artist's paintbrush, palette, and easel. It also has a wolf for Grumps, a history book for Mom, and a bunch of stuff that presumably represents her life in New Hampshire: a log cabin, a woodstove, a bear, an eagle, a maple leaf, a powwow drum, an arrowhead, a moccasin, a robin, a trout, a spider's web, a key, a mushroom, and an eight-pointed star. Before she gave it to me, she added two new charms, a guitar and a musical note. Every time I jangle this bracelet, I know Bilki can hear me.

On the ride north, I sleep soundly until my head slams into the car window. I feel like I'm careening down a ski slope. This sensation tells me we must have crossed into mountainous Vermont. I pull myself up and notice a sign pointing east that says "Lake Winnipesaukee — 100 miles." That's not far. This must be fate. I've never hitchhiked but I'm willing to try it; people do it in old movies all the time. Only in modern films does it result in rape, robbery, or murder. Besides, we're in Nowhere, Vermont. What could possibly happen here?

The silver car-door handle gleams, beckoning me. I contemplate my odds of surviving a jump from a moving Volvo at seventy miles an hour. I picture Beetle by the lake. He's tanned, shirtless, wrapped in a designer beach towel, surrounded by a harem of perfect hair. My fingertips wind around the warm door handle. I put a hand on my already sore head to protect it from impact with the road, and lean in.

"Lila! Do you know it's already three o'clock?" booms Dad, tapping his vintage Soviet wristwatch.

I jerk my hand back from the door and wilt into the corner of the backseat. In the rearview mirror, the road sign for Lake Winnipesaukee shrinks behind me, along with my hopes for the summer.

"We'll make it on time, Bryer," she says, while fiddling with the radio knob to locate a station with decent reception.

Dad baritones, "We don't have time to stop and chat with your father."

Mom holds up both palms, defensively. "Not to worry. None of us wants that." She connects Dad's phone to the car speakers. "Let's listen to your Mongolian music medley."

The stampeding drumbeat sets Dad's narrow shoulders bouncing up and down. Frankly, even this is better than endless talk shows on National Public Radio. None of us speak while the Native drums thunder. We all fall into it. Mom and I are accustomed to heavy drumming. We've heard it every summer since I can remember—at the Mohegan Wigwam Festival—her annual pilgrimage to Grumps' traditional territory to remind me of my Native American roots. I've run into a few Abenakis there. But not as many as you might think. Mom says most of Bilki's folks keep to the northern woods, thanks to the colonists offering bounties on Abenaki scalps in New Hampshire. Naturally, that made them wary of outsiders. Of course that was a long time ago. But Mom is a historian and often confuses the past with the present.

Our mighty red Volvo—which I fondly call Red Bully because it either seems to have plenty of energy or refuses to budge—syncs to the beat, rising and falling as it winds around the mountain roads. I feel like I've entered one of Bilki's painted portals, swirling through time and space. My stomach churns from all the swaying. Acid lurches into my throat. Mom pales. That's when it hits me—a memory I'd rather forget. I try and push it out of my mind, hoping Mom and I aren't thinking the same thing.

She turns down the music. "Bryer, don't these winding roads remind you of that awful Goliath hypercoaster we rode when we visited your parents in Montreal?"

Oh, no. We're thinking exactly the same thing. This nauseating drive reminds us both of the day I rode that amusement park ride and threw up all over my French-Canadian grandparents. I was four years old, and we haven't received an invitation from Ma-mère and Pa-père since.

Dad's normally pasty skin turns the color of the evergreens that now line the roads. This is one of those times when I know he's cursing his photographic memory, grimly envisioning every detail of that ill-fated family trip to Montreal. He opens his window. I do the same. The road straightens, and I'm relieved. Yet Dad's nauseated look remains. In fact, it worsens.

"Lila, you should have told my parents the truth about everything, right from the beginning. They had a right to know."

"When we were first married, you said they wouldn't care."

This is a mysterious conversation. It sounds like there's more behind my grandparents' rejection of me than kiddy puke. I'm not surprised to hear Mom lied to her in-laws about something. She's never up front about anything. Dad is just as bad. When I asked him why digging up bear pits was more important than my high school graduation, he told me, "because the universe depends on it." Can you believe it? My parents care about their weird secrets more than anything, certainly more than they care about each other, or me. I have no idea why Mom married Dad. She's half his age, and she doesn't give a hoot about Russian anything.

Dad resumes speaking with forced calm, "I never said my parents wouldn't care, Lila. What I said was—"

"Look out, Dad!" I shout.

A logging truck careens around the corner, on our side of the road. Dad swerves away to a spot where the pavement has eroded, with only a chasm beyond. My body turns cold. Our tire slips into the abyss, tilting the car toward the passenger side. This is it. I tell Bilki I'll be seeing her soon. Rocks grind beneath our churning wheels. We slip lower. I kiss Rosalita good-bye. Dad revs the engine and somehow grinds back out, avoiding disaster. Yay, Dad! Yay, Red Bully!

We, three, remain soundless for the next few hours, until he turns off onto a road plagued with jarring potholes and frost heaves. Mom breaks the silence with a strong series of curses as she cranes her ballerina neck out the window, searching for the turn to Grumps' place. There are no street signs, only a dense skyline of spruce, pine, and hemlock, broken by leafy patches of oak, sugar maple, and white birch.

After one false alarm, during which Mom gives Dad bad directions that nearly send us off another abyss, she shouts, "This is *definitely* it!"

We turn at a cluster of four white birch trees onto what looks to me like a flooded hiking trail. Mom shrieks. Dad hits the brakes, splattering the windshield with mud. Through the muck, I expect to see another fatal cliff. Instead, I spot a giant charcoal-colored dog, bounding through the sloppy trail ahead of us. Only, he doesn't look quite like a dog, and I catch a whiff of musky honey. Dad and I are speechless at the sight of this huge animal that is gone before we can get a good look.

"That's a female black bear," Mom explains, as if she's lecturing to one of her idiot freshmen classes. The scar on her cheek reddens. "Bryer, you should drive more carefully or you'll hit one of your research subjects!"

"*I* should drive more carefully? That's pretty funny, coming from you," he says.

A sudden lump forms in my chest. Dad just broke our family taboo. No one jokes about Mom's poor driving. She had a bad truck accident as a teenager in which she killed an animal—a dog or deer or something. The details are never clear. Bilki said it devastated her. According to Dad, that incident is what kicked off Mom's PETA passion and her depression.

Mom rummages in her pleather purse. "Where is my medication?"

Mom believes her meds are the solution to everything, when in fact there are some simple lifestyle changes that would make her instantly happier. For example, we could move out of our refurbished cattle slaughterhouse apartment. Were that to happen, I might give up vegetarianism. But I doubt that will ever happen because when I once asked her how she could stand living there, considering how much she loves animals, she said she felt compelled to keep the unhappy animal spirits company. No wonder she needs antidepressants.

Dad gestures down a muddy sewage-brown trail through the forest that's barely the width of a single car. "This is it,

Mona. Your grandfather's house is right through here. We'll get stuck in the mud if we go any farther."

"Bryer, you can't expect Mona to walk through these terrible woods alone. I swear you treat her as if…"

He interrupts. "Watch it, Lila. Neither of us wants to get into that discussion right now."

Mom reburies her head in her purse. "Here it is!" She retrieves a plastic medicine bottle, lifting it into the sunlight like an idol. After fumbling to open the lid, she gags down a pill without water and squeezes my cheeks so I can't look away. "Mona, I have to be back in Hartford for a fund-raiser in mid-July, for International Homeless Animal's Day. We'll see you then."

I pull her hand off my face. "What about International Homeless Teenager's Day? You can't leave me here." I jiggle my bear charm in her face. "We just saw a real bear. I'm not getting out of this car."

Mom is stone-faced. I shake my bracelet harder, hoping to get Bilki's attention. My grandmother needs to witness her daughter's neglect.

"Bears are rare in New England," scoffs Dad.

My mouth freezes wide open.

Mom pops a second pill.

Dad speaks between clenched teeth. "If you're frightened, Mona, perhaps your mother should stay here with you."

Mom chews out her words, "Don't you dare start that again, Bryer."

"I'm serious, Lila. You need to face your demons. We both know you only married me to get away from this place. God knows, you don't want to go on this dig. I'm sure your old hometown buddy, Will, would be happy to let you move in with him."

"Mom, who is Will?" I ask.

"Your father is talking nonsense, Mona. There was never anything between Will and me."

Mom whispers something to Dad. They pull apart and lean against opposite car doors, fuming.

I perform a three hundred and sixty-degree scan of my surroundings. "How about we ditch this plan. You can drop me at the nearest train station. I'll find my way home and stay out of trouble. I promise."

Mom's smile quivers. "Dr. Zee says you shouldn't be alone, Mona. Besides, what would you live on? You don't have a job. We're broke. Remember?"

I doubt Dr. Zee was consulted about my summer banishment. But Mom is definitely right about the money thing. I saw Dad Skype the folks in Russia, last night, begging them for a cash advance.

"You'll be fine here, Mona," she continues. "The animals won't bother you, if you don't bother them. You need to take a reality check and start walking."

This woman, who just dry-swallowed two la la pills, is telling me to take a "reality check." I picture myself gathering her mountain of precious research notes into a pile and burning them in a beautiful bonfire.

Dad pats my arm with the back of his hand, in a careless farewell. According to him, hugging and kissing is for folks with more brawn than brains. He could be right. Beetle and I both got D's in Algebra. I love to picture Beetle's muscular arms wrapped around me while he presses his smirking lips into mine, even if there is no point in daydreaming about him anymore.

I shake myself back to consciousness and try to sound reasonable. "Let's call Grumps to make sure he's home."

My father wipes his fogged-up glasses. "There's no need. Your grandfather is expecting you. We're here a bit early but he never goes anywhere."

Mom arches her perfect eyebrows at him. "Your father is right. Nobody up here ever leaves."

Dad's pupils start moving, not quite flipping all the way back into his head, but bouncing upwards. After briefly searching his brain for the right file, he says, "Nobody up here ever leaves, eh? Unless, she's a beautiful young woman who cons an older man into helping her escape from a crazy family that believes their Native American myths are real."

"So now you were conned into marrying me," Mom snivels into a tissue.

"Wait just one minute, Lila Sassafras Elmwood..."

This could go on for hours. Their arguments loiter into doomsday. A forest full of hungry bears suddenly doesn't seem so bad. I open my door and hop out of the gear-stuffed car, landing with a muddy splash, splattering myself up to Etta's eyebrows. I grab Rosalita and my duffel bag and slog through the brown goo.

I check the bars on my cell phone and notice there's no reception. "Please don't tell me there's no service here."

They take a break in bickering to shake their heads no, like two bobbleheads from the Disney villains collection.

"That's great," I groan.

Something black slithers past my muddy ankle, and I shriek. "Was that a deadly water moccasin snake?" My eyes follow the slimy ripple into the shadowy woods.

Mom hangs out the window for a look. "Reality check, Mona. There are no water moccasins this far north. That was only a black racer snake. Scary, but harmless."

Before today, I'd never seen a bear or a snake outside the Roger Williams Zoo in Providence. I react like any dufus confronting danger in the wilderness: I crack a joke. "Bears, snakes. I'm guessing the flesh-eating *Windigo* will be next. Right?"

Mom wrinkles her nose at me as if I've failed to research the correct assignment for her Native American history class. "*Windigo?*" She speaks this northern Indian word with a Canadian accent. "*Chenoo* is the only monster people talk about around here. You should know that. But don't worry. It's been years since anybody's seen one."

I think hard, trying to remember anything about a *Chenoo* from summer camp story time on the Mohegan reservation. Nothing comes to mind. It must be a northern Indian thing. Mom is notoriously stingy about sharing her mother's traditions.

Dad waves limply. "Farewell Mona. You'll be fine."

He steers into a tight U-turn. Red Bully thumps over a couple of boulders and sprays my face with mud. Mom waves at my mud-freckles until her strained face disappears past the familiar cluster of four birches. I wonder if she's really going to Russia, or checking into some drug rehab facility.

Something shifts the moment my parents disappear and it's just me alone in these woods. I may be what Grumps calls a "City Gal," but I sure don't hate trees or fall foliage, like Mom. The mud engulfing my feet isn't that bad either. It's warm and soft, welcoming actually. Like the trees. The sun has just slipped below the horizon, and suddenly everything is illuminated, glowing, like each tree radiates its own light from deep inside. The general lack of manmade noise adds to this effect. There are no beeping crosswalks, no squealing brakes, and no blasting car stereos. There's not another human being in earshot, like I'm in one of those religious movies where all the good people rocket off planet Earth and leave us losers behind. But it's not really silent. The sounds, here, are simply new ones. These woods have their own melody. My soaked Chuck Taylor sneakers gurgle and pop in the mud. Bee-boppa-loo-bop. Not far away, something grinds low and throaty, in a real Ray Charles whiskey growl. That growl is coming from a different direction than the black bear we saw earlier. How many bears can there be up here? Until today I thought they were extinct in New England. Surprise on me. I focus on more comforting sounds. A whippoorwill whistles its shrill evening cry, and a redheaded woodpecker offers a jazz downbeat—ratta-tat, ratta-tat-tat. This place may not be as much of a blues haven as Shankdaddy's neighborhood at the other end of Manburn Street, but it's definitely got strains and rhythms.

I'm probably noticing more sounds because I can see less and less. The sun has dropped like a stone, turning the sky from passion pink to grizzly gray. Everything appears in shadow or silhouette. I pull a peanut butter, honey, and banana sandwich from my duffel and consider dropping bits of it along this trail, in case I need to find my way back. Then I remember those videos of Yellowstone National Park where stupid campers leave out food and hungry bears attack them.

The animals won't bother you, if you don't bother them. That's what Mom said. But what does she know? It's better not to lure the bears.

I pass a boulder shaped like a giant turtle. Yellow cat eyes pop out from behind it. It's a mountain lion but it merely blinks at me, disinterested, like I'm a fellow homey from the 'hood. I can see why Grumps stayed up here after Bilki died and didn't return to tribal elder housing on the Mohegan Reservation. This place draws you in. Plus, considering my grandfather's rough temperament, I realize how fortunate we are he chose to stay up here, in these woods.

Wait a minute...*these* woods? What if these woods are nowhere near Bilki's house? What if my parents dropped me off on the wrong road? Mom had a lot of trouble locating the turn off the main road. A sharp chill begins in my neck and skitters to my toes. Mom is heavily medicated. She could have easily picked the wrong road.

I keep moving because stopping will get me nothing. A hum fills the air, maybe from a swarm of insects? Maybe from the wind? Maybe from the whispers of the trees? Are they guiding me? Either way, it's soothing. The last gleams of sunlight twinkle through the white pines, like holiday lightbulbs going out on this land full of Christmas trees, one by one. My eyes adjust to see things in a strange gloaming blue light. The mountain lion that was behind the boulder has moved closer but still doesn't feel threatening. A bull moose saunters past me and nods. Orange pineo mushrooms on the side of an oak stump expand before my eyes. I recognize them from nature class at tribal camp. Soft moss spreads across the forest floor. I can see things growing! I avoid an anthill because my eyes peer through the earth, into the bustling insect metropolis. I belong to this forest like I've never belonged anywhere. I am these oaks and pines. I am the moss. I am the mushrooms. I am the wildcat. I am the moose. I am the ants. I'm all of it. Okay, I'm also overtired.

I trip and fall on a flat stone with a sharp edge that bruises my foot. So much for my cosmic unification with the Great North Woods. I check Rosalita. Fortunately, she remains undamaged because I dropped her onto my duffel. I don't bother to get up. What's the point? I have no idea where I'm going or where I am. I sit, rubbing my sore and injured foot. In my exuberance over these woods, I got careless and stupid. I should have been more careful.

I don't dare try and stand. What if I can't get up? What if nobody comes looking for me for a month? That's what happened to Mia Delaney, wasn't it? Her classmates assumed she rode off with her lover into the sunset, when in fact he must have circled back to the school basement and locked her inside. Her parents didn't search for her at her own high school. If they did, they could have saved her. What kind of parents don't comb every inch of their kid's territory after they disappear? What kind of parents drop their daughter off in the middle of the New Hampshire woods without making sure she gets to her grandfather's cabin safely?

My foot throbs. I lay my head on my duffel and stare up at the stars. There are so many here. I pick out the few constellations I know.

The temperature drops, sending shivers through me.

"Bilki, what am I supposed to do?" I ask, lifting my arm to the stars and jangling my charm bracelet.

My grandmother comes through with only one word, "Reach."

What does she mean? Reach for the stars? Reach inside myself? Reach around me? I'm about to curse her vagueness when my reaching hand touches another flat stone with a sharp straight edge that was clearly cut by some machine. This is definitely a step. My tripping stone is a step, attached to another step. I scramble up them on my muddy hands and knees. There has to be something beyond these steps.

I remember the tiny flashlight on my keychain. Lizzy gave it to me last September when I freaked out after a hurricane killed our power for a week. I raise my beam of light to reveal a panel of wood covered with a swirl of crimson and gold. I wave the light around and see it's a door painted with fall leaves. Only Bilki could have created this. I've found my grandparents' cabin!

I hobble to my feet and tap the door with my good foot. It flies open, which is a sign to call the cops where I come from. My narrow beam of light reveals a room littered with flannel-lined jeans, thick wool socks, leatherwork gloves, rubber fish waders, cotton union suits, and crewneck sweaters, all tossed around like an L.L. Bean showroom in late December. In Hartford, this sort of strewn-about mess would suggest the thieves had already come and gone.

"Hey Grumps!" I pull on the nearest sweater. It smells smoky, like firewood.

There's no reply.

I lay Rosalita against the cabin's log wall and push a torn goose down vest off a rocking chair. A flurry of feathers falls past my tiny flashlight beam like light snow. I collapse on the rocker and gobble my peanut butter, banana, and honey sandwich amid this feather snowstorm. I realize I need a bathroom and stand without much trouble, flashing my beam around. This cabin has only two rooms beyond the central living space. One has a pumpkin-colored door with a mushroom painted on it. Bilki loved the color pumpkin. She used to call it the marriage of sunlight and cherries. I walk over and push this door open. The room doesn't smell bright and fruity. It smells as if Grumps has not changed the sheets since his wife died. I close it, quickly, gagging.

The other bedroom has a blue door with a spider web painted on it. The wall opposite the bed features a mural depicting deep blue woods with Bilki's signature vortex at the center. A swirl of leaves, also in blue, covers the floor. In this dim light, everything appears bruised. Mom definitely chose the colors in here. I dump my stuff on the bed, which is covered with flannel sheets and a scratchy wool blanket. At least the room smells okay and the blues complement my personality and musical persuasion. There are a few unexpected drawbacks. I can't find a light switch, and neither bedroom has a bathroom.

I return to the main room where my weak flashlight beam glints against something metallic on the rough plank kitchen counter. It's a jailor's-style key ring loaded with heavy iron skeleton keys. There are no locks on these bedroom doors or anywhere else in here that I can see. I jingle the keys and think about all the horror movies that use skeleton keys as props. Those movies generally feature half-seen monsters slashing teenagers. I swallow hard. What does Grumps use them for?

I sit back down on the feather-coated rocker and fold my muddy legs, pretzel-style. With every passing minute, my knees press tighter together. I really need a bathroom. Plus, it's getting colder by the minute. Apparently summer nights are not always that summery this close to the Canadian border.

The distant sound of someone singing catches my ear. It's the old "Indian Hunter's Song" and it's definitely Grumps who is singing it because he emphasizes the line: "Oh why does the white man follow my path, like the hounds on the tiger's track?"

I wonder if I should tell him my dad keeps a Siberian tiger's skull inside a locked box in our basement storage unit. I wonder how violently Mom would explode, if she ever found it. What am I saying? My mind must be rambling because I'm exhausted and overjoyed to hear Grumps' voice.

Overjoyed to hear Grumps' voice. Who would have thought I'd ever think that?

I wag my itsy bitsy flashlight in the direction of his singing and gulp. He's wearing overalls that look as though they've never been washed. His long ponytail has faded to white and his belly hangs real low, like an honest-to-God Native American Santa Claus, minus the good nature and clean suit.

"Do you have a bathroom?" I holler, now bruising my knees with pressure.

"Hello to you, too, City Gal," he says roughly. "I'm sorry you found the place deserted. I thought you'd be here a bit later. As far as an indoor bathroom goes, there ain't any. But there's an outhouse out back. Or there's always the woods."

He unclips an industrial-sized flashlight from a loop on his overalls and hands it to me. "Your mom should have given you a proper flashlight to bring along. I guess she forgot we don't have streetlamps up here. I'm glad to see you kept your wits about you and weren't spooked by the dark. These woods are Abenaki country, your territory. They'll always keep you safe."

"No problem," I lie. "Which direction is the outhouse?"

He points to a nearby knoll.

I push though a tangle of overgrown bull briars that tell me Grumps prefers the woods to this outhouse.

"Remember to keep an eye out for poison ivy," he calls. "You know the old saying: leaves of three, turn and flee."

He doesn't need to warn me to watch out; tripping on his front step taught me to observe my footing. But it appears I have bigger worries than itchy plants. A skunk scampers out a burrowed hole under the outhouse door. I gently tug a few vines off the door handle and check for more stray animals before entering. Inside, I find only a splintered wooden seat covering a hole that hangs over a bottomless pit. In lieu of toilet paper, there's a pile of torn newspapers, filled with small-town personal ads. My flashlight catches one that says, "Logger Looking for Big Love." I groan, fully realizing how far away from Hartford I really am. So far, the trees and animals feel great but the people up here may be another story.

Grumps' cabin windows shine with a melted caramel glow that tells me he's lit his woodstove. I recognize that glow from the lantern light tours of Mystic Seaport's nineteenth-century village. Dad took us there because he loves outdated stuff. I have to wonder about Grumps' motives for living in the past. Does he do it because his wife was alive in the past?

My flashlight beam falls on a patch of burnt-looking chaga mushrooms. I know these fungi because a kid at tribal camp picked some off a birch tree and ate them. Our counselor phoned the Connecticut Poison Control Center. But they told her he'd be fine, more than fine, actually, as these things are some kind of super-cure. I want to bring a bag of these home to fix whatever is wrong with Mom.

Bilki chimes in loud and clear, inside my head. "The flora, fauna, and fungi of these woods are all sentient beings."

I decide to leave the mushrooms alone and head inside the glowing cabin.

"Where do I wash my hands?" I ask, arms outstretched.

Grumps directs me to an iron hand pump built into the kitchen counter over a tin washbasin with a hard clump of handmade soap beside it.

"This jewelweed soap will take care of your poison ivy."

I notice the black flecks in it. "I don't have any poison ivy. I was careful where I stepped."

"What about where you put your hands? Were there any vines on the outhouse door?"

I decide to lather up with the nasty soap while Grumps jingles his keys, searching for a particular one. He finds it and sticks it into the wall. I don't see any door in front of him, never mind a keyhole. Yet, unbelievably, a full-sized door opens in the wall before him. I shake my hands dry and shuffle closer. Upon careful examination, I find the well-concealed keyhole. I caress the door's knotty pine wood panels. They match those on the wall, making the door nearly invisible until opened. I wonder if this is Grumps' fine carpentry work.

Inside his secret door, Grumps moves a stack of yellowing art magazines to retrieve a faded rainbow tower of towels. I can't understand why he bothers locking up these grungy things. He hands me a frayed pink one that looks like it used to be red. Moving to the other side of the room, he sticks another skeleton key into the wall and opens an even larger hidden door that leads outdoors. He points his flashlight at a generator and steps outside to fill it with gasoline. I fall to my knees over the sight of this lifesaving modern contraption. Maybe he's not so old-fashioned after all.

He chuckles over my worshipful stance. "Forget it, City Gal. I know what you're thinking. This isn't some luxury camping trip. The generator is only for things that matter, like refrigeration and tools. That's it. There'll be no electric lights, television, phone, or computers in this cabin. We don't need hot water this time of year, either. You can wash up and do your laundry in Second Connecticut Lake, out back."

This remark about bathing and washing in a lake is clearly a joke. I open a window to check if there's even a real lake outside. Regrettably, something glistens, like moonlit waters.

I try to smoke Grumps out, "Why would a body of water be called 'Second Connecticut Lake' way up here in northern New Hampshire?"

He twitches, appearing to have something annoying stuck in his eye. "They don't teach much geography in Hartford, do they, City Gal? There are four Connecticut lakes in New Hampshire. Their water flows south into the Connecticut River that runs through your hometown of Hartford into The Great Salt Sea. 'Connecticut' is the Algonquian Indian word for long, tidal river. It was our east coast superhighway, back when we got around everywhere by canoe."

Lucky me. I get a geography lesson *and* a history lesson. Granted, I feel ignorant for not knowing all this—considering Mom teaches Native American history—but I hope these sorts of wise-old-man lessons won't go on all summer. I read *Heidi* in the sixth grade. It's a story about an abandoned Swiss girl from the city who goes to live with her grouchy know-it-all grandfather in the mountains. I hated that book.

Grumps lights an oil lamp on the counter. He opens my guitar case and removes Rosalita. The hairs on my arm leap to attention. I rarely let anybody touch my axe. But I remind myself she was a gift from him and try to remain respectful.

He strums a few bars from the 1970s tune, "Come and Get Your Love," by the American Indian singer Redbone. The iridescent shell tones on the mother of pearl "R" reflect a rainbow of color in the lamplight. I wonder if this colorful "R" stands for Redbone. After all, I was the one who named the guitar Rosalita. I never asked my grandparents if the instrument had a former name. I would ask this question now if I didn't have bigger concerns. What if I'm really spending my whole summer with no lights, no phone, no computer, no television, and no hot running water?

I can't live like that. A knife block glinting on the kitchen counter catches my eye. Grumps notices my interest in it. He unlocks another hidden door and stuffs the knife block inside, then relocks it protectively. I wonder how much Mom said about me telling her I considered jumping off the roof of City Place last year. I also wonder what's up with all his locked doors.

The old man tucks the key ring under his armpit and turns to look me in the eye, like he's reading my mind. "Curious about my locked doors, aren't you, City Gal? One day they'll be yours to open, and you'll wish you'd kept them shut. For now, all you need to know is that they contain several treasures, including The Secret of Wabanaki."

"The Secret of Wah?" I say. "All I've seen so far are household goods. I'm not twelve anymore, Grumps. I can't be enticed by magic doors filled with secrets."

I know he's trying to inveigle me, a trick he learned from Bilki. My phone beeps to signal it's nearly lost power. I realize there's no way to recharge it, no way to text anyone or call for help if he decides to lock me inside one of these cupboards. I sneak a peek at his wristwatch to check the time. It's got a big white plastic domed face and winds by hand. It's the kind of watch that was popular in the early 1970s. Currently, it reads nine o'clock.

Grumps catches me looking and glances at his watch. "Look at the time! You should hit the hay, City Gal. Things always look better in the morning."

"It's too early for me to go to sleep."

"Not when you have to get up at five."

"Why would I get up at five?"

"To feed the bears. Up here, we make sacrifices for the animals and the trees. They do the same for us." He points to the woodstove. "This stove is fueled with wood, and we cook animal meat on it. That's two sacrifices the trees and animals have made for us. In return, we do things for them, like feeding the bears."

"I don't eat meat and we heat our Hartford apartment with gas," I quip.

He shakes his head and unlocks another secret door. From inside, he pulls out a huge bunch of bananas and lays them on the kitchen counter. "I know you enjoy bananas. But remember, they're mostly for the bears. Still, we don't want them to become tame, so we let them find their own nuts and honey."

I gawk slack-jawed at the bananas. "Couldn't you poison a bear from New England by giving it tropical fruit?"

"Why? You're a Native of New England, and you love banana with your peanut butter and honey sandwiches. Right?"

I close my eyes, reminding myself that my city logic is bunk in these woods.

"You let me worry about what to feed the bears, City Gal. I know a bit more about the creatures of these woods than you do. Your grandmother's family has protected this place for a long time. I also learned about the woods, growing up with the old-timers at Mohegan. But I learned much more up here, from the deep woods themselves. Of course, I'm only the interim caretaker of these northern woods until one of your grandmother's Wabanaki people steps in to take over."

"That won't be me," I say, patting my chest, worried by his mispronnuntiation of her tribe's name.

"We'll see," he replies.

I've had enough of this old man. I put in my earbuds. With the last juice in my phone, I listen to the full-length version of blues' goddess Bessie Smith's "St. Louis Blues." Her words suggest an option for me, if things get too weird here.

"Feel tomorrow like I feel today, I'll pack my trunk, make my getaway."

Three

The Secrets of Indian Stream

Pots and pans clank at dawn. I stumble out of my room to use the outhouse and smell something cooking on the stove that's definitely not vegetarian. Bull briars catch my ankle, and I focus on my footsteps. Something smacks into my forehead. It's big, furry, alive, and smells like musky honey. Everything goes blurry. My legs wobble. My body throbs. I've run into Chenoo. Chenoo, for sure. Chenoo, the cold-hearted, the flesh-eater, the killer-terror. So much for my friendly woods. The creature's voice grumbles like a 1970s muscle car. I quake from head to toe. My eyes begin to clear, and I see what this thing looks like.

What I'm facing is not Chenoo. It's a bear's rump and it's enormous. Chenoo might have been better. I pat my thumping heart to keep it from breaking through my heaving chest. Grumps' fantasy about friendly bears is absurd. I was insane to feel safe in these woods. This thing will turn around and start mauling me any second now. I hate bananas. Thanks to them, my life will end at seventeen. I mentally say good-bye to Lizzy, Beetle, and my guitar, Rosalita. At least I left her inside where she's safe. After I'm gone, I hope my parents don't give her to Lizzy. Her finger work sucks, her turnarounds bite, and she doesn't get the blues. But they probably will give her my guitar because they always exercise poor judgment. Look at their neglect in leaving me here. The thick scent of animal musk gags me. I picture our Mohegan chief offering the eulogy at my funeral. I see her searching for words to avoid stating the butt-obvious: that a foolish Indian girl died because she wasn't paying attention when she went frolicking in the northern woods and got eaten by a bear.

Amidst the mourners—who are far fewer than normal for a funeral on the Mohegan Reservation—I notice Rasima cuddling Beetle. She pulls him closer, and closer....

Adrenaline shoots through me. I pull myself together and focus on finding a solution to this problem as if it's the last five minutes of my algebra final. Sadly, the only idea I come up with is begging Bilki for help.

She responds to my supplication with the words: "Thankfulness is the most important virtue."

Really? That's all I get in this emergency? I understand that she wants me to appreciate the fact that I'm still alive, and that this bear has not immediately turned and torn me to pieces, or risen up on its two hind legs and roared, or made a single threatening gesture. Wait! Come to think of it, the creature hasn't budged.

A cautious optimism creeps into my mind. Why would this woodland animal like me any less than the others who greeted me like one of its own when I arrived? Plus, a bear bumping into a human being is like me tripping over a puppy, or more likely, a hamster. I suddenly feel sympathetic toward household pets. A warm mist rises off the bear's sleek back, which is flecked with hairs ranging from chocolate to toffee-colored. Apparently, black bears are not always black. The creature gracefully ambles around to eye me, still on all fours. A shock of blond fur pokes out from the top of its head like a bad punk rock dye job.

Its ears pop up like soft round homespun mittens. Its copper penny eyes blink with curiosity. The pointed golden-brown claws on its paws appear almost manicured.

I'm thinking I might be okay, when its eyes flare. This bear thinks it knows me, in a bad way. The hairs on its mitten ears prickle, alight with energy. Its eyes flash metallically. It quivers back its snout, exposing raw pink and black gums, baring a full range of healthy teeth, including canines sharpened to dagger-points. This is no friendly moose or mellow mountain lion. I don't dare take a breath. It's ready to pounce.

"Marilynn!" Grumps calls out from behind me.

The bear's quivering jaw snaps shut.

"You'll have to excuse my city gal granddaughter," he continues. "She's a bit of a klutz, not accustomed to looking out for other creatures."

There's so much adrenaline running through me that my sentences run over one another. "You talk to bears? You call this one Marilyn? Is it because she's blond, like Marilyn Monroe?"

"No, of course not," Grumps steps forward. After some difficulty bending, he mashes half a dozen bananas in front of the bear and speaks under his breath, as if I've embarrassed him in front of her. "This lovely creature spells her name differently than that old-time Hollywood actress. She uses two n's, and her last name is Awasos. You know the word. It means black bear in Abenaki and Mohegan. Her first name is a recent addition. I chose it to honor our Mohegan chief."

"I would have asked our chief if she wanted a bear named

after her. Besides, shouldn't you have named this bear after an Abenaki Chief, considering she's living in their territory?"

Grumps eyes me curiously, as if I'm an exotic bug. "Don't you know that animals have their own territories?" He pulls his loose white hair back into a ponytail and wraps it with a red rubber band. "For somebody as special as your relatives up here claim you to be, you sure don't know much."

"What folks up here would be talking about me? I don't know a soul in this town."

"We can talk about that later. Right now, I'd like to present Marilynn Awasos," He bows ceremoniously to the bear. "Marilynn is a lineal descendant of The Great Bear, the most ancient and powerful creature in all these woods, in the whole world, in fact. Someday, you might meet The Great Bear yourself. But let's hope it doesn't come to that."

Marilynn's mitten ears perk up. So do mine. This Great Bear sounds worse than *Chenoo* and *Windigo* put together. I hope to avoid it.

Grumps dumps another bunch of peeled bananas on the back steps. Marilynn blinks her coppery eyes in thanks. Her muscular shoulders roil like a bodybuilder's, as she pushes the fruit with her paws and dips her broad snout to chomp down the yellow mush. I watch for any sign that this tropical fruit does not agree with her. I'm secretly hoping she might keel over and vomit from an allergic reaction, or run away, disgusted by the taste. Sadly, the fruit seems to go down fine. Once she's finished, she rolls back her gums and bares her glistening teeth at me again. This time, her snout is twitching and she licks her canines. The shiver that runs through me feels like a minor electrocution. I don't think Marilynn and I will ever be friends.

Grumps steps right up and speaks into her mitten ear, "That's the last of the bananas, Marilynn. It looks like me and City Gal need to make a trip to the general store to pick up more."

The bear is eyeing me suspiciously. No matter what he says, this creature doesn't feel friendly like the other animals in these woods. This bear is dangerous. The combination of my adrenaline rush and Marilynn's munching and slurping makes my stomach growl.

"Grumps, I'm hungry."

We bid Marilynn good-bye and head inside. The sun has risen. I now see the cabin fully for the first time. The bright mismatched glassware on the windowsill looks like somebody spilled a bag of Skittles. The dishes on the wall rack are decorated with woodland animals, like some of the ones on my bracelet. There's a plate featuring baby bears eating blueberries. Another shows a huge black bear catching a lake trout. I'm sure these are supposed to be cute portraits. But I have trouble thinking of bears as cute.

I search for a place to sit. The only seats appear to be two straight-backed maple chairs set beside a rough-hewn pine kitchen table and two rockers that face the woodstove. One of the rockers is stained strawberry, the other mustard. I'm guessing the strawberry one belonged to Bilki because Grumps always raved about her strawberry smile, not to mention that mustard suits Grumps' disposition. I never thought I'd miss Mom's relic of a navy futon, but I do. At least it has a plush cushion. In contrast to the sparse furniture, there are far too many oil lamps in here. The lamp I most admire sits taller than the rest, on the kitchen countertop. It's two-toned, with a swirling lime-green bottom and a cerise glass top. It reminds me of those Bob Marley cocktails that Mom slings down like water. The table boasts a tin lamp the colors of my favorite apples—granny smith, golden, and red delicious.

I see two cooked venison steaks in a cast iron pan on the stove. That explains the smell I noticed earlier. Yuck.

"Do you have any pancake mix?" I ask.

"Sorry, I forgot you don't eat red meat." He lowers his head and wraps the steaks. "I got this venison from my pal, Sadie. She still hunts. I gave up hunting after your mother's accident."

Ah, mom's car accident. It was bound to come up eventually. It drifts into family conversations like an unknown scent, vaguely threatening, always mysterious. All I know for sure is that it gave mom a scar and a hatred for this place.

I try to focus on the positive. "I see you've picked up most of the clothes from the floor. The room looks great."

What I don't say is that I grimly noticed the cast iron woodstove that warms the place appears to be his only cooking device. I should have taken a hint from the cast iron stove charm on my bracelet. It follows that the iron hand pump and speckled tin washbasin constitute his only sink and faucet. I really am living in the past. I can't hide my disappointment.

Grumps pours coffee from a black iron pot into a blue speckled tin cup, like I'm in a scene from an old cowboy movie. Other speckled cups hang from wooden pegs on the wall. None of them match. He hands my cup to me, grinning. "Try this. It's my specialty."

I hesitate.

"Smell it, if you're skeptical."

I sniff and swoon. It's so rich and smoky, almost chocolaty. I sip it. "This is the best coffee I've ever had." The song "Home on the Range" pops into my head and sticks.

I raise my cup to salute Grumps but he's already staring into another time, his hand resting on the picture of Bilki behind his rocker.

I open the fridge to put the meat away and notice two glassy-eyed lake trout lying on a newspaper on the top rack.

"I like fish," I say. I want to explain that I only avoid eating land animals due to my slaughterhouse apartment building. But that statement would just give him another opportunity to take a dig at my City Gal lifestyle. So instead I say, "You can fry this fish and I can make Bilki's baked beans to go with it. She taught me how.

"You'll make your grandmother's beans?" Grumps eyes twinkle. "Get dressed and we'll pick up the ingredients at the general store. You can also get what you need to make your peanut butter, honey, and banana sandwiches."

Uplifted by the prospect of edible food, more awake, and enjoying the illumination of bright summer sunlight, I find my bedroom delightfully transformed. My scratchy wool blanket is the color of overripe blueberries. The woodland wall mural includes plants and animals made with brushstrokes of glittering silver and electric indigo. Azure cornflowers cover the corners of the dresser. Teal ivy vines wrap the bedposts. The ceiling is midnight blue, dappled with pale cobalt stars, including the bold constellations of The Hunter and The Great Bear. The leaves on the floor are a vibrant swirling sapphire, so odd and so un-autumn-like. Imagine mom hating New England fall foliage so much that she made her mother paint the leaves in her room blue—the one color they never turn.

I emerge into the main room, wearing a tee shirt that's not my usual grim black. It's tie-dyed, featuring a peace sign riddled with bullet holes, the logo for the band "Shooting for Peace."

"Grumps," I ask, "what ingredients do we already have for the baked beans?"

He unlocks a new door in the wall with his skeleton keys. This one is stuffed with old recipe books, along with mason jars full of home-canned vegetables, and a bin of dried herbs, which he pushes aside. "I've got your dried beans right here. We can start soaking them now. I've also got plenty of maple syrup to sweeten them." He pulls out a mason jar, hand-labeled "Chief's Private Syrup Stash," and smiles.

"What's up with the locked doors? Do you think somebody is going to steal food from a cabin in the middle of the woods? Who would do that? The bears?"

"I'm guarding the Secret of Wabanaki for your grandmother."

"Wabanaki. Sure." I'm figuring his mind is going and he's forgotten how to say "Abenaki." I refocus him on the task at hand. "By the way, Bilki always threw an onion and a dash of ketchup and mustard into her beans."

"We'll add those to the list, City Gal," he says, shoving Rosalita at me, as if she's a kid sister who needs watching.

He drops a key in my free hand, and waves me outside, around the backside of his woodpile and whips a dirty canvas cover off a sky-blue Ford pickup truck with two white doors. The hood and front end are a slightly darker blue than the truck bed. My guess is this vehicle dates back to the 1980s.

"Whad'ya think?"

"I think it looks like two clouds on a sunny day."

He slaps his knee. "I'll be darned if that's not exactly what your mother said when I bought it for her! Blue was her favorite color when she was young."

"It still is," I respond. "We share a bluesy mindset. It's the one thing we have in common."

"You got more than that in common with your mom. You'll learn that one day." Grumps hitches up his overalls gruffly. "Go ahead and take the wheel. My eyesight's going."

"I don't have a driver's license." I eye the hard metal dashboard and the unfamiliar standard-style shifter and clutch.

"Nobody cares about that up here. Most folks in Indian Stream are driving snowmobiles before they can read. You're seventeen. Time you learned to handle a truck." He points to the pedals. "Press the left one, pump the right one twice, put your right foot on the middle one, and twist the key in the dashboard."

I try it. The engine revs in a choking, sputtering, twentieth-century kind of way.

"Whoo-wee!" he says. "Now pull the lever forward and down. Step your foot on the skinny pedal, and let off on the left."

I hold my breath at each instruction, not daring to miss a word, trying to coordinate the motions. I need groceries. I need to stay alive. We jerk forward. I lurch downhill over the frost heaves in the road, and my teeth rattle. Grumps' great belly bounces like a barrel full of Jell-O. Sweat glazes my eyes but I exhale. I'm shaken but I'm also driving for the first time.

I expect him to complain about me abusing his antique truck with my amateur driving technique. Instead, he pumps his fists over his head and yells, "Here we go!" as if he is a ten-year-old, riding the Goliath hypercoaster in Montreal.

We're headed uphill now. I shake my wrist till the charms on my bracelet tinkle like sleigh bells. It's my way of asking my grandmother to please keep us on the road. She definitely hears me. Everything disappears, except for the center lines and gritty pavement before me. I feel focused. I'm grateful not to see any stray bears, considering all the road signs warning us we're passing through their favorite haunts. Coming down the first hill, Grumps asks me to pump the brakes, to make sure they work. I scream inside, but I do it, and to my relief the truck slows down.

Calmer, I ask, "Is this land all part of the Abenaki reservation?"

"Nope. All the Abenaki First Nations' reserves are located in Canada. Things are different here in northern New England than they are down in Connecticut, City Gal. The land is broader, and the history is darker and deeper, like the woods."

"But Bilki always said the Abenaki territory here was huge."

"It is. That's the problem. There's enough land to make a colossal reservation, which is why the government won't let your relatives have it."

I mutter, "I can't help thinking about our tiny Mohegan reservation and all the things we have squeezed onto it: a pharmacy, casino, restaurants, hotels, shops, gardens, elder housing, museum, church, ceremonial grounds, sacred sites, and burial grounds. It's a small piece of land, and I'm grateful for it. Yet we hardly have any trees. These Abenakis may not have a reservation but they sure have us Mohegans beat when it comes to trees in their territory."

"Indeed they do. But protecting those trees comes at a high cost. Remember that."

I nod; too busy focusing on my driving to engage in further philosophical debate about protecting trees. At the bottom of the next hill, Grumps signals me to stop.

"You made it, City Gal. Welcome to downtown Indian Stream."

I lay a hand on his shoulder. "*We* made it, thanks. Mom never let me drive."

"She has her reasons." His words catch in his throat. "You'll be a pro in no time."

I take in Indian Stream's Main Street. This is not the Currier and Ives quaint New English small-town center I expected. There's not a single white church or wood clapboard colonial house anywhere in sight. It's nothing but a cluster of jaundiced yellow warehouses. A dozen beat-up pickups sit parked in this gravel lot. I wonder who repairs Grumps' truck. It has to be forty years old but it looks better maintained than all the others, despite its multicolored bodywork.

I pull up to one of the yellow warehouses and park beside a dented pickup with a muddy ATV loaded in the bed. The hand-painted sign in front of the warehouse says, "Indian Stream General Store." The adjacent warehouse has a dent in it the size of a semi. A flimsy banner roped across the front reads: "Black Bear Bar and Grill."

One warehouse has sliding doors big enough to move tractors or snowmobiles in and out. The town municipal building has a sign hammered into the ground out front that says, "-own -all," with the first letter of each word amusingly missing. I see a parking spot that says "-ax Collector." Now I know what teenagers around here do for fun.

The fourth yellow warehouse is so bad it makes me give thanks for Colt High for the first time. Hanging out front is a ragged piece of scrap lumber, wood-burned with the words "Indian Stream School K-12." Apparently, the students made the sign themselves. I'm guessing Mom went here, which explains why she hates yellow. At least Colt High has a pro-fessional-looking sign out front, and we didn't have to hang out with elementary school kids. COLT HIGH. I realize I'm missing my graduation tomorrow and mentally slip downhill.

Grumps pulls me back up, with a shake of my arm. "Time to visit our fancy Indian Stream general store," he snickers. "C'mon."

I leave Rosalita in the truck because I don't want to make a bad first impression on his friends. I know what people think of musician chicks. *They do drugs. They're easy.* The store smells oily and rusty like an auto-repair shop. Rows of red metal industrial shelves rise from a cracked linoleum floor to a water-stained ceiling. The shelves are piled high with fishing and hunting gear, car parts, tools, DVDs, locally made maple syrup, handmade quilts and mittens, yellowing books, wrapping paper, and weird Canadian food products, ranging from pork brains to a whole chicken in a can. These oddities shouldn't surprise me. When I looked up the history of Indian Stream before I left, I read that it's frontier territory. People in this place have been fighting over their rights to land for centuries. The colonists who came here were so ornery they formed their own republic and stayed independent from both Canada and the United States for years. The Indians tried to keep their independence, too, but that didn't work out as well as they'd hoped.

One side of a cloudy glass refrigerator contains microbrew beers with depressing names like Grim Reaper and Last Chance Lager. The other side holds milk, eggs, butter, and locally produced sodas, which come in red, pink, or blue. Their names are sweet enough to make my teeth hurt. Black Cherry Charmer. Wild Blueberry Fizz. Razzamatazzberry. I crave a Diet Coke.

Grumps stands next to a DVD rack and shakes a copy of the movie *Smoke Signals* at me. I watched this movie like a thousand times. It's about a couple of Indians who come from the boondocks out West, a place not all that different from this one. The movie is hysterical. I presume Grumps picked it off the rack because there's a pretty Indian woman on the cover.

"We ain't got no way to play movies," he says. "But help yourself to the books." He continues staring at his DVD. "They loan them out, here, like a library."

I rifle through the yellowed books that smell like my dad

and review their titles. Not a bestseller in the bunch. They're about local subject matter with titles like *Logging the Modern Way*, *How to Dress a Moose in Thirty Minutes*, and *Foraging for Beginners*. I choose one called *Wabanaki Tales*. The introduction says "Wabanaki means 'people of the dawn land.' It refers to the ancient confederacy of the Mi'kmaq, Maliseet, Passamaquoddy, Abenaki and Penobscot tribes of the northeastern United States."

At least he didn't make up the word. I'm hoping the text might tell me something about Grumps' big "secret."

I start to read an Indian story about how a bear saved all the people of the northeast woodlands.

Grumps clears his throat, makes a fake pompous face, and imitates my father's professor voice. "I'm glad to see you researching your heritage." He points to my book. "But don't believe anything in there. A book can't teach you our real Indian traditions—excuse me, what your Ph.D. mother calls Native American or Indigenous lifeways. You don't want to read about our people in books by folks who get their information secondhand. They're all gobbledygook. All you need are these woods for a true Indian education." He leans backward. "Books are misleading when it comes to our ancient stories. Too many people believe what they say, literally–like some of your lunatic relations."

I assume he's talking about my dad, who's chasing down Russian bear legends from old books. I tuck the book under my arm, debating whether or not to borrow it. I don't want to put it back, mainly because Grumps made fun of it. But he is right about Dad. I follow him to the meat section, which turns out to be nothing but a dented chest freezer full of Ziploc bags, with labels like "rabbit parts," and "ground moose." Venison suddenly sounds as ordinary as hamburger.

Grumps pulls aside a guy in a blood-splattered white coat who is carrying a cleaver. He mumbles something to my grandfather about the "stash out back." Thanks to my slaughterhouse apartment, I'm not big on blood and so feeling green, not to mention this guy makes me think I'm in the middle of a crack deal. Three minutes later, the same blood-splattered man—who I hope to God is a butcher—slaps a fresh turkey on a piece of brown butcher paper at the checkout counter along with a half dozen bunches of bananas and two sealed boxes, marked "Elmwood." A list, scotch-taped to one box, says, "2 loaves of whole wheat bread, flour, vegetable oil, dried yellow eye beans, yeast, pancake mix, crunchy peanut butter, and wildflower honey." I grab a bag of onions, a bottle of ketchup and a jar of mustard. I've got all I need—as long as I can keep a few bananas away from Marilynn.

The boy at the checkout wraps the turkey for Grumps and rings up our order, slapping the outdated cash register as if it's a video game. He is short, not much taller than me, and maybe a year or two older. I catch him staring at my tie-dyed tee shirt, biting his lip, trying not to laugh. I wonder if he's a pervert or simply amused by the design—a peace sign riddled with bullet holes. I don't want to stare back at him but it's hard not to. His black hair spikes in a jagged way, as if he cut it with a dull knife. His eyes remind me of the pale green lichen on tree bark, and his bushy black eyebrows rise up to a point over his nose like a furry teepee. His noxious attitude and offbeat looks give the impression of a snarky leprechaun. He's no Beetle.

Grumps reads the notices on the community bulletin board, aloud. "Used Snowmobile For Sale. Mel's Worms, Crawlers & Dillies. Free Horse Manure. Tag Sale of Biblical Proportions. Veterans Ham and Bean Supper. Over-Fifty's Singles Dance."

This all sounds depressingly hick to me. The leprechaun chuckles at my pained expression and limps out from behind the counter to bag my groceries. I want to ask him if he has hurt his leg tripping over a pot of gold. Instead, I ask, "What's so funny?"

He points at my tee shirt. "What's so funny," he repeats, "is you. You're obviously not from around here." I try to ignore his buttery voice. Its smooth and melodic quality reminds me of Shankdaddy, the amazing old blues man from the other end of my street.

"No, I'm from Hartford, Connecticut." I say proudly for the first time in my life.

I examine the cartoon drawing on his tee shirt. It shows a sexy blond bear with long eyelashes and pillowy red lips. He watches my curious reaction to it, and his lichen-green eyes darken to the color of the twilight trees.

"What's your name, Hartford?"

I sigh at the way he says, "Hartford." It makes my dinky city sound sophisticated. Invisible fire ants run up my arms. I've never felt this sharp sensation before. Of course, there are no actual fire ants in New Hampshire, or anywhere in New England, for that matter. I only imagine this is how they must feel.

I swallow and reply, "I'm Mona LaPierre," carefully omitting my dreaded middle name. My heart is fluttering like a baby bird, and it pisses me off.

He clomps out from behind the counter in the heaviest black boots I've ever seen. Besides the boots, he's weighed down with nothing but muscle, like you'd expect for a guy who chops his own firewood. He also smells woodsy, like smoke and musky honey.

"I'm Del Pyne," he says. "Too bad a pretty girl like you has to spend the summer up here in the sticks with us backwoods folks."

I step away from him. Nobody has ever stooped low enough to call me pretty, not even jokingly, especially not my parents. They pride themselves on being realists.

Del's eyes flash with horror at the sight of my quivering chin. Now, I'm completely confused. Can he seriously think I'm pretty? Might squinty eyes the color of deep-woods mud and tree bark hair be considered attractive up here because they give me a woodsy look. He lowers his flushing face, pretending to review a grocery price book. Oh my God, he *does* think I'm pretty.

I muster the courage to ask him a question. "Do you go to school?" I picture the yellow warehouse next to this one. For his sake, I hope he's already graduated.

He flashes the most inveigling smile I've ever seen—not a sarcastic smirk like Beetle's—a full-blown, I-really-like-you smile with a brain attached. I've only seen smiles like this in my dreams.

"I'm nineteen. I'll be twenty in August" he says, "if that's what you're asking. I just finished my third year of forestry school at Yale. How about you?" Del folds his arms, signaling it's my turn to dish on my background information.

I don't know what to say. He's smug, and he's obviously a liar. Like he goes to Yale. Like anyone could finish three years at Yale by nineteen. Nobody from Colt High has ever attended Yale. It's one of those mystical places in Connecticut that everybody has heard about but nobody actually goes. And seriously, why would Yale have a forestry school in the city of New Haven?

I don't mention that I have birthday coming up in late July, as I don't want him to know I'm only seventeen. "Let's see what you like to read." He pulls out the book from under my arm. "*Wabanaki Legends*. So you have an interest in the stories of these woods? I'm not surprised. Your relatives are the keepers of its most ancient tales."

I grab the book back. "That's not why I chose this book. I like reading about lots of things. You don't have to go to Yale to like reading, you know." I decide to smoke out his lie. "What do you plan to do with a degree from Yale Forestry School?"

He gently lifts my chin. "Look around you, Mona. All we've got up here is woods. Your grandfather made me realize the importance of this place. I'm on the fast track to finish college in one more year. Then, I can come back to Indian Stream for good."

I squint my already squinty eyes, wondering if he's for real, loving the feel of his hand on my chin. "That's a pretty big sacrifice, to live here with a Yale degree. You could go anywhere."

"Your grandparents taught me these woods would be long gone if people hadn't sacrificed to protect them."

"You sound just like them."

"That's because they practically raised me." Del drops his head, as if he's said more than he meant to.

Grumps yells at the butcher. "Are you out of your mind?"

We snap our heads in his direction.

"It looks like your grandfather is getting into it with my boss over our recent price hike on bananas," says Del. "Maybe you should distract him."

"Hey Grumps, it's time to go!" I say, still feeling the touch of Del's hand on my chin.

Grumps breaks away from his quarrel and sidles up to the leprechaun like he's his favorite grandkid. "Morning, Del. I see you've met my big city granddaughter. As you may have noticed, Mona Lisa ain't the smiley type."

I shrivel at hearing my middle name.

Del's eyebrows form that furry teepee shape, indicating keen fascination with this disclosure. "I was just telling Mona *Lisa* that I go to college in her home state."

I concentrate hard on not sighing again. His voice is not only buttery; it's melted butter dripping over steamed corn on the cob. When he says "Mona Lisa," it sounds luscious.

"We're proud of you attending Yale, Del," says Grumps. "I know your father is glad to see you doing so well at his alma mater. Don't drop out like your ole dad."

Grumps lowers his head exactly like Del did when he realized he'd said more than he meant to. What are they both hiding?

Del replies quickly. "You know I'll graduate, Mr. Elmwood." He eyes Grumps admiringly, the way I'm sure I used to look at Bilki. Plus, it appears he actually *does* attend Yale.

Del's lichen-green eyes open wide, like one of Bilki's vortexes, pulling me in. Thousands of fire ants inflame my skin from head to toe. I've never been the object of anyone's stare—except when Beetle obsessed over my guitar-playing hands or my dumb cupcake-pink tee shirt. I don't know how to behave when I'm nervous, especially without Rosalita by my side. I try to remember the reactions of pretty girls like Rasima when guys checked them out. I recall her focusing on a page in *To Kill a Mockingbird* when Brick Rodman couldn't take his eyes off her. I pretend to examine my Indian legends book and continue to read a section of my bear story, subtitled "Animal Sacrifice." Unfortunately, the subject matter reminds me of my parents' stupid bear sacrifice trip and why I'm stuck here in the first place. I slam the book shut and shove it back on the shelf.

Grumps speaks loudly enough to Del for me to overhear. "Did you know my granddaughter just finished high school?

But college isn't her thing. She plans to go on tour with her music as soon as she turns eighteen, next month.

My tree bark hair falls over my cowering face. Why did Grumps tell Del I'm a musician? Why did he tell him I'm only seventeen? So much for me trying to impress my first admirer. Not only does this guy now know I'm underage and not headed for college, he can feel free to further disrespect me because I'm a musician chick.

Del's smile spreads wide, and I think I know why. I want to die of embarrassment.

I return to the register, and he punches my arm, lightly. "Hey, since you play guitar, you should hook up with my band, The Blond Bear. I could pick you up on Saturday afternoon for practice."

Sometimes, it feels great to be wrong. His stupid red-lipsticked blond bear tee shirt finally makes sense. It's for his band. It's no stupider than my Dead Kittens tee shirt. The trouble is that I'm now mute. A smart guy, or leprechaun, or whatever he is, has invited me to his band practice. This is totally unexpected. It never occurred to me that I would run into another musician way up here, never mind one with a dream smile, teepee eyebrows, a buttery voice, and magnetic lichen eyes, who thinks I'm pretty. The trouble is that I can't squeak out a sound. What I'm feeling is a lot like what I felt on that Goliath hypercoaster in Montreal: somewhere between terrified and terrific.

Grumps rolls the grocery cart toward the exit. I have yet to reply to Del's invitation. We're leaving, and I've blown it because I'm too flustered to speak. My life can't possibly suck more.

"She'll see you Saturday afternoon," Grumps calls back to Del, unexpectedly.

"Great!" he shouts.

I know I should be angry at Grumps for speaking *for* me. But I'm not. I'm grateful.

Once we're back in the truck, I whisper, "Thank you, Grumps."

"My pleasure, City Gal. I know what you're going through. I had some awkward speechless moments myself, when I first met your grandmother." His eyes drift away.

Whoa. I'm not sure what to think about his comparison of Del and me to him and Bilki. I only met this guy half an hour ago.

I start driving and try to stay focused on the road. A young moose leaps over the guardrail in front of me like a prize-winning filly, and I slow down to twenty miles an hour. A fluffy red fox skitters across the road, and I slow to fifteen. My mother's obsession with helping animal accident victims finally makes sense. Human roads are nothing more than intrusions into shared animal trails. All living creatures walked these trails together in the days before pavement. No human creature has earned a special lethal right-of-way in these woods, or anywhere.

A splash of canary-yellow sow thistles spills over the curb, as if someone has tossed a bucket of sunshine. Beside it lies a patch of wild strawberries wobbling their red heads in the wind. I hear Bilki whisper, "Strawberries are a natural love charm that Indian men give to the women they love." I can't help noticing Grumps crank his head out the window to keep the strawberries in his rearview mirror as we pass. I find myself daydreaming about Del giving me those strawberries and swerve to avoid a ginger cottontail hopping in front of the truck. Now I'm down to ten miles per hour. We might as well be walking home.

I turn onto the still-mucky path to our cabin and stop for a moment to avoid a slinking tabby cat holding a squirming flaxen mouse between its teeth. I eye Grumps' pockets, looking for the bulging rocks he usually keeps to ward off cats. I fully expect him to toss one at the animal. But he doesn't budge. His face remains relaxed, almost devoid of wrinkles. I feel a warm rush as I realize he is content, and I have a band date for Saturday. Not to mention I just learned how to drive.

We unload our groceries, and I get busy boiling beans. They bake in the woodstove all afternoon and I'm grateful it's cool for a summer day. The beans come out of the oven candy-crunchy in their maple glaze. Grumps fries the fish outside over a fire in a cast-iron pan. It turns out crisp and delicious. This meal is a miracle, as I'm no cook. Sandwiches are usually all I make. I can't help wondering if my inveigling dead grandmother had a hand in all this.

Grumps thanks me, pats his impressive stomach, and settles into his rocking chair to read *Yankee* magazine. I bring Rosalita into my bedroom and happily bang away at James Taylor's *Steamroller Blues*. It's the most upbeat blues song I know. My world brightens with each verse. *Yes, I'm a steamroller now, baby, I'm bound to roll all over you.* I think of Del's teepee eyebrows, his lichen-green eyes, his spiked dark hair. I'm surrounded by beauty in this room. The woodland wall mural, floor leaves, cornflower dresser, ivy covered bedposts, and ceiling dappled with constellations. This bedroom is gorgeous. Hell, my world is gorgeous. I sing my song louder. *Yes, I'm a cement mixer for you, baby, a churning urn of burning funk.* I try to simmer down, telling myself not to fall in love with a guy I've just met. But James Taylor's lyrics speak for me. *And if I can't have your love for my own, sweet child, won't be nothing left behind.*

Perhaps I've fallen into one of Bilki's vortexes. Don't get me wrong; I miss Shandkaddy and the bluesy end of Hartford. But here in Indian Stream, I've found a musical guy who's perfect for me, and woods that make me feel like I'm part of them surround me. I feel closer to Bilki. The fact that one of us is living and the other dead doesn't matter.

Four

Blond Bear

I'm sporting the neon yellow George Harrison "Here Comes the Sun" tee shirt that Lizzy gave me. This shirt always seemed too loud and hopeful, until today, when it's sunny outside, eighty degrees, and I have a band date. Del steps out of a Saab as old as he is in his kick-ass black boots, wearing a tee shirt with an emerald-eyed leprechaun peering through a shower of glittering gold coins. It's a tour shirt for the band Leprechaun Gold. Seeing Del in that tee shirt is like seeing Grumps sporting a Bad Santa shirt or Mom with an Indian butter girl on her chest—redundant.

I glance back at Grumps' cabin door, painted with colorful fall leaves. I'm expecting him to burst through it, any second, to greet his favorite grandson, but the door remains shut. It's the middle of the day yet he's nowhere in sight. I wonder if he's visiting his bears.

Del lays Rosalita in the backseat atop a messy pile of papers beside an expensive-looking electric guitar with ghostly gray wings.

I step inside the vehicle and pat the dashboard. "Nice car. They don't make these anymore. Do they?"

"What you mean is that this is an *outdated* car."

I want to tell him it's a nice car, period. But after hearing his melted butter voice again, nothing comes out.

"My dad is an amateur mechanic," he explains. "I never know what sort of antique I'll be driving. Next time we hang out, I could be cruising a 1960s Volkswagen Beetle. So beware."

My heart skips two beats. First, when he says, "next time we hang out," and second, when he uses the "B" word. I wonder what Beetle and the cool kids on Lake Winnipesaukee are doing right now for fun.

He points to his guitar in the backseat. "This is Angel."

I touch the feathery gray wings around the sound hole. "She's a work of art." I open my guitar case and point to the mother of pearl letter "R" inlaid into the spruce body. "I call mine Rosalita."

He touches the "R" reverently. His lichen eyes gleam. "She's a classic."

I lean in to examine the papers in his backseat. They appear to be poetry or song lyrics.

Del catches me checking out his stuff. "As you can see, I write the words to songs but I can't read or write music. I never took lessons, and we didn't get Internet service up here for online lessons until this year."

The haphazard guitar lessons I received from Mom's graduate students suddenly feel like a gift. I endeavor to say something positive. "Paul McCartney doesn't read music either. Did you know that?"

He makes that curious teepee expression with his eyebrows, only it's fiercer than usual, like he's transformed into a clurichaun—one of those nasty leprechauns that nobody talks about. Del grinds his teeth like there's something he can't chew through. "But I *should* have learned." His voice turns from butter to gristle. "My dad knows how to read music, and he never taught me." He slams the car into gear and we bounce along the bumpy road.

"Can't your mom talk to him about it?"

"She passed away."

He forgets to slow down as we pass over a bump and my head hits the roof. "I'm sorry to hear that," I say, realizing this may explain why my grandparents practically raised him. "I know what you mean about having a difficult dad. When mine thinks too hard, his eyeballs roll up into his head and turn white." I lean into him and offer my best imitation of Dad's weird eye habit. It's something I've had years to perfect, trying it out on Lizzy.

Del closes his mouth super-tight, trying not to laugh. His face has relaxed. We pass the cluster of four birches, the one woodsy landmark I know around here.

"Speaking of bad dads," I say. "The only reason my dad left me here this summer was so he could study bear sacrifice in Russia."

"Bear sacrifice?" Del's expression becomes momentarily grave, but he recovers. "Does having crazy dads make us crazy too?"

"Maybe." I revel in our shared drama and, especially, the word "us."

"Here we are," Del points at the building in front of us. "Home sweet home."

We roll into a semicircular gravel driveway in front of a huge contemporary barn-style house with exterior boards stained in streaks of pumpkin, cherry, and golden custard—like fall pies. My stomach tumbles from skipping breakfast. But

I don't care. I'm speechless over the colors and design of this place. It's hard to believe the owner is a troubled man.

An old motorcycle tire, studded with nailheads forming the word "Welcome," serves as a wreath for the front door. Del drives into an attached garage that's twice the size of our Hartford apartment. There's nothing amateurish about his dad's car repair hobby. One of the three garage bays has a hydraulic lift. Racks of tires, engines, welding tanks, and hand tools line the back wall. I'm guessing I've found Grump's secret truck mechanic.

A trendy chandelier overhead seems to be made from discarded Harley-Davidson parts. This kind of biker chic would fetch big money in Hartford. Del is smiling again; he can tell I'm impressed. He throws open the door connecting the garage to the main barn-house. We enter a huge open room that echoes the fall palette of the exterior, only in brighter shades of tiger lily, goldenrod, and trillium red.

Del lays an arm across my shoulder and points overhead. "My dad painted these."

The feel of his arm unsteadies me. I follow his finger to the ceiling and stare, gaga, at a series of giant photos, printed on canvas and overlaid with swirling painted designs, somewhat reminiscent of Bilki's vortexes, but with very different subject matter and a dissimilar style of paint application. These are painted photographs of cityscapes, not painted scenes of woodland animals and trees. Each apartment or townhouse door has a vortex over it, made of slashed swirled lines of color, applied with a paint-dipped scalpel, like the artist is trying to cut the doors open. His paintings don't draw you in. They push you away, like concertina wire.

"Did you know your grandmother was my dad's art teacher?" he asks.

"I figured as much."

Some of the painted photos remind me of places in downtown Hartford. Others I don't recognize. There are no people walking these streets. There is only one portrait of a human being in this entire art display. It shows a close-up of a man's face with a cityscape superimposed on his putrid green eye. The face resembles Del, only it's older and more corroded-looking. This may be the artist's self-portrait. But if his eyes represent a window to his soul, then his soul is putrefied.

Del leads me past several electrical outlets. I can't believe I forgot to bring my phone to charge. We pass a normal bathroom, which I'm dying to use. But Del pulls me forward, pointing out a wall of industrial steel racks, loaded with a painter's arsenal of color tubes, brushes, powders, and canvases.

"These art supplies were a gift from your grandmother," he explains.

"How is it they haven't run out by now? She's been dead for years."

"She left my dad a lifetime gift certificate for some online company in her will. Your grandmother really believed in Dad and didn't want him to have any excuse to give up."

I'm thinking Bilki was overly generous with her gift to Del's dad, considering my grandfather's lousy living conditions. I'm stewing over this when I notice three people about my age, hooking up a sound system in a far corner of the room.

"Time for you to meet the band, City Gal." Del emphasizes my nickname from Grumps. He must have caught me ogling the cityscapes.

He points to each member of the group and their heads pivot my way. "Mona Lisa, this is Sponge, Bear, and Scales."

I take a moment to connect the names with the faces. Scales is the only other female in the room. She acknowledges my presence with a glower. Her round head is pasted with short rippled bleached-blond hair that reminds me of a lemon. Irritating hair clips protrude from it that say things like "Mine," "Yours," Now" and "Never." She wears big hoop earrings that make me think of the pretty graffiti girl with the LOVE earrings at school. When she bends over to adjust the speaker volume, I notice she's wearing the same distressed leather shorts as the lead singer of The Dead Kittens band. Apparently, we share some musical preferences.

Then there's Bear. He is a gigantic male version of me, with shoulder-length tree bark hair, mudwood eyes and all. He's definitely Abenaki. The more I look at him, the more I'm stunned by our resemblance—in everything but size.

He raises his fist in a "red power" sign and leans down to press his cheek into mine, so we can pose as twins for a selfie, which he immediately posts to some website. "We are a beautiful pair. Ain't we, Tribal Sista?" he whispers in my ear. "Just so you know, word is all around the tribe about you being here. My dad was psyched when I told him I'd be seeing 'Lila Elmwood's daughter' today at band practice. Him and your mom used to be tight, back in the day." He squeezes his palms together for emphasis.

I swallow hard. "His name wouldn't happen to be Will, would it?"

"Hell no. I'm Bear Junior, and my dad is Bear Senior."

"Papa bear and baby bear? You must have had a rough childhood."

"Tell me about it."

Sponge leaps forward from behind a gorgeous Mini Moog keyboard and bounces toward me with his arms flopping like a rag doll. He is a way-too-skinny dude with long dirty-blond hair shaved off on one side of his head.

"Mona Lisa, *amore mio.*" He wraps himself around me, reeking of weed.

I'm glad I don't know what he called me in Italian. I dislike him knowing my middle name.

Del turns to me, leprechaun smug. "Sponge is okay. He can turn any melody into a wall of sound in seconds. You'll see."

"Go ahead and test me, sweet thing," says Sponge, flipping his half-head of hair. "Play one of your lil' tunes."

He licks the electronic keyboard like a dog lapping its water bowl. I try to give him the benefit of the doubt that this action somehow enhances the quality of his music. Meanwhile, Scales darts over to the opposite corner of the room—as far away from me as possible. She settles into a couch made from the sawed-off back of an old Ford Mustang. It's the one piece of furniture in the room designed to cozily accommodate two people but nobody joins her. She and I have become instant adversaries, thanks to the way Del keeps staring at me. Bear winks, supportively, telling me to ignore her. Only I can't do that because I sense she's a qualified music critic.

"Go ahead. Mona Lisa," says Del, in a voice that's butterier than ever. "Show us what you've got."

Caressing Rosalita's scrawny neck, I whisper to her, "I need your magic more than ever now, girl." A million riffs twang inside my throbbing head. Nothing seems good enough. I finger a few bars of Beatles music and notice Scales' mouth slip into a victorious smirk. She thinks I have nothing to play but the tired old standards. Yet her smirk is kismet. It reminds me of Beetle and sparks an idea. I decide to perform the song I wrote for him called "Thunder and Lighting." It was good enough to make the finals of Swamp Toad's Songwriting Contest. I received word my song was in the running for their big prize, via email, right before I left home. That means it has to be decent.

I stumble into my quick four and nearly knock Scales out of her Mustang seat. "I'm ready, Sponge. After I run through the first verse, jump in and show me what you've got."

He wags his tongue like an eager bloodhound.

After two more false starts, the song itself gets me going. I wail the first verse.

Thunder and lightning fall down from the sky.
Since time began no one has ever asked why.
The crashing cymbals the big brass drum,
Just like you, baby, they're big, loud, and dumb.

Scales' smirk turns into a chuckle. She gets that this pays homage to James Taylor's sarcastic "Steamroller Blues." I knew she understood music. She is foot-tapping by the end of the chorus. The second time around, Sponge transforms my song into a Dixieland Blues rhapsody with droning horns, twanging strings, and pounding drums. Everybody claps, feeling the rhythm. We finish with an exchange of congratulatory fist bumps. Del and Bear clap rowdily. Sponge kisses Rosalita with slurp-dog lips, and I feel myself stiffen, wiping off his saliva with my sleeve.

He places his pinky on his jagged front tooth. "We are a magnificent team. No?"

I shudder at the thought of teaming up with him and can't respond. Luckily, Bear scoops Sponge out of the way like an extra dining room chair and muscles in to hug me.

"I'm impressed, Tribal Sista!" He wraps his tree trunk arms around me.

Somehow, Bear feels like family. Knowing him makes Indian Stream seem more like home.

Scales marches forward to formally shake my hand. "Serious guitar chops, Mona. Nice melody. Hot lyrics. Your voice is, um, fair."

First-class megabitch or not, her familiar leather shorts and the fact that we both like the same sort of lyrics—not to mention the same guy—tell me we have plenty in common.

"Scales, I'm guessing there isn't a musical note you can't hit," I say, trying on friendly.

"True." She wiggles her well-manicured pink fingernails high in the air and sings the clearest, cleanest, Julie Andrews' high notes that I've ever heard.

"Serious pipes," I say with genuine admiration.

Scales releases an odd hiccup-laugh that could be interpreted as snooty, sweet, sarcastic, or all three, depending.

"She goes to Baa-ston Conservatory," Bear says in a fake Boston accent.

Del punches Scales like a kid sister. "She's okay."

I catch the way she licks her lips at him.

"Bear has the real talent," says Del, hugging his buddy and ignoring Scales. "He plays drums and writes amazing melodies. I generally stick to lyrics, as you know. Neither of us do both as well as you, Mona Lisa."

Scales raises a well-plucked eyebrow. It makes her lemony head look like a narrow slice has been cut into it.

There's a painful silence following Del's compliment. We are all standing in a circle. Sponge's bloodshot eyes ping-pong between Del and me and Scales. The quiet becomes unbearable.

Sponge lays a limp backhand against his forehead, pretending to faint, and imitating Del's voice. "Oh Mo-na Lisa, you are so mu-si-cal. You are so won-der-ful. I think I love you." He smacks his lips, making a kissy face.

I try not to blush. A grape-colored vein bulges in the middle of Scales' pale forehead. Del turns his back on everyone and pretends to tune Angel.

I fail in my best attempt to relax the muscles in my face. "So Bear, about the band's name—The Blond Bear—I get that Sponge and Scales are blond and that they incorporated your name into it. But how does Del fit in?"

Bear hesitates. "Actually Mona, we named the band after Del. You might want to ask your great aunt why we chose that name, in his honor."

Before I can explain that I don't have a great aunt, Del whirls around on his good leg and cuts me off. "It's time for us to perform our theme song for Mona Lisa." He picks me up by the waist and hoists me onto a nearby stool made from a leather-padded wheel hub. I grab his shoulders and feel his warm hands on me. My arms tingle worse than ever—my whole body tingles. Del wiggles a furry teepee eyebrow at me. I toss back my hair.

He strums a chord on Angel that sounds like a woman screaming. My former glee evaporates.

"The song Scales and I are going to sing is called 'Growl,'" he announces.

Scales drops down on all fours in those overly short shorts and releases a half-rabid snarl, scraping her fingernails on the pine floorboards. Del bends over her with Angel, hitting another screaming chord, squatting till he's practically sitting on top of her, grinding out the most guttural sounds I've ever heard. He stands straight and spins on his good leg so fast I swear the wings on his guitar start flapping. My bones ache. Del and Scales sing in such tight harmony that the room vibrates. Their lyrics describe the search for the perfect mate. I try to remember they are only performing, especially when they both drop to the floor, groaning and snarling at one another, nose-to-nose on all fours, like mating bears.

The song spins into reverb. I collapse on an ottoman made from a padded monster truck wheel, clapping painfully.

Sponge pulls a blanket off a frosty case of Grim Reaper beer and slaps one into my hand. I thank him and guzzle it.

"Your song was great, guys," I yell to Scales and Del, before recoiling at the microbrew's taste—which is somewhere between Guinness and prune juice. Scales reacts to my disgust with a high-pitched hiccup-giggle that morphs into a trilling war whoop. What a voice she has.

She steps between Del and me, brushing her lips against his earlobe and whispering something. Bear hands me another Reaper and I down it, remembering too late that I skipped breakfast. Del breaks away from Scales and pulls Rosalita and me onto the ottoman with him and Angel. Scales stomps back over to her Mustang couch, pouting. Sponge nestles in beside her, and she tries to shove him off. He pokes at her playfully, refusing to budge.

The neck of Del's guitar touches mine sharply. Bear looms over us, like a Victorian chaperone. I try to ignore him and turn my eyes to Del's guitar. The artist's signature on Angel says "Will Pyne." I wonder if Del's dad is Mom's mysterious friend.

"Del, your dad paints guitars, portraits, and cityscapes. He's one seriously talented man. Does he have a gallery in Boston or New York or something?"

"Nah, he sells everything on the Internet. That way he gets to keep his privacy."

"Can I meet him?"

He sets down his beer as if it's his worst enemy and limps away. "I think he's busy today, Mona Lisa."

Bear overhears him and shakes his head negatively.

Missing the warmth of Del sitting beside me on the ottoman, I follow him over to a desk. The top is painted with artificial clutter: a spilled coffee cup, a newspaper from 1994, a scatter of colored pencils and two pseudo-dripping paintbrushes. My head feels dizzy. It must be the cheap rotgut beer.

"What's wrong Mona Lisa?" he asks.

"Yes, Mona Lisa, why aren't you smiling?" asks Scales, giggling.

I groan inwardly at this tired joke, and point to the desk. "I see your dad paints furniture, Del."

"He paints anything when he runs out of canvas…" His voice cracks. "Or whiskey."

So Del's dad is a drunk, and he has no mom. That explains my grandparents' involvement in his upbringing. Stones rumble in the driveway, along with the distinctive motor sound of a Harley pulling in. Everyone springs into action as if an alarm has sounded. This must be Mr. Pyne. Sponge falls off her Mustang couch with a thud. Scales rushes to scoop up our beer bottles. Bear leaps around like a ballet dancer stashing unopened beers in his gym bag. Del kicks his dad's painted desk with his overly heavy black boots, scuffing the chair leg. His eyes scour the room as if he doesn't recognize his own house. I've seen this same look on Lizzy's face, whenever her deadbeat dad visited her apartment. On those days, I felt protective of her, realizing her Cherry Coke attitude was really a mask.

I slurp one last mouthful of Grim Reaper right before Scales grabs my bottle and tosses it. Before I can swallow, I notice one real photograph among the faux-clutter on the desk. I pull it out and beer spews from my lips. It shows a dark-haired man, who looks like Del, standing beside a Harley with green flames. I'm desperate to look out the window to check out what kind of bike just drove in, but I hear the electric garage door already grinding closed.

I hold my forehead.

"You okay?" Del asks.

I don't respond right away. I try and tell myself there must be hundreds of Harleys with green flames in New England, not just the one that belonged to the guy who killed Mia Delaney. Still, I've never seen another bike that matched this notorious description before. Grumps did say Del's dad went to Yale—which is only a half-hour away from Hartford. I'm hoping this is all a dark coincidence.

I pick a few triads on Rosalita and finally reply in half-sung lyrics. "Sometimes you laugh. Sometimes you lie."

I think I meant to say, "cry," but it's hard to be sure what I meant.

Scale sucks air between her teeth as Del leans into me.

He re-sings the lyrics I started and adds a new line. "Sometimes you laugh. Sometimes you lie. Sometimes you're wishful when an angel walks by."

This guy really likes angels. I've never been called an angel. It sounds like something a guy says to inveigle a girl. Or scarier, Del means it.

He slugs his beer before Scales whisks it away. "Wait a minute, Mona Lisa, my muse! I think we got us a song here."

I'm pretty sure Del's dad is about to appear, and they don't get along. So why is he taking the time to write a song right now? This is insane. It's obvious his dad makes him nervous. Hell, the guy's self-portrait makes me nervous, never mind his green-flamed bike. Then again, the whole point of songwriting is to cope with life's emotional challenges. Right? Bear seems to appreciate this fact. He remains calm and strums a few chords to go with the lyrics, encouraging Del to add more words to the tune. Del tries his burgeoning lyrics with Bear's third line:

Sometimes you laugh, sometimes you lie.
Sometimes you're wishful when an angel walks by.
Sometimes you need her, sometimes you know...

Del lifts his furry teepee eyebrows at me, indicating I'm responsible for completing the final line of the stanza.

I swing Rosalita into position and jump in with a single country-western style chord, "*Where there's an angel, a devil must go.*"

Bear nods, approvingly. Del wraps his arm around me like a blanket infused with fire ants. I'm sure he is going to kiss me. I want him to kiss me. I don't care if his friends see, or if his drunken father walks in, or even if his dad is Mia Delaney's murderer. The fire ants are climbing up my neck, choking me. I'm a seventeen-year-old high school graduate, and no guy has ever kissed me.

Del pulls me closer. I sink a few inches, like I'm sucked down into this woodsy earth. A door between the house and the garage bangs open and shut. Del presses his forehead to mine and his lichen eyes fade. "What a team we made." He pushes me away, as if he's saying good-bye forever.

"Daddy's home!" comes a shout from the newly opened door. Those words rattle out of this guy's mouth, like a dumped bucket of used car parts.

He staggers in, wearing a tee shirt with a picture of an exploding planet on the front. It says, "Apocalypse Survivors" in flaming letters. That's Mom's favorite Hartford band. This must be *her* Will. He resembles a rotting and decomposed version of Del with axle grease hair, bile-green monster gumball eyes, and skin that shines as if it's spread with a thin layer of mayonnaise. Great taste, Mom.

Del's dad approaches Sponge, unsteadily. "Lemme guess, you're stoned again, aren't ya boy?"

Sponge shakes his head like a Muppet. "No sir, Mr. Pyne."

Mr. Pyne circles Sponge, head-bobbing and singing Lady Ga Ga. "Daddy I'm so sorry, I'm so s-s-sorry yeah. We just like to party, like to p-p-party, yeah."

He stops singing. "Well, well, well. Looks like we got us a new troublemaker in town." He approaches me, bugeyed, spewing whiskey breath. "You're Lila Elmwood's kid. My condolences on being trapped here for the summer, little Lila." He presses his smelly chest against my shoulder. "Ain't nothing worse than getting trapped in Indian Stream."

Mom's friend is a creep. I try and focus on the fact that he controls my only access to running water and the Internet.

Sometimes you lie.

"Your artwork is beautiful, Mr. Pyne," I cringe.

"I know. I'm a genius." Those emphatic words blow a whiskey hurricane my way. "But I'm no mister to you, Babe. Your mom and I go way back. Call me Will."

I was afraid of this. He thinks his connection with Mom makes him my instant pal. I feel the thumping pulse of his heart pressed against me; he's that close. His stale alcohol smell makes my stomach convulse. I'm grateful when he stumbles backwards. I scan the room for help. Bear, Scales and Sponge are already packing their musical equipment. Del stands still and lifeless like a helpless clone of himself.

Will heads for the open kitchen area and slams a pot of something from the fridge on the stove. "Listen, Lila Elmwood's kid..." He stirs the pot with one paint-splattered hand and shakes the other paint-splattered arm at the ceiling. "I'm going to take your picture, and then I'm gonna blow it up, and paint it, and make you immortal. He flings his arms upward, including the one holding the spoon. He splatters the wall with red sauce from the pot.

I don't move or speak.

"Well, all right then, Little Lila!" He drops the spoon back on the stove and heads my way, more upbeat, as though I've agreed to his proposal.

Running his paint and sauce-speckled hands through his axle-grease hair, he grabs a camera from a kitchen drawer. Stumbling, he circles me and snaps photos of my mudwood eyes, tree bark hair, and unsmiling face.

Will hauls up his sagging pants, weighed down by too many paint tubes, paintbrushes, and flasks, paid for by my grandmother who somehow couldn't afford running water or electricity for her husband. He leans over to grab Angel, and I eye Rosalita warily. If he touches her, I swear that I'll stab him with one of Scales' "Now" or "Never" hair clips. He strums a stunningly complex Chuck Berry-style chord, which shows me he really can play guitar. Del was right: Will should have given him lessons.

Will tosses Angel back on the futon and yells. "Listen up, you monster rocker wannabees! I made some fine bear chili last night. You gotta try it."

Now that I've met Marilynn Awasos, the idea of eating bear chili sounds not only disgusting but also dangerous. My stomach flip-flops and my head reels. I don't know if it's my fear of Marilynn or eating bear chili, or the digestion of cheap beer that's making me ill. I double over from a sudden wave of nausea. The shadow of a girl with a hoop earring slides across my feet. I assume it's Scales. I lift my head to regain composure and see she's still packing equipment, across the room. It wasn't her.

Something is wrong here. My body becomes weightless, as if something has yanked me under Second Connecticut Lake. I stagger to the ottoman and sit with my head between my knees, hoping not to pass out. The girl's shadow crosses my sneakers again, more slowly this time. The outline shows a head full of curls, just like Mia, the graffiti girl.

I feel like hell. Del rushes to my side, gently caressing my head with the back of his hand. "Relax, Mona Lisa. Take a deep breath. There's no actual bear in Dad's chili. It doesn't even contain real meat. He's a vegetarian. The name is a joke. People always freak the first time they hear him say 'bear chili.' I would have warned you, if I'd known he'd be showing up."

This news is somewhat of a relief. I think about how few murderers must be vegetarians, and then I recall that Hitler was one.

"Willy's chili is coming out!" calls Del's dad, carrying the heated pot to the table and shaking his vulgar hips, making his pants fall lower than I want to see.

He slips, slopping chili on the floor and splattering it onto a kitchen corkboard. So what if he's a pathetic drunk? That doesn't make him a murderer. I remind myself that thousands of Harley-Davidson motorcycles must have been painted with green flames back in the 1990s. The odds of Will Pyne being Mia Delaney's murderer are a million to one. Still, if ever there was a world-class, drunken psycho, whack-job, murdering son of a bitch, it's Will Pyne.

My eyes follow his chili splatter from the kitchen corkboard to the floor, and my wooziness subsides. "I'll clean it up," I offer, hustling toward the paper towels.

My eye catches several worn and faded snapshots tacked onto the kitchen corkboard splattered with chili. I wipe them clean. One shows Del as a baby with the same spiky hair. He's wearing a white pillowcase with holes cut out for his arms. It's a lousy ghost costume. Another photo depicts a much younger Will, wearing a cap and gown and holding a plaque. He's standing beside Mom, Bilki, and Grumps, in front of the yellow warehouse that is Indian Stream School. I remove the picture from the board to examine it more closely. A palette and paintbrush adorn the plaque, suggesting it's some kind of high school art award. My grandmother proudly beams beside her protégé. Mom hugs Will like a baby brother. What is it with my family and the Pynes? When Grumps is around Del, the old man acts perkier. It appears the whole Pyne family has a weird emotional lock on my mother and grandparents. Or maybe that was in the past, and whatever charm Will once held has been eaten away by alcoholism, leaving nothing behind but the foul-smelling slimeball that I now see.

The corner of another picture peeks out from underneath the graduation photo. I lift the top photo and the image underneath stops my heart. It's the dark curly-haired graffiti girl from school with the Rush band tee shirt and the LOVE hoop earrings. I turn it over, and it says, "Mia."

Will snatches the photo from my hand before I can examine it closely.

He bends down and sniffs me. "You losers have been drinking beer again. Haven't you?"

Del steps up to shield me.

His dad fumes, "Big Lila wouldn't like to hear that I allowed my boy to get her little girl drunk. Now would she? Besides, Del, you know my rules about college guys and high school girlfriends."

The word "girlfriend" is one I've never heard used in reference to me. I'm ashamed to admit I love hearing it, even coming from Will Pyne.

"She's already graduated, Pops," says Del, clenching his knuckles as if he wants to hit his dad. Yet oddly, he pulls his own face back, as though he expects to be struck first.

Will snarls, "But she ain't old enough to drink, and neither are you." He pounds the countertop and hollers, "That's it, kiddies! Band practice is over! Since you've all been drinking, you can all walk home."

The band scatters like their anthill got stomped on. Will grabs a whiskey bottle from a cardboard box full of them, like it's a party case of soda. He fills a huge glass with whiskey and slugs half of it.

I clutch Rosalita and totter through a side door. My vision gets splotchy like I'm swimming in mud. My guts wriggle. My thoughts slosh in rolling waves, overlapping and crashing onto one another. I have so many questions. How does Will know the graffiti girl at school? Is he a pedophile? Is it a coincidence that her name is Mia and he has a photo of a green-flamed Harley? Either way, I have to find a way to warn this girl that she has a stalker, but I'm feeling sicker by the minute.

Once outside, I ask Bilki, "Can you please help me get home?"

"Where is home?" she responds.

Her response is as annoying as always. Nonetheless, I consider some appropriate answers to her question. *My family rents an apartment in Hartford, Connecticut. The Mohegan Reservation is located forty-five miles southeast of that city, in Uncasville. Abenaki territory spreads all over the northeastern United States and into Canada. Grumps' cabin is situated in Indian Stream, New Hampshire, a three-minute drive from here and a fifteen-minute walk. So that's home for now. Home is where you feel safe—unless you live with someone like Will Pyne.*

I walk down the road we came on, and my head floods with images of other people's homes. Lizzy's apartment. Beetle's legendary mansion, even though I've never been there.

A new wave of nausea makes me wonder if perhaps this whole scene is taking place inside my head. Maybe I'm in a hospital bed, suffering from a concussion or a coma, thanks to that logging truck pushing Red Bully off the cliff. Maybe everything that's happened since that moment is a figment of my imagination.

Distracted by this thought, I trip over a pile of rocks and fall, scraping my elbow. The burning ache in my arm tells me I'm not imagining any of this. I'm somewhere real, somewhere I can be hurt. I panic and check Rosalita. She's fine.

Del catches up to me. "You can't walk home alone, like this."

He tries to scoop me up. I briefly feel safe, supported by his thick solid arms, arms that chop wood and play heavy-duty guitar. But then I remember that green-flamed Harley and Will's picture of the graffiti girl, and I don't want to stick around.

He tries to cradle my bleeding elbow, but I yank my arm away. "I have to go!"

"Fine, then I'm tagging along for a while. It's easy to get lost in these woods."

I hear Scales' nervous giggle, coming from somewhere nearby. After an uncertain minute, a lemon blur fades into the woods.

Bear steps into the clearing where I can see his large form, however fuzzy. "Should I stick around, Mona Lisa?"

Del responds for me, in a throatier voice than usual, "You don't need to do that, Bear."

I clench my fists at my sides. "Will both of you please leave me alone?" I turn to Del "Your father is a maniac, and I don't feel well. Please go away."

"You don't feel right because you guzzled your beer too quickly—probably on an empty stomach."

I ignore his logical deduction and keep trudging. A large shadow moves behind the pines. Another smaller shadow follows it. Then another. I thought the other members of the band were gone, but apparently not. We have an audience. Every direction I turn, I detect a moving shadow. These can't all be Del's bandmates. There are too many of them. This must be another hallucination, like the shadow of that girl I thought I saw at band practice. I need to shake this one away, too.

"I'm seeing things that can't be real."

"Beer doesn't make you hallucinate," says Bear, who hasn't left.

"No it doesn't," echoes Del. "I don't like the idea of you being alone right now, Mona Lisa."

"No!" I insist. "Get away from me!"

I hear Will's voice, whispering, not far away in the woods. "I can take Little Lila home."

I picture the photo of the young graffiti girl on his bulletin board and run, more like stagger, away. My balance is off. I feel lousy, like water moccasins are slithering through my brain. I should never have come here. The last thing I want is a ride from Will Pyne.

I pick up the pace and make it about a quarter-mile down the road. My head is still sloshing, my stomach churning, my mind everywhere and nowhere at the same time. My legs buckle as I try to support myself on a tree trunk. I lose my balance, slide to my knees on the still-damp but no longer mucky ground and scrape my arm on the bark.

I put my hand to my arm and come away with blood. "Del. I could use some help."

No answer. He must have done as I asked and left. I don't dare shout in case Will is out there, somewhere, stalking me, like he does the girl from school.

The next sound I hear is something between a growl and a snarl. I want to run. But I'm stuck on two immovable knees. The out of focus woods shimmer like sun-drenched water. If there's a bear lurking nearby, I don't expect to be lucky a second time. I manage to pull myself to my feet and stumble away.

A blur of yellow and red twirls before me, like a French impressionist painting. The image clears for a moment. I see it's the sow thistles and strawberries I saw on my drive with Grumps. This means I'm headed in the right direction. If I can just keep going a little further, I'll make it.

I stand but instantly fall back down onto my unreliable knees. An inky blob moves my way. My vision comes and goes. Something warm and moist bumps my face. I'm trembling, breathless. It smells like musky honey; I don't have to see clearly to know this is a bear. Its tongue laps my face, relishing me, licking my head like a lollipop. A dagger-sharp canine cuts my cheek. It licks the dripping blood with its long leathery tongue. This is it: my last moment of life.

The bear's broad haunch knocks into my shoulder. His paw and forearm swat at my leg like a baseball bat. I can imagine what that bruise will look like, if I live long enough for it to turn blue. The next swat may snap my neck or rip open my throat. Something pale catches my eye. It's a patch of blond fur. This is Marilynn! I don't know if this is good or bad. She shoves my shoulder again, pushing a haunch under my armpit for leverage. She's not trying to kill me. She only wants to get me up and on my feet. I don't kid myself that it's because she likes me. I'm guessing she feels obligated to Grumps, as her food source.

I prop an arm on Marilynn's enormous haunch. The haze before my eyes is clearing. I can see her expression of disgust. I look around and discover the worst: she's not alone. There are at least three more bears gathering nearby, circling. Could these be her cubs? That's a best-case scenario. I can also think of a worst case. What if some bears here got wind of my parents' trip to study bear sacrifice in Russia and decided to sacrifice me, as payback?

I hear yipping and squealing, along with a deep moan. Three cubs race in front of me. But that moan did not come from a cub. I see them scamper toward a gray lump. The lump rises to turn and face me. It's an ancient bear. I see its balding head and rows of sloppy loose flesh drooping beneath its chestnut brown eyes. There's a crack in its bulbous nose. Its haunches are saggy and its claws are broken and yellowed. The smell coming from this creature reminds me of the dying fall woods. If God is a Bear, he looks like this one. I think of the adorable bear charm on my bracelet. This creature looks nothing like it.

Bilki murmurs, "This is The Great Bear."

So this is the creature Grumps mentioned with such fore-boding. My arm is still propped on Marilynn for support as the gray withered titan lumbers my way. The little bears back off, clearing a path. The Great Bear drags himself over to Marilynn and me, huffing with weak shallow breath. The young bears lower their snouts to the ground and whimper submissively before The Great Bear. I don't smell musky honey coming from this creature; I smell rotting leaves. I'm frozen, not with fear but with amazement. This bear must be a thousand years old, maybe a million. He somehow remains on all fours, albeit unsteadily. I'm still on my knees.

We're close now, eye-to-eye. He taps my crown lightly, and the entire world illuminates, like I've been kissed by a falling star. The Great Bear bows his head, and then drags himself backwards, into a circle formed by Marilynn's cubs, the loose skin of his arms and legs slapping against the sides of his decrepit torso, until he collapses in the center.

I'm wired now. The path home appears laser clear. Marilynn continues to accompany me back to the cabin, growling cantankerously. We reach the cluster of four birch trees, and she dumps me onto my sore arm, exiting into the pines.

Grumps is fixing something in the kitchen. I cover my scraped arm and muddied knees with Rosalita, grunt a hello and head straight for my room.

"Just a minute, City Gal," he calls through my closed door. "I did not see Del Pyne drive you home. Why is that?"

"His dad is messed up. I bolted."

Grumps tsks. "Poor Del. You are like all the other gals that boy has lost to his father's bad manners."

Other gals. An unexpected rush of envy overtakes me. I start playing a blues riff I learned from Shankdaddy, hoping to free my mind of anything related to Del Pyne. But it's impossible. His world is a classic blues song. He's got a mean drunk daddy livin' at the bottom of a whiskey jug. Wait! That's a good line. I try writing more lyrics for a song I call "Big Bad No-good Daddy." But whenever I think too hard about Will Pyne, it feels like someone is grinding broken glass into my skin. Then it hits me, the part of what happened today that truly merits a song. I let my fingers find the notes and chords. The lyrics follow. Tonight, I sing "The Great Bear Blues."

Five

Otherworldly Relations

A daytime examination of my bedroom mural reveals a decrepit bear with saggy haunches, sloppy loose flesh, a cracked bulbous nose, and broken yellow claws. This painting—bolstered by Del's rotgut Grim Reaper beer—inspired my imaginary Great Bear from the woods. I can't believe I didn't put this together yesterday. I not only imagined the bear, I probably imagined that shadow-girl at Del's, as well.

In my mind, I hear Mom saying, "Reality check."

Fine, so I imagined it all. But I came way from the experience with a decent blues song. Perhaps I need to view this summer sojourn in the woods as a musical retreat. I notice my duffel remains packed and decide to make my peace with moving in. Stuffing my clothes into Mom's maple dresser, I run across a shoebox full of her old pictures. The one on top is a black-and-white art photo of me as a frowning kid. Bilki must have hated this colorless picture. I turn it over. It says, "Bilki–1944." Whoa, I've made a mistake; this is a photo of my grandmother as a child. What a stunning resemblance there is between us. People say she was pretty as a young woman, so this picture gives me hope. Without the notation on the back, I never would have guessed it was her because I never saw her frown. Everybody loved her smile. I wonder what turned her frown around. It certainly wasn't marrying Grumps.

The next photo in the pile is in color. It's a shot of two young women hugging one another. The one wearing the Yale sweatshirt is definitely Mom. She looks about twenty-five. There's no mistaking that perfect butter-girl face. Fringed leather hairties wrap around her twin braids à la late-twentieth-century Indian chic. I imagine what Beetle would say if I wore those leather hair things to school. He'd probably call me a hillbilly. I push that thought out of my mind because Beetle is gone from my life for good, now that we've graduated. Hair covers the other girl's face, but she has the same great curly hair as the girl in the photo at Will's house. I carry the picture into the main room to question Grumps about it.

Sunlight streaks through the smoke from the open woodstove door like heavenly rays. Grumps slouches in his mustard-colored rocking chair, caressing the arm of the empty strawberry rocker beside him. He's wearing another new shirt, still creased from the package. I wonder how many Christmas, birthday, and Father's Day gift shirts remain unopened behind his secret locked doors. He doesn't look half bad, now, considering the way he appeared when I arrived, with his hermit beard and filthy clothes. The cabin looks better, too. The floor is clean and the place smells all right. I almost hate to hinder his recovery with this blast from the past.

I shake his arm, which clenches a ring full of skeleton keys like it's the launch codes for America's nuclear arsenal.

"Can you tell me who this is?" I ask.

He half-opens one eye and hacks out a few coughs—not sick coughs—fake coughs, the kind you make when you want to avoid speaking. "I can't remember the gal's name," he says, letting his chin fall to his chest, pretending to drift back to sleep.

I shake the picture at him. "I'm curious because she looks like somebody I know from school."

"I doubt that."

"Then you *do* know who this is." I press the photo into his limp hand.

He wipes the sleep from his eyes and raises a firm hand signaling me to stop. "City Gal, I was up with the birds this morning while you slept in late, after playing your guitar all night. I've earned my nap. I'm guessing this rude wake-up of yours has something to do with whatever went on at that band practice yesterday." He narrows his eyes, "Did something unsavory happen that I should know about?"

I assume by "unsavory" he means did I have sex or use drugs or alcohol? I ignore the part about the alcohol and answer honestly about the sex and drugs. "No Grumps, nothing unsavory happened. Like I said before, I left because I wanted to get away from Will Pyne."

He folds his arms tightly over his broad belly. "Poor Del. He dropped off my groceries this morning looking like a lost bear cub. He wanted to see you. He'll be back."

I slap the photo on his chest. "Right now, I'm more concerned with this."

He squints, fumbling his taped-together reading glasses, beckoning me to show him the picture again. I wonder when he last saw an eye doctor.

"I don't recall who took it." He returns to fussing with the skeleton keys on his ring, as if pondering which secret door to open next.

"Who is the girl?" I flap the photo at him.

"Some old friend of Lila's. She's probably the one who talked your mom into leaving that nice local boy to marry that old Canuck professor."

I recall my parents' conversation on the way up here. *Nobody up here ever leaves... Unless she's a beautiful young woman who cons an older man into helping her escape...*

Fire surges through me. Mom wanted to escape Indian Stream at any cost. Yet she sent me here for a month—a real sign of affection on her part. From Grumps' droopy face, I can tell he realizes he shouldn't have said what he did.

He forces a fake-chipper expression. "Seeing how your parents' union gave me an artistic granddaughter, I guess everything turned out all right."

"Please try and remember this girl's name," I insist.

"It was a long time ago." He turns away.

It dawns on me that I haven't turned this picture over, to look for inscriptions. So I flip it, and read the words, "Me & Mia."

"Mia!" I burst out.

I support myself with an arm on the wall. My mind races to piece together the facts. This can't be my friend. But obviously Mom had a friend named Mia in the 1990s, when she went to Yale. Is it possible this could be the same Mia who was murdered at my high school?

"May I take this picture back to Hartford?" I ask Grumps.

"Why?" he grumbles.

"It says 'Mia' on it. A girl name Mia died eighteen years ago at my school. Her killer was never caught. I know somebody who dated her. He's the father of a guy at school. I'd like to show it to Mom and see if there's any connection. So may I take it?"

Grumps snatches the picture from me. "No, you may not take it. A death in Hartford has got nothing to do with us folks, way up here."

I snatch it back. "But what if it does?" I shake the picture. "Mom obviously knew a girl named Mia. That means her friend, Will Pyne, may have known her. What if this is the same Mia as the one who died at my high school? I've seen a photo of a Harley with green flames at Will's house. That's the bike they say the killer rode. What if he picked her up on her last day of school and they took a ride on his bike and something went wrong? Maybe she told him she was in love with somebody else, like Worthy Dill. Worthy's son told me they had a thing. Maybe Will locked her in the school basement to die, as punishment."

"Whoa now, City Gal. You got all that from some hazy old photos?" Grumps drops his jailor's keys. "Just because Will owns a bike that is similar…"

"So Will does own a Harley with green flames?"

"Well sure, but that doesn't mean anything. There are no murderers around here."

"C'mon Grumps! I'm sure there are plenty of murder cases that never get solved up here because nobody follows through or the killer slips the border to Canada. I'll bet Indian Stream doesn't even have a real police department. Besides, I've met Will Pyne. I know what he's like. Any decent cop would pin him as a suspect for something hideous."

"The fact that Will's peculiar doesn't make him a murderer. Besides, you don't even know this girl's full name." He flicks the photo in my hand with his fingernail. "She could be Mia Smith or Jones. Probably not the same gal at all."

I'm almost inclined to agree with him, when a shadow crosses my feet. Only it's more than a shadow. It's a woman, and she appears in living color, with wide emerald eyes, heavy dark curls, and huge silver hoop earrings with the word

"LOVE" carved across the center. Her Rush band tee shirt shows a rabbit coming out of a hat.

Not caring if Grumps overhears, I ask her, straight up, out loud, "Are you Mia Delaney?"

She points to her chest, then the photo of the girl with Mom, and nods.

I wonder why she doesn't speak to me like Bilki does. I'm curious because I believe all Indians can talk to the dead, even Grumps. They just need to remember how.

He holds his head with both hands and directs his stiff and imploring gaze upward, as if Bilki better weigh in on this sticky situation.

"Now you're talking to ghosts. You better get a grip, City Gal. Stop acting crazy like some of your northern relations." He rubs his hands together like he's wringing someone's neck. "You've always had a dark side. It's the musician's curse. You need to get over it! Sometimes I imagine seeing your grandmother. Then I pull myself together. You should, too. Take a reality check."

Now I know where Mom gets her favorite annoying expression. He slumps in his rocker, deflated. I've likewise discovered where I get my slumping habit.

Grumps isn't really with me anymore. Talking about my grandmother has made his eyes cloud over like the morning fog on Second Connecticut Lake.

Hoping to shift his focus away from Bilki, I return to Mia, "I saw the same dead girl at the Pyne house."

"This was after you'd been partying, no doubt."

"After two beers," I admit.

Grumps snorts. "Are you claiming that it's reasonable to believe in what you see when you're drunk?"

"I had two beers. I wasn't drunk." My face heats up. I can't hold back to protect his feelings, anymore. "You feed bananas to bears, and you think it's weird that I saw a dead girl?"

He rumbles like an earthquake. "Bears are real living creatures. They need to eat, just like you. They protect these woods, the whole planet, the universe in fact. You can't see the dead. You can't talk to the dead. Our people used to have those skills. But that was long ago." Grumps thumps back down in his rocker and shoves his nose deep into *The Farmer's Almanac*. The magazine is upside down.

I don't know what to say. For the first time it occurs to me that I haven't actually *seen* Bilki since she died. Sure, we chat inside my head. But, thanks to my Great Bear hallucination, my head is a less reliable place than I once thought. Still, it's got to be more reliable than the head of a man who feeds bananas to New Hampshire bears because he thinks they protect the universe.

I try to force him to take a reality check. "If I didn't see a dead girl then how do you explain the fact that I've seen a teenager who looks like the one in this photo from decades ago?"

He peeks over the top of his magazine. "Coincidence. Doppelganger. Dead people don't wander around as white wispy ghosts. That's Hollywood."

"I didn't say I saw a ghost. I said…" The sound of a Harley interrupts our conversation. I pray it's not Will.

"Maybe that's your ghost," Grumps grouses, still reading his magazine upside down.

Through the window, I can't see any bike but I do catch a dark tuft of leprechaun hair moving through the trees.

"It's nobody I want to see."

"Then I guess we'll leave the door shut," Grumps says with fake complacency.

Del's voice slips through the walls. "Mona Lisa, I know you're home. Please let me in."

If only he had a different voice. If only I didn't suspect his father of murder.

He calls again, his voice cracking. "I need to see you. I have something important to tell you."

It sounds like he hasn't moved on to those "other gals" or defaulted back to lemonhead. What if Sponge's joke about Del's serious romantic feelings for me was no joke at all? What if Del tried to jump off a tall building like City Place, right after I left his band practice? I know how it feels to consider such options, even though I never actually went there. Lucky for Del, there's nothing over two stories high within three hundred miles of this middle-of-nowhere hellhole.

"Please let me in," he pleads. "I won't stay long. I promise. I have to get to work."

I'm about to peek out the door to see his dad's Harley with green flames, when Grumps throws down his Almanac, leaps out of his rocking chair, and flings the front door open. A rush of cool pine-scented air clears out some of the wood smoke from the room.

The old man drags Del inside. "My granddaughter claims to have seen a ghost after drinking beer at your house yesterday."

Del's lichen-green eyes glower, suggesting I'm a snitch, and a wackadoo one at that.

I realize I need to backpeddle. "I saw lots of crazy stuff yesterday. I wasn't feeling well. I even thought I saw an ancient bear in the woods."

Del and Grumps exchange bizarre looks.

Grumps refolds his arms tightly over his great stomach, "You never know what you'll see when it comes to bears. They're complex. But ghosts! I'll bet you get your whacky notions about them from that Canuck father of yours. I read in the newspaper that twice as many Canadians believe in ghosts as Americans. They ain't got nothing to do up there in that big empty frozen wasteland but let their imaginations run wild."

My head flies back in shock at how blind he is. "You're making fun of Canadians because they live in the northern boonies?"

"No, I'm saying they've got strange notions up there—like lower standards for maple syrup and believing in ghosts."

"I know it's possible to talk to the dead because Bilki talks to me all the time!" As soon as I announce this, I wish I hadn't.

Grumps sinks, and Del eyes me coldly, like I've said something unforgivable.

So instead of shutting up, I babble. "She's not the only dead person who visits me. I've been visited by Mia, as well." I hand Del the picture. "This is my mother, Lila, and Mia. I think it's the same Mia who was found dead at my high school back in the 1990s."

Grumps rumbles, "Be careful what you say, City Gal."

Del stands frozen and somber.

Grumps throws an arm around him, "Never mind her, Del. She has an overactive imagination."

"Why would I make this up, Grumps?" I ask. "Do you think I like being stalked by Mia Delaney?"

Grumps storms away into his bedroom, slamming the door.

Del's eyes trail Grumps, as if he wants to follow him. His words tumble over one another awkwardly. "There's something at my house I want to show you."

"There's no way I'm going back there."

He speaks soothingly, "Don't worry. Dad leaves for Maine to deliver a painting around noon tomorrow. Please don't say no."

"Honestly, Del. I can't think of anything you could say that would make me want to go back to your house."

"What if I tell you that Mia Delaney was my mom?"

Six

The Devil Must Go

Del appears at my door wearing crumpled clothes and a cautious smile, in a newly washed and vacuumed Saab. This means his dad took the Harley. That must have been one small painting to fit on the back of Will's motorcycle. Del has cleared out everything from the backseat but a single piece of paper that contains the lyrics to the song we wrote together. I wonder if his older song lyrics were about Scales. I pick up the paper and read the last line:

The devil must go.

Those lyrics make my throat swell. I don't know a worse devil than Will Pyne. Yet Mia Delaney must have seen something in him, once upon a time. I picture his mayonnaise slick skin, his bile-green eyes, his axle-grease hair. But perhaps looks are deceiving. If he had a child with Mia then maybe Will Pyne was not the devil that locked her in the janitor's closet at Colt High, after all. Still, he's a mean drunk and I don't want to be around him. But I do want to be around Del, so I've got a problem.

"You say Mia was your mom," I say, picking up at the earth-shattering place where we left off.

"Yes, she gave birth to me in late August after her junior year of high school. She didn't show during the school year, so nobody at school knew she was pregnant. She went back her senior year like nothing had happened. She planned to get her diploma and then come back here for good."

Del's Saab rumbles toward his house, its multi-colored siding shining in all its autumnal painted glory.

"So this was Mia Delaney's house?" I ask.

"Yes," Del chokes.

I scan the driveway for vehicles. "You're sure that your dad left for Maine?"

"He headed out over an hour ago." Del lays a reassuring hand on my shoulder. "You're safe with me."

My head throbs at his words. I can't help but wonder if this is what Will Pyne said to Mia Delaney before he locked her in the school basement closet. *You're safe with me.* Then I remember Mia is Del's mom. She and Will had a child together. They loved one another. I'm probably all wrong in my assumptions about him. I'm sure that's what Del is dragging me to his house to prove.

Del taps the paper I'm holding. "Those lyrics we wrote aren't half bad." He spreads his hands like they're framing a lit-up marquis. "LaPierre and Pyne, I can see it now. We could be the next Lennon and McCartney."

"Lennon and McCartney," I drone. "You like the Beatles?"

His beaming lichen-green eyes tell me that I should already know that. And of course I do. I feel like he was made for me, which is dangerous, and another reason I want to find out what really happened to his mom.

We pull into the Pynes' garage.

"Mona Lisa, this is what I need to show you." He beckons me toward a cheap beige vinyl door at the back of the garage. This door doesn't appear to get much use; it has cobwebs on the padlock. My nose detects the scent of whiskey and blood beneath the aroma of axle grease. Del smiles at me, inveiglingly. I move closer to him and smell musky honey.

Then it hits me. I'm facing a padlocked door at the home of a man with a green-flamed Harley who keeps a photo of a girl who was murdered at my high school. I picture her getting waved into this locked room, like somebody waved her into the school janitor's basement closet and then locked her inside. Panic sets in. Is Del more like his dad than I want to believe? *Like father, like son?* I can't go inside this locked room.

"Why do you have this room padlocked, Del?" My heart thumps inside my chest. I listen hard for any warning from Bilki.

He holds out the open padlock. "I know this seems weird. But you'll understand when you see what's inside." He hands me the lock, and it feels like an ice cube. "Inside this room is a gift my dad made for my mom. It will prove to you that he didn't kill her."

He pulls me inside the secret room. My clenched heart melts. I'm in the middle of what appears to be a colossal bouquet. Four wall-size canvases fill the room, each painted with interior designs of rooms made from oversized flowers. The dining room features daisy chairs set beside a sunflower dining room table. Stuffed lounge chairs in the living room are constructed of velvety iris; the carpet is made from delicate cherry blossoms and lady slippers. Purple hydrangeas form poufy couches. The kitchen sink is composed of Borneo silvers, the bathtub of passionate red peonies; everything in these paintings is soft, supple, and scented. Will has painted a fantasy home, a sweet and idealized place to start a family, the kind of place you see inside a dream. His signature sits in the bottom right corner of each of the four paintings, written steadfastly in all caps: WILL.

Del drops down on the floor and pats the boards beside him. "Lie down here, beside me. You haven't seen the best painting, yet."

A knot cramps my gut and tightness spreads down my legs. No guy has ever asked me to lie down beside him. I slowly lower myself to a sitting position and hold my knees.

Del takes a hand off my leg and kisses it. "Relax. You can't see the best painting unless you lie on your back. It's on the ceiling." He wiggles into a comfortable position and points upward.

I stiffly recline, trying to focus on the ceiling and not on the padlock still in my sweaty hand, or Del's warm body beside me.

"What do you think, Mona Lisa?"

The canvas overhead depicts a bedroom without color. It's white on white. There's a bed made of calla lilies, down-turned sheets made of Queen Anne's lace and a comforter of stephanotis. White tulips form the pillows and the headboard overflows with bellflowers and baby's breath. A painted faux frame of white roses surrounds the whole picture. There are no noticeable shadows in the artwork. But they must be there. Right? Or I couldn't see the white flowers. You have to have shadows to notice light.

Del prods me with a gentle elbow. "What's your opinion of this work?"

"I can't believe your dad painted this for your mom.

"I know. Me, either."

"What did Bilki say when she saw this painting?"

He rolls over and kisses my shoulder, electrifyingly, shockingly. My body stiffens like rigor mortis.

"She never saw it," he says, gulping. "Nobody has seen it, except Dad and me. I only found out about this room after Dad was on one of his drunken rants He'd been going on about the surprise wedding/graduation gift in the garage that he'd made for Mom before she died." Then one day, I happened upon the padlock key in a junk drawer.

I feel like a peeping Tom, viewing this secret painting meant for someone else. While I'm obsessing over my guilty conscience, Del rolls over and kisses my open mouth, mid-thought, pressing me into the floor. I melt into him. I want this. My heart pounds through my chest so hard I know he can feel it. His lips are velvety, like those flower petals. His tongue tastes fiery, like shooting stars. His rock hard hands wrap around me so tightly that I'm not sure where they begin and I end, and I don't care. Everything spins. One minute I'm lying on the floor, the next I'm on that white flowerbed inside the rose picture frame on the ceiling, its white-hot flowers burning through me like flares from a newborn sun.

Del pulls away and sits up, abruptly. "Whoa, Mona Lisa. That was wild. I'm sorry. I've got to remember how old you are and slow down."

I flush, resenting his self-control. "We're only a couple of years apart."

"I don't think that's how our parents would see it."

I want to be back in his arms, melting into him under that white-hot sun. I fight for composure and walk away toward a corner bookcase. It's painted white and set between the paintings. The doors on the front are glass and I can see a single book inside. It has a yellow and black bumblebee cover. The cover says "Colt High Yearbook 1994."

"This is your mom's Colt High yearbook!" I say.

Del shouts, "Yes! but before you open that, I need to explain!"

I'm already flipping for the senior portraits. One stands out from the rest: a girl with dark curls, wide emerald eyes, and big hoop earrings with LOVE carved across the center. Underneath her photo, it says, "Mia Delaney—destined to follow her star, or some rock star. Wherever Mia goes, there will be music." The senior pictures follow in alphabetical order. The photo beside hers is labeled, "Worthy Dill." The guy's face is violently scratched out, as if with a scalpel.

My hands shake. "Your dad really hated Worthy. Didn't he, Del? It seems he reacted poorly to Mia's relationship with him."

"No! It's not what it seems. Mom is the one who despised Worthy. That's why I wanted you to see this room. Maybe he killed her. You need to know the whole story. Mom mailed Dad this yearbook near the end of senior year. He was living up here with me, waiting for her to complete high school so we could all be together, for good. Everything was all set."

I point to Worthy's scratched-out picture. "It looks to me like Will did this. Maybe he was mad at your mom because of her relationship with Worthy and killed her."

"No! Dad says Mom scratched out the picture because Worthy was always bothering her."

"That's your dad's version of the story."

I pull the picture that I pilfered from Grumps' cabin out of my pocket. "This photo of my mom with Mia proves a connection between Hartford and Indian Stream, between Mia, Worthy, and Will. I think my mom hid it to protect your dad, to keep people from linking him with Mia after her death. If your dad is innocent, it can't hurt to show the picture to the police."

"I've never seen that picture of our moms together. I think it's great. But now that you know my family's dark secret, I'd prefer you keep it to yourself."

I whip around. "But what if your dad actually killed your mom over her relationship with Worthy Dill?"

He falls limp. "He didn't do it, Mona Lisa. The picture will just put unwarranted suspicion on Dad."

"How can you be sure it's unwarranted?"

He slaps the picture. "He goes to sleep every night with her picture and a bottle of whiskey."

"That's not good enough. If your dad didn't murder her then why didn't he look for her killer?"

"He became a drunk after she died. You've seen him. He would be convicted instantly of something, if he went to the police. Your grandparents convinced him to lie low."

A shadow passes over my feet. I catch the curve of a hoop earring in the corner of my eye. My body temperature falls. "Your mom wants justice, Del. For some reason, she has chosen me to ensure that she gets it. When I return to Hartford, I'm telling the police I've found the mysterious biker with the green-flamed Harley that they've been seeking for the last eighteen years."

"If you truly believe my dad killed my mom, then you should leave—right now," he says icily.

The white flowers overhead transform into a blanket of snow. It's no longer summer in Indian Stream. What are the odds the first guy who likes me has a dead mother who only I can see, and a murderous father whose guilt only I can perceive? It's a good thing I love the blues.

The drive back to my cabin is a blur. The next thing I know, I'm sitting on my bed, tired and lonely, with Rosalita beside me, her strings hanging loose. I tighten them and tune her, toughening my fingers on a few guitar drills. My George Harrison tee shirt lies soiled on the floor. I pick it up. It's an omen, a sign to focus on my music and follow in George's footsteps, toward virtuosity. It's time for me to do what George and all the great axe men and women have done throughout time. I'll start woodshedding, intensely practicing on my guitar without distraction. Considering the fact that Del and Grumps won't listen to reason about Will Pyne, I believe woodshedding is my best option. It'll be just Rosalita and me, practicing bluesy twelve bars by oil lamps until the end of July.

"We've still got a few weeks here, girl," I tell her. "We might as well make good use of the time and kick the finger work up a notch."

I press George's sunny yellow cotton face to my heart and try not to think about the padlocked room at the back of the Pyne's garage with the ceiling filled with white flowers and pure promises of things that will never be. Instead, I take solace in some of George's best lyrics:

With every mistake we must surely be learning
Still my guitar gently weeps.

Seven

Wabanaki Blues

Grumps' leather steampunk goggles prevent flying bone bits from salting his eyes as he carves moose antlers with his electric knife. His generator purrs like a well-fed kitten. I used to resent him using electricity for tools when there was no hot water or lights. Now I'm more concerned with what he's making. He's been carving the entire ten days since I arrived; his pile of finished antlers stands taller than I do. All of them depict black bears. So much for Dad's notion that they're rare around here. Some show natural scenes, with bears swatting at bees' nests and snatching trout from streams. Most offer more fantastical images. One antler is etched with a group of bears playing ice hockey, another shows two bears snowmobiling. These antlers must be intended as knickknacks for tourists. I wonder where he plans to unload them. I wonder where he got the antlers in the first place. But I won't ask him.

"Your mom never appreciated my art," Grumps says, spitting out antler dust. "Madame Professor said she saw no beauty in carving up animal parts. Yet she's the one who behaved recklessly toward the creatures of these woods. Not me." His jaw quavers.

The reckless behavior he is referring to is her infamous truck accident, and I don't know enough about that event to judge whether she was at fault. I run my fingers over a raised groove in one of the antlers. It reminds me of her scar.

"Maybe I should take up some kind of art, like you and Bilki."

Grumps drops his work. "Are you kidding? You're already a top-notch artist! Don't think I don't hear you playing Rosalita all night long. You may make it to the big time, City Gal. Your bent notes ain't half bad and your turnarounds are great. Though I gotta say it. Your music has improved recently. It sounds different—deeper."

I can't tell him that these woods have changed my music because they feel like my long lost home. Besides, his compliment is hollow. Grumps has no idea what good guitar playing sounds like. He knows nothing about turnarounds.

I examine one of the antlers and picture it on the mantle of somebody's log cabin. "Do you plan to sell these antlers at the general store?"

"Heck, no, I usually let Will sell them for me online along with his paintings." He scrutinizes my face for signs that I'm giving in on the issue of Will Pyne.

I stiffen my jaw, not only because of Will but because I'm trying not to think about Del's kisses.

Grumps turns off the electric knife and the generator. "There's a powwow this weekend down south. I sometimes set up a vendor table, there. I wouldn't have remembered it, this year, if somebody hadn't shoved a flyer under my door this morning. Maybe we can head south and make us some mad money."

A powwow. I groan inwardly. Sure, I go to the Twain Campus Powwow and Mohegan Wigwam Festival every year with Mom. There are things I like about them and things I don't. The drumming is great. I love the frybread. But the dancing is a big problem for me. My feet never follow the drum exactly. It's not about me lacking a sense of rhythm; I'm a musician for God's sake. My rhythm is fine. There is something else going on with me and my inability to dance in the traditional woodlands Indian style. I've heard Indians say Native dancing is like sweetgrass or sage, a barometer and guarantor of personal spiritual cleanliness. To be in step with the earth is to walk purely, in oneness with all creation. That's more than likely my problem: something about me has always felt ugly, dirty, and out of step with this world. Besides, I don't have any of my proper Mohegan regalia with me, which means I can't dance in the powwow circle, even if I want to.

Grumps peers at me as if he's reading my mind. He bends low and grunts to unlock a hidden cabinet behind the kitchen table. He pushes the chairs aside and drags out a psychedelic trunk with a neon orange sticker stamped with his family name, "The Elmwoods."

He pats the trunk. "This contains your grandmother's old Abenaki regalia. It's time you acknowledged not only your Mohegan blood but your Abenaki roots, too. You're what I'd call a true Wabanaki gal.

"Wabanaki? As in The Secret of Wabanaki?"

"Yes. That's the ancient name for the confederation of Native people in the northeast. Mohegans used to live further north. It includes us, the Abenaki, and others. The symbol of the confederation is a star."

"Is that why Bilki talked so much about stars?"

"In part. There's a bit more to that. You need to learn about Bilki's side of your family. There's a whole lot more Abenaki in you than you think." He bites his lip as if he'd said something he shouldn't have, and his voice grows solemn. "You need to remember that two nations live inside you, City Gal."

Two nations? I already know I'm Mohegan and Abenaki. I want to tell him there are plenty of other nations that also live inside me, from my dad's side of the family. But he tries to forget that.

The inside of the open trunk smells like Lizzy's dog Hank when he's wet. I turn my head and hold my breath.

"That mustiness will air out in no time," Grumps promises, swatting his nose.

The handcrafted Indian clothes folded inside the trunk are mingled with sweet-scented cedar shavings to keep the moths from gnawing them, but this stuff still doesn't smell or look very wholesome. He pulls out a crimson wool skirt beaded with a wavy golden design, that I know represents the path to the stars. *I guess tribal camp taught me a few things.* There are a couple of tiny moth holes in the matching crimson leggings, and there's a tall peaked cap to go with it, that I'm uncomfortable about wearing. You don't see tall pointed headdresses like this one in southern New England. I picture Bilki wearing this red ensemble with her strawberry smile, and it seems appropriate. I recall the photo I saw of her as a kid, resembling me, and try to remain optimistic about how this regalia will look on me.

"Did Bilki bead this skirt and leggings?" I ask.

He grumbles out some Mohegan cuss words, leading me to assume the answer is no, and that he isn't fond of whoever did bead them.

Nestled in the bottom of the trunk are several pairs of moccasins, ranging in size from newborn to Sasquatch. Grumps hands me a medium-sized pair lined with patchy rabbit fur. I check them for mites before trying them on. They look remarkably like the moccasins on my charm bracelet. From another locked wall compartment overhead, he pulls out a varnished wooden hatbox containing a turkey feather headdress. He ties it on his head. The leather headband is crackled. One of the feathers is droopy. None of this regalia appears very regal. But there is something about it that feels important.

"This headdress belonged to your Mohegan great-great grandfather, Eliphalet Elmwood, City Gal. It's the Elmwood family's finest." He adjusts the headdress, failing to make it look any more centered. "If you want, you can wear some sarcastic tee shirt, like the rest of the summer tourists. Or, you can wear the proud traditional Abenaki clothes that Bilkimizi saved for you."

Bilkimizi. I never heard him say my grandmother's full Abenaki name before. *Bilkimizi...Maple Tree.*

He hunches down low, over his belly, and dances in a circle, toe heel, toe heel, in the ancient step.

"I'll be powwowing in my ancestor's fancy feathers this weekend," he says. "Good thing that gal slipped the powwow flyer under our door today. I suppose that your Abenaki relatives sent her here because they all want to see you at the powwow."

I recall what Bear said about word getting around the tribe about me. "Who did you say dropped off the flyer?"

"No clue. All I can tell you is that I saw her blue fingernails under the door."

I hope I look less pale than I feel. I picture the electric blue fingernails of the graffiti girl at school. I know there are a million logical possibilities but I'm pretty sure Mia dropped off that flyer. I wonder why Mia thinks it's important for us to go to this powwow. This makes me far more excited about attending it. I tell Grumps to turn around while I busy myself with trying on Bilki's Abenaki clothing.

He turns his back, anxious. "Let me know when I can look."

After fumbling all the old buttons and ties, I say, "Ready." I'm surprised at how well Bilki's clothes fit, even the pointed cap.

Grumps grins broadly. "Wow! Indian clothes suit you." He taps my headdress. "This cap shows where you're from: the place where the white pines touch the sky." He makes a peak over his head with his fingers. "Now you've learned something."

The cap feels great, like Bilki is holding my head in her lap. But I'm certain he's lying about it looking good. It reminds me of something worn by a medieval princess, a class dunce, or a Scandinavian gnome. I step in front of the kitchen looking glass and blink in surprise. Actually, I look half-hot. Older perhaps? Or from an older time?

I examine my full reflection in the window and have to admit these clothes are perfect for me. Best of all, I don't look short anymore. The hood gives me several much-needed inches.

"Your grandmother called that cap her Abenaki crown." Grumps swallows hard.

I march over to Bilki's picture and thank her with a kiss. Sometimes she doesn't need to speak inside my head for me to feel her presence. With this regalia, she's conveyed something heartfelt, even though she's not here. Grumps sniffles. I won't turn around and embarrass him. Instead, I stare at my reflection in the picture's glass. What would Beetle think if he saw me wearing these clothes? He only shops at high-end stores. I know Lizzy would say something like "Baby It's You," in our steady habit of quoting Beatles' lyrics for everything. If only this place had cell phone service so I could text her a photo of me.

"Well, whad'ya say, City Gal?" asks Grumps. "Are we pow-wowing together this weekend?"

He performs a "sneak-up" dance step, behind me, chasing me around the room. A squeal escapes my lips.

I signal for him to stop and point to the three giant mounds of carved antlers. "You really think you can sell all of these at the powwow?"

He sticks his thumbs in his belt loops, cockily. "Yep, as long as you help me man the vendor table. Young ladies always improve sales."

I squint my eyes, questioningly.

"Seriously," he swears. "It's a time-honored fact. We'll split the profits."

I picture the vintage Beatles tee shirt I saw before I left, on eBay. It's probably sold already. If not, it probably costs more than I'll earn at any powwow, but my share of the profits could give me a start.

"Let's do it," I say, shaking hands.

His eyes dance with fond memories. "Yes, Ma'am. We're going to have a fine time on Lake Winnipesaukee."

"We're going to Lake Winnipesaukee?" My heart roars. Everything is different now. I'm travelling to a legendary vacation oasis—Beetle's crystal blue summer heaven—an enchanted place frequented for centuries by New Englanders with overflowing bank accounts. I feel certain I'll see Beetle. My summer is saved.

I grab Rosalita, sling her over my shoulder and rock a few bars of "Let the Good Times Roll" by blues legend Muddy Waters. I hit it hard on the turnaround and the repeating music reminds me of dancing the never-ending circle at a powwow. Grumps taps his foot and does a modified version of the toe-heel. We sing together, with Grumps picking up the harmony. I stare down at my new Abenaki regalia, think of Bilki, nod at Grumps, and add a modified song line:

Who'd ever know, I got the Wabanaki blues.

Eight

Embedded in the New Hampshire Dust

Enticing islands lay sprinkled across the waters of Lake Winnipesaukee like jimmies, making me want to steal a raft and ford the waves in a candy-hopping adventure. I wonder how many of these delicious islands Beetle has visited? I wonder if Rasima went with him.

Drumbeats rise somewhere along the shore, pounding in sync with my anxious heart. Grumps turns at a hand-painted sign for the powwow. We back the truck into the crowded vendor area, which smells of face paint, frybread, and something fetid. The vendor booths are lined up behind the roped-off dance circle where drum groups, firekeepers, judges, and other event staff are making their last-minute preparations for Grand Entry. Standing in the center of the dance circle is a master of ceremonies wearing a red, white, and blue satin ribbon shirt with five neck bandannas—one for each different branch of the military. He's debating the dance contest rules with a group of scowling judges who keep examining their watches. Grand Entries always run late. That's a good thing because my slow driving put us here nearly an hour behind schedule.

I figure out the source of the nasty smell. Vendors here sell more dead animal parts than I'm accustomed to seeing at our southern New England powwows. I have a sensitive nose when it comes to dead critters. Porcupine quills, bear claws, bird skulls, deerskins, antlers, raccoon, fox and rabbit skins all lay in heaps, ready to be transformed into Native American regalia and ceremonial items. Bark boxes are also more popular because these northerners have bigger trees. I don't see anyone selling southwest turquoise, probably because New Hampshire is farther away from Arizona than Connecticut. Still, there's the ubiquitous Ecuadorian table, with its bright weavings, exotic Andean flutes, and miniature clay trolls. Two booths are already crowded with buyers. One is selling wood-burned guitar straps, computer tablet covers, and iPhone cases. The other has a sign that says, "Black Racer Woman – Love Charms." It's overflowing with teenage girls.

A woman with a clipboard rushes toward us, her thin oyster hair flying. I notice her tee shirt says "Waki Wabanaki."

"*Kwai!* About time you arrived, Elmwood!" she says to Grumps. "There's only one vendor spot left and it's right next to the frybread vendor with the fryolater that smokes," she huffs, out of breath. "Take it or leave it."

"*Aquy,*" Grumps replies, greeting her in Mohegan. "Glad to see you, too, Sandy."

She turns to me and squeezes my face like Mom does when she bothers to notice me. "Mona Lisa LaPierre! I recognize your grandmother's regalia. You look beautiful." Her eyes blink too much, as if she's holding back tears. "Everyone is so pleased to have you home! I'm sure you know how much you mean to us."

"Careful, Sandy. We don't want to scare the girl away." Grumps wags a scolding finger.

Sandy keeps blinking. "Mona, you look exactly like your grandmother. She hardly smiled at your age either. What a sourpuss. I think she developed her wonderful smile after she brought joy into the world with her paintings." She slaps Grumps on the back. "It sure wasn't you who made her smile, old man. Still, I was grateful when you brought her back home to New Hampshire, where she belonged." She squeezes my face again, so I now know from whom Mom gets this irritating habit. "Just so you know Mona Lisa: this is the center of the universe, home to the most beautiful fall leaves on the planet."

"That's enough, Sandy." Grumps tries to pull her away from me, and she resists, moving closer.

Sandy whispers in my ear and I smell smoky blankets. "No matter what those fools in the rest of New England like to boast, our leaves are better here in New Hampshire than anywhere else. Our maple syrup is better, too."

"Enough," grumbles Grumps. "City Gal here has better things to do than worry about who's got the best foliage and maple syrup. She's a blues musician and a good one."

"Another artist! How wonderful!" Sandy touches my unsmiling lips, fondly. "Mona Lisa, you run off and have a look around. I'll help your grouchy old grandpa set up his booth."

Before I can get away, half a dozen other elder Abenaki women pile in for kissy introductions. They all look a little like me. It's funny: seeing people with the same face as mine makes me feel better about the way I look. They are joined by clusters of women from Mi'kmaq, Maliseet, Passamaquoddy, and Penobscot, all wishing me well. I'd never seen people be this friendly at a powwow before. They all call me their Wabanaki sister.

I finally get a break when bees swarm us, and we disperse. Bees are a fixture at powwows. I bustle past them toward a dusty cloud of sage because I know bees avoid smoke. Waving to a familiar Wampanoag potter, I pass other vendors and pause to admire a wampum eagle barrette that would look amazing in anyone's hair but mine.

Wind whirls at my feet, creating dust devils that seem to smile at me. I don't know if it's the fact that I'm wearing Bilki's regalia or what, but I feel comfortable here. I search the crowd for familiar faces and spot my cousin Aaron Elmwood from Mohegan. He never misses a New England powwow and nobody ever misses him; he is the biggest Indian around, bigger than Bear. I wave at him but he doesn't see me, most likely because of my Abenaki disguise. It's somewhat unusual for an Indian to wear the traditional clothes of more than one tribe, like I'm doing. Seeing me in Abenaki regalia is bound to shock some folks who only know me as a Mohegan who wears the regalia of that tribe. Like lots of Mohegan teenagers, I made my Mohegan ceremonial clothes in the arts and crafts room on the reservation. Now I own clothes I presume Bilki made, as well. They are my heirlooms. I'm proud to come from two tribes, and wearing the clothes that Bilki left me makes me feel closer to her.

The midday crowd bulges at the ticket entrance, a fragrant cocoa butter wind blows my way. My heart skips one…two… three scheduled beats as a group of floppy-haired boys from Lake Winnipesaukee blasts in wearing loud plaid shorts and glowing summer tans. They swing their arms freely, as if they they can snatch whatever or whoever they choose. Maybe they're right about that. I don't spot Beetle with this group, and my heart sinks. Even if he is here, somewhere, with what I'm wearing, he'll never recognize me, or want to.

I head for the love charm booth, which is overflowing with girls my age. The sign says the vendor's name is Black Racer

Woman. I remember the black racer snake I spotted on my first day in Indian Stream. Mom said it wasn't poisonous but Black Racer Woman still seems like a spine-chilling name for an Indian woman to choose. Of course in all fairness, she probably didn't pick out that name herself. Traditional Indian names often come from parents or other elders, like mine did. Take my Indian name, it's worse than Black Racer Woman, as far as I'm concerned. In fact, it's so bad I'd rather not discuss it. But I can tell you that I blame my mainstream first and middle names on my old-school, boring, French Canadian father who couldn't stop himself from giving me an old-school, boring, French name.

A high-pitched cackle erupts from a lean elderly woman seated behind the love charms booth. I assume this is Black Racer Woman. A heavy rope of iron hair creeps down onto her beaded buckskin vest like a boa constrictor. Her wrinkled lips pinch an ancient stone pipe that looks as if it could've come from one of my father's archaeological digs. She wears grimy moose hide moccasins that make me wonder if she lives in a wigwam with a dirt floor. The more I examine the beadwork on her buckskin vest, skirt, and hood, the more familiar it looks. I check the design on my skirt and shiver; it's the same pattern.

A lemonheaded girl buys a ball of vines from her table and stuffs it in a brown paper bag. When she turns around, I recognize her.

"Hey, Scales!" I yell.

She doesn't notice me, or maybe doesn't want to.

I gag on the strong scent of fake strawberries and trace it to a freckle-faced girl with a frizzy red ponytail. She pushes in front of me, into Black Racer Woman's wares, and grasps another ball of vines just like the one that Scales bought. Up close, I see it's labeled "Love Winder Charm." I feel my cheeks burn.

The freckled girl rails at the old woman, "I know what your little note says. But is this a *real* love charm?"

Black Racer Woman responds by tapping the handwritten card attached to the charmed ball with her fingernail that's been filed to a fang-point. "Read for yourself, kid." The gold rims on her oak-colored eyes flare as bright and fierce as the hot August sun overhead. It occurs to me that Mom's eyes are the same oaky color, minus the solar flare effect.

The girl sneers and rolls her eyes.

Black Racer Woman cocks her head. "Oh, I see. You can't read. Poor thing. I'll help you." She chants:

Here before you lies a way, a man's affections for to sway.

This Winder Charm, which costs a fee, when e'er unwinds shall romance see.

These words sound more like Shakespearean hocus-pocus than Native American magic. Or perhaps the two are more similar than I thought. After hearing exactly how this charm lures men, I am twice as irritated at Scales for buying it. When the freckled frizzy red-haired girl hears Black Racer Woman's words, she loses color and her freckles stand out like constellations in an albino sky. She clutches the ball to her chest, tosses a twenty-dollar bill at Black Racer Woman, and races off with her prize.

Black Racer Woman shrugs at me, as if to say, "another one bites the dust."

I'm eyeing the small red leather pouches beaded with the eight-pointed stars, on the other end of her table, each one bulging with enchantment. I feel an unexpected tug at my heartstrings when I notice there's only one left. Another Abenaki girl reaches for it at the same time I do. Black Racer Woman slaps the girl's hand and points her fang-finger in my direction. "This last pouch is meant for you. It carries the Wabanaki star."

I know she can't be talking to me, so I turn to the brilliantly feathered dancer waiting in line behind me, tilting my head to indicate that this old woman is obviously speaking to her, but the dancer shrugs innocently.

Black Racer Woman taps one of the charms on the bracelet on my wrist. "I am speaking to you, Mona Lisa LaPierre. I recognize your charms. I bought that star charm for your grandmother."

I'm suddenly less fond of my bracelet.

"How do you know my name?" I ask.

She chews her pipe stem and takes a long draft of her smoking mixture before answering. The air fills with the aroma of bearberry. "The man who chose your name was my father, your great grandfather. He named you Mona Lisa, after that great painting because he wished for you to paint these woods, just as your mother did."

I know Black Racer Woman meant to say, "Just as your *grandmother* did." Mom has never painted anything. But Black Racer Woman is old so I let her mistake slide. Besides, I'm stunned to discover I was named after a famous painting because my Abenaki great grandfather wanted me to become a painter. I was sure my name came from my dad's French heritage. How come I haven't heard about this art-loving Abenaki great grandfather before? It dawns on me that I should be grateful he didn't name me after Edvard Munch's *The Scream* or Salvador Dali's *Skull*. Although, *Starry Night* by Van Gogh would have made for a cool Hollywood-style Indian name that Beetle would love and Mom would hate—which still works.

She leans over and grabs my wrist, shaking my charm

bracelet. She clearly has no idea that jingling this bracelet calls her sister. Her fractious dark medicine can't harm me.

She pulls on my paintbrush charm. "Your great grandfather bought this charm. He also wanted you to become a painter, like your mother, but he misspoke his wish for you and said the word 'artist.' It was an easy mistake but a significant one. It will make things trickier for you when it comes time to fulfill your destiny, my dear grand niece."

I ignore her idiotic remark about my destiny. "So you're my great aunt?" I sputter.

"Yes." She holds the "s" a little too long, making it hiss.

"Bear mentioned me having a great aunt. That must be you," I say. "Why haven't we met before?"

She scrapes her fang-tipped fingernail back and forth across her neck as if she wants to shed her second skin. I hope this hair-raising woman is no indication of what I can expect from the rest of my northern relations. I rub my neck. It feels like something is winding around it, tightening its grip.

"Are you some kind of Medicine Woman?" I ask, suspiciously.

She cackles. "I am many things, Mona Lisa. Your grandfather thinks I'm a snake. But not all snakes are poisonous. Just because something has frightful qualities, that doesn't make it bad. Snakes can be healing creatures. Rattlesnake tails eliminate pain during childbirth. Did you know that?"

She didn't answer my question. But then, old-time Indians never do. A group of teen tourists buffets me, pushing for a better look at her inveigling wares. She leans way over her table to hand me the red leather pouch before any of them try and take it. My hands stiffen around it, like they have been bitten or stung, and I drop the pouch on the dusty ground.

Black Racer Woman lets loose another one of her flock

of crows' cackles. "I knew you would feel its medicine. This pouch will help you fulfill your destiny."

I pick up the pouch again, gingerly. I can't stop looking at its eight-pointed beaded star. "I don't have a destiny," I tell her.

"Of course you do." Her oaky eyes catch fire again. "It is marked by the colors on your regalia. "I ought to know; I beaded it." She leans back, gauging my reaction.

"What's inside the pouch?" I ask, holding it out, trying not to think about her hand in making my regalia.

Her fanglike fingertip snags three pieces of withered gray root from inside. "This is May apple root. It's different from my other wares. It's not a love charm, so it causes no deception. It's merely an ancient fortune-telling tool." She rolls the pieces of root around on her well-lined palm. "When you are caught between two love interests, you name a piece of this root after each of them. The third piece you name after yourself." Her irises fleck gold, orange and yellow, like burning embers. Her intense eyes make me think she is peering into another realm beyond this one. She continues to roll the threesome around in her deeply lined palm. "Whichever piece of root winds up closest to your piece is the one that represents your one true love. It's all about where your roots land."

My heart quickens at the thought of learning my romantic fate until I hear a mockingbird laugh inside my head. "She's tricking you," says Bilki.

Sometimes Bilki can be a nuisance. I try and ignore her. But I can't ignore Grumps.

I overhear him arguing with some swamp Yankee about the price of his antlers, and I realize I'll need to pay for this pouch. But I'm broke. My hand shakes as I place it back on the table.

"Don't you want it?" my great aunt asks, disbelieving.

"How much is it?"

"My pouches are always free." She pushes the roots back inside the tiny red leather sack and squeezes my fingers around it. "That way, if they don't work, you can't complain."

The pouch begins to warm in my hand. I hope using it will clear up my plaguing questions about Beetle and Del. That's why I want this stupid pouch so badly.

"*Wliwni!*" I say, thanking her in Abenaki. It's one of the few words Bilki taught me. She lowers her eyes approvingly. I hang the pouch around my neck and tuck it under my shirt.

Dust fills the air, signaling the approach of someone in a great hurry. I turn and find Grumps at my heels, his shoulders squared off like a moose in rut.

"What mischief are you up to with my granddaughter, witch?" he asks Black Racer Woman. "Are you filling her head with the same crazy stories that ruined her mother? Only a lunatic believes every old Indian story, word for word, like you do. Our tales are allegories. If a story talks about sacrifice, it means to work hard to do the right thing. You don't need to slaughter anything. Don't you dare fill my granddaughter's head with your primitive sacrificial nonsense."

Black Racer Woman pokes her thousand-year-old pipe stem into Grumps' tight shoulder. "Stay out of this, Mohegan. Your people lost their Connecticut woods long ago because you watered down the old beliefs! I'm protecting my land the old way! We both know what Mona needs to do to save these woods."

He grabs her pipe and pokes the stem back into her chest. "Mona Lisa is none of your affair. Keep away from her. You've already done more than enough damage for one wicked lifetime. It's your fault Lila left here. Don't you dare drive Mona away."

"You need only look in the mirror to see who drove Lila away, old man. You'll probably scare this one away, too. Then who will save these woods?"

Black Racer Woman retrieves her pipe and sucks down smoke like a greedy chimney and then exhales upward, creating a brand new storm cloud.

Grumps drags me back to his booth, fuming about how crazy he was to marry an Abenaki woman and get mixed up with these backwoods people. He is so angry he knocks five bucks off the price of his antlers—all except the one he finished last night depicting baby bears playing in a pile of fall leaves. He puts a sold sticker on that one and sticks it back in his truck bed.

Del's bandmate, Bear, appears at our booth before we have a chance to stop vibrating from the intense energy of our volcanic encounter with my great aunt.

He grabs me with his enormous hands and spins me around. "Tribal Sista is lookin' fine!"

I'm relieved to see his familiar face, even if he is wearing a Blond Bear band tee shirt. Black Racer Woman blows a kiss our way and Bear pushes me behind him. He shouts in her direction, "Be careful about the company you keep, Mona Lisa. Some Indians are dangerous!"

"What do you mean by that, exactly?" I ask.

He waves off my question. "Just promise you'll tell me if your great aunt asks you to do anything stupid. Okay?"

"Sure. Whatever. Speaking of no-good Indians, why aren't you dressed in your Abenaki regalia?"

He puts a finger to his lips, his eyes teasing, "Shhh! Quiet. I am temporarily disguised as a tourist. I'll soon be changing into my powwow best."

I can't help but notice, once again, how much he looks like me, and he isn't bad-looking. How is this possible?

He flaps his giant elbows in a funky chicken kind of way. "Keep an eye out for my dance moves during the northern men's traditional competition. You're looking at the winner, right here. I got somebody to impress today."

He slides his mudwood eyes suggestively toward a group of long-haired Navajo women who are putting the finishing touches on their magnificent regalia, decorated with hummingbirds, butterflies, and other exotic flying creatures, beaded in unnaturally vibrant colors. I wonder which one of these beauties he's after. To me they are an irritating shampoo commercial. My hair will never be long, shiny, or silky. Choppy tree bark is all that will grow from this head. One of the women has combed a lightning bolt part into her perfect raven mien. It reminds me of the "Thunder and Lightning" song I wrote for Beetle. I scan the growing crowd for the boys from Winnipesaukee but can't find them.

Bear nudges me. "Speaking of impressing people, did you work things out with Del?"

"No." I squeeze my new pouch. "His father is a dangerous nut job."

Bear twists his mouth in a quirky way, hopelessly trying to make me crack a smile. "For the record, I don't believe people should be judged by their parents' actions. My dad has made some colossal mistakes. I'm sure your parents have, too."

"I doubt they've done anything as bad as Will Pyne."

He pulls at his smooth chin. "Don't be too sure. Besides, there's something special between you and Del. It would be a shame to waste it." He stretches up onto his tiptoes to scan the powwow grounds, "I thought for sure he'd be here today. Sometimes he conducts summer research in the Yale woods in northern Connecticut. But there's usually no set date for that. I've still got six weeks of freedom before the University of Maine reclaims my soul. But I hope to spend some time in Arizona, first." He jiggles his eyebrows like Groucho Marx. "I want to convince somebody from there to come back east with me in the fall, if you know what I mean." His eyes widen at the sight of a new girl stepping into the well-groomed Navajo crowd. "Bin-go! There she is! I *gots* to go, Tribal Sista." He kisses the top of my Abenaki cap.

I feel like I've lost a brother but don't have time to mope about it, as our booth fills up fast. We sell nine sets of antlers in fifteen minutes, and these things aren't cheap. Grand Entry hasn't even begun and we've already cashed in—big-time. Grumps tosses me an "I told you so" look and asks me to count out the contents of his cash box while he chats with a friend. I'm up to eight hundred and sixty-five dollars when a little girl clenching a powdered sugar-coated piece of frybread rushes toward me and slams into our booth, dusting my laid-out cash like a first snow. The careless kid is wearing a Disney princess tee shirt with ALL of the princesses on it, like she's the official keeper of princessdom.

"Mommy! Pretty costume!" She sticks a chubby pinky finger in my direction.

Her mom has dark circles under her eyes. She doesn't apologize for the mess her kid made and grabs the hem of my skirt as if I'm a mannequin. "Louisiana, maybe we can find a costume like this for you to wear for Halloween. With a better hat. You can be mommy's little Indian princess."

I am about to explain that my hat is actually a traditional peaked cap, and that I am not a mannequin or a princess, and that what I'm wearing is not called a costume. But the kid's father picks up one of Grumps' antlers, and I don't want to blow a sale. Just as the man pulls out his wallet, Princess Louisiana gets bored with me and drags both of her parents back in the direction of Black Racer Woman's booth.

Grumps returns as the loudspeaker booms with the lineup instructions for Grand Entry. The master of ceremonies speaks from a raised wooden platform. He's wearing the same clothes he had on earlier, with the addition of a buckskin vest beaded with a glittering American Flag. I whisper to Grumps that I think he's an Iraqi War vet. He says he guesses the man more likely served in Afghanistan because of his eagle-eyed look.

The master of ceremonies speaks like a drill sergeant. "All First Nations line up at the entrance to the big tent. Royalty up front!"

There's a funny look on some of the spectators' faces when they hear the word "royalty" used to indicate Chiefs and other traditional tribal leaders. Watching the tourists' curious expressions over these unfamiliar Indian customs is half the fun of attending powwows.

Grumps tosses a plastic red checkered tablecloth to cover his antlers and offers me his arm like an old-fashioned gentleman. "I'm privileged to dance this year's powwow Grand Entry with my well-dressed granddaughter. Let's you and me make some Good Medicine in that dance circle. We're going to need all the good spirits we can muster after dealing with your poisonous snake of a great aunt. Get in line, City Gal."

As I mentioned, I'm not crazy about dancing. Thankfully, Bilki offers some timely advice. "The point of powwows is to dance on somebody else's territory and realize it's all part of the same dusty earth. We humans are huddled together on a tiny blue bead, spinning through the star-studded universe."

That was trippy. My head is still spinning from her words, as the dancers start shaking their feathered headdresses, ankle bells, and gourd rattles to warm up. The women dancers bob straight up and down, the men begin to stomp, and the earth itself feels wobbly, as if it's moving with them.

A serious-faced little boy flashing a lime feather bustle and tangerine ribbon shirt carries a shell filled with smoking sage past our line of waiting dancers. I ask him for an extra-thorough smudge, and he circles me up and down with sweet smoke. I need a good spiritual cleansing after meeting tiny Princess Louisiana and Black Racer Woman. They're standing in front of my aunt's booth, laughing together, and sharing some demonic joke. My heart flutters fearfully at the thought of them teaming up and conquering the known universe, snuffing out the light of every star in the sky.

Grumps strays out of line to greet a few more friends. I spot a guy standing beside our vendor booth with spiked dark hair and lichen-green eyes. It's Del! The first drumbeat thunders. Our eyes meet. A second loud drumbeat sounds. I lunge out of the dance line.

Someone grabs my arm and brings me back. "There's no stepping out now, City Gal, says Grumps. "The circle has begun. You can't break it."

I feel the pressure of my grandfather's hand on my arm. His pulse is keeping pace with the rhythm of the drum, urging my legs to do the same. Del's lichen eyes plead with me to step out of the circle. But I can't, even though he's a magnet for me. I'm thinking maybe Bear is right and it's unfair of me to have blamed Del for his dad's addiction. My guilt and longing make me fall out of step. I want his arms around me. I want his soft, fiery lips on mine. I stumble and realize I need to pay more attention to my feet. When we circle around again, Del is gone from our booth. An elder from Shinnecock waves at me reassuringly with her turkey feather fan. I miss a beat. Her smoky eyes pull my concentration back to the circle.

My steps are suddenly in sync for the first time. The earth's heartbeat surges through my feet—toe heel, toe heel. I take sure steps. The dance circle resonates through my mind, body and spirit. I'm fully connected with it all: toddlers waddling to their first drumbeats, jingle dancers clanging rhythmically, grass dancers spinning into a blur of color, proud grandmothers swishing their long-fringed shawls, old warriors shaking ceremonial clubs and making every arthritic step count. There are Indians here today from across the four winds of this hemisphere—from the Wabanaki people of the eastern dawn, to as far south as mountainous Ecuador, to as far west as the adobe Pueblos and as far north as the Inupiat of the Arctic. I am one with them, one with the circle, one with the universe. I am dancing in step with it all. Toe heel, toe heel. I climb upward into the air and leap on the back of a swooping eagle, toe heel, toe heel. I jump off and fly higher, on my own, beyond the birds and into the heavens.

Out of the corner of my eye, I look down and catch sight of Del again. His back is turned; he's walking away. My mind leaves the circle with him. I tumble like a shooting star and crash back toward earth, past the MC, the drummers, the tourists, the ever-watchful tribal elders, the mothers, fathers, babies, and ancestors, toe heel, toe heel. My foot lands hard and the last drumbeat sounds. My eyes dart everywhere. There is no sign of Del. My spirit runs dry.

I spring from the circle, searching. Someone tugs on my Abenaki cap from overhead. I raise my uncertain eyes and tremble, realizing I almost forgot how delicious butterscotch bangs and licorice eyes can be. It's Beetle! I shake from the sight of him, from the power of dancing the circle, from feeling the living beat of the drum, from seeing Del and losing Del. Thunder and lightning are falling from the sky, and I am the only one who realizes it.

"What's up with the pointy witches' hat, Guitar Girl?" Beetle asks, yanking me back to a world without ceremony.

I'm suddenly embarrassed. I'm dressed in moth-eaten wool garments from my grandfather's hoary trunk. Yet Beetle appears confident, donning his riot of candy plaids and checks, a ridiculous style reserved for the frolicking preppy New England summer elite. Both of us wear our respective regalias. I shudder as the worlds of Indian Stream and Hartford collide.

Beetle's super-buff, super-jerk friend Brick Rodman hovers behind him, jeering at my clothes. Auspiciously, two girls in string bikini tops lure him away.

Beetle continues to tug at my hood until Grumps comes and snatches him by the shoulder.

"Excuse me, young man," he says, terse. "You must be careful of that headdress. It belonged to my late wife. I'm Mona's grandfather, Mr. Elmwood. Who might you be?"

Before Beetle can respond, I lay a gentle hand on Grumps heaving chest. "Grumps, I know him from school, back in Hartford."

Beetle turns on the charm. "The name's Barrington Dill, sir. My friends call me Beetle." He reaches for Grumps' hand but my grandfather swats it away like it's a bug and sways unsteadily.

"Maybe you should sit down, chief," says Beetle, reaching to help him.

"I'm no chief, boy. I'm Mr. Elmwood to you."

Beetle eyes Grumps worriedly and pulls a plastic chair close. "Please, have a seat, Mr. Elmwood."

Grumps snarls out a "thank you."

Beetle points to Rosalita lying in the other chair at our antler booth. "She's how I knew you were here, Mona. I recognized your guitar." He continues to view Grumps, cautiously. "I didn't know you were spending the summer at Winnipesaukee with your gramps."

"We're staying on a different lake, a little farther north."

Grumps' fist slams on our vendor table. He must have overheard me say, *a little farther north.* He knows that's a lie. It's like saying I live in the ritzy Upper East Side of New York City when I live in the Bronx—which is also up and east, technically speaking. For all they have in common, the people of Indian Stream and Lake Winnipesaukee might as well exist on different planets.

Beetle scans back and forth from Rosalita and me to Grumps. "I missed seeing you at graduation."

I roll my eyes. "It wasn't my idea to miss it."

"I didn't think so." He grins. "But just so you know, it was a disaster. Some jackweed called in a threat to kill the principal only a few minutes into the event. We never got our diplomas. All we got was Dibble's speech about how we should all be kinder to animals. Can you believe it?"

"I can't believe everybody at Colt High missed having a decent graduation this year. That shouldn't make me happy but it does. In fact, I'm inspired to play you a tune." I climb behind the table, take up my guitar, and play a few lines from "Thunder and Lightning," the song I wrote about him, daring to expose my true feelings. This powwow dance circle has given me strength and nerve.

Beetle elbows me. "That tune rocks. Got any lyrics for it?"

My throat closes up because the lyrics are about him. Yet he has no way of knowing that. Besides, I'm desperate to hear his awesome voice. Beetle performed the title roles in our school musicals of *Les Misérables*, *Pippin*, and *Jesus Christ Superstar*. I don't want to miss hearing him sing my best composition.

I grab a pen and paper from our booth. "I'll write the words down. You can sing them. My voice stinks."

Grumps grunts at that comment and struts away to chat with a Mohegan vendor selling carved gourds.

Beetle and I launch into "Thunder and Lightning," my original blues song. A few people crowd around the minute I start playing. There's a guy our age with an arm tattoo that says "Mi'kmaq," a skinny little kid wearing beautiful brain-tanned buckskin, and a grimacing Narragansett elder, all listening intently.

Thunder and lightning fall down from the sky, badum, badum
Since time began, no one has ever asked why, badum, badum
The crashing symbols, the big brass drum, badum, badum
Just like you baby, they're big loud and dumb, badum, badum

While we perform, Beetle stares at my hands as if he is worshipping them. We finish and a few bystanders clap. The grimacing Narragansett elder steps in front of us and speaks loud enough for everyone to hear. "A Mohegan can't be expected to know enough not to play blues at a powwow." A smile flickers across her lips. "But at least you both have talent."

Her mixed review is fair. Nobody puts on this sort of display. My decision to perform with Beetle was straight up selfish, regardless of any trumped-up justification I might devise about making good medicine with dance and song.

Beetle spontaneously touches my chord hand to thank me for our song. His tan is glowing and he's beaming at me like he's my own personal sun. He leaves his hand on mine.

"Your guitar playing gets better and better. You and Rosalita will be famous one day soon."

Grumps returns and clears his throat. Beetle's hand lifts off of mine.

I put a finger to Beetle's soft lips, "Your voice is great."

Brick Rodman leaps in front of us, performing a made-up Hollywood Indian dance. "Princess Many Strings, 'sup?" He plucks Rosalita's strings.

I swing her behind my back, protectively. "So Beetle, I see you invited your classy friend to stay at Winnipesaukee with you."

"Don't you know it," says Brick, tossing an arm around Beetle. That gesture makes me feel like I've been violated.

"Yo, Beetleman, time to hit it," says Brick. "Rasima is helping your mom throw a barbeque at the house, tonight. She told me she invited some local girls. We gots to go."

Beetle doesn't respond to him. He stares at my hands, like he always does, only this time his face is strained. "Mona, we'll practice together when we get back to Hartford. Right?"

I say nothing and cast my eyes down. I'm not sure this is a good idea, with him headed for college.

"Peace out, Injun scout!" salutes Brick, grabbing his friend's arm and heading off.

Grumps starts coughing up a lung, which I presume is a show of disdain over that remark. But he keeps coughing well after Brick leaves.

"You okay?" I ask.

"I am, but you may not be. This was on your chair." He hands me a folded powwow flyer with a message scribbled on the back.

Hey Dancing Lady,

Sorry to have missed you. Deeply sorry. Great dancing, by the way. Keep on swinging that blues axe. I expect to see your name in lights soon. I apologize for being such an idiot.
Love always,
Del

My heart sinks deep into the dusty earth. Why did he leave before talking to me?

I picture Del's smile, the one true, smirk-free smile I've ever known. If Grumps and Bilki love the Pynes, why am I so critical of them? I run to the parking lot at a full clip, my chest and throat afire. In the distance, I spot a lemony head inside a Saab beside a tuft of spiked black hair. I hate that lemony head because I know it's thinking about utilizing a love charm.

I guess my face tells the whole story when I get back to the booth because Grumps hugs me with all his might.

He shakes a finger in the direction of my great aunt's booth. "Anything bad happening here is her fault. That snake creature is Bad Medicine. You want better luck, stay away from her." He snatches a bee from the air, squeezing the life out of the poor creature with his fingertips. He buries it in the dirt with his toe and covers it with a sprinkle of tobacco. "That was probably another one of *her* friends."

I squeeze the red leather pouch under my shirt. His blaming my great aunt doesn't help. I slouch into a sorry lump of wool. Something rustles on the ground beside me, and I reach for it. It's a bouquet of indigo blue cornflowers with a card addressed to M.L. The question is: are these from Del, too? Do those initials stand for Mona Lisa? Or Mona LaPierre? It matters. Del calls me Mona Lisa. Beetle knows me as Mona LaPierre. So who is it from? The note says, "Blue flowers for a Blues woman." Both guys are musicians, so the note doesn't help identify the gift-giver.

No guy has ever paid attention to me until this summer. Now I don't know which one is leaving me flowers. Maybe my creepy new great aunt isn't such bad luck after all. I study the note on the flowers for a clue to their sender. I can't figure it out. But I realize I have something that may help!

I pull out Black Racer Woman's pouch filled with May apple root. As she instructed, I name one piece of root "Mona," one "Del," and one "Beetle." The idea is to draw together the two roots of the people who are meant for each other. I roll the three withered pieces of root around, and they vibrate in my palm. This is it. I feel like I'm choosing between two life-styles rather than two guys. Beetle globetrots the planet like a celebrity. Del burrows into The Great North Woods, like a bear in winter. I roll the roots in my palm one last time for good measure and then squeeze my fist, holding my breath as I begin to open my palm.

Someone shouts, "Louisiana!" and I look up, just as the number one Disney princess girl slams into my booth, knocking me and the three pieces of May apple root out of my hand and into the dust. The girl's mother lunges forward, swoops up her daughter and storms off, trampling two of the roots to smithereens. The third piece, she kicks away, out of sight. I comb the ground with my fingernails, searching for my ruined fortune. But there is no trace of the May apple root. My future is forever embedded in the New Hampshire dust.

Nine

Headed for a Good Fall

It's mid July, nearly a month since I arrived in Indian Stream. Grumps shifts his chin, cutting a ragged new trail into his earth-brown skin. "I hear distant thunder. A storm is coming."

What he means is that my parents will be picking me up today. I think about how I'll soon be able to use my cell phone again. Funny, I almost don't care. This summer, I learned to appreciate the woods. I even learned to accept Grumps' odd relationship with black bears, though they still maintain a wary distance from me, always posturing, like the friends of your enemies. There is one thing that hasn't changed—despite the upturn in our relationship—I still hate that *Heidi* book.

Outside, the liquid silver sky grumbles like a waking spring bear, tarnishing to squirrel gray, then charcoal, as thunderheads march overhead like an army of sky warriors. A mighty west wind sweeps in, bowing down the tallest pines until their needles brush the forest floor like giant brooms. A golden crack of electricity unzips the grizzly sky, illuminating explosive sheets of rain that turn paths and roads into sputtering white-capped streams. Grumps mumbles something about how lucky we are not to have to worry about losing power. I ignore that remark and retreat to my room, moved by the fierce weather to add a third verse to the song, "You are My Lightning." I think about Beetle, the guy who inspired its lyrics, and wonder if I'll ever see him again.

Outside my window, a slate-colored thunderhead darkens and expands. That sight is perfect for a bluesy recluse like me. I'm not kidding about the recluse part. Since the powwow, over a week ago, I've stayed home. Maybe I've been woodshedding because I realize my music is all that matters. Maybe I've been afraid I might see Del and Scales together somewhere around town. Either way, I've plucked and picked at Rosalita till her strings frayed. A worn spot on her body reflects the pressure of my wrist. Occasionally, I've heard Grumps sing along when I strum an old Beatles song. Otherwise, he's kept his distance. He's been getting rides to the general store from a mysterious gal pal he calls Sadie. All I know about her is she drives a biodiesel beater that smells like french fries.

I'd be lying if I said I've spent all my time indoors. The other day, Grumps took me on a hike to identify sugar maple fungus. He showed me the ugly pockmarks on the leaves. I was inspired to write a song in honor of these sick maples, called "Too Sweet to Die." It may be that he's obsessed with keeping the maples alive because they're my grandmother's namesakes. Protecting them matters to me for a different reason: I want to keep eating pancakes with real maple syrup. While I've been here, I've probably eaten a hundred.

Considering my recent woodland excursion, you may find it odd that Grumps still calls me City Gal. But now it's a joke. He doesn't treat me like a kid anymore, either. He knows these woods have changed me, taken root under my skin. In fact, I've been thinking about writing a new blues song, inspired by my arrival here, called "Lost in the Woods." The only line I have so far is "I lost the trail and found where I was going."

I'm thinking about that new song, and in the midst of trying to rhyme a line with "showing," "glowing" or "knowing," when Grumps calls out Del's name. I shoot my head out my bedroom door, eyes and ears alert. Yes, Del Pyne is here, inside our cabin. His heavy black boots are sodden, his clothes are dripping into a puddle big enough to spawn a lake trout, and his spiky black hair is matted down to an oil slick. Grumps hands him a towel and shoves a stack of papers on the table in front of him. He doesn't even touch the towels or the papers because he's distracted, beaming at me with the world's truest smile.

"It's great to see you, Del." I say, more tenderly than I planned. "I thought you were back at Yale."

"I was. Something came up. I had to come home. I'm glad I did. I'm so happy to see you." He steps forward and opens his arms to hug me. I also move forward. But Grumps steps between us and speaks in a fatherly tone, like I'm a kid again, "Mona Lisa, I have a private business matter to discuss with Del Pyne. He graciously drove all the way back here from New Haven today in this storm. He doesn't have much time and neither do you. You need to finish packing. Your mother will be here any minute to take you back to Hartford."

Del shudders at that last word. "Can't our business wait a couple of minutes, so I can talk to Mona Lisa, Mr. Elmwood?"

Grumps shakes the papers at him. "No, Son. There's no time left."

Del scribbles his signature on one of the papers, and turns to Grumps. "Fine, then I agree to your terms, Mr. Pyne, with the stipulation previously discussed."

Grumps shoves the signed paper in an envelope and seals it. "You need to get this to Sadie right now, before her office closes for the day."

I wonder where this mysterious Sadie works. The post office? The bank?

Del pushes past Grumps toward me. He puts a hand on my arm, setting it afire. "Good-bye, Mona Lisa." His eyes sink as he turns and heads out. I think I hear him whisper, "I'll miss you."

Wind and rain whistle and splatter into the room until he slams the door behind him. Why did he leave so suddenly? I tell myself the only consoling thing I can. That I'll soon be back in Hartford, where I can put Delaney Pyne and the rest of Indian Stream behind me for good. Del's world is ugly and complicated. His mother is the walking dead, his father is a murderer, and his lemonheaded girlfriend hexed him, whether he knows it or not. I'm sick of these backwoods people and their dark secrets.

Before I can confront Grumps about what he was doing with Del, the door bangs open and my heart leaps with hope Del has returned. Rain sprays sideways, and in blows a mud-plastered, dangerously tanned woman—my mom.

I feel like I've been shot.

"Let me guess, Mona," she hurls her words at me like daggers. "From the lousy look on your face and the lousy expression that Delaney Pyne wore when he just passed me, I'll bet my father, here, is doing something secretive he won't explain to you."

I finger the picture of Mom and Mia in my pocket.

My mother storms around the room, soaking everything. "I see you still have no running water or adequate electricity, Dad." She turns to me, "Mona, I apologize for leaving you here in this hellhole while your father wasted my time studying his ridiculous bear sacrifices. Even your grandfather knows animal sacrifice is nonsense." She scowls at Grumps. "Don't worry, Dad. We'll be out of your hair in no time."

Water sprays off her as bitingly as her sarcasm. Grumps opens his arms, but she storms toward my room, arms swinging like flying hatchets. An alien may as well have landed in this log cabin; that's how strange and out of place she seems. I cautiously follow her inside my room where she shoves dirty clothes into my duffel along with my clean stuff and wraps the handle around her arm, tightly, like a tourniquet. Her choice to soil clean clothes seems super-callous to me. She's obviously forgotten how long it takes to wash them when you're doing it in a lake.

"Lila Sassafras Elmwood!!" belts Grumps. "You can't come here for the first time in decades, insult me and my home, rudely snatch up your daughter, and then run back to the big city without a decent word to me."

"Reality check, Dad. Reality check," Mom twists the duffel handle further, making her wrist red. "I live in the twenty-first century. Stop pretending you live in the nineteenth, then maybe we can talk."

Grumps body slumps. I cringe at the thought of him morphing back into the miserable, lonely, filthy old man I saw when I first arrived.

He converts his remorse to rage. "You better look in the mirror, missy. For a pretty gal, you ain't looking so good, these days. Misery is taking its toll. I'm not the only one who is stuck in the past because someone I cared about died. I work out my feelings for your mother the old-fashioned way. I'll admit, I cry a lot, because that's natural. You dope yourself up with medications so you don't have to think about your past."

Mom storms to the kitchen counter where she picks up a bunch of bananas and shakes them at Grumps. "At least my mourning process doesn't include delusions about magical bears."

"How dare you speak that way about The Great Bear?" says Grumps.

Mom unwraps the duffel from her wrist and throws it on the ground so she can fling her arms around, lunatic-style. "Don't go there, Dad. I hit a bear once, a normal bear, and I'm sorry. It was an accident. It wasn't my intention or my great aunt's intention for that to happen, and it had nothing to do with any woodland curse. So just drop the issue, once and for all."

"Mom, you hit a *bear*?" This stuns me more than her sideways confirmation about knowing Mia Delaney.

She waves off my question as insignificant, even though I've never heard of anyone hitting a bear. I wonder if she killed it, if this murdered bear was a relative of Marilynn, maybe even her parent. Now I know Marilynn dislikes me because she sees me as "the murderer's kid." I suddenly feel guilty about judging Del for having a murdering father. I imagine what animal-loving Principal Dibble would think of my mom if she knew she killed a bear.

Grumps continues, his voice shaking. "We have more in common than you want to admit, Lila. Neither one of us finds it easy to mourn the loved ones we have lost. Bears, mothers, friends…."

"Maybe you're right, Dad." Mom eyes me furtively. "But, you know I can't talk about that right now."

I speak up. "I know about Mia, Mom. Don't avoid talking about her on my account."

"What? How did you find out?" Mom's face is veiled in shame, as if she's been stripped naked.

"I pieced it together from things I heard," I explain, thinking it imprudent to bring up my interaction with the dead, at this moment.

Grumps presses Mom. "There's no reason for us to quarrel, Lila. Neither of us is comfortable with the sacrifices these woods have asked of us. That bear..."

"Stop it, Dad. You're prattling like some yogi mystic again. These woods did not ask anything of anyone. They did not ask you to move here so you could be bored to tears. You moved here because Bilki wanted to be near her relatives. That was your mistake. It made you miserable and it ruined my life. Fare thee well."

I'm still in shock over learning Mom killed a bear when she drags me outside into the sopping downpour and shoves me inside Red Bully. I feel a sharp physical pain in my chest at not having a chance to say a proper good-bye to Grumps. Her soggy head shakes with fury. She shuffles inside her pleather purse, through bundles of crumpled receipts, keys, and pill bottles, to locate her nerve medicine. Dad raises a finger to acknowledge my return and hits the gas. Through the rear window, I can barely make out Grumps' sad Santa frame, waving from the doorway through the torrents of water. Marilynn materializes and ambles toward him. I take a deep breath. Her odd blond tuft of head fur drips water into her copper penny eyes, making it look like she's crying, which I know is not the case. In the trees, I spot what look like three moving boulders. That's probably her cubs. But they quickly fade from view.

The cluster of four birch trees that guided us here from the main road comes into sight. We pass it, and I know I'm leaving Indian Stream. Not everything that happened here was bad.

Some of it was miraculous. I met Del, and some interesting Abenaki relatives. Best of all, I got to know Grumps.

All too fast, we are up the road and gone. I sink into the backseat behind the wicked queen who is my mother and the evil robot who is my father. Once we're beyond the bumpy back roads of northern New Hampshire, the weather quiets and the sky turns cornflower blue, reminding me of the flowers from Beetle at the powwow. *At least I hope they were from him.* I picture us singing together when I get back to Hartford. I fantasize about taking him on the road with me, even though I expect he's headed for a life as the big man on campus at some small ritzy New England college. I quell all romantic thoughts about Del. He and I will be finished for good the instant I report my suspicions about his father's role in Mia Delaney's death to the Hartford police.

Dad wipes his ever-dripping forehead. "Phew, am I glad to be out of that mess. Wild weather, wild animals, wild people. Are they all as crazy up there as your grandfather, Mona?" His eyeglasses flash in the rearview mirror.

I fold my arms in defense of Grumps. "He graciously took me in while you played Indiana Jones. You should be grateful to him. All you and Mom can think about is how much you hate him. I have more serious matters to consider, like how Mom's friend, Will Pyne, may have murdered a girl from Hartford."

Mom jumps in. "Don't be ridiculous. Will did no such thing. He makes a bad first impression. That's all. Consequently, he has always suffered at the hands of ignorant people who look at the surface and don't see him for the wonderful heartfelt genius he is. He's an artistic miracle and probably the only truly sane person in Indian Stream." She turns, trying to wrangle my trust. "He used to be a good guitarist. You two have a lot in common."

"I'm certain I don't have anything in common with Mia Delaney's murderer."

"That's enough! Stop the car, Bryer."

Dad screeches to a halt on the side of a cliff. I wonder if this choice of location is meant to intimidate me or if his eyeballs have rolled up into his head and he has no idea where we are.

"Mona, listen to me," says Mom. "Don't be duped by those insane rumors. If there's one thing I can guarantee, it's that Will Pyne never hurt my friend Mia Delaney. Don't you dare get mixed up in that awful case."

"It's been a few years since you've seen Will, Mom. He's pretty messed up."

"Will is harmless. If you cross me on this, Mona, I swear…"

"Don't you want to find Mia's killer?"

"There's no point in continuing this conversation." Mom coils up in a ball and leans on her car door.

A sick feeling surges through me at the thought that my mom may know something about Mia's murder that she won't reveal. The car goes silent for a few minutes.

Dad finally speaks. "I suppose you rode in that multicolored jalopy your grandfather calls a truck."

"Actually, Grumps taught me how to drive it. Thanks to him, I'm ready to take my driver's test as soon as we get home."

Mom eyes Dad in an unnaturally alarmed way.

Dad rolls up his tattered oxford shirtsleeve. "I almost forgot, Mona. Wait till you see this." He flashes a freshly inked tattoo on his wrist. It's an interlocking braid that probably signals his membership in some secret Russian tribal group. I refuse to like it and wish I could stop eyeing it. I never asked my parents if I could get a tattoo, and now that he has one, tattoos suck.

Mom swats Dad's still-swollen wrist. "He just got it to impress his graduate students, Mona."

Dad starts the car and kneads the steering wheel. I hope there are no more cliffs around.

I try out a joke. "Principal Dibble has an opinion of where you go in the afterlife with a tattoo." I point my thumb straight down.

Dad explodes. "That woman has no sense of humor." He eyes Mom. "Thank goodness you're done with her, Mona."

Continuing the playground one-upmanship, Mom rolls up her sleeves and flexes her toned biceps, "Would you believe I dug up twice as many artifacts as the rest of your dad's graduate students, combined?"

I'm not in the mood to hear how many bear bones she scooped out of the dirt. So I insert a conversation-stopper. "This summer, I fed bananas to a blond bear named Marilynn, and I met my fortune-telling great aunt, Black Racer Woman, whom some folks call a witch."

Mom rolls her sleeves down over her bulging biceps. Dad turns the dial to National Public Radio and cranks it up despite the spotty signal. I relax and let my eyes follow the Connecticut River. It's the lifeline between where I'm going and where I've been.

Dad is the first to speak again, two hours later. "We're out of the mountains, Lila. You should have decent phone reception now."

They gaze at one another with crinkled brows. I can see they're desperate for hopeful employment news. My professor parents have spent every September of their lives inside a classroom. They won't know where else to go when the leaves start to turn.

Mom checks her emails and giggles. Dad and I simultaneously draw our heads back in shock at hearing girlish sounds coming from Lila Elmwood's mouth. Mom presses the numbers on her phone frantically and then shifts to her haughty professor voice, stretching out each word as if it has an extra syllable known only to smart people.

After five minutes of this phony prattle, she hangs up and screams. "Twain College wants me back! You'll never believe what else, Bryer? They want me to head up their new Native American Studies Department!"

"Isn't that fine, Lila."

His flat tone tells me he wonders how Twain College can support a whole program based on the boring Natives of this continent when his research on the fascinating indigenous rituals of Russia remains so poorly funded. He hasn't caught on to the fact that American Indians are the least understood, most important people on the planet—according to Mom, anyway.

On the crowded I-91 highway between Springfield, Massachusetts, and Hartford, Connecticut, we hit super gridlock. It's nearly a hundred degrees, and our air-conditioning is busted. We're stuck in a noxious cloud of gas fumes that my parents don't seem to notice. I can see the churning waters of the Connecticut River out my window and feel comforted, knowing they come from the lakes of Indian Stream.

Dad reads emails on his phone while Mom makes a zillion work calls.

"Go ahead and text your friend, Lizzy," Mom offers. "We can afford an unlimited plan now!"

I had almost forgotten I own a phone. I connect my long dead phone to the car charger. The battery slowly revives, and I text Lizzy. "Listen. Do you want to know a secret?" I hope she hasn't forgotten our Beatles code. I want to tell her about running into Beetle at the powwow.

She writes back, "Honey, don't."

Lizzy has somehow read my mind all the way from Toronto. But she shouldn't worry about me falling back into depression. I accept the fact that my summer encounter with Beetle was a onetime thing. He will never be my boyfriend, and neither will my summer fling, Del Pyne. Yet I'm entitled to my dreams. It's head-in-the-clouds moments like these that keep young women like me from crowding the edges of the roof at City Place. I text Lizzy again to tell her that I'm trying to "take a sad song and make it better." I know she loves the lyrics to "Hey Jude."

She writes back, "That'll Be the Day."

Ha! I want to tell her she's an idiot because Buddy Holly wrote "That'll Be the Day," not the Beatles. While the Fab Four recorded it, they did it before they were even called the Beatles. Her text technically breaks our rules.

I force myself to push away my mental nonsense and take her words to heart: Lizzy wants me to lower my sights, to realize there's no reason to suppose this year will be different than any other. I'm still Mona Lisa LaPierre, the girl with the last face on earth that anyone would want to paint—who never, ever, smiles. I have tree bark hair, mudwood eyes, and dresser drawers stuffed with black band tee shirts.

The traffic is moving but we aren't. Dad doesn't press the pedal. Mom and I exchange irritated looks. He's reading his phone and patting it, like a good dog, while chuckling like the mad scientist that we know he is. Horns beep madly all around us. He ignores them.

Mom shakes Dad harshly, "Bryer, what's the matter with you?"

He unsteadily hands her his phone.

She speaks in a shrill tone as she reads his email aloud, "'We at Twain University Press would like to offer you a ten thousand-dollar advance for your book on Russian bear sacrifice.' Bryer, this is wonderful news!"

I recognize fake glee when I hear it. Apparently, Dad's archeological dig was more successful than Mom let on. This news will surely compel her to shoot for a bigger advance on her next book. Dr. Lila Elmwood doesn't like anyone to beat her at anything. Sadly, she's in for bitter disappointment. Her current research—on the bitten birch bark designs of Eastern Woodland Indians—won't do it for her.

"Mona, I almost forgot." She pulls a mottled green envelope from her purse and slaps it in my hand. "You got something from Swamp Toad Records."

I read the letter, written on bumpy toad-green stationary. *"Congratulations! I'm pleased to inform you…"*

I can't believe this. I won their songwriting contest. I pull out a check for five thousand dollars. FIVE THOUSAND DOLLARS. We've been driving FOUR hours and only now does Mom mention this letter. There's no point in getting angry. It's more sensible to imagine that I'm an orphan who has no parents with whom to share my success.

I write a cryptic text to Lizzy, "From this moment on I know, exactly where my life will go." I realize this lyric will confuse her. I delete it before sending because it comes from a John Lennon song that was reworked by the three surviving Beatles in the 1990s after he died. It's considered the very last Beatles song, and you have to be a serious Beatles fan to know about it. Lizzy isn't serious about anything. I change my text to "Maybe I'm Amazed" along with a picture of the check. She'll get that.

Lizzy texts back immediately. "Money don't get everything it's true. What it don't get, I can't use."

Wow! Lizzy's rich new stepdad has certainly changed her worldview. But am I any better? All I can think about is my check from the recording company.

I pull up eBay on my phone and look for the rare Beatles tee shirt I drooled over in June. It's still there. I already have five hundred dollars from my cut of Grumps' antler sales, but it costs twice that to "Buy It Now." If I make an auction bid I know I can stall the seller for payment for a couple days while the Swamp Toad check clears at Beetle's dad's bank.

I hold back a moment. This is not the kind of shirt most teenage girls would want, never mind a shirt that any guy wants to see a girl wearing. It features the Beatles dressed as butchers holding raw meat and dismembered baby dolls. Only those in-the-know understand the historic value of this slightly sick bit of memorabilia. Normally, I wouldn't go for a slaughterhouse motif, considering my apartment building. But this shirt is a rare and exotic treasure. Almost all the original shirts were yanked from the shelves before anyone could buy them. Wearing it is a blow against censorship, a blow against narrow-minded people like Principal Millicent Dibble.

I offer a thousand bucks. Successful musicians need hot clothes. Unfortunately, I realize I also need to tell my parents about my big songwriting win. Otherwise, if they see me wearing the tee shirt, they'll think I stole it.

I spill the news. "I just won five thousand dollars in a songwriting contest."

Mom reacts with unprecedented cheers. I'm guessing she thinks this check will make me forget my suspicions about Will Pyne. I maintain a stern expression to assure her that it won't. The traffic picks up enthusiastically as if not wishing to hamper our car full of winners on our stampede toward success.

"Can we hear the prize-winning tune before you leave us and take it on the road?" Dad asks, showing uncharacteristic interest. Mom manages a pretty grin, probably thinking this boost to my musical career will make it easier for her to get rid of me.

I play the bluesy chorus to "You Are My Lightning." It isn't too long before Mom is snapping her fingers and bobbing her head. Dad car-dances, and he really does have good rhythm. I breathe into the music, keeping my eyes on Rosalita's vibrating strings. They are the only truly magical thing in this universe because they can take me wherever I want to go.

Part II

Ten

Stale Sole

I receive a strange text that day after I return home.

I wrote a song for you. - Beetle

I laugh at this text, knowing it's a prank, most likely from Brick Rodman. I won't give him the satisfaction of a response. A second text beeps.

Can you come over for dinner? - Beetle

No way. I won't fall for this. Brick's reign as the High Priest of Humiliation ended on his last day of high school.

I hear my ringtone sound. It's Bonnie Raitt's "Right Down the Line." I swear the music stops my heart. I fumble to turn on the phone. The caller has the same number as the texts. I choke out a hello.

"Hey, Mona," says a golden voice that can only belong to Beetle.

I allow myself a brief celebratory fist-squeeze. Then a mental image of the City Place rooftop forces me to calm down and exercise caution. Beetle said he wrote a song *for* me, not necessarily *about* me. There's a big difference. It's probably about the glamorous girls of Lake Winnipesaukee. I need to remain aloof, which is easy, as I haven't spoken.

"Did you get my texts?" he asks.

"I've been busy working on a song," I reply, because this is one lie that is always half-true. "It's called 'Lost in the Woods.'"

"Sounds like you had quite the summer. I'll bet your song is amazing. I'd love to hear it. I have something to play for you that I wrote on vacation. Can you come over my house for dinner?"

———

Beetle's house comes up first on Google images when you type in "world's hottest houses." The silver trim on its green glass siding reminds me of newly minted quarters. Most Colt High students live in cheap renovated apartment buildings that used to be something industrial, like mine. This house should belong to somebody from Loomis Chaffee, Suffield Academy, Westminster, or some other overpriced Connecticut boarding school. My personal, professional, and paranormal lives have merged into one outrageous burst of late summer sunshine. Going to Beetle's house represents not only hope for romance and musical collaboration, but also a chance to find clues to Mia's murder, all in a single location. Plus, meeting Beetle's parents may clear up the mystery of why Barrington Dill was slumming it at Colt High for the last four years.

Mrs. Dill and Beetle greet me at their green glass front door. Her blinding blue eyes gaze right through me, as though she needs to look past the person who is ruining her otherwise pristine entryway. This blank staring woman is famine thin with California hair that shines brighter than the sun. Beetle introduces me, and she pushes a stray blond hair behind her ear then fiddles with her hemline—which is shorter than moms usually wear—without uttering a word of greeting, like she's trying to impersonate a teenager.

Beetle introduces me a second time, and her intense eyes snap to attention, widening at first sight of my butchered baby-dolls Beatles tee shirt. She obviously doesn't know it's an expensive collector's item.

Her eyes remain stuck on my chest as she speaks, "Nice to meet you, Mona. Our Beetle has been going on about how talented you are. I was once a musician. I played French horn in the Colt High band. Mr. Dill was a linebacker on the football team, when we were seniors back in 1994. Beetle takes after me with his preference for music. Of course, I never considered it as a potential career." She heaves her chest and breaks eye contact with my shirt. "Worthy and I have such fond memories of Colt High. We are sorry to hear it will be torn down soon. It's such a wonderful place. We are planning to host a Farewell Dance there for all the alumni, including all you recent grads, before the demolition. We think Colt High is the best school in Connecticut."

I inhale and hold it. There is no appropriate response to this. Mrs. Dill is either kidding or crazy. Colt High ranks 148th out of 150 high schools in the state. When my parents sent me there, they insisted it was a school on the rise. So much for their judgment. The truth is they couldn't afford private school and—unlike other professors' kids—I wasn't academic scholarship material. I'm hoping Mrs. Dill is joking about her adoration for our school because otherwise she's nuts, and Will Pyne has filled my wacky parent quotient for a lifetime.

She flips her hair, adolescently, "Please come in."

I smell stale fish.

"Where will you be attending college in the fall, Mona?" she asks.

The rising fish stench makes it impossible not to gag. After making a harsh hacking sound, I recover. "I was accepted at Berklee College of Music but I've decided not to go." I picture the framed acceptance letter that Mom hung on our living room wall.

"Not attending college? With two Ph.D. parents, no less? Perhaps the fact that your parents are professors makes it difficult for you to realize that attending college is a privilege—a privilege that Beetle's father and I did not enjoy."

So she's Googled my family and me. I wonder if Mrs. Dill does this sort of snooping on all of Beetle's friends. Meanwhile, I can't believe the Dills never went to college. This stuns me more than her nosiness. I don't know much about Mrs. Dill's background. But I assumed Worthy's family was Old Hartford Money, the kind of money that automatically buys a ticket to a decent liberal arts college. Honestly, what uneducated person names their kid Barrington Dill? It's beyond curious that Worthington Dill never went to college. I feel guilty over the idea that he might be a self-made man when all this time I thought he was just another spoiled rich asshole.

Mrs. Dill continues. "I'm sure you feel it's acceptable to skip college because you're an artist and one of your songs just sold for a tidy sum. But music is not a stable way to make a living, dear. I keep trying to explain that to Beetle." Her blinding eyes blaze a deeper blue. "But he's determined to skip college to pursue a musical path, just like you."

Thank God I don't ever smile, or I'd turn into Alice's Cheshire Cat, right now. This is the best news I've had since finding out that Marilynn the Bear was not going to eat me. I nudge Rosalita warmly, the way you do a friend when you hear something awesome.

"We're almost ready to eat. I suppose you can bring your instrument into the dining room," she says, curling her lip at my guitar.

The fishy smell follows us, like the ghost of an ancient fisherman is tagging along.

Beetle rubs his nose uncomfortably. "Mom, what's for dinner?"

"Poached gray sole and steamed white rice."

Beetle and I share a worried glance. That explains the smell. This fish is nothing like the fresh lake trout Grumps fried outdoors, and I only eat brown rice. But it doesn't matter. I'm at Beetle's house. Monkey brains would be fine.

He waves me into the dining room. "Check this out, Mona." Beetle opens a guitar case that's sitting in a corner as though it's being punished. From it, he pulls out a fireglo red Rickenbacker, its strap etched with a series of Wabanaki stars. This strap was for sale at the Winnipesaukee powwow. He probably bought it to make him look cool, and it does.

Beetle introduces our instruments to one another. "Rosalita, may I present Dark Horse." He lowers his dark eyes flirtatiously. "I named him in honor of George Harrison's old album."

"Dark Horse," I repeat. What an ironic name for anything associated with someone as popular as Beetle. That name would be perfect for Will Pyne's guitar, if he had one. My thoughts shift to envisaging the battle between Will Pyne and Worthy Dill for Mia Delaney's affections. Worthy, the handsome prince. Will, the dark horse. There's no way Will won fairly. I need to tell the Hartford Police what I know about him. Maybe the Dills will tell me something that sheds more light on this cold case.

My fingers slide across the rosewood fret board and maple body of Beetle's new axe. "It reminds me of George Harrison's twelve-string."

"I know, right?" says Beetle, trying out a lick on his tight new guitar. He plays rigidly, as if he's mimicking a session from YouTube that he's practiced a thousand times. A dinner bell interrupts him, and he huffs, frustrated. I want to laugh at the sound of that bell. If my parents heard a bell like that at our apartment, they'd think the place was on fire.

"I'll play your song after we eat," he smirks.

So now it's *my song*. I force myself to imagine the deadly view from the top of City Place but all I can get is an image of Beetle dancing with me on that rooftop, like we're in some dipshit Broadway musical.

A dozen yellow roses fill a cut crystal vase at the center of a gleaming glass dinner table with Worthy Dill seated at its head. I recognized Worthy right away from his magnificent portrait at the bank. He could pass for Beetle's slightly overweight older brother: butterscotch bangs, licorice eyes, fabulous smirk, drop-dead shoulders, and all. It's easy to imagine what Mia Delaney and Mrs. Dill saw in him when he was young. He's not bad-looking now. Maybe I'm not so different from Mia.

Worthy rises to kiss my hand. "Lovely to meet you, Mona."

Hastening toward the stereo, he puts on the Beatles song, "Can't Buy Me Love." If only Lizzy could see this. Beetle and the Beatles together, in the same heavenly space. Seriously, the ambiance really *is* heavenly. The Dills' dining room is the color of whipped cream. Daddy Dill and Beetle are wearing butter-colored polos. Mommy Dill places a snowy platter of steaming food beside gold-plated serving dishes and flatware. In their pale clothes, lit by the golden crystal teardrop chandelier over the dining room table, the Dills shine like three glorious suns. I represent the proverbial sunspot, in my ripped black jeans, beat-up Chuck Taylors, and butchered baby dolls tee shirt.

Two huge wedding portraits hang on the wall behind Mrs. Dill's head. The faces of the bride and groom rest in separate oval gold frames that resemble halos. A brass plaque under the groom's photo says "Worthington 'Worthy' Dill." The bride's photo plaque includes her maiden name, saying "Carrie Arquette 'Cricket' Dill." So Carrie Arquette was mashed together to form "Cricket." What odd nicknames they manufacture in this family. It explains how they got "Beetle" out of Barrington Dill.

"Mona is quite the musician," Mrs. Dill informs her husband, curling her lip over every syllable of that last word.

I keep my head down. "I work hard at my music but I never expected to make money from it."

"Certainly not!" Mrs. Dill eyes Beetle harshly. "That's very sensible. We keep telling Beetle that he should rethink his plan to take a year off from college to pursue his musical interests."

Beetle stares at my hands. "If anyone deserves to get rich from playing the guitar, it's Mona. She is amazing. I don't think she would speak to me if I didn't play an instrument."

Worthy's brow spasms like he's going to be sick. He groans softly and then lunges forward to remove a yellow rose from the centerpiece. He presents it to me on two open palms, as if to atone for his poorly timed outburst. "Thank you for supporting Beetle's little hobby."

"My pleasure," I say, accepting the rose, and trying to put aside his condescending remark. "Lovely wedding photos." I sit straighter, shooting for a semblance of upper-class propriety.

Mrs. Dill crinkles her pencil-thin mouth, in what I suppose is a refined version of a thank you. "You'll have to excuse this informal dinner," she says, absurdly. "I had to throw it together because we only returned from Lake Winnipesaukee this afternoon. Mr. Dill and I have gone there for a month every summer since we were in high school. Our parents were good friends. In fact, we just brought this gray sole back from our favorite fishmonger by the lake." Telling this tale brings a warm glow to her cheeks.

Meanwhile, I turn green and instinctively cover my mouth. No wonder the fish smells off. It takes over three hours to get from Lake Winnipesaukee to Hartford. There is an awkward silence as the fish is passed.

"Mona, did you vacation anywhere after school got out?" asks Mr. Dill.

I put the yellow rose to my nose to alleviate the fish smell. "I also visited New Hampshire," I say. My grandfather has a cabin way up north, near Canada."

"Oh! My poor child, it must have been terrible, staying in a border town." Mrs. Dill shudders.

This is my chance. I shake the rose at her and a petal falls off. "Funny who you meet in border towns. I ran into the son of Mr. Dill's old girlfriend, Mia Delaney." I lean back in my chair, expecting the Dills to get into it over Worthy's old high school girlfriend, the way my parents fight over dad's flirtations with his graduate students.

Mrs. Dill's face sags and crinkles, as if the sands of time have rushed in all at once. She throws her napkin at me and stomps out. Mr. Dill rubs his chest, grumbling out the words, "Excuse me," and strides out of the room after her.

I expected a petty argument, not a full-on exodus. I can't believe I've just blown my chance to question Mr. Dill about Mia's death.

Beetle's head flops on the table and the fringe of his bangs pokes through his fingers. "Oh, man, I should have warned you. You couldn't know how sensitive my parents are on the subject of Mia Delaney. Everyone at school thinks of her as some tragic character in a distant old story. It's personal with my parents. She was their classmate. Dad kicks himself for going away on vacation to Winnipesaukee instead of searching for Mia after she disappeared, even though people said she left him for another guy. Now you tell him she also left a child behind which must make his guilt worse."

I'm shocked to hear Worthington Dill ever pined over anybody. I realize that I'm unfairly prejudiced, assuming Worthy only cares about money, when I really know nothing about him. The fact is, Worthy has been nice enough to me.

Beetle continues, "I should never have asked you over here, today. I wasn't thinking. My parents always act wacky when they return from Lake Winnipesaukee. It's some kind of flashback PTSD or something. Coming home always reminds them of when they returned to hear about Mia's murder."

"I understand. I can imagine the chaos and horror when Mia's body was discovered. It must have been awful—but still nothing compared to what Mia suffered."

I try to stay focused on finding out more information that can help her.

"I need to excuse myself to clear the dishes," says Beetle.

I frankly expected a housekeeper to appear. "Can I help you?' I ask.

"No thanks. I got this. Just listen to the music and relax. I'll be done in a few minutes."

The stereo blares the Beatles' song "I Should Have Known Better." I reexamine Cricket and Worthy Dill's headshot-only wedding photos. The date on the plaque says "September 30,

1994." A baby picture of Beetle on the opposite dining room wall has a plaque that reads, "Baby Barry, Our Blessing. March 14, 1995." He's older than me, graduating at eighteen, like most seniors. The dates on his parents' plaques tell the story of his birth.

Cricket graduated in the summer of 1994, so if Beetle was born in March of the following year, that means she got pregnant during her family summer vacation with the Dills, right after graduation. That's why she and Worthy were married that autumn. That's why they never went to college. I reexamine their wedding pictures. Her face appears swollen, and something about Worthy's eyes reminds me of a trapped and wounded animal. I'm probably imagining these things because of what I now know about their teen pregnancy. I can't believe the Dills were my age when they got married and had a kid, or that Mia was only a junior when she gave birth to Del.

Beetle returns, wagging a sponge. "There's something else you should know about Mia Delaney. When she disappeared at the end of her senior year, it wasn't the first time. That's why the authorities didn't search for her right away. She also went missing after her junior year. They say she liked to spend her summers with musicians. Who knows what groupie bus tour she crashed that got her killed?"

"We don't know for sure that she was a groupie," I snap, knowing that was the summer she had Del.

He takes a few steps back. "Fine. Maybe she wasn't a groupie. Let's just say she was attracted to musicians. That's why nobody hunted her down once they heard she'd taken off with some lowlife on a Harley. Her own father didn't bother to search for her." He removes the cut crystal water glasses from the table and curls his lip exactly like his mom does when she's disgusted. "Of course her family came from sketchy Manburn Street."

Ouch. I bite the rose between my teeth and snap it while playing a few bars on Rosalita. What he's said is insulting but also correct. My street *is* sketchy. I don't belong in this expensive glass house. I live in a former cattle slaughterhouse, next door to a former funeral parlor and a former orphanage. No designer mom waits on me, carrying platters of steamed food into a formal dining area where we eat with gold utensils. Our plates and glasses are a mishmash of whatever the dollar stores have on sale. I usually scarf down pancakes, or peanut butter, honey, and banana sandwiches in front of the computer, while Mom and Dad meet with their students, and research endless boring documents.

I want to put aside what Beetle said about my street, if only for Mia's sake. But my heart is shattered. I picture his glass house exploding into a million tiny shards. I don't want to hear the crappy song he wrote for me. I need to move, to get away, and to think. I lay what's left of my yellow rose atop Cricket's wedding picture and move Rosalita away from Dark Horse, into the living room. The delicate chandelier in here is made of interwoven gold circles, like tangled wedding bands. I sit on a powder blue velvet sofa beside a glass coffee table with a flowery letter D etched in the center. The rug beneath depicts pastel cherubs. A winsome porcelain teddy bear with a lavender ribbon circling its chubby neck sits atop the coffee table. Everything here is faint and fragile. Who lives like this?

From where I sit, I'm able to view Beetle's ashen face when he emerges from doing the dishes and finds I'm not where he left me. His eyes search frantically until he sees I've moved to the living room. He hurries to sit beside me. I bristle at his touch.

"What do you know about Mia's family?" I ask, determined to find out everything he knows.

"Mia's dad was some kind of down-and-out blues musician," he says. "He went by the name of Sugardaddy or something."

My fingers react first, strumming Rosalita fiercely, forcing out notes that make me double over and groan. "His name is not Sugardaddy."

He's talking about Shankdaddy. I'm stunned to hear he's Mia's father, although that connection explains why I saw her hanging around him. It also explains where Del gets his buttery voice. My fingers slip into a real nasty E bar chord. It's bad enough that he insults my neighborhood, now he's insulting a musician I idolize. I want to tell him he should stay away from me because I prefer the artful, murky side of this city, that my life is not so different from Mia's, that my dad is also careless and neglectful. In fact, he's in Russia again, offering Mom no timetable for his return. Mom is just as bad: she doesn't care about me or worry about her aging father, living alone in the middle of the New Hampshire woods. Neither of my parents would search for me if I got locked in the janitor's closet. They might not even notice I was gone. I want to tell Beetle that he's lucky to have a dad who cares about him. I reserve judgment on his mom. I shudder at the thought of what she'd say about Shankdaddy if she met him. I worry about what Beetle would say, as well. Mia and Shankdaddy Delaney are real people, like me. People with messy lives, not fake perfect ones. Beetle is in no position to judge Mia or Shankdaddy.

But I don't say anything. The riot inside my head pours out my fingers instead of my lips. I slam into the raucous melody of Orianthi's "According to You." I'm hoping Beetle will sense he's making assumptions I don't like. For some reason I can't be straightforward and launch a protest through words. It's easier to express myself through music. That's what it's for, isn't it?

He puts a heavy hand on mine, and I lose it. That poorly timed gesture gives me the courage to say what I feel.

"I've met Shankdaddy and he's not sketchy," I explode. "He's a music legend in my part of town. And Mia wasn't a slut." I don't know that last bit for sure, but I feel compelled to defend a dead friend's honor, the way you do with all your friends—slutty, chaste, living, or dead.

He removes his hand, shakily. "Fine, maybe Shankdaddy isn't sketchy. But his name still sounds dangerous."

From where I sit, slumped in this wispy blue room, I have a direct line of sight to the golden halo frames surrounding Cricket Dill's puffer fish bridal picture and Worthy's deer-in-the-headlights groom photo. Neither of them deserves their halos any more than Shankdaddy and Mia deserve to be demonized.

On the stereo, George Harrison's twelve-string lets loose the impressive opening chord to "A Hard Day's Night." Beetle will never play a single chord with heart like that. But Shankdaddy can easily do it, and I'm getting there. Who cares if Shankdaddy and George Harrison were neglectful or irresponsible in their personal lives? They're virtuosos. Beetle will never achieve that status. He is in no position to judge someone like Shankdaddy.

I sit tall. "Shankdaddy is a genius. I met him two years ago. His grandson—Mia's son—is quite charming. We jammed together this summer."

Beetle kicks the glass table beside me. The porcelain teddy bear with the lavender satin ribbon topples over and chips his ear. I'm glad. I've been dying to see something around here break. Beetle's too preoccupied to notice the bear's damage or care about it. He's pulling his bangs, trying to piece things together.

"Are you telling me that Mia's kid was that gimpy dude who was hanging around your vendor booth at the powwow? I knew there was something I didn't like about that guy."

Uh-oh. This I did not expect. A more naive girl might interpret this remark as a show of affection or possessiveness or worse. But the thought of the City Place roof keeps me grounded.

Beetle starts pulling his bangs, again. "Wait a minute. Wait a minute. I've seen Mia's senior yearbook. That hottie didn't look pregnant to me."

I don't bother to explain that she gave birth to Del at the end of the summer after her junior year, well before her yearbook photo was taken. That information would give away that I know more than I'm letting on. Besides, we're both picturing Mia in divergent ways. He imagines a sexy slut from a bad part of town who's broken his dad's heart. I picture a beautiful young woman from a talented musical family whose life was unfairly cut short. My Mia isn't part of a distant bygone tragedy. Her friends' and family's suffering lingers in my present. I recall the angel on Del's guitar that represents his mother, the deep sorrow I heard in Shankdaddy's voice when he sang the blues. I can still see Mom frozen in agony at the doorway to the janitor's closet where Mia's dead body was found. To Beetle, Mia Delaney is a tawdry player in a twisted, trashy, timeworn tale. To me and those who loved her, she is a real human being with a complicated life and afterlife, who is deeply mourned.

Now for some ugly honesty: despite how angry Beetle makes me feel or how much he insults the Delaney family's lifestyle, a part of me enjoys being a guest in the world's hottest house, and I hate myself for it. I'm not rich or beautiful but I have information about Mia Delaney's murder that may matter to Beetle's dad. If I share what I know, might the Dills think better of me? I want them to like me. If I make a connection with them that also helps Mia; is that wrong?

I test the waters. "Beetle, I know who killed Mia Delaney. I need your dad's help to nail her killer." After saying this, I immediately need some air and step out the green glass French doors. But instead of relief, the searing August heat sucks my breath away.

"What are you talking about, Mona?" he asks.

I force out the words. "I met a man this summer with a photo of an old Harley with green flames, like the one they say belonged to Mia's killer."

"You sure had a busy summer," mutters Beetle, tugging on his bangs, still trying to stimulate his brain. "I don't know if that bike means anything. They must have made hundreds of those stupid flame-painted motorcycles, back in the 1990s. Right?"

I'm already outside. I could run to Del in New Haven, or run to St. Louis to jumpstart my blues career and escape what I know about this murder case, or run home to the sketchy street where I belong and hang out with musicians I already know. Instead I step back inside, shut the green glass door, return to the cool and comfortable central air-conditioning, and betray the Pyne family.

"I've seen Mia's photo in a 1994 Colt High yearbook at this motorcycle guy's house. It had your dad's face scratched out."

"What!"

I realize too late that I've said more than I should have. Mentioning the yearbook in Will's secret room could get Del in trouble. Not to mention that I can't tell Beetle what

I was doing in that secret room made of flowers, or that I recognized Mia's picture because I'd seen her. I can't say any of this because I'm from Manburn Street, a place that Beetle has already dubbed the home of lunatics and losers.

He grabs my hand again, only this time, he kisses my fingers. His palm is sweaty. He's jealous and...desperate? I'm willing to overlook this sweat and his heartless snooty view of the world if he genuinely cares for me. My defenses tumble. I'm prepared to drop the subject of Mia Delaney until the end of time if he keeps holding my hand. An untimely wave of nausea rolls over me. I pray it's only a lingering effect of the fishy-smelling sole. I shut my eyes tight, afraid that if I open them I'll see the shadow of a hoop earring or a cascade of dark curls. I let go of his hand and drop my head between my knees.

"What's wrong, Mona? Do you have a migraine or something? My mom gets a lot of those." He rubs my back, tenderly. "How about a glass of water?"

I finally let it register in my brain that Beetle likes me as more than a friend. I try not to focus on how much I want to throw up. I concentrate on breathing slowly. Man, do I hate fishy-smelling sole. I'm not crazy about soggy white rice either. Beetle's mom is as bad a cook as mine.

"I'll be fine in a minute," I say, waving him away, while still keeping my head down.

He grabs my hand again, which seems overly clingy—a problem I never imagined having with Barrington Dill. At least his hand is no longer sweaty.

"Maybe this glass of water will help," he calls from the kitchen.

I stop breathing. Beetle is no longer in this room but someone is holding my hand. I open my eyes gradually and see the fingernails lying in my palm are painted electric blue.

The powder blue couch dissolves around them. I am floating in the pure deep darkness of outer space. The lights have blinked out in the entire Milky Way galaxy; nothing cuts the void but those electric blue fingertips, glowing like stellar blue stars. I'm hovering between the living and the dead, between the earth and sky. I lift my head and spy the glint of a hoop earring engraved with the word "LOVE" poking out from a head of dark curls. I want those curls to fade away, those blue-tipped fingers to leave my hand. I can't hear the Beatles' music on the stereo anymore. I can't hear anything. I'm light-years away, adrift in the in-betweens of this world and the next. I want to hear something that is earthly, for Ringo to bang out a wanton drum solo, or George to strum an exotic eastern chord, or Paul to croon my heart away, or John to waken my political soul.

Those stellar blue fingernails dig into my skin and then release, letting me go. The inky cosmos fades away and I'm back in the Dill's light-drenched living room, my outstretched hand lying empty. Mia is gone, but her fingernails have injected courage into my veins. I rise as Beetle returns from the kitchen carrying my glass of water. I swallow the drink greedily and feel energized. The music has resumed and the Beatles are singing, "Things We Said Today."

Adopting Mom's bossy professor tone I announce, "The man who killed Mia lives in New Hampshire. He needs to go to jail. I should tell your dad about this guy right away."

Before Beetle can respond, his dad enters the room, having overheard I don't know how much. "Tell me about what guy?" Mr. Dill wheezes. I wonder if he has been working out, but he isn't wearing sneakers, and his butter-colored polo shirt remains crisp.

I approach him. "I ran into someone this past summer who may be responsible for Mia Delaney's death. I'm telling you because I know she was your girlfriend."

"She was never my girlfriend!" Worthy bursts out. "She only cared about musicians."

From the beaten look on his face, this rejection happened yesterday.

"Worthy, where did you go?" calls Cricket from another room.

"In here, dear."

Cricket storms in and notices Worthy rubbing his brow. Her head whips at me. "You are still here, causing trouble! You are a heartless girl to bring that dead girl's name into our house. I think you'd better leave."

"No way, Mom," Beetle protests. "Mona hasn't even heard her song."

"Is that all you care about? Young man, let me tell you something about the kind of lowdown lives that musicians lead."

"I wished I'd been a musician instead of an athlete," mumbled Worthy.

"You would. Then all those loose groupie chicks would have loved you even more than they already did."

"That's not true, dear. I never got serious about any groupies."

"Only because an unfortunate circumstance nipped that in the bud."

I tune out their argument and exit as gracefully as possible. The new information I've learned warrants consideration. Worthy Dill said he was not Mia's boyfriend, and I believe him. This contradicts the story Beetle has spread around school for years. Why did he make it up? Girlfriend or not, the Dills dislike the subjects of Mia Delaney and musicians. Still, that's not my issue. My job is to tell the Hartford Police everything I know about Mia's murder. Unfortunately, without Worthy's help, I doubt they'll listen to me. He pulls a lot of weight in this city. I'm just another blues musician from Manburn Street. Nevertheless, I'm determined to find Mia Delaney's killer. I only hope Mia is patient.

Eleven

It's All in the Stars

Hartford Police Headquarters is a tidy contemporary brick building that looks the way Colt High should. The duty officer at the reception desk wears a steel-wool buzz cut and the glow of impending retirement.

He shakes his head disgustedly, as he writes down my name. "That's LaPierre with a capital 'P,' as in 'Problem Child,' right?"

I ignore his sarcasm and tell him about my discovery of the infamous Harley with green flames from the Mia Delaney case.

He yawns in a rudely exaggerated fashion, patting his open mouth. "Which crazy cold case murder site have you been following on the Internet, girly?"

I push through his insult. "I need to make a statement regarding new evidence in the Mia Delaney case."

The cop licks the tip of his pen. "Let 'er rip."

I offer a statement about Will Pyne: where he lives, that he owns a picture of a green-flamed Harley, that he sleeps with a picture of Mia.

I finish and the cop says, "Okey dokey," more like I'd just

bought a raffle ticket rather than submitted critical evidence in a cold case murder.

I exit this brick box full of morons out a side door that leads me past a fragrant stew of sidewalk garbage. My whole world stinks. I'm almost home when a white Escalade rolls up alongside me, its wheels so shiny they catch the hot August sun and blind me. I figure the car belongs to a drug dealer and hug Rosalita. Nobody is stealing my baby and selling her for crack. The vehicle stops and the car door swings open. I stiffen. Out steps Worthington Dill, sporting khaki Bermuda shorts and lime-green Docksiders. A drug dealer would have been preferable. I wish I could snap my fingers and make him disappear. I never wanted the Dills to see where I live.

"Greetings, Mona!" Worthy hugs me; his broad shoulders remind me too much of Beetle. His eyes stay fixed on my face, seemingly oblivious to my neighborhood.

After a few uneasy throat clearings, he continues, "I am here to apologize for the incident at my home last week. My wife knows I find the subject of Mia Delaney a difficult one. She tends to react overly harshly when people mention that girl's name around me."

"She doesn't care much for musicians, either, does she?"

"No," he smirks. "Speaking of which, how is your budding music career coming along?"

I notice he stutters on the word "music."

"I need a partner who can sing. My voice is mediocre."

He raises his eyebrows cheerfully. "I'm sure you'll find one, soon. Meanwhile, I want to hear all about this New Hampshire biker whom you suspect of foul play."

My palms moisten. I wipe them on my jeans, recalling that day at his house when Mia's electric blue fingernails replaced Beetle's sweaty hand. Mia's nowhere in sight, but she could reappear at any minute as long as Will Pyne remains free. I know I am her messenger, standing alone, as her sole hope for justice.

"I told the police everything," I explain. "The man's name is Will Pyne. He lives in Indian Stream, New Hampshire. He owns a Harley with green flames. That's all I know."

"So I heard—the police just called me. But I think there's something you overlooked mentioning, something more convincing that would have triggered a search warrant." His mouth puckers, and his eyes divert. Worthy Dill has a shitty poker face for a rich businessman.

I slouch, fold my arms and wait for him to come clean about whatever it is he is hiding.

He raises a hand in front of his face, "All right, all right. I'll tell you the whole truth. I owe you that much. I heard from Beetle that you had a special relationship with the suspect's son. Beetle is afraid you're keeping information from the police out of loyalty to this young man. He believes you intentionally neglected to mention a mutilated picture of me that you found in an old yearbook at the Pyne house, a picture that suggests Will Pyne has violent tendencies, however misplaced, as we both know Mia had no use for me."

I'm speechless. I forgot I told Beetle about that yearbook. Mr. Dill is right. I didn't mention his mutilated picture to the police, perhaps because the duty officer was in such a hurry to get rid of me at the station, or because I knew that disclosing it could get Del in trouble with his dad for invading his secret room. Either way, Beetle and Worthy think I'm withholding evidence to keep Will from being arrested, which isn't true.

"You're right," I swallow. "I didn't mention the yearbook."

"I've already talked to the police but I'm going to urge them to apprehend Will. He pats my shoulder. "I'm so sorry for the rift between you and my son. It was entirely his parents' fault. On behalf of Mrs. Dill and myself, I apologize. But when it comes to that Pyne boy, I'm concerned for you. His family is dangerous."

A blues song brews inside my head. *His mama and his papa, they're from the baddest part of town. His mama and his papa, they come from the baddest part of town. Don't tell me he's a good man, baby, when I know he's just a lowdown clown.*

I tap the beat on my guitar case. Mr. Dill's eyes fall to my tapping hands, as Beetle's always do, and they linger. You can tell he's wanted to play guitar since he was a teenager, and I can guess why. From his perspective, the musician always gets the girl, even if the guy is a loser. I mean, look at Worthy compared to Will. There's definitely some truth to that. Meanwhile, I can't help picturing Del's smile, the only true smile I've ever known—the one smile I'll never see again, once the police find out about that yearbook.

Mr. Dill lightly kisses my hand. "Now that we're done with our official business, someone wishes to speak to you. Good-bye, Mona."

Worthy steps into the Escalade, and Beetle steps out the other side. His hair is lumpy and the heavy bags under his eyes suggest he hasn't slept. Yet, the minute he sees me, his face gleams pale like a sun pushing through a blizzard. He's wearing a torn white tee shirt with stylishly faded Nantucket red shorts. He's perfect, as always.

Beetle removes Dark Horse from its case, and hangs it in front of his chest in all its blazing fireglo red summer glory. He starts strumming, awkwardly, singing a melancholy song called "My Mona." The senior citizens living in the renovated funeral parlor next door peek out of their open windows. A few are curious enough about my crooner to step onto their stoops in their bare feet. Several kids mosey our way, emerging from the orphanage-turned-condos. This show is a bonanza for the early birds in my neighborhood. Nobody sings outdoors at this end of Manburn Street, especially nobody who arrives in an Escalade. It reminds me of a scene from a bad music video, where a swank car cruises into a sloppy neighborhood and a well-dressed model steps out—except Beetle doesn't look like a model today.

This brave song must be what he wanted to sing to me the night I went over his house. He definitely wrote it himself. The melody sounds like background music for a lame reality show and the repetitive lyrics remind me of *The Little Engine That Could*. The composition has nothing to recommend it except the singer's amazing vocal range. Don't ask me why, but every time he hits a high note it feels like hot sauce is running through my veins.

When he finishes, claps erupt from my nosy neighbors, mostly to support his bravery. An old lady in a pink robe that is missing most of its buttons yells, "You got golden pipes, Son."

He bows, which prompts more clapping and hooting. I surprise myself by rushing forward and brushing a kiss across his cheek. This prompts the loudest cheers from the old folks, remembering when.

He grabs my hand. "Let's go for a walk."

"I know just the place." I wave good-bye to the whistling crowd, and his father drives away. "I'm going to show you the best part of my street."

Beetle dons an apologetic smile that shows me how sorry he is to have insulted me that day at his house when he dissed my street.

He tugs at my sleeve, "Lead on, Mona."

I'm ready to forgive him for pre-judging my neighborhood if he is willing to give it a fair chance. Rosalita and Dark Horse bounce against our backs as I lead him toward the thumping car stereos, quarreling couples, squealing children, and otherwise boldly drumming human hearts that always congregate at the other end of Manburn Street. We walk past a woman with no teeth dancing on the sidewalk barefoot beneath a neon sign that flashes the words "Beautiful Dancing Girls!" A fire hydrant catches my eye: it's painted with lush red lips and a thickly lashed winking eye that reminds me of The Blond Bear's band tee shirts. I flinch at the memory of Del and Scales singing their growling duo. I hate myself for thinking about him, and him with her—especially right now.

Beetle sniffs the air with interest. "Something smells awesome!"

The scent of burnt-sweet scotch bonnet peppers wafts our way from Jam's Jerk shop. I've experienced Beetle's mom's lame cooking, and my mom never cooks anything edible, either. We share excitement over the smell of wonderful food. Beetle and I step under the shop's flaming red awning and belly up to the busy counter, where he buys himself a jerk chicken stick and me some fried plantains. We nibble them while watching a cluster of chattering tween girls eye the half-price summer dresses in the window of Montego Bay ladies' apparel store. Waves of crackling laughter flow out of Kingston Beauty Shop as we pass. Steam rolls off the pavement under the cars and trucks. I enjoy watching Beetle lick the last of the jerk goo off his lips. Late summer in the city was never so delicious.

After we finish, I lead him down another block to show him a sign that says "Madame Celine, Astrologer" in glittery gold lettering. The steps leading up to it are also painted gold.

"This is the last place I saw Shankdaddy." I point at the black, green and gold door painted to resemble a Jamaican flag.

I race him to the top of the golden steps. A zodiac mobile hangs in the front window, spinning constellations of celestial rams, crabs, and lions. I pat an old gray stool by the door. "Right here, Shankdaddy picked out a bluesy tune that made the earth rumble beneath my feet."

"Is he inside?" asks Beetle, cautiously climbing the golden steps.

"Maybe." I pull the door handle and the shop bell tinkles.

"Guitar Girl!" wails the shopkeeper. "I remember you."

"Hello, Celine," I say.

She is radiant with abundant sapphire braids and appears cool despite the lack of air-conditioning. Astrological charts, music posters, and pictures of Jamaica cover walls painted the colors of tropical fruit.

I look around for Shankdaddy but Celine is alone, except for a black cat with one gold eye and a second empty eye socket filled with matted scars. The cat brushes against my leg and I pet him. I wish Millicent Dibble were here to see me showing this kitty kindness.

"Nobody could forget your musical gifts, Mona. Old Damerae remembers you. He liked your style." She pets the cat.

Damerae limply lifts a paw to my knee in a seeming attempt to shake hands like a dog. I bend down to grasp the frail paw, and he mews weakly but earnestly. I introduce Beetle, and Celine doesn't acknowledge him. She's busy watching Damerae scratch the wall, like he's writing something.

Celine slaps the air in irritation. "Damerae says you have a special connection to the stars, Mona. He wants me to read your horoscope, right now, on the house." She kisses her cat on the forehead. "I have to obey Damerae's wishes. He's never been healthy, so I'm inclined to think his thoughts are directly connected to the other side, if you know what I mean."

I want to say I'm a Mohegan and Abenaki Indian who talks to her dead grandmother and sees a dead teenager named Mia, so of course I know what she means. But I only nod so as not to make things any weirder for Beetle, who already appears bedazzled by Celine's place.

She pats one of her astrological star charts, continuing to ignore him. He doesn't care. His eyes are glued to the posters of twentieth-century Hartford bands, and he's mumbling bits of trivia about each one. His parents are Hartford natives, so he knows far more about the musical history of our city than me—the girl with the Canuck dad and New Hampshire-born mom.

Celine gathers her braids and knots them atop her head— as if prepping to perform surgery—before reading my star chart. "You're a typical Leo, Mona, preferring to stand alone." She clucks her tongue. "No matter. Even loners sometimes get noticed. I see you're already somewhat famous and about to become a star!"

"Celine, I won one songwriting contest."

"Child, you're about to climb higher." She grabs a pen from the counter, whirls around in her floral dress and taps me on the head, as if it's a wand. "Celine is your fairy godmother. You're headed for the big time. You've been chosen for great things. The stars don't lie. They say you have an important future ahead. Prepare for a wild ride in this great big universe. It all belongs to you." She lets loose a laugh as wide as the Jamaican sky.

Damerae scratches at the wall again and mews.

"No!" Celine wails and lifts him. "It can't be." She presses her silky copper cheek against the cat's ebony face and acknowledges Beetle for the first time. "Young man, come here." She pulls Beetle in front of a different chart and slaps it. "It would appear Damerae has noticed something I missed. The stars say you're about to become famous, as well."

Beetle radiates like a supernova. "Awesome!" he says, flabbergasted.

"Don't thank me!" She tears the chart off the wall and rips it in half as if to punish it. "It would seem the stars have a mind of their own."

Beetle points to a framed photo on a shelf that shows a younger Celine with natural mahogany hair, seated beside a man in a scarlet straw hat.

"Is this Shankdaddy, the old blues man who jammed here with Mona?" he asks.

Her rum-colored eyes swell, and she slips into a heavier Jamaican accent. "Lord no, child, Mona never played with him. I buried my poor fadda a dozen years ago." She touches the picture and closes her eyes prayerfully. "Yes indeed, he is long gone to the other side. But he would have liked Mona."

I'm thunderstruck by Celine's revelation. First, she's saying that Shankdaddy is her father. Worst, she claims I played guitar with him a decade after he died.

Beetle taps a yellowed newspaper clipping tacked on the wall that says, "Dead Girl's Sister Vows to Solve Case." A memorial candle in a glass holder flickers beside the clipping.

"Are you Mia Delaney's sister?" he asks, breathless.

"Yes, I am." Celine's speech is clipped. "Her short life shows how our lucky stars can sometimes turn cruel. Mia's fortunes started out as good ones, just like yours. She, too, was a lovely and talented free spirit. So be careful."

Beetle's licorice eyes form a black hole, sucking in everything around him with new urgency. Mia has become real to him.

Celine touches Rosalita. "It's too bad you didn't actually play guitar with my father, Mona. You two would have made beautiful music together. She raises a judgmental eyebrow at Beetle. You deserve a good musical partner."

Celine passes a finger through the flame of the memorial candle and puts a tissue to her eye. "I'm sorry." She opens the door and waves us out. "I'm afraid that we must speak another time."

The door tinkles shut behind us.

Beetle bites his sarcastic lips closed, but fails to keep his mouth shut. "I can't believe we just met Mia Delaney's sister, and you jammed with her dead father. I didn't know you were so tight with the dead." His hands wave like a magician's.

I turn to him with the eye squint of all eye squints. "You know what, Barrington Dill? I think it's entirely possible that Shankdaddy jammed with me. Maybe we made music together in a way beyond our knowing. Astrology is outside our realm of understanding. Yet you can't tell me that you didn't love hearing you're about to become a star."

"Sure Mona, but how is that going to happen?"

I hop down the golden stairs, jubilant. "Perhaps there is a way to honor my late friend, Shankdaddy, and fulfill Celine's prophecy at the same time." I almost manage a smirk. "Wanna start a band?"

Beetle trips on the last step, catching himself on the railing. He slaps a hand on his chest. "You want to start a band with me?"

"Actually more like a bluesy duo. Your voice is golden. I play a decent guitar and write good songs. What have we got to lose?"

He pulls my hips toward him and meets my lips in a feathery kiss. Briefly, I taste a world far from the sultry blues, a pop music realm of sun-struck parties beside glittering lakes with first-class jet trips to Stadt. It quickly sours on my tongue, along with his feeble kiss. I discreetly wipe my mouth, underwhelmed. Beetle beams brightly. I guess that kiss wasn't as bad for him.

The lyrics to "Day Tripper" run through my head. They may be running through Beetle's head as well, but for a different reason. It's that kind of song. That's the beauty of John, Paul, George, and Ringo's musical magic. Their songs can mean different things to various people. Some say the lyrics to "Day Tripper" represent an ode to acid. Others say they pay homage to light love. I say they're the postscript to every first kiss that ever was, a reaction to that perilous exploration into the unknown frontier of another human body.

"It took me so long to find out...and I found out."

Twelve

Forever

Over the last few days, I've revised my review of Beetle's kissing. Good kissing is sometimes a matter of practice. I wouldn't dare tell Mom that, and not just because she's my mom. She's skipping Twain College's annual Freshman Frolic due to the fact there's nothing she currently despises more than young lovers. This attitude stems from Dad's email saying he isn't leaving Russia until he's confirmed a connection between ancient bear sacrifices and celestial phenomena. In the words of blues great Curtis Griffin, her man "ain't never coming back."

In other news, Saturday, July twenty-seventh, is my eighteenth birthday. This is a day most mothers remember. But given the fact that it's Friday afternoon and mom's lying in bed moping, I'm not expecting much of a party.

I make a half-joking suggestion. "Why don't you visit Celine's Fortune-telling Parlor for an astrological reading? It might cheer you up."

"Why not?" She leaps to her feet. "I haven't seen my old friend Celine in years."

This is not the response I expected. I had hoped for

something like, "No, I need to get ready for your birthday celebration." But maybe, this is the response I should have expected. Of course Mom knows Celine. She was friends with her sister, Mia.

Ah, Mia.

I decide to give up dreaming about a birthday party and write more blues.

Mom and Celine stumble into our apartment well after midnight, giggling loudly enough to wake me. Clearly, their reunion went well. Saturday morning, I wake to more of Celine's bold laughter rolling out of the living room. She and Mom lie sprawled across our futon, surrounded by an empty bag of tortilla chips, a paper plate piled with a mountain of cigarette butts, along with bottles of grenadine, crème de menthe, banana liqueur, and rum. Mom must have been making Bob Marley cocktails again. Now I'm wondering if Celine gave her the recipe.

"Men are no better than moldy bologna," Celine wails. "Toss 'em out! Toss 'em out I say! Before they stink up the house and make you sick from their rotten, garlicky smell!" Celine throws a pillow at Mom, and they start tossing pillows at one another like kids at a slumber party.

I'm steamed. Clearly, Mom has forgotten that today is my birthday. I stand over them, knowing how Zeus feels when he gazes down upon wretched humanity.

Celine kicks Mom when she sees me. "Happy birthday, Guitar Girl," she says, warmly. "In case you are wondering why I am still here, I have chosen to save you from your mom's cooking on your special day."

I think of the fragrant jerk chicken and plantain smell from her end of Manburn Street and decide to take her at her word. By dinnertime, balloons fill the house along with the head-spinning smell of a homemade Jamaican meal. She cooks lipsmacking Jamaican patties, both beef and soy, and a gooey rum cake that packs a punch.

I hear a knock at the apartment door and open it to find Beetle staring up at the rusty hooks, heavy chains, and bone saws dangling from the ceiling. He may not appreciate the fact the local historical society dubs these pieces industrial art. This is the first time he's visited my slaughterhouse apartment. I wonder what he thought of the crying marble angel in front of the ash gray Victorian funeral parlor-turned-senior housing next door. At least he didn't see the "historic" iron rings used to restrain troublesome children hanging inside Lizzy's place—the former orphanage.

Beetle seems delighted to get out of the hallway and enter our living area, such as it is, with the cheap navy futon, yard sale dining room set, and outdated big box television. We sit down to eat and he raves about the meal. After we finish,, Mom hands me a card from Dad with twenty bucks inside. The handwriting on it looks suspiciously like hers. Mom's other gift is an IOU for six months' rent in a St. Louis apartment. This is her way of hinting that it's time for me to move out and move on with my musical career.

Beetle pushes an expensive-looking red velvet box my way—which can't be good. I take my time opening it, remembering that his parents got married at our age. The box contains a gold heart locket with his picture in it, which is somewhat of a relief. But it's still an absurdly expensive piece of jewelry, not to mention that I hate it. Why would he think a heart-shaped necklace would go with my butchered baby-dolls Beatles tee shirt, or any of my other band tee shirts?

I turn the heart over and read the inscription. "Beetle and Mona Forever."

He kisses my cheek because Mom is watching, and says, "Forever, Mona, like the sun, the moon, and the stars."

I imagine Black Racer Woman's boa constrictor braid wrapping around my neck, strangling me. I can't speak. I jangle my wrist in a call for help. I hear Bilki say, "Don't worry. Even the sun and the moon don't last forever. The web of the universe is always changing."

Celine grumbles some folksy Jamaican saying. "If yu wan somebody lov you, yu mus lov dem fus."

She doesn't normally speak with such a heavy accent. I know what she's up to. I've heard this type of sneaky ethnic commentary before. It happened one Christmas, years ago. Bilki made beans with doughboys (which all Indians outside of New England call frybread), and everybody chowed down—except Dad, who barely touched his food.

Grumps shook a fist at Dad and shouted in Mohegan, "K'kunôk sawáyuw!"

He and Bilki had both studied their Native languages, as a form of semi-secret communication. I had to know what he said in Mohegan so I whipped out my language phrasebook and intuitively opened it to the "Insults" section. I translated aloud: "There is no brain in his head!" My words ended all discussion at the table. But I don't need a translation of what Celine just said. It's straightforward: she thinks Beetle and I are more in love with our music than each other.

I re-read the inscription on the locket, "Beetle and Mona Forever."

I whisper to Celine, "Forever seems like a long time when your band is going nowhere."

Celine whispers back, "Picture something that makes you happy. It will get you through this awkward moment."

I picture my amazing thirteenth birthday with Bilki. It

was the last time I saw her. She cut her long silver hair to her chin, claiming it was wearing her down. Illness had already reduced her strawberry smile to ashes. After Mom served her sorry-lump-of-a-homemade-sponge-cake, Lizzy gave me that neon yellow George Harrison "Here Comes the Sun" tee shirt. Mom and Dad handed me a cheap new cell phone, Ma-mère and Pa-père sent me fifty Canadian dollars, and Grumps unveiled a headboard with my full name wood-burned into it. None of these presents was exactly what I desired. Fortunately, Bilki wanted her present to be private. She shooed everybody else away and handed me a heavy box containing a bright red Pendleton blanket with an eagle on it—the Indian symbol of virtue and high ideals. She wrapped it around my shoulders, grabbed a BIC lighter, tucked a roll of paper towels under her arm, and led me into the back courtyard behind our apartment building—formerly known as the livestock corral.

She dumped out the water in the stone birdbath and filled it with sticks and shreds of paper towel. After she lit it, we sat together on an iron bench and watched the rising flames. She pulled that eagle blanket tightly around my shoulders and told me to look hard into the fire. Shaking a gourd rattle from her purse, she sang an old Abenaki song. I recognized the word *Wliwni,* for "thanks." I watched those flames and saw fluttering autumn leaves, an entire sky raining crimson and gold. This didn't seem like a very earth-shattering image for my coming-of-age. I'd expected a spirit animal or some white-haired ancestor to appear and deliver wise words about my future path in life. But my vision revealed colorful fall leaves, pure and simple. When Bilki finished her song, she told me that I was officially a woman. I didn't feel any taller or sexier. But I did feel more peaceful, like I'd joined a great circle of people who wrapped their arms around me. That's the only birthday memory I treasure. My grandmother gave me a real gift that took more trouble than picking up some junk at the mall or tossing a gift card in the mail.

Just like Bilki, Celine saves her present for last. She hands me an old Robert Johnson record album tied with a blue raffia ribbon.

"This is amazing," I say. "Too bad I have no way to play it."

"Foolish Leo," she says, smug. "You always think you're the center of the universe, that everything relates to you and your creative endeavors. You follow the sun because it is the nearest star. And a star you shall become yourself. But you miss the obvious, much of the time. This record is not for playing; it's a spirit offering for Shankdaddy. If you leave it by your bed tonight and think of him, he will visit your dreams and give you a new hit song."

Beetle and I shrug at one another, as if to say, "What have we got to lose?"

I go to bed early, pulling my Beatles comforter over my head, concentrating on the buttery sound of Shankdaddy's voice. The speckled shadows of near-sleep eventually give way to clear images. An old gray wooden stool appears. Blue smoke swirls around it like a tornado. When it clears, I see myself sitting on the stool with Rosalita. A man with high and mighty cheekbones carved of granite and big white mocking teeth strides my way. He tips his straw hat rakishly to one side. Following him is a girl wearing LOVE hoop earrings and a cropped Rush band tee shirt. She points to Rosalita with her electric blue fingernails, indicating that I should play something. I perform one of my songs while she and the man play an eerie game of patty-cake. After I finish the song, they halt their game and turn their thumbs down. I try another song, and they resume their game. When I finish, they indicate I've failed, again. And so it goes. I play every song I've ever written. Nothing pleases them.

Blue smoke envelops the girl. A giant blue tear forms in the man's eye. He reaches into the smoke but can't grasp her. As he reaches, the blue smoke surges through him. His lips turn teal, his eyes turn turquoise. Indigos ripple through his veins and into his fingertips, until all the blue smoke is inside him. He wraps his bluesy arms around me from behind and places his long-suffering hands onto mine. Our hands blend, playing serious blues on blues. We rage through the chords of a song about a father who mourns the loss of his dead daughter. The song is throaty, gut-busting, downstreet Manburn blues, with an added sweet note that scrapes the bottom of your soul.

My mind wakes bursting with Shankdaddy's tune. I call Beetle and tell him to get to my place, fast. He arrives, self-assured in the misconception that his gift rocked my world because I'm exuberant and still wearing his locket. I play my dream song and he scribbles down the music and lyrics.

I walked into her room, wasn't nobody there
The place it smelled real empty, the shelves they were all bare
Because she's gone, way down to the deep red clay
Hope you know I love you, darlin, why'd you ever go away?

Her car was at the junkyard; the gas light was on E
I pushed the rusted shifter, but I couldn't set it free
'Cause she's long gone, taken oh so far away
Hope you know I love you, baby, and that devil he will pay!

I set you in the ground, 'neath a pile of rolling stones
I want to hold your hand, but it's a heap o' skinny bones
I know you're gone. Gone to where the blues don't play
Where you'll never get no older. Just a child all your days.

On the second go-through, Beetle sings along with me. His earthy pipes take right to this tune, transforming it from a dreamy blues melody into a mourner's anthem that grabs your heart and shakes the blood from it till your spirit screams. Who knew Beetle had soul?

We perform the dream song for Mom and Celine. By the time we hit the turnaround, Mom is crying as if I've made the honor roll.

Celine folds her arms and says, "Anybody who can produce music this divine needs to be in touch with Orpheus Gray. He was Shankdaddy's manager."

Beetle and I tell her to contact him. In fifteen minutes, we hear a bold knock at the door, made by the rapping of a hard object. A rigid pencil of a man with a snowy Afro and silver dollar eyes appears. He's carrying a wooden cane with an ivory skull handle and wearing an outdated tuxedo with a Jamaican green bow tie. He reminds me of a medicine man. Beetle whispers that he looks like a math professor. Celine introduces him as our new talent manager. I'm surprised when he pulls out his phone to record us on video.

"You may begin," he says, formally.

While listening to us perform "Skinny Bones," his stiffness softens. Orpheus does not clap. He rises, lean and long like his cane, and thumps the cane three times, "Well done! You are on the verge of glory. But like great marathon runners nearing the finish line, you must take great care in making your last steps count. My job is to make sure you don't trip before you reach your goal. To do this, I need to pick a good name for your band. A band's name is everything."

I think about The Beatles' lousy name and have to wonder if he's right. Sure, there have been other successful bug band names—the Locusts, Atom and the Ants, the Crickets—but

I don't think their names were key to their success. He raises his cane heavenward and squeezes it, concentrating with his eyes closed, as if casting off *haints*. I straighten up, respectfully. But Celine signals me to relax.

"This is not a religious ceremony," she claims, "just Orpheus' way of doing things."

Not seconds, but minutes pass, dozens of minutes. I fidget. I don't care what she says about this not being a ceremony; it feels like one to me.

Orpheus' silver dollar eyes pop open. "Bonepile!" He spits out the word, swiping gushing perspiration from his forehead with a jade satin handkerchief.

Bonepile. Beetle and I exchange comfortable glances.

I speak first. "It makes me think of T-Bone Burnett, so I'm good with it."

"It's dark and edgy, like you, Mona." Beetle smirks with delight.

Orpheus sends some of his music business buddies our video and everything begins to swirl like I've step into one of Bilki's vortexes. He hooks us up with a studio to record "Skinny Bones," "Thunder and Lightning," "Too Sweet to Die," "Lost in the Woods, "Big Bad No-good Daddy," and "Great Bear Blues," along with a few standards to fill out an album. I enter an unknown world of synchronization licenses, statutory rates, derivative works, split ownership, and endless starbursts of lights, lights, lights.

Thirteen

Farewell Dance

The theme of the Colt High Alumni Farewell Dance is "Stars of 1980s Rock." This is the first school event for which I haven't faked allergies or the flu. I text Lizzy the photos of our themed outfits. She insists I've Photoshopped them because they're too ridiculous to be true. Beetle sports a vest and cane à la Lindsey Buckingham on Fleetwood Mac's "Rumours" album. I don Stevie Nicks' signature top hat and a flouncy black halter dress. Beetle's heart locket hangs from my neck. Nobody made me wear it tonight. I don't need Black racer Woman's pouch anymore. Recording an album together has been a dream; hearing our music playing on the radio is as surreal as seeing that Great Bear in Grumps' woods. We're supposed to go on tour in a week, after spending Labor Day weekend with the Dills at Lake Winnipesaukee. The idea of me staying there with the Dills make me feel the need to perform a reality check.

The Dills went all-out in their sponsorship of this event. Cricket booked a celebrity caterer, and Worthy hired Orpheus as the disc jockey. From behind the turntable, our manager waves a Michael Jackson rhinestone glove at my former principal. Smitten Millicent Dibble giggles grotesquely. She is sporting a one-piece pantsuit and faded yellow shag, which she claims is her costume homage to Cherrie Curry of the *Runaways*. To me, she looks more like a hoary Blanche Dubois, not to mention that her B.B. is wearing a punk rock metal-studded cat collar.

Orpheus calls Millicent and B.B. over to him. "Your cat is divine," he says to her. "I'd like to feature him on Bonepile's new album cover and tee shirts. His King Cat image screams the blues. So whad'ya say, honey? Can we make your cat famous?"

She bats her thickly made-up bottomless eyes at him. Beetle and I exchange barfing expressions and escape to greet his parents. The Dills have come dressed as The Carpenters. Mrs. Dill wears a flippy brown Karen Carpenter wig, and Mr. Dill's hair is ready-made for his Richard Carpenter part. Mr. Dill compliments us on our costumes, and we compliment him on what his people have done with this gym. It's unrecognizable. Worthy splurged for a great dance floor, blacklights, and rock star banners, including special ones for dead 1980s music icons—Bob Marley, Stevie Ray Vaughn, Jerry Garcia, Karen Carpenter, Michael Jackson, and Whitney Houston—surrounded by white carnations that say RIP.

Like we need any more dead people at Colt High.

Posters for period record albums cover the walls, featuring Rush, Guns and Roses, AC/DC, and Metallica. The Rush poster draws my eye. It shows a rabbit coming out of a hat. The sound of Brick Rodman yelling breaks my fixation. He's muscling his way through this ridiculous crowd of '80s rock star replicas, ages seventeen to seventy, holding Rasima with one arm and pushing away old guys gawking at his date's blacklit white Madonna cone bra with the other. He tries to get Beetle's attention, but too many people are pressing my band partner for autographs. Half of our musical duo is already a star. Brick pops a colorful pill and Rasima shrinks when he offers her one. I help Beetle break away so he can rejoin us.

"When are you guys going on tour?" Brick asks.

"Talk to Orpheus," we both say, simultaneously. Beetle kisses my top hat, his eyes dancing. I know he's imagining a music legends' dance like this one, thirty years from now, when people come dressed as him.

Rasima won't lift her head. She presses her arms tight to her sides, as if she's barely holding herself together.

"What are you doing this fall, Rasima?" I ask, trying not to stare at the blacklit illumination of her white cone bra.

"Some of us need to get real jobs. My parents are making me join the army."

"You'll be a great soldier," I say, in a disingenuous way that makes me realize I've been spending too much time with publicists.

The only thing stupider than Rasima in this cone bra is the prospect of Rasima in fatigues. After hearing that her parents forced her into joining the army, mine don't seem so bad. Sure Mom ignores me, and Dad only emails when he has newly discovered bear bones to show off. But the only thing they ever made me do was spend time in Indian Stream with Grumps, and that I don't regret.

Rasima's hive of ex-bumblebee cheerleaders swarms our way. They're dressed in a matching group outfit of white tutus and tiaras, like the waterskiing girls on the cover of the Go Go's 1980s "Vacation" album.

"One of your fans is looking for you, Mona," says the tallest tutu girl. "I think he wants an autograph. Should I have the security guard tell him to get lost?"

"No, Mona loves her fans," says Rasima. "She said so on Twitter. She'll be happy to give him whatever he wants while I dance with her boyfriend." She pulls Beetle away.

Brick pops another colorful pill, after his girlfriend deserts him. I follow the tutus, determined to be as kind to my lone fan as Beetle is to his many worshipful minions.

Before I can get a good look at him, I notice the guy's white tee shirt, glowing in the blacklight. Then I catch the jeans and clodhopper black boots. Those boots. It's Del, and he's wearing Bruce Springsteen's killer classic 1980s look. Nobody besides Lizzy knows Springsteen's song, "Rosalita," inspired the name for my guitar. Fire ants once again cover me from head to toe.

Someone slips their arms around my shoulders from behind, startling me. I turn and see it's Beetle.

"Rasima can't dance," he says, pulling me away from Del, who turns his back to remain incognito.

"Besides, I never liked Madonna, Mona." He offers Del his best smirk. "Sorry fan boy." Del won't look up; he won't let Beetle recognize him.

Beetle and I dance to "Emotional Rescue" by the Rolling Stones. The lyrics seem surreal. *You're in too deep, You can't get out, You're just a poor girl in a rich man's house.* I worry Del might leave. But every time I look his way I see he hasn't taken his eyes off me.

Near the end of the song, the cool scent of musky honey breezes my way. Del grabs my hand, solidly, like it's an axe handle. "I believe it's my turn to cut in."

"Whatever you say, fan boy." Beetle ignores Del, flipping his bangs coolly, and strutting off.

I lean in and latch on. Del strokes my arm. Every nerve ending comes alive.

"I can't believe I'm dancing with the woman who told the Hartford police my dad killed my mom," he says. "I think you should be more suspect of the people attending this event. I'll bet Mom's killer lurks somewhere in this very gym."

I survey the alums in their thirties who knew Mia. "I see Paul Simon, Lionel Ritchie, The Pointer Sisters, Elton John, Aretha Franklin, Billy Ocean, Olivia Newton-John, and the Carpenters. None of them strike me as very lethal."

Del pulls my ear to his lips. "I admit I'm obsessing over my mom's case. But so are you. I can see it in those beautiful maple eyes."

"Yes, I am," I reply, wanting to hear more about my eyes. No one has ever complimented them before. But *maple*? Like my grandmother's name? I'd laugh at how unappealing that sounds if it didn't make my heart so full it feels it's about to explode.

Del clearly mistakes my self-conscious silence for disapproval. "I'm sorry I brought up the case," he says. "I'm not here to discuss that. I'm here because it's my twentieth birthday, and all I want is to be with you. Sorry I missed your eighteenth. My father got wind of it from your mom. But she said your boyfriend was celebrating it with you. He points to Beetle. "You don't belong with that guy."

Beetle is playing with the golden streaks in Rasima's raven hair and staring at her cone bra.

Del's eyes follow mine, my eyes that appear special to him, my eyes that remind him of maple, instead of mudwood.

"Let's go somewhere private and talk," he says.

I follow his scent of musky honey down the chessboard of the main hallway and into an empty science lab. You'd think the bumblebees would be buzzing about my mystery man and me. But no one even snaps our picture as we pass. They're all watching Rasima and Beetle, the rightful king and queen of Colt High. Del and I move through the crowd like ghosts.

He hoists me onto a lab table. It's just like the time he lifted me onto the stool at band practice. I feel the same fiery tingling; nothing has changed.

"How did you know I was here?" I sit tight beside him.

He wraps his arm around my waist. "I told you, our parents talk. That's what friends are supposed to do."

It occurs to me he may be sweet-talking me to get me off investigating his dad.

Del lifts my chin, reading my mind. "Mona, I'm not here for my dad. I had to see you. We need to straighten things out between us, even though I know we both have complications."

Complications. That hurtful word can only mean one thing. My heart takes an unexpected plunge. He's seeing someone else, and I think I know who. The jealousy I feel is a hundred times worse than how I feel about whatever's going on between Rasima and Beetle. What I feel with Del is magic, not the phony kind created by rock posters, cheesy eighties' costumes, and mood lighting. Del slides me onto his lap. I put my arms around his neck and melt into him, offering my lips, my arms, all of me. We blend together, like rhythm and blues.

"I guess this means I shouldn't give up on you," he says, coming up for air. "I knew you were thinking about me when I heard you growl at the end of Great Bear Blues. I saw you perform it on YouTube. Pretty sexy. I wonder where you got the idea to growl?"

I flush. "I credited the Blond Bear with that on the album."

"No worries. You can growl for me anytime." He caresses my horrible hair as if it's made of spun gold. We kiss hard and my head spins. I'm thinking I want to be somewhere more private, when the door to the lab bursts open. I'm terrified it's Beetle. But it's worse than that; it's Worthy Dill.

I hide my face in Del's shirt but notice my top hat sits in plain sight.

"Excuse me. My apologies for intruding." Mr. Dill says. "I'm looking for my wife. The last time I saw her she was chatting with Millicent Dibble. Have you seen either of them?"

Neither of us say a word. He gets the hint and leaves.

"Let's go, Del," I say.

Guilt washes over me as we slip out the back door. I ask him if we can drive his Saab the two blocks to my apartment. I can't stand the thought of getting caught twice.

He pulls in front of my parents' building and smiles, like I'm all that matters. "I love you, Mona Lisa." His words flow out and into one another. "I'm tired of living without you. I want us to be together, forever."

A minute ago he was talking about his complications. Now he's talking about staying together *forever*. I'm wearing Beetle's locket with his promise of forever. I think of my parents' shaky promise of forever and how much better off they'd be if they'd forgone that promise.

"I love you, Mona Lisa." Del repeats, more urgently.

I run my hand through his black spiky hair. It reminds me of the prickly pine trees of Indian Stream, that welcoming forest so far removed from here. He leans his head on my hand and kisses it.

I can hear the unhappy spirits from my slaughterhouse apartment, the funeral parlor, and the orphanage wailing in my ear, "Say that you love him, Mona! Speak up!"

I roll my fingers near my stomach, as if plucking Rosalita. Why didn't I bring her with me tonight? I miss her. I can't imagine life without her.

Unexpected words fall out of my mouth. "I have to put my music first."

"That's it? I tell you that I love you, and that's all you say?" Del collapses against the driver's seat like he's been shot. He leans over me and pushes open my car door. "Good-bye, Mona Lisa."

I get out, and his tires squeal away. I didn't even wish him Happy Birthday.

Fourteen

Solo

Beetle swears he forgives me for deserting him at the Farewell Dance. He has to forgive me because our band tour starts in a week. For the sake of our music, I've tried to put aside my own curiousity about what happened between Rasima and him. Orpheus is calling this Bonepile's "Haunted Fall" tour. The promotional tee shirts show an orange pumpkin-headed B.B., surrounded by dancing skeletons. Naturally, Mom had a fit. Bones are sacred to Indians.

I told her, "Worry about taking care of yourself and allow me to focus on prepping for my tour."

What I don't tell her is that I definitely know the dead are more than a bonepile. I'm hoping Mia skips the tour. But I wouldn't mind if Bilki came along and visited Grumps. He agreed to attend our concert in Manchester, New Hampshire. I just hope someone else is driving him there.

Beetle and I are working on a new song in my bedroom but neither of us is sitting on my bed. There's an invisible wall between us since the dance. He's on one side, pulling his bangs, trying to nail a B chord. I'm on the other, staring into the swirling vortex of leaves on Bilki's wall mural, wondering if it leads to an alternate universe, when Mom bursts in and throws a balled-up printout of an email at my head.

"Will sent this. Grumps is gone." She storms out, wimpering.

Grumps is gone. These words act like a hydrogen bomb. I realize I wanted my grandfather to see me on stage more than anything in the world. This may seem like a strange thing to think at a time like this. But who else do I care to impress? Who else actually cared about me and my music?

"He can't be gone!" I shout, at the place where Mom had been standing.

Through the shattered racket inside my mind, I hear Beetle say, "I'm sorry, Mona."

I nuzzle my wet face into his lavender polo. He reads the crumpled email. "It was his heart…There will be no funeral or memorial service…Sadie tossed his ashes into the Connecticut River… The reading of the will is Friday…You have to be there. What do they mean 'you have to be there.'?"

"I want to be there."

"Why? Somebody can attend for you and mail you your cut of his estate. My parents expect you to come with us to Winnipesaukee this weekend. It's a big deal. We never miss the annual Labor Day party. First, your parents make you miss graduation. Now this! Does your family make you miss everything in your life that matters? I'm sorry about your grandfather, really I am. But this is my family's last outing before we go on tour together, maybe our last family outing, period."

"Consider this: this is definitely my last outing with Grumps." I play with the log cabin charm on my bracelet and realize I need to say good-bye to him properly.

I hear Bilki say, "Break the tie that binds him." This tells me what I need to do for my grandfather. I remove a pair of scissors from my desk drawer and crawl into bed with them. Beetle gasps, obviously worried I'll do something to harm myself. But I pull back my Beatles comforter and snip my bed sheet. He relaxes. I continue snipping and transform a piece of cotton sheeting into a star.

I wait till his eyes drift away, before reaching for my head. I snip through a bunch of hair in front, creating hideously uneven bangs. Cutting my hair actually hurts. My head and hand both feel sore. Once Beetle sees what I've done, he snatches the scissors from me. I wish he hadn't. This is what Indians do in mourning: we cut our hair to break ties with the past.

He is pulsating with concern, trying to say something, but the words catch in his throat, like he has developed laryngitis.

Even in the midst of my grief, I tell him, "Take care of your pipes. Go home and rest."

"You need time to yourself," he manages to say, scuffling out of my room.

I lay a hand on my Ikea headboard and picture Grumps' homemade headboard wood burned with my first and middle name. It has never left our basement storage unit. I feel guilty about hiding it there but my middle name is not public knowledge, neither is a wood-burned North Country headboard exactly my style. The toy wigwam he made for me when I was a kid is another story. I rummage through my closet to find it. Aha! Here it is!

This miniature structure is domed with a leather flap for a door, a bent spruce frame, and a papery white birch bark covering. That covering was surely Bilki's touch. I've seen the poplar bark on the wigwams at our historic Mohegan village on the reservation. This is different. It's a model of an Indian house from way up north; it's more Abenaki-style. I drag this northern wigwam, with all its accessories, from my closet to the bed. When other kids fussed over Victorian dollhouses filled with velvet furniture and porcelain tea sets, I preferred this wigwam with its tiny black kettle hanging over a pebble-stone fire pit. I love the little wooden dolls Grumps carved to go with it, not to mention the thimble-sized clay pots, splint baskets, wooden bowls, bows, arrows, fishing spears the size of toothpicks, and cots made from matchsticks and rawhide scraps.

I retrieve my scissors and clip squares of sheeting to make tiny funeral shawls for the wooden mother and daughter of the little wigwam family. The wooden father serves as a stand-in for Grumps' corpse. I cut out a star and place it over him as a funeral blanket. I shuffle into the kitchen and grab a chipped yellow rose teacup from Mom's misfit china collection and fill it with sweetgrass, sage, and matches, building a funeral fire inside. I place the cup on my nightstand and sprinkle loose tobacco in the flames. This is the only way I can hold a traditional funeral fire for Grumps, here in our Hartford apartment.

I whisper to Bilki in the stars above, "I'm improvising a ceremony, like you did for my thirteenth birthday."

In my tiny teacup fire, I watch visions flicker against the porcelain. A grandfather teaches me how to drive a pickup through the wooded wilderness. A grimy Santa Claus greets me outside a lamp-lit log cabin that's trapped in the past. A talented carver demonstrates how to make funny images of black bears on antlers. A tribal elder dances me through the dusty steps of a powwow Grand Entry. An experienced woodsman shows me how to protect maple trees. A mournful widower enjoys my baked beans. A caring friend speaks to a handsome young man on my behalf. A blind fool protects a villainous murderer because he's his friend. A delusional father thinks his daughter killed a black bear on purpose.

The fire dies out. I want to write some death letter blues for Grumps, to offer him a good send-off, but I fall asleep beside the smoldering teacup. Mom shows up at breakfast wearing a self-inflicted pixie haircut and a peaceful glow. We don't speak. I point to my uneven bangs, signaling that I tried to cut my own hair. She flutters her hands, indicating that the time for such things has passed. Beetle calls to check on me, his voice barely audible. I whisper I'm fine. He wishes me a safe journey and says he'll text me his plans.

I've nearly finished packing when my phone buzzes, breaking the crushing stillness of our apartment. The text says, "I'll be at Lake Winnie. Mom invited the Joneses to spend a few days with us before Rasima joins the army. I'd rather be with you."

This information returns my focus to the land of the living. Everyone knows Lake Winnipesaukee is a romantic place. Look what happened on Worthy Dill's trip there with Cricket after his high school graduation. I want to text Beetle a warning about what Rasima might do to get out of joining the army. But sanity and caution grab me, just in time. I remember it was Will's unfounded jealousy that provoked Mia Delaney's murder. The scratched-out yearbook picture I found at his house told me he wound up killing her because he thought she loved Worthy. Even though, according to Worthy, Mia hardly knew he existed. Maybe there's nothing between Beetle and Rasima, either. I try and calm down and not let history repeat itself.

I feel the weight of being eighteen. I need to adopt a broader perspective on the world. I will start by acknowledging the suffering of the Dill family. Worthy struggled to keep Beetle away from musicians because Mia disappeared with one. Cricket hid her pregnant teenage shame by showing headshot-only photos of her wedding. The Dills forced their son to attend a lousy high school because they romanticized their last years of teenage freedom. Cricket and Worthy are simply a couple of dumb kids who were forced to grow up too soon and resent it.

Struggles have also molded how Beetle and I see the world and each other. We keep secrets that divide us. I see how he looks at Rasima. It isn't her hands he stares at. I know another secret we both hate to admit: Bonepile is toast. It's not that we never should have gotten together as a duo. We blended well for a while. The ability to create beautiful music is usually fleeting. Hence the many one-hit wonders in this world.

I remember reading an old interview with John Lennon in *Rolling Stone* in which he talked about his band, THE band, after they broke up. John wasn't nostalgic or bitter. He simply said, "We all had roles to play." Each one of the Beatles played a part in making their music, but they only made magic when they played well *together*. And Beetle and I have never really been *together*.

The last time Orpheus stopped by, he revealed something that compounded my concern. "Shankdaddy should have gone solo," he said. "He had more talent than the rest of the Hoodoo Chickens combined. But he wasn't willing to sacrifice his buddies for his art. Art requires sacrifice, and music is the most fragile of all the arts. Personalities can make or break a composition in a flash; people are musical notes that sometimes blend beautifully and other times twang in discordant tones. It's time for you to quit, or go solo. Remember that. I know a club in St. Louis that would love to book you as a solo act, whenever you're ready, Mona."

Whenever you're ready, Mona.

I'm feeling pretty ready.

My musical taste leans toward songs about ugly lies, dirty streets, and long-dead bones. Beetle prefers songs about sparkling sapphire lakes lined with sunbathing beauties wearing lockets shaped like golden hearts. That's why he feels it neccessary to keep a part of himself from me, no matter how much he claims to care for me. People always guard their most interesting secrets. My grandfather is an extreme case in point. What's behind all those hidden doors in his cabin? What's this "Secret of Wabanaki" that he never shared with me? Now that he is gone, I may never find out.

Fifteen

Secret Doors

It's early September and the leaves look the same as they did when I first arrived in June. But everything else has changed. I can't smell Grumps' musty blue jeans or hear him calling me City Gal like it's the worst name on earth. I can't drive with him in his mismatched Ford pickup to his useless excuse for a general store and listen to him bicker with his idiot friends. I can't hear him call my crazy snake of a great aunt "a witch," or argue with me about whether or not ghosts are real. I miss all that.

Overgrown vines seal the front door to Grumps' cabin. Mom gives the door handle a few useless yanks. I ponder the purpose of these impenetrable plants. Are they protecting the cabin from us, or us from the cabin? I consider this to be a warning from the woods and take it to heart. Mom doesn't; she scoots around to the back door and barges in. I pause beside Grumps' woodpile, sensing a peaceful, out-of-body stillness. The woods are in mourning. A silent robin redbreast rests on a split log with its head bowed. I wonder what this robin charm on my bracelet meant to Bilki. A sign of spring perhaps? A southwest wind rustles the maples, and their leaves wave gently, fanning my sorrow.

Mom shouts my name like I'm a tardy student. I tiptoe inside the muggy cabin, not wanting to disturb the dust in the air. It contains microscopic bits of Grumps. A small pile of carved antlers lies on the floor, and my throat closes. I picture Grumps carving them, antler bits flying into his bundled white hair. None of them shows a hockey-playing bear or a bear riding a snowmobile. Those fantastical ones sold out first. All that remain are antlers carved with scenes from the real woods. A mother bear leading her baby toward a loaded blueberry bush. Two young bears playing in a pile of fall leaves. I don't see any antlers depicting an ancient bear with flabby haunches, a cracked bulbous nose, and rows of loose, sloppy flesh drooping beneath his eyes. That's because The Great Bear isn't real.

Dust mutes everything inside the cabin. The strawberry and mustard rocking chairs have dulled to rust and putty. The animals on the woodland dinner plates appear stuffed and forgotten. Even the Bob Marley oil lamp I remembered as cerise and lime now appears bloody and putrid. Color and life are synonymous. One can't survive without the other.

I touch Grumps' favorite photo of Bilki on the wall—just as he used to do. It was silly for me to worry about his mental health when he made this loving gesture. Now I see it as a natural thing to do, a way of saying "I remember." The door to his bedroom is ajar but I won't go in. It's still his private place, *his* bedroom. I peek inside and find the bed is made. I wonder if he left it that way or if his mysterious lady friend, Sadie, tidied up after he died. Did she find his lifeless body? Was it Will who found him? I say a silent prayer. *Oh, please don't let it be Del.*

A gruff grandfatherly voice says, "Go on in, City Gal."

I push open Grumps' door and step into his pumpkin-colored room. Mom calls my name a second time but she can wait. I kiss the corner of his chenille bedspread. The moment lingers. I hold that bedspread to my cheek, squeezing it hard inside my fist, wrinkling it, welding it into my palm, not wanting to let go. Then, for an instant—so swift I can't be sure it happened—I feel someone squeeze back.

I drift back into the main room where Mom sits cross-legged in front of several opened doors in the wall, with a handful of skeleton keys dangling from the ring in her hand.

"Wherever is that paper?" she mutters, tossing things about.

She's already flung open two hidden doors, located at different heights in the knotty pine-paneled wall. They remind me of flaps on a Christmas Advent calendar, opened carelessly by an impatient kid who can't wait to claim her prizes. On the floor lies the dreary domestic contents of the doors she's opened: old plates, bowls, cups, and saucers. She tries another wall opening near the ground and pulls out a set of narrow velvet-lined drawers, like you'd find at a jewelers, filled with Indian children's toys, including a game made from a stick and corncobs, and turkey wishbone dolls dressed in buckskin. These things remind me of something Bilki once said: "Indians make treasures from things that most people consider junk, things that come from the earth."

"Dad, what have you done with it?" Mom mutters to herself, fumbling a new lock. She opens a door that is tall and narrow and yanks out easels, canvases, rag paper, paintbrushes, tubes, powders, colored chalks, and pencils. A fiery fall landscape covers one of the canvases. She holds it up and mumbles something about giving this painting to Will Pyne. I feel my blood rise.

Her eyes flit my way, acknowledging my presence. "Mona, I'm trying to find a drawer that contains a single piece of painted parchment paper. This paper is very dangerous. Grumps has locked everything else in this cabin as a diversion, to conceal this one piece of paper. I need to destroy it." She turns her back on me and returns to removing things from her latest door. "Tell me as soon as you find it." She flaps an anxious hand behind her, signaling me to get on with it and check out another door.

I find a key that matches an especially wide door near Grumps' bedroom. Like Mom, I crawl inside to retrieve its contents. Mouse droppings stick to my palms. I pull out three round tin bins, containing reel-to-reel movies, music cassettes, eight track tapes, and vinyl records—all of which are useless, with or without electricity. I read a song title on one of the bricklike 1970s eight-track tapes: "Give It To Me" by J. Giles Band. *And people say today's music is dirty.*

She turns to me. "I could use some help with this one, Mona." She's examining several rusted cabinets inside one of her open doors.

I describe the items inside, as I find them. "There's an Abenaki tribal member roll, handwritten on index cards and a box of legal papers from some twentieth-century land claim case."

"What's that pile of letters on top?"

I briefly examine one and close it. "They're love letters between Grumps and Bilki."

"Useless," she says.

I thumb through the book that's beneath them. "I found your baby book, Mom."

Instead of putting simple baby snapshots inside, like normal mothers, Bilki included hand-painted watercolor portraits of "Our Lila Sassafras," inserted between rainbow layers of pastel tissue paper. There's one painting for every year from birth until her spoiled brat turned eighteen.

She grabs it from me and squeals with delight.

I want my kid to squeal like that over something I've created. But I can't paint. All I can do is write blues songs, and even the best blues songs don't make anybody squeal with delight.

While Mom gets sentimental over Bilki's paintings, I explore another wide-flung door. This one is stuffed with boxes of chipped arrowheads and broken clay pottery. These are archaeological items, the kind of stuff that makes my father rapturous. Why isn't he here when Mom needs him?

I poke Mom with an arrowhead—which dad calls a projectile point, "How is it that Dad missed coming with us? This is the ultimate archaeological dig."

She doesn't seem to feel the sharp tip jabbing into her arm. She's busy making sour facial expressions at Bilki's painted rendition of one of her 1990s hairstyles with high-rise gelled bangs.

"Why didn't Dad come with us?" I repeat, poking her again, hoping to confirm my suspicions about the defunct status of my parents' marriage.

She tears up a portrait of her, painted by Bilki, with colorful falling leaves fluttering in the background. She rips the torn halves into quarters and groans. I don't know what this behavior is all about. The portrait appears fine, unless she's vainer than I think.

"Bryer knew Grumps wouldn't have wanted him here," she finally responds to my earlier question.

"Fair enough." I swallow. "However, I haven't seen my father for months."

She violently rips the remaining picture bits into confetti.

I take advantage of her distraction to slip in my big question. "Are you divorced?"

"Not yet."

I push harder. "Why did you and Dad get married?"

She squeezes her lips shut, hoping nothing will escape. But something does. "You remember how your Ma-mère—as you called her—was always rubbing her rosary beads when we were around?"

I say "yes," three times, for encouragement, because getting Mom to yak long enough to find out anything about our family is like coaxing a UFO to stay still long enough to shoot a clear video.

"She was a religious woman," Mom declares, scooping her torn-up paper mess into a tin garbage can. "When she found out I was pregnant, she insisted I marry your father." Staring into the tin can, her beautiful face takes a twisted turn. "Even though my true love was Bear St. Jean."

My heart thumps to a standstill.

Her eyes gleam with memories. "Not to disrespect your dad. But Bear was an amazing man. His son goes by the same name. Maybe you met him during your summer visit here."

I collapse into Grumps' rocker. Mom dated Bear's dad. So I *was* almost his tribal sista.

"I see that you know him." she says. "Don't feel bad. I'm content with my choice." She pats the rocker instead of me. "Marrying your father got me out of these vile woods. Bear St. Jean would have trapped me here forever. That would have been a nightmare. I couldn't take being around my parents. I was a failure to them. I couldn't paint, sing, or play an instrument, like they wanted. You are the one they were waiting for. I never even liked the animals here, or anywhere, until after I killed that bear. That accident changed me. It made me realize how precious animals are. But it still didn't make me love these woods."

I wonder about this bear she killed. I think of the heartless thoughts that ran through my mind when I first saw Dibble's cat, and then I remember how much I love Damerae. I don't think it's possible to love all animals, any more than it's possible to love all people. Some are simply better friends than others.

Mom reaches for me then pulls back, as though she planned to tell me something earth-shattering, and then changed her mind.

Her voice softens like a hushed lullaby, "Grumps wrote me a letter, telling me how proud he was of you, how he admired your musical talents and your concern for the woods." She pats my chair in lieu of my arm. "He even remarked on your great dancing at the Winnipesaukee Powwow, not to mention your male admirers."

"I don't recall seeing this letter from Grumps."

Mom's dainty nose snivels but her eyes carry no tears. "I'm ashamed to tell you that I burned that letter after you ratted out my friend, Will Pyne, to the police. I was furious at you for that." She stops rocking me. "Actually, I'm still pissed."

I gape at the stranger I call Mom. "You burned the last letter about me from Grumps, and you're mad at *me*."

I need a whole sweetgrass bonfire to burn away the bad spirits growing inside me. I have to settle for lighting the single sweetgrass braid I find lying on the kitchen windowsill. I don't recall seeing it here when I was living at this cabin. The top on this piece is partially burned. My guess is that someone lit it after Grumps died to clear his house of bad spirits. I wonder if Del is the one who did it. He surely learned that Indian custom, growing up with my grandparents. I light what remains of the braid and let it burn over the speckled washbasin. The glowing green stalk quickly disintegrates into ash.

Mom gags on the smoke. I blow harder on the lighted tip to create more.

"What on earth?" She swats away the smoke.

"It gets rid of bad spirits."

"I know what it's supposed to do! Honestly, Mona. Reality check. Reality check."

Mom resumes investigating the contents of her open doors. It's clear there will be no more family revelations today. I let the sweetgrass braid burn out.

A growling rumble from the woods suggests Marilynn has arrived. I grab a couple browning bananas from the counter and step out to find her nudging Grumps' woodpile. Tears the size of pennies run down her enormous nose. I toss the bananas to her. Her rounded mitten ears snap back at the sight of me. I cautiously step back. I'm ashamed of my cowardice but I can't bring myself to go any nearer than I already am, a dozen feet away. We will never be close like she is with Del. Still I'm glad she came by to pay her respects, even if I'm hampered by my city gal notion that she might turn and devour me. Marilynn nudges the bananas but doesn't eat them. She blinks her eyes, in a kind of good-bye, before lumbering back into the woods to mourn Grumps' passing in privacy.

"Mona! It's nearly time to visit the lawyer's office. We need to get going before the locals snatch up your grandparents' fortune."

I wave an arm around the sparse cabin. "I don't think Grumps had much money."

"Ha! Are you kidding? Do you have any idea what kind of money your grandmother made as a painter?"

I've entered an alternate universe in which Bilki and

Grumps were rich. Now I wish I'd made Grumps turn on the generator more often and pick up better groceries.

"If Grumps had a lot of money, why was he such a hermit?"

"He wasn't a hermit when he was young. Have a look in here." She reaches inside the door that I know contains the trunk with the neon orange Elmwoods' sticker on it.

"This is Grumps' old band trunk. I remember his crazy musician friends: Diz, Goober, Brownie, and Mongo. The Elmwoods travelled across New England when I was young. Bilki didn't like Grumps going too far away. The band toured more distant cities before I came along. Babies are band killers."

I gape at The Elmwoods' sticker. In my mind, it transforms into a 1970s black light band poster featuring four scraggly-haired seventies dudes wearing silky Qiana shirts and platform-heeled shoes, performing The Hustle.

I lean into Mom. "Grumps had a band called The Elmwoods?"

Her face softens, almost lovingly. "I'm surprised he never mentioned it. He gave up playing his guitar after Mongo died of a heroin overdose. You should keep this trunk, Mona. You're the family musician now." Mom pushes the musty trunk my way. "Back in the seventies, The Elmwoods were a big deal in the Hartford music scene. Grumps was the lead guitarist. He loved performing before large crowds. He moved up here grudgingly, after Bilki's dad died and left her this godforsaken cabin. Your grandfather never fully adapted to these woods. That's when he came to be known as 'Grumps.'"

"So Grumps was a musician who liked Hartford?" I cough out the words because the whole cabin is now filled with sweetgrass smoke.

Mom's eyes sparkle dreamily. "You should have seen Hartford back in the 1980s and 1990s. The Russian Lady

Nightclub. The Whalers Hockey Team. The Civic Center concerts. All the big groups played Hartford—Van Halen, The Grateful Dead, Rush…"

Upon hearing the band name "Rush," my heart stumbles over its next few beats. I remember Mia's Rush band tee shirt with the rabbit coming out of a hat. I also notice the sweetgrass braid is out. A wispy trail of white smoke above it lingers and expands, curling into a larger cloud that wafts through the room like a faceless apparition. Of course, I know the dead look nothing like this cloud of smoke. They definitely have faces, not to mention hands that you can feel. Sometimes, they even wear band tee shirts.

Mom tries to discreetly clear her throat of smoke before speaking. "My father made a decent living as a musician. He saw a lot of himself in you. That's why ole Reggie gave you his guitar."

I slump onto the band trunk. "So my guitar belonged to Grumps, and the 'R' on it stands for 'Reggie.' Why didn't Grumps say anything when I named her Rosalita?"

"He was proud you gave your guitar her own name, like all the greats. Jimi Hendrix had 'Betty Jean,' B.B. King had 'Lucille.'" She holds her head with two hands, as if it's gained weight. "Well, you know all that."

Indeed I do. I feel exhilarated, knowing Rosalita played concerts, far and wide. I grab her and play the opening chords to *Hey Jude*. I inhale the last of the lingering sweetgrass smoke. I don't cough. I breathe more clearly than ever before. I'm not mad at Mom any longer. I start singing the lyrics, and Mom joins in on the line, "take a sad song and make it better." We sing the rest of the song together between sniffles. This time real tears flow down her cheeks. By the time we get to the part that goes, "Remember to let her into your heart," my voice is cracking and Mom's singing off-key. Her parents were right: she has no talent, whatsoever. But we're singing along to Reggie Elmwood's guitar, and that's what matters. This is his musical funeral. It may not be a flamboyant New Orleans affair with a brass band parade but it's not bad for a musician who died in the middle of the New Hampshire woods.

Out of the blue, our harmony improves, like a new voice has joined our awkward duo, producing a lip-buzzing hum. Mom shoots me one of those Indian looks that tells me she acknowledges we have stepped out of our everyday world into what Bilki called "the in-betweens," the swirling space within the vortex that connects earth and sky. We both know this new sound is actually the voice of Grumps, singing and playing with us. We feel his presence. We join him in belting out the line, "And any time you feel the pain..." Now I swear John Lennon and George Harrison are backing us up.

This is not the first time I've sung with amazing spirits. They may not always be visible, like Shankdaddy and Mia, or talk inside my head like Bilki, but they are definitely here in this cabin with us, in the vibration of every string and vocal cord. This is not macabre. It's joyful. When the living and the dead sing side by side, there is nothing more harmonious. I think of Marilynn Awasos, a black bear from New Hampshire, crying over the passing of an old Mohegan Indian man. After seeing that and hearing this, I can believe anything. Maybe Dad will make the archaeological find of the century. Maybe Mom will overcome her depression. Maybe I'll make it to St. Louis with my blues music, after all.

Sixteen

The Will of Grumps

A woman about Grumps' age paces outside a rundown log cabin beneath a sign that says "Indian Stream Legal Services." Her battleship gray hair is cropped above the ears, even shorter than Mom's new pixie. She's perspiring in a long-sleeved button-down Vermont Country Store dress and sensible loafers. Another woman seated under the office sign smokes a fragrant tobacco mix with her back turned.

The pacing woman heads our way, and I smell French fries. "Attorney Sadie Barnes is the name. I am terribly sorry for your loss." She shakes hands with Mom and me, as though she means it.

This has got to be Grumps' lady friend with the biodiesel beater. Not exactly "sexy Sadie," if you know what I mean. I'm thrilled to finally meet his mystery driver. I never guessed she was an attorney.

Sadie walks over and taps the shoulder of the smoking woman, who whirls around and enshrouds her in a cloud. She's chewing the stem of her pipe as if it's a tough moose steak, and her silver braid gleams in the September sun. It's Black Racer Woman.

I elbow Mom. There must be some mistake. I can't imagine Grumps leaving Black Racer Woman anything in his will. Mom appears equally stunned.

"My condolences, gals," says Black Racer Woman, tossing the harsh rope of her braid back on her shoulder. "Surprised to see me? No more surprised than I am to be here. I didn't know the old man had a bad heart. Did you?"

Mom shakes her head.

"It's good to see you, Lila," says her aunt, "even if you won't be here for long. I know how you feel about the woods. It's all right. You've done your duty by raising Mona Lisa. Now it's her turn."

I dislike the sound of whatever it is that she's suggesting. Black Racer Woman hugs us both in her slithery way.

"The other folks are already inside," announces Sadie, marching past us to the cabin door. "Let's get started."

I mouth the words "other folks," and Mom smiles acridly.

A fusty smell fills the foyer of Sadie's law office. The temperature is well into the eighties and there's no air-conditioning or open windows. A fan is running, spreading the fusty smell around. I pinch my nose as I pass a bookcase filled with yellowed law books. On top lies a vase filled with dried faded roses beside a dozen or so familiar-looking carved moose antlers. We pass the bookshelves and cross an ancient shag carpet on which lies a heavy mahogany desk that commands the central room space like a casket. Two people are seated on a brown plaid couch in front of the desk. One of their heads has spiked dark hair and the other is lemon yellow.

I step rigidly toward them, like I'm walking the plank. Del and Scales stand simultaneously, holding hands. A sweetheart candy hair clip with three conjoined pastel hearts, saying "My Baby," "Real Love," and "Be True," holds back Scales' bangs.

She flashes a gold ring topped with a modest diamond. It appears that Del's complication is a serious one.

Del offers his seat to Mom, but she refuses to sit. The baby fat has shed from his face, revealing strong bones, and his hair has been stylishly cut, definitely in New Haven, not Indian Stream. He's wearing wing tips instead of his usual clodhopper boots. I saw him two weeks ago, and he's changed so much. His dream smile is gone, and his once-beautiful lichen-green eyes have turned the color of toad skin. I toy with the notion he always had this drab urbane appearance, that I only imagined him to be better looking. He eyes my unevenly chopped bangs as if he's thinking something equally negative about me.

Scales presses me with a hug that makes me feel like the tail end of a tube of toothpaste. "Mona, I'm so sorry about your grandfather." She touches my Bonepile tee shirt reverently. "You are such a musical beast. I can't believe you played with The Blond Bear this summer and this fall you're a star. Del says you are dedicated to your music one hundred percent. You deserve your success. Congratulations on making the big-time, baby."

"Thanks," I say weakly. I don't correct her on the fact that I never actually played with the entire Blond Bear band, only Sponge. I figure she has already bragged about it on Facebook to everyone she knows, so there's no point.

"That Beetle dude you sing with is sizzling hot." She bites her ring.

I picture her breaking her front tooth.

Del looks over my shoulder. "Why isn't your sidekick here?" He eyes my heart locket bitterly.

"Beetle is suffering vocal problems," I explain.

Scales sticks out her lower lip and says, "Aw."

A wicked clurichaun smile flutters across Del's lips.

Sadie shuffles through the piles of papers on her cluttered desk, seemingly unable to find something. We all sense it may be a while before our meeting here is concluded.

Mom reaches out to hold Del and Scales' hands, at a distance. "Congratulations on your engagement."

"Thank you, Dr. Elmwood." Scales lunges in to squeeze-hug Mom. "Bear St. Jean, Senior asked me to send his regards."

Mom flushes and gossips with Scales about Bear's dad. Mom never gossips.

I'm grateful for this chance to chat with Del. I move in close enough to smell his skin. "Hi, there."

He maintains a steel expression. "Did you know that after you rejected me at the Farewell Dance, the police came by and searched our house? They found Dad's secret painted room for Mom, which prompted him to call you and me names I can't repeat. That was the week I got engaged. They also found Mom's yearbook with the picture of Worthless Dill scratched out. Thanks to you, my dad is once again a suspect in my mom's case."

I grab his wrists, selfishly, before he leaves my life forever. "Don't blame me for your decision to get engaged."

Fire ants march up and down my arms. I remember our lips melting together. Why didn't I tell him that I loved him?

"I didn't intentionally tell the police about your dad's secret room," I explain. "I accidentally mentioned it to Beetle. He told his dad. After he saw us together at the dance, he must have gone to the police about the yearbook. I'm sorry. Worthy probably did it to break us up and protect his son's relationship with me. I guess it worked." Jealousy surges through me as I catch sight of Scales' glittering ring hand. "He might not have bothered, had he known you were planning to get engaged."

He squeezes my arms. "Don't you dare turn this around. I opened my heart to you the minute we met. I introduced you to my friends. We made music together. I showed you Dad's secret room of flowers because I wished I'd made it for you. I told you that I loved you. You tried everything you could to shut me out. You rejected me."

"So you asked Scales to marry you to spite me?" My hands vibrate. We're still holding one another.

He yanks me closer, and the room shrinks around us. The dilapidated plaid couch, the casket-style desk, the shelves topped with dead animals, wilted flowers, and castaway antlers all converge, driving us closer together on the musty shag carpet, pushing us nose to nose, wedging us into a tight space smaller than the janitor's closet. He touches my lips lightly with a finger and we jolt from a small electrical shock.

Scales and Mom don't seem to notice. They're effusing over how much they both love cities. I wonder if Black Racer Woman has cast a spell on them. She is spinning around on a swivel chair in the corner of the room, humming a strange tune and tapping her grimy moccasined feet.

"You should never have told me that you loved me if you planned to marry someone else," I say to Del.

"You shouldn't have told me you were unavailable, if you didn't mean it."

"All I said was, *I have to put my music first.*"

"Fine. But you didn't say you loved me, either."

"There's no sense in me trying to remedy that now, with you rushing into marriage, like we're living in the twentieth century. My mom rushed into marriage with my dad, and look where it got her—miserable."

"Well, my dad would have given anything to marry my mom when they were young, and he never got the chance.

Look where that decision got him. There is no right and wrong answer to this. There is no correct life plan. You should try going with your heart, Mona Lisa."

I squeeze my heart locket. It feels icy. "Then why didn't you go with your heart, Del Pyne?" I raise my voice, "Why didn't you?"

That last sentence was too loud. Everyone turns our way.

Mom slaps Del on the back and sticks a tongue in her cheek, "Del, your dad tells me you can take Mona in a guitar duel."

"Dad is exaggerating. I still suck at guitar almost as bad as Mona's friend, Beetle boy. Of course, he does have a decent set of pipes." He wraps his arm around Scales' waist. "Almost as good as Scales'."

I feel like I've been punched in the chest.

Scales slaps her fiancé's arm. "Stop it, Delsy. That's rude." She pulls him closer. "Anyway, I know this is an awful time to ask but we have an important request. We want you both to come to our wedding on Halloween."

"Congrats," I sputter, wondering what it is with Halloween and me. I try not to think too hard about why Scales might be choosing to get married so young and so soon. I can't help but picture a newborn baby girl with lichen-green eyes and spiked blond hair, singing shrill soprano notes while playing the ukulele. "How's the rest of the Blond Bear gang? All happily married as well?" I ask.

Del's nostrils flare.

"Mona, you are too funny," Scales hiccup-laughs. "Bear may be the next to go. He took off for Arizona with some fancy dancer after the Winnipesaukee Powwow. She transferred to U of Maine. He already calls her 'the Missus.' His dad is encouraging them to get married soon because he insists true love doesn't come along every day."

Mom reacts to this by flopping onto the couch, glassy-eyed. She's gone on one of her mental retreats.

"Good for Bear," I say to close out that topic.

Scales whispers, "Did you hear Sponge is in prison for trying to sell drugs to kids at Little League practice?"

I clap my hands. "I couldn't be happier to see him gone."

Del's leg buckles, and he groans.

"You okay, Delsy?" asks Scales. She turns to me, confidentially. "His leg hurts him terribly sometimes. But I tell him he should feel blessed. I mean, who else takes a bullet meant for a bear, and survives?" She turns to Black Racer Woman and gasps, "Oops. I'm sorry. I forgot you were the one who shot him. I'm sure it was an accident."

Black Racer Woman stares down Scales. "Your fiancé should not have tried to protect that bear. That creature needed to die to save these woods."

I recall my great aunt's argument with Grumps at the powwow. "Auntie, you know my grandfather didn't agree with your ideas about bear sacrifice. We should drop that subject, out of respect for him. We are here for the reading of his will."

"Agreed, Mona Lisa, I apologize," says Black Racer Woman.

Sadie harrumphs, "I should think so!" She gathers four mangled file folders that have obviously been reused numerous times and swipes her nose with a tissue. "Now let's skip the legal blah, blah, blah, and get down to brass tacks." She shakes Mom's limp shoulder. "Lila dear, we will begin with you. Your father has left you four hundred and twenty thousand dollars. Spend it wisely, but be sure to spend it." Sadie eyes the carved antlers on top of her bookcase, despondently. "I wish he had." She hands Mom a check that falls in her lap.

Sadie addresses Del, next. "Upon your graduation from forestry school, you are to receive nine hundred acres of woodlands, in trust, along with an annual stipend of seventy-five thousand dollars for your labor and a separate stipend for property maintenance. Should you accept this gift, you are also accepting a lifetime responsibility. These woods can never be sold. They must remain under your care. This is quite a sacrifice you will be making."

Now I know what Del and Grumps were discussing on that stormy August day when I left Indian Stream: it was Grumps' will. He must have known that he didn't have much time left. It hurts me to think the only ones he told about his final wishes were Del and Sadie.

"I told Mr. Elmwood I wouldn't accept his terms without family approval." He turns to Mom and me, only looking her in the eye. "Is this acceptable to you, Dr. Elmwood? Mona Lisa?"

Mom hugs him limply. "You love these woods like my mother did. Who better to protect them?"

I haul up the sides of my mouth, as best I can. I wouldn't call my expression a smile.

Sadie's voice turns raw. "As for you, Mona Lisa LaPierre, your grandfather has left you his cabin, his truck and three hundred acres. If you wish to sell it, he stipulates Del Pyne must be given the right of first refusal."

"If you don't want the cabin, we are interested in buying it," Scales injects.

"We'll see," I say, recalling her recent endorsement of city life.

Black Racer Woman clucks her tongue. "Excuse me, Sadie. My sister had 1,500 acres of woodlands. Del received nine hundred acres and Mona received three. Who got the rest?"

"Reggie sold that land. I realize you would have preferred that your brother-in-law left it to you. But this is all he designated as your bequest." Sadie passes Black Racer Woman a thin file folder.

Black Racer Woman examines the file's contents with disdain. "This is only a copy! I suppose he still has the real thing locked up like Fort Knox." She turns to me. "Your grandpa Reggie thought that locking things up could stop the natural course of events. When you discover what he's hidden for you, you won't be very happy with him."

My great aunt exits and nobody says good-bye. I wonder about this mystery stash of his that she's warned me about.

"That's it, folks," concludes Sadie. "I'll help you iron out your details independently."

The realization of the finality of Grumps' death and Del's marriage makes me babble. "Now that Grumps' mystical woods and magical bears are safe once again, thanks to Del, we can all go home." I salute everyone stiffly.

Scales whispers something to Del that clearly agitates him, then turns back to Mom and me. "Mona, Dr. Elmwood, we want you to come to our engagement party on Sunday. I know you both have busy careers and that this has been an awful week, but we would be honored if you'd come. Vegetarian chili for all!"

I turn to Del with raised eyebrows. "You really want me to come to your party?"

"I would like both you and your mother to attend." His words are clipped. We lock eyes for an instant too long and the fire ants start marching. I try to think of Beetle, my pretty baby with the sweet soulful voice that makes women swoon and wonder why there has never been a single burning fire ant between us.

Mom comes back to life. "I would love to attend your engagement party. You know how fond I am of you and your father. But I have to head back home tomorrow for my volunteer service at the Hartford Animal Shelter. They're terribly short-staffed." She elbows me hard enough to leave a bruise. "But surely Mona can stay. She has her own truck now."

I'd love to," I burst out, surprising myself with my affirmative answer. "I can take a few days off to let Beetle's voice heal. Orpheus has already cancelled our Manchester concert. He only booked it so Grumps could attend."

Scales screeches in her shrill soprano voice. "Of course you can come. You're a rock star and rock stars can do whatever they want!" She hiccup-giggles uncontrollably. Del squeezes her arm to make her stop.

"Thanks, Scales. I appreciate that. But I play blues, not rock, and even the best blues singers wind up somewhere south of stardom. In fact, I think your term 'blues star' is an oxymoron." I take a seat on the plaid couch.

She whispers in Del's ear, asking him if I just called her a moron. I wish I could laugh, but I'm picturing Del and me at the Farewell Dance, enjoying those unforgettable moments. The only moron here is me.

Seventeen

Young and Stupid

The Pyne house reeks of wedding cake. Four tasting samplers cut in matchbook-sized pieces lay on a white tablecloth covered in pale pink tissue-paper rose petals. An artfully painted sign invites guests to vote on their favorite cake for the big event. There's a Blond Bear cake with lemon frosting and a chili chocolate center, an Indian Stream cake topped with a blue Skittles stream with a gooey maple fudge frosting, a Winter Woods cake made from white fondant covered with gummy pine trees, and a Mad Guitar cake with red licorice strings, black licorice tuners, a peanut butter pick guard and a banana pudding center. I'm sure I'd pick that one if I could choke down a bite of anything. But I've lost my appetite because Scales is pressing herself so tightly against Del that it looks like she is frosting him.

Will Pyne stumbles by wearing his usual whiskey cologne. I hoped he'd be rotting in jail, thanks to the police finding that yearbook in his secret room. I head in the opposite direction, pushing my way through a crowd of weather-burned faces topped with baseball caps advertising lumber companies, real maple syrup, and organic microbrews. I have a hard time getting past Scales' Boston Conservatory friends, crowded by the bathroom. I hate to admit it but Will's out-of-town artist buddies are the most interesting people in the crowd, with their silk-screened scarves and rainbow dreadlocks that remind me of Celine. I reach the kitchen and search the corkboard for Mia's photo but find it gone.

I lift my head skyward, seeking guidance from Bilki and find the ceiling covered with cupcake-pink balloons. They make me wonder if Del and Scales are expecting a baby girl. The center of the room features a life-sized cardboard stand-up of the happy couple, surrounded by a cupcake-pink cloud. I feel melancholy as I recall wearing my cupcake-pink Dead Kittens tee shirt on my last day of high school. Getting in trouble over that cupcake-pink shirt is what led me here, to Indian Stream, in the first place. Now it appears that cupcake-pink will usher me out of here—for good.

My eyes follow the sound of Bear's booming voice. A western Indian girl wearing turquoise bling and a red leather skirt accompanies him. Her crow-colored hair swooshes back and forth, like freshly trimmed leather fringe. I figure she knows how to bead her own regalia and make the world's best frybread. She is probably working on a cure for cancer in her spare time. I turn away, but it's too late.

Miss Arizona points at my face and shouts, "Mona from Bonepile! Axe woman extraordinaire! I love your band! I have a ticket for your upcoming concert in Boston. Don't you dare cancel that one."

"I'll see you there, in two weeks.

Bear throws a tree trunk-sized arm around my head. "Hey, Tribal Sista. I'm coming too."

I want to tell him how close I came to actually being his sister but now is not the time.

"This is Nomi," he says introducing his companion. "She's a musician." Bear nudges me. "She's also pre-med."

Naturally.

Before I can reply, she says, "I wouldn't be at college if I had your chops, Mona." She strums an air guitar. "Seriously, your fingers are amazing. I'm Guitar Hero garbage compared to you."

Her worn fingertips tell me that's bunk. I may have exaggerated her beadwork and frybread-making skills, but I'm willing to bet this woman can play a mean guitar. And look at her! This may be East-West Injun envy on my part, but if I were Orpheus, I'd hire Nomi to perform all my songs and lock me up in the janitor's closet.

She grabs my hand. "I loved your songs on YouTube. I play 'You are my Lightning.' all the time. Or try to anyway." She hugs Bear affectionately, "Don't I, Bear?"

"She does," he sighs.

I hug her, because "You are my Lighting" is the one song that's all mine, written without help from the living or the dead.

A squealing microphone interferes with our bonding.

Will Pyne stands unsteadily on a milk crate and shouts, "Welcome to our Wang Dang Doodle!"

Scales gasps and shrinks. Her lemony head looks like it's been squeezed. I believe she thinks Will said something obscene. I snort, bemused by his use of that old blues' expression for a party. Bear and Nomi respond to Will's remark by sneaking into a corner for a passionate make-out session, as if his words were somehow romantic.

Will raises a magnum bottle of champagne. "Let's toast the happy couple." His monster gumball eyes appear almost kind today. "To Del and Scales." He signals us to lift our glasses.

His head sinks down, as if he's passed out for a second, and then revives to speak forcefully. "On behalf of Del's late mom and myself, I wish you two a magical life together."

His words trigger a skull-splitting headache that forces my eyes shut. I hold my forehead, and feel an arm fall over my shoulder. I know it's Mia. I keep my eyes closed and think of all the things that I should have been doing to help her, things to make sure that Will went to jail, things for which she should rightly chastise me. I deserve whatever punishment Mia Delaney's ghost has in store for me. I open my eyes and discover the fingernails attached to the hand on the arm aren't blue. But things are still bad because the arm on my shoulder is covered with paint splatter.

"Well, well, well, if it isn't Little Lila, still stalking the big bad murderer man." Will wipes his palms together, as if making a clean break from something. "Would you like a drink?"

In lieu of the champagne he gave everyone else, he offers me a hit of whiskey from his pocket flask. "No thanks, Will."

He tosses a gulp of whiskey down his throat and shakes the flask at me. "Excuse me for being friendly. I thought you might be looking for a strong beverage today—considering your predicament." He winks in Del and Scales' direction.

Scales watches us. Will pours whiskey from his flask over his head, trickling it directly down his throat like a leaky faucet. His eyeballs redden as he gargles and swallows hard. "I suppose you can't help the fact that you are young and stupid, Little Lila. I was young and stupid once. Look where it got me."

Will cups a hand around my ear, to prevent Del and Scales from lip-reading his words as he whispers, "By the way, you're wrong about me being a murderer. No matter how much pressure the cops get from your boyfriend's big daddy, they won't sentence me for Mia's death because I didn't do it." He points at Del and Scales. "Yet, you're about to sentence the love of your life to a fate worse than death just because you don't like me."

He's drawing my focus away from the murder, which isn't difficult right now, as Scales floats through the crowd like cotton candy in a ridiculous soft pink sundress.

"Any feelings I have for your son are irrelevant," I tell Will. "My upcoming tour is my priority."

"You'll be missing the big wedding then?"

I'm about to reply when Del storms into us.

"I know you two aren't having a social chat. This has to stop now. Mona, it's time for the three us to talk. C'mon." He leads his dad and me to the Mustang couch and sits Will between us, so we can prop him upright, not to mention keep the fire ants at bay.

"Dad, tell her your version of what happened between you and Mom. Start when you were a nineteen-year-old Yale sophomore, and Mom was a sixteen-year-old junior at Colt High."

Will's torso lilts my way. I push him back.

His words flow fast, like a dammed-up river, bursting, "After I met Mia at a Rush concert in Hartford, I was hooked. We talked about starting a band that would rival her father's band, the Hoodoo Chickens. But that plan fizzled when Mia got pregnant during her junior year. Babies are band killers."

I recall Mom saying this same thing. Now I believe it.

Will continues, "She wasn't due till late August and she hardly showed until summer, so nobody at school knew about the pregnancy. We moved up here the summer before her senior year to have Del in secret. It was a good plan because her father often went on tour during the summer and she could do as she pleased."

"After Del was born, I dropped out of college to care for my baby boy so Mia could finish high school. On the last day of Mia's senior year, I was supposed to pick her up and bring her back here to live with us for good. I painted her something that was going to blow her away. Something that would make her forget about all the other guys that were after her." He grumbles, "But then you already know about that special painted room, as does the entire Hartford Police force."

I mutter an apology.

Will digs a dog-eared photo from his wallet that shows a cluster of 1990s-era teenagers standing in front of Colt High sporting high-waisted jeans and gelled hair. Every guy is leaning toward Mia.

He points to her. "Beautiful, wasn't she? I took this photo on the morning of her last day of school. She didn't know I was there." He rubs the well-worn photo.

I now believe what Del said about Will sleeping with his mom's picture, every night.

"What happened on Mia's last day of school? " I ask.

"The students gathered in the parking lot. I overheard a group of girls mention Mia's name and pulled my bike beside them. One of them claimed Mia had fallen in love with Worthy Dill. This hit me hard. I knew who Worthy was. I'd heard Mia talk about him, far too much. When I heard this gossip, I lost it. One of them started talking about how nervous Mia was about telling her old boyfriend she was dumping him for Worthy. I waited a little while, hoping that girl was wrong. But she and her friends all turned and laughed at me. I knew Mia had played me and gloated about it to her friends. I figured if Del's momma wanted a happily-ever-after with Richie Rich, then baby Del and me were better off without her."

"When you found out about her death, later on, why didn't you come forward and tell the police this story?"

He shakes his flask at me. "By the end of that summer, I'd replaced Mia with whiskey as my new love. Your grandparents were doing most of the diaper-changing and bottle-feeding. Imagine how freaked I was when I got a call from your mom at the end of the summer, telling me that the police were looking for me in connection with Mia's death.

"I thought she was nuts. I couldn't process the fact that Mia had died at Colt High. Lila said she had a hard time believing it, too. She'd assumed she hadn't heard from me because Mia and I had ridden off happily into the sunset with baby Del."

Will doubles over onto my arm. "The truth is, Little Lila, I wanted to die when I found out Mia had been murdered. But your grandmother encouraged me to paint my way through the darkness." He points to the paintings overhead, obscured by cupcake-pink balloons. "That's when I began to draw these doors with swirling portals, to help Mia escape from her basement closet prison. I tried to repaint the past. Even though, deep down, I knew it didn't matter because she'd already moved on from our relationship, when she died. I figure that Worthy guy was in bad shape, like me. So I left him alone."

I feel like I'm holding an unpinned grenade. I had no idea Will thought Mia loved Worthy when she died. I gently remove the flask from Will's hand, so he can't throw it at me. "Will, Mia never loved Worthy. She didn't even like him. He told me that himself."

"He must be lying!" Will's bloodshot eyes bulge like a dissected frog. He slides off the couch onto the floor.

"Why would Worthy lie about that?" I kneel beside him. "It makes him sound suspect."

"Maybe he *is* suspect," says Del. "Or maybe there was some-body else. Dad and I have spent our lives hiding. It's time we faced this thing head on and uncovered the truth. I'm going to ask some hard questions around Hartford, regardless of how important this Dill guy is."

My heart pounds at the thought of Del coming to Hartford.

"Del, if anyone finds out you're Will Pyne's son, they'll clam up."

"Then you can ask the questions and I'll help you anony-mously." His smile is harsh, sizing me up for trustworthiness. "Do you believe Dad now? Are you willing to help us find Mom's real killer?"

"Yes."

Will's face changes as he processes the emancipating rev-elation that Mia has never betrayed him. The wrinkles around his eyes run deeper, yet the eyes, themselves, soften, and he chuckles grimly.

Scales rushes toward us and snatches Del's hand, as if he's a stray toddler. "What's going on, guys?" Her lemonhead looks terribly squeezed.

Del pulls her away where I can't overhear. She holds her hands over her ears, clearly displeased with whatever he is saying. I'm guessing nobody told her that Del's mom was murdered.

I overhear her squeal. "Murdered! Why investigate the murder now? Why does Beetle have to do it with Mona? Can't this wait until after our wedding?"

Del shouts back, "I need to do this before Mona Lisa goes on tour."

"I'm not sticking around while you take a trip with another woman. I'm heading back to the Cape."

"I'll be back for our wedding, Scales. I promised you we'd get married on Halloween and I'll keep that promise."

Will speaks to me, confidentially. "That ain't real love between those two. We both know it. Make your move now, Little Lila. Save my boy from himself. Save yourself, too. Go where your true feelings lie. You can stop being young and stupid any time you want. Now would be good."

"Will, Del is engaged. I'm going to help you both find out who killed Mia. But I plan to remain young and stupid when it comes to my relationship with Del."

"That's a damn shame for all of us, and for the universe. You may be a nuisance but so am I. That's because we've got depth. As it stands, I'm getting a daughter-in-law who wades in the shallow water." He offers me a glass of champagne—not more whiskey or a plastic cup like he gave everybody else—a real crystal glass of champagne, and I accept. He dumps the remaining contents of his flask down the sink, and fills a matching champagne glass for himself.

"To justice, for Mia," he toasts.

"To justice, for Mia," I echo. A hand brushes mine. No one is near me.

Will taps his temple. "Now that you're working for our side, I feel guilty about tossing your portrait into the landfill after the cops came to the house to grab Mia's yearbook." He strokes his chin, contemplatively. "I'm surprised I didn't burn it. Fortunately, my work is too good for anyone to trash. One of the locals fished it out of the muck and sold it. I need to buy it back for you."

"Gee, thanks, Will. Just what I've always wanted, a painting of my glorious face that's been in the dump."

He bows. "You're welcome."

Will strolls over to Scales. She and Del have their backs turned to one another. Will tosses an arm around her quivering shoulder. "Bride-y! Mona and I were just saying this is one hell of an engagement party."

He pours the rest of his magnum bottle of champagne on his slick, axle-grease head and yowls like a wild animal, newly unbound from his chains.

Eighteen

Graffiti Girl

Hartford Police Headquarters appears darker and dirtier than the last time I was here. Perhaps some lights are out, or I'm seeing the place through Del's more critical eyes. The same cop as last time mans the reception desk, rubbing his steel-wool buzz cut. I notice him checking out our guitars.

"You again?" he says. "Don't you have enough to worry about, writing hit blues songs? We checked out the lead you gave us and even the added information from Worthy Dill. We still came up with squat. Bring something fresh and valid to the table and we'll talk.

Del steps in front of me. "I am the victim's son, Delaney Pyne. Is that fresh and valid enough for you?"

I drop my head to my hands. "So much for you staying anonymous."

The officer practically jumps out from behind the desk and offers his hand to Del. "My name's Mealy, and I'm truly sorry to hear that, kid." He bangs his fist against his forehead.

"What's wrong?" Del asks.

"We should have solved your mom's case."

"So why didn't you?"

I put a hand on Del, worried that he's already losing his temper.

Mealy takes my hand off him. "It's all right. I deserve tough talk. Son, what I'm about to say, I will surely regret." He kisses some saint's medal hanging from his neck. "We botched the evidence in your mom's case."

Del's lichen eyes transform into Saint Elmo's fire.

Mealy crosses himself. "The janitor who found your mom's corpse tampered with the crime scene."

"What exactly did he do?" asks Del.

"I'm not sure, exactly. I was a rookie back when it happened, not in the full loop."

Del rattles the man's shoulder. "How did he get away with it? He could be my mom's murderer!"

"Maybe, but I doubt it. Irving Stone was a decorated veteran of The Gulf War. Trouble was, so was our late chief of police. The two of them were loyal comrades-at-arms." He scribbles Stone's phone number on a yellow sticky note, hands it to Del, and walks away. "Talk to him. Find out what really happened. But do it soon, before it's too late. He's real sick. Maybe he wants to clear his conscience."

He turns to Del, " I should have paid better attention to what your friend had to say. I should have reopened this case. But its easier to live in denial." He hands Del one of his business cards and writes Stone's number on the back.

Del dials Stone's number. He presses the phone to my ear and huddles with me so we can both hear. A nurse at the Veteran's Administration hospital answers and tells us we can visit Irving Stone right away, and "the sooner the better." We run red lights the whole way there. Del focuses like a flaming arrow.

"Please let me ask the questions," I urge. "You may scare Stone into silence."

"That's fine, as long as I see you making progress." He remains icy. "This may be it, Mona Lisa, our one and only chance to uncover the truth."

The signs posted in the hospice wing insist on quiet, and the walls are painted the pinkish-orange of a New England sunset. Yet there is nothing peaceful about Irving Stone's sick room. It smells like a pharmacy, a frat house, and a zoo. The complexity of the scent gives away the severity of his condition.

The nurse who greets us is middle-aged and sturdy. You might say "fat" at first glance but only because she wields every ounce of flesh like a barricade, blocking Del and me from seeing Stone until we've signed in. Of course, Del doesn't write his real name. He wants to meet Stone anonymously.

Sometimes you lie.

Irving Stone is a tissue-paper ghost of a man. He pushes his body up into a sitting position, like he's a kid hoisting open a heavy garage door. "Greetings, Ms. LaPierre and Mr. Woods."

I roll my eyes over Del's chosen pseudonym. "Greetings, Mr. Stone," I say for both of us. "We're researching the Mia Delaney case and hope you can shed some light on the subject."

Stone signals his nurse to leave—which she does grudgingly. He tries to clear his throat in order to speak, but fails. His blue-spotted hand reaches for a short paper cup of water—the kind found in dentist's offices and kindergartens—but he can't grasp it on his own.

"Allow me to help you, Mr. Stone," I say, assisting him with his drink, even though I know that he may be a well-camouflaged monster.

After taking a sputtering sip, Irving speaks to us through faintly purple lips, his rumpled eyelids fluttering, "Of course they ruled Mia's death an accident. They figured she got locked in the basement unintentionally. Maybe some kids were fooling around, locking doors, and didn't know she was there. There were no wounds, no harm done to the body. But you must already know those technical details from your research. Right?"

"Right, right," urges Del.

Stone pulls himself away from him, toward me. "One of the students told me it was that motorcycle bastard boyfriend of hers who did it. He was the one who locked her up in my closet."

"I think we both know that's not the real story," says Del, leaning into Irving's bed aggressively, like he's prepared to squeeze the last teaspoonful of life out of the old man if that's what's necessary to get him to admit to Mia's murder. "I think you locked her in. You had the keys."

"No! That's just it. I didn't have them. They weren't hanging on my key rack that Friday."

"That sounds pretty convenient."

"Not for me. The principal gave me a bad mark on my personnel file and laid me off. I was the first to go with the city cutbacks."

Stone's fists tighten beside his emaciated cheeks and his eyes widen into a silent scream. He is obviously remembering some terror, perhaps his own violent actions in the war or something worse.

He stutters, "If it hadn't been for the school board and their budget cuts, I would have been working at Colt as a janitor that summer. I would have found Mia in time. Damn those budget cuts. Damn them."

I try to prop Stone back up on his drool-stained pillow, to help him take another drink, to keep him talking. His eyes drift in different directions as if he is having another flashback, or a spell, or his heavy medication is taking its toll. He appears to have lost track of his surroundings.

I try to bring him back. "Tell me what Colt High was like back then."

Stone's hands clap in recognition as if everything has realigned. "Poor Millicent Dibble! I felt terrible for her during the investigation." His voice fades. "If it weren't for her rheumatism, she'd have never found herself in the center of that messy murder."

"Dibble was principal when Mia Delaney died?"

"Yes, indeed. She had been a music teacher and was promoted when Principal Wheeler retired. It was more charity than promotion. Her fingers were no longer nimble enough to play her music very well."

The revelation that Dibble was principal at the time of Mia's murder is only overshadowed by the news that she was once a music teacher.

"What instruments did she play?" I ask, spilling the remaining contents of his water cup on the floor.

Irving sways, remembering some absent tune. "She played keyboard and a mean axe. It was sad, what happened to her."

Del rubs his bad leg from standing still for so long. I'm being insensitive with this digression but I can't help it. "Could she sing? Did she write music? Did she have her own band? Was she any good?"

Irving slips down on his pillow, flustered by my barrage of questions. He needs help to sit up again, to remain alert. But I'm afraid to grip his arm. Red marks remain on his skin from the last time I helped him. I worry his nurse might accuse me of abuse.

Del grabs him and hoists him up, refocusing the questioning. "What did the janitor's closet look like when you first found Mia's body?"

Irving re-settles himself. "That's the foolish part. I was determined to be the perfect worker when they brought me back at the end of August, so they could never lay me off again. I headed back to that school, ready to make it shine. I was focused on that one goal." Stone makes a weak fist. "That's why, when I saw the graffiti all over my closet walls, I attacked it with a vengeance. I couldn't believe somebody had broken into my office and made such a mess. I assumed the vandal was the same person who took my keys."

"Graffiti? What did it say?" Del hulks over the man's bed. I'm leaning in, exactly the same way.

"Stupid, stupid, stupid me!" Irving beats the bed. "I hate myself for what I did next. I'm so sorry, so very sorry." Stone grows visibly weaker. A full deathbed confession appears to be cresting on the crusty edges of his purple lips. Del kneads his fists while Stone slobbers drool down his neck. "You'll hate me when I tell you what happened."

Del's fists clench so tight his entire body quakes. I reach out and hold his hands with all my strength.

Stone's face loses all tension as if he's letting go of something painful. "You see, I began washing the walls without bothering to read what was on them. I was nearly done cleaning before I spotted that skeleton face peeking out from what I thought was a pile of rags on the floor. I might not have noticed it at all if that face hadn't been wriggling with maggots."

This image makes me weak. I've always pictured Mia as perfect, even in death, a fairy tale princess in a glass coffin. The vision of Mia reduced to a rotting corpse sickens me.

"What was written on those walls?" asks Del, still firm.

"That's just it. I don't know. I went into shock when I saw the body. It wiped my mind clean. That information has never come back to me, not since I saw Mia. My buddy the police chief said if I told anyone I washed the walls I'd be fired from my job. He kept that information out of the police record."

My hand falls over my nose. "Didn't you smell the decomposing body as soon as you entered the room?"

"No ma'am," shrugs Irv. "I got no sense of smell. I lost it in an accident back in the army. I figured it was a blessing when I started scrubbing toilets and mopping up kids' puke for a living, after I came home from Iraq."

Del rips into the conversation. "Can't you remember even one word of what was written on that wall?" His words are frostbitten and demanding.

"No sir, not a thing, except that it was written in reddish-brown, like dried blood." Irving turns to the side of his bed and vomits into a bag. He gags and has trouble catching his breath. I instinctively reach for the nurse's emergency button. Before I touch it, he comes back to us, sitting up on his own, revived.

"Oh my God!" He pokes a finger toward the ceiling. "I remember something. For the first time since that day, I remember. One of the words on that wall had something to do with a bug."

"A bug?" My mind races to fill in the blanks. "Like an ant, or a bumblebee, or a beetle or...a cricket?"

Irving slaps his head with the sheet, clearly relieved. "Yes, that's it! A cricket! After all these years I remember. Bless you, youngsters!" He waves us in for a hug.

But Del can't move. His eyes are pogoing around the room, putting it all together. "Mr. Stone," he asks, "who claimed to have seen Mia leave with Will?"

"I don't recall," says Stone.

Del pulls out Mealy's card and phones him. "Hey Mealy, it's Del Pyne. What was the name of the student who claimed to see Mia leave with Will?

There is a silent pause while he listens.

"So it was Cricket Dill." Del's face inflames. "Thanks, Mealy. I think I'm onto something. We'll talk soon."

"We're going to the Dill house." He turns to Stone, "Goodbye and thank you, sir. You may have just solved the Mia Delaney case."

"I don't think it's a good idea for us to go there, Del."

"Probably not. But I already know where the Dill home is located. The address for Beetle's house was linked to your Bonepile website by some stalker fan. It's your choice whether or not you want to join me."

"Can you at least explain why we are going there?"

"I want to confront Cricket before she has time to lawyer up, to see the look on her face and hear what she has to say, for myself. I want to catch her off guard."

We carry our guitars to the front door of the green glass house with steel trim. Our cover story is that Del's just another musician friend, stopping by to jam with Beetle. Del strangles Angel's neck while we wait on the Dills' doorstep.

Mrs. Dill cracks open her money-green glass door and begins her strange adolescent ritual of putting a stray blond hair behind her ear and fiddling with her hemline before saying a word. It's as though I possess super invisibility powers that work on her for a good ten seconds every time we meet. Now that I know she is responsible for Mia Delaney's death, her ritual appears sinister.

After my ten seconds of oblivion is up, she speaks as though interrupted in the middle of an important task. "My goodness, Mona. It's you. I thought you were still up in the boondocks of New Hampshire. Beetle was expecting Rasima to come by today, not you." Mrs. Dill drops her eyelids in the direction of Del's guitar. "Are you another musician?"

"Yes, Beetle invited him to our band practice," I reply, resolved not to respond emotionally to anything she says. The stakes are too high.

Del can't hold it in any longer. "I've heard a lot about you, Mrs. Dill."

She raises her finely penciled eyebrow, "From whom, may I ask?"

"Irving Stone, the old janitor at Colt High. He says your name was written on the walls of the janitor's closet where Mia Delaney died."

Cricket mimes the words, "My name?" She flattens an imperceptible wrinkle on her blouse and nearly loses her balance as she reaches for her hem.

"Mom, who's at the door?" shouts Beetle from behind. He appears, dressed in an ice-blue polo. As soon as he sees us, his deep licorice eyes turn to sludge. "Mona, I recognize this guy from the Winnipesaukee Powwow." He turns to Del. "You're Del Pyne, the guy who stole Mona away from me at the Farewell Dance."

Beetle's licorice eyes plead with me to explain my cruelty.

Cricket grabs her golden hair and pulls it, exactly like Beetle. "Your name is Del? As in Delaney?" She pulls two hundred dollar bills out of a nearby drawer. "If this is some kind of paternity blackmail scheme against Worthy, I'll pay. He never needs to know about you. But if he's your father, you deserve compensation."

I have to hand it to Cricket for making the name connection

between Del and Delaney so quickly. I couldn't do it. But the fact that she thinks he is Worthy's kid shows her paranoia about the nature of Mia's relationship with her husband.

Del raises his palms, "Keep your money, Mrs. Dill. I'm not claiming to be your husband's son. I only want to know why your name was written on the wall of the room where my mother died."

Cricket steps outside, gasping for air, mouthing the words, "My name? Mia is your mother?"

Beetle supports his mother's arm. "Forget it, Mom. Even if what he says is true, it means nothing except that Mia was jealous of you because she had a thing for Dad."

"Beetle, that's a lie," I say. "You heard your dad say Mia rejected him!"

Cricket tugs harder at her hair, turning her scalp pink. "No! Mia loved Worthy. I know she did."

"No, Mrs. Dill. Mia never cared for Worthy," I interject.

She groans and yanks her hair with all her might. "This can't be true! No one would reject my Worthy! I had to fight for him. It was the only way! I needed to keep Mia away from him." Her scalp and cheeks flush crimson.

"So you admit to telling my dad Mia was cheating on him with Worthy, so he wouldn't look for her."

Both of Beetle's arms now support his mom to keep her from collapsing. "Don't answer that, Mom. I don't want to hear another word."

Cricket's face reddens to the point where I'm afraid she'll collapse. She spits words and water, as though she might drown if she doesn't expel them both rapidly. "I never meant to hurt a soul!" She pulls away from Beetle to grab the collar of Del's shirt and shake him. "Locking Mia up was a prank."

"How did you do it?" I ask.

"I stole the principal's key from her desk. I couldn't believe it when I heard nobody found Mia all summer, that she died in that closet. It was an accident. The janitor always came in on Mondays. I was sure he'd find her. How was I to know the school board would lay him off?" She slips down onto her knees on the neatly cropped grass in her front yard. "I'm no murderer. I can't even set a mousetrap, or fly paper. I could not kill anything on purpose."

Invisible fingertips pat my arm, supportively, but I see no one.

Beetle punches the green glass of the front door until it cracks. "That's enough, Mom. Shut up!"

Cricket ignores her son and focuses on Del and me. "I thought if I locked Mia up, I could get my chance with Worthy. You see? That's all. I was sure somebody would find her."

Beetle slaps a hand over her mouth and shouts, "I'm calling a lawyer."

Cricket's eyes deepen like an ocean trench. She pushes him away. "This young man has grown up motherless because of me! I need to make it right!"

Beetle shakes her. "So what happens now, Mom? He gets to take my mother away from me? What's the point?"

Beetle's bangs are disheveled and sweaty and his licorice eyes lay vacant. His smirk is nowhere to be found. "You can't bring your mother back. What happened to her was an accident. You heard what my mom said. Nobody meant to kill anybody. She locked up a girl, to keep her from going out with some guy she liked. It was a stupid high school prank gone wrong. We all do stupid stuff."

Del lunges for Beetle's throat. "Your mom's stupid prank ruined my dad's life!"

I insert myself between them. "Del's right, Beetle. This is serious." I lower my voice because several neighbors have stepped out onto their lawns with their cell phones raised. I hope at least one of them has already called the police.

Worthy appears and rushes to his wife, still kneeling on the grass. "Cricket, what's all this commotion? Dear God, sweetheart, what has happened to you?"

"It's nothing," she says, patting her cheeks as he lifts her to her feet. "I need to freshen up a little, is all. Everything will be fine."

Worthy speaks in his most fatherly voice. "It's obvious Mrs. Dill is unwell. I'm taking her to the doctor." He glances at Del's heaving chest. "Young man, did you provoke this incident?"

Del stands as tall as he is able. "Yes, sir, I did. I am Mia Delaney's son. My name is Delaney Pyne. Your wife killed my mother."

Worthy shoots me a hangman's glare. "Dear God, what kind of game are you playing, Mona? You told me the culprit was Will Pyne." He waves his finger between Del and me. "After what I saw you two doing at the Farewell Dance, why should I trust either of you?'"

Beetle thunders forward. "After you saw them doing *what* at the dance, Dad?"

"Your girlfriend was kissing this boy."

"What! Mona, is this true?" Beetle grabs me.

"Yes, I admit it. But do you really want us to get into what either of us did that night?"

Beetle silently pulls his bangs, confirming my worst suspicions about him and Rasima.

Worthy shakes his cell phone at Del and me. "I'm phoning the police. This is some sort of blackmail game, cooked up by you two young lovers. I've had enough. Cricket had nothing to do with Mia's death. How could little Cricket have forced Mia Delaney into the school basement? She has always been delicate."

Mrs. Dill bobs her head up. "I convinced her that her father was on his way to school because he found out about her secret baby. I guessed she'd been pregnant, junior year, because I'd seen her vomiting in the bathroom. My theory was a long shot. But the panicked reaction I saw in her eyes confirmed my suspicions. I told her she'd be safe in the janitor's closet and she believed me. Once she was inside, I locked her in. I was certain the janitor would find her on Monday. By then Worthy and I would be away together on Lake Winnipesaukee." She turns to Del, "Please phone the police. I need to tell them I am responsible for the death of your mother. It's the least I can do."

Del lurches at her violently. Worthy and I both grab him. Worthy Dill agrees to phone the police. I listen to him disclose everything. His honest action makes me feel worse about the fact that he caught Del and me making out at the dance. Del appears frozen in shock. I bring him around the side of the house, away from the Dills. I hold him in my arms while we wait for this thing to be over. Instead of fire ants, I absorb his burning rage, something more intimate than any lovemaking. I feel his devotion to his mother, his fury at Cricket, and his shock over discovering the ugly truth. He has no one else to console him but me. His mother is long gone. His surrogate parents—Bilki and Grumps—they're gone, too. His loser dad is five hours away. His stoner best friend is a pin brain. His fiancé is who-knows-where. I'm all he's got. Del wants to see this thing through to closure. He fears the Dills will bolt. But none of them budge.

The police show up in two minutes. Cricket waives her right to a lawyer and delivers a full confession on the spot. Neither

Worthy nor Beetle objects. Del and I offer the police a quick summary of how we pieced things together. The last thing I hear Worthy do is call his office to ask his administrative assistant to reserve Beetle a one-way ticket to Stadt.

Del phones Will to tell him what's happened. I phone Mom and she offers to pass the information on to Celine. There is some gasping and sobbing, along with a stream of thank yous.

"What now?" Del asks, beaming at me like I'm his shining star.

I won't take advantage of his vulnerability. I kiss him warmly on the cheek, with all the love and friendship in my heart. He pulls me to him, kissing my mouth so fully I'm not sure I can ever sing another blues song. This is the kind of powerful kiss that could ruin me for anyone else. But I perform a reality check. I remind myself that this isn't a romantic kiss; it's a kiss born of an impossible goal achieved through teamwork, like a kiss after an underdog team wins a state playoff game or a group of doctors and nurses saves a hopeless life on the operating table. Together, Del and I have solved an infamous Hartford murder case that involved his Mom. What he's feeling is the rush of having avenged her and maybe saved his dad's life. I can't take advantage of that.

I pull away from him, overwhelmed, wanting more but afraid to make his wedding more painful for both of us than it already is. Still, there is much to celebrate. Mia Delaney's killer is in custody. The Hartford Police let Mealy perform the arrest honors, as senior officer. After he handcuffs Cricket, he tells me he's giving his two weeks' notice. I imagine Mom dumping her depression medication and Will tossing his whiskey bottles over the news. I see Celine blowing out Mia's memorial candle because her sister finally knows justice. As for me, there remains one more thing I need to do with Del Pyne, before he heads north and walks his bride down the aisle, into forever.

Nineteen

A Tale of Yellow Roses

The gold metallic words "Madame Celine, Astrologer" gleam in the fall sun. Del examines the zodiac mobile spinning in the window and points warily at the scorpion, the lion, and the crab, questioning the sociability of a person who displays such creatures. He scowls, like Bilki might, at the uneven brushstrokes of green, gold, and black paint on the Jamaican flag on her door. So Del is an art critic. It's clear he was more of a grandchild to my painter grandmother than I was.

"Your aunt Celine lives here," I explain.

The door flies open, bells tinkling. Out bursts Celine, like a tossed bridal bouquet in a dress covered with fuchsia hibiscus flowers. "Welcome, Nephew! I knew you would stop by. After all you've been through, you need to be with family." She kisses Del's head. "Seeing you is a dream come true."

"How do you know who I am?"

"I could say the stars told me but..." She points to a news alert running at the bottom of the television that says, "Hartford Socialite Jailed for Delaney Murder." The screen is showing high school yearbook photos of Del and me. "Besides, Lila phoned to tell me the good news."

She shakes her head. "What on earth was that Cricket woman thinking?"

"Celine, Cricket thought Mia loved Worthy Dill."

She throws her hands into the air. "She must have been blind. Mia never gave that Worthless Dill boy the time of day." She shakes a finger at Del. "That's what she called him: Worthless Dill."

Del chuckles nervously. "My dad called him that, too."

I scan the room and find Mia's remembrance candle, still lit.

Celine catches me looking and retrieves it, placing it before Del. "This candle is for you to extinguish, Delaney Pyne. I have kept it for your mother since she died, waiting for justice. I would like you to be the one to blow out this flame, now that her killer sits behind bars."

He hesitates—perhaps preparing to say some silent prayer.

"Mona Lisa," he says. "You did most of the work finding Mom's killer. You need to do this with me."

I nod. We both blow on the flame, hard. It flickers for an instant before snuffing out and sending a phantomlike trail of smoke all the way across the room.

I feel a jolt when I notice who is missing. "Where is Damerae?"

Celine points to the sky. "When the stars come out, you can see him shine." She squeezes Del's hand, "like your beautiful mother, Mia." Celine plucks Angel's strings and eyes the painted wings on Del's guitar, dubiously. What's this, Nephew?"

"This is my guitar. I named her Angel, after my mother."

"I see." Celine shakes off something, before patting Rosalita. "Mona also has her guitar with her. This is good. The three of us will sing today for Mia and Shankdaddy. He was your grandfather, and a great musician. Mona's grandfather, Reggie, was not a bad musician, either. They jammed together, back in the day. But enough about yesterday. Today is about moving forward. We three will sing together beside the Delaney graves. Their burial ground is a short way from here." Celine opens a closet by the front door and grabs some things that she stuffs into her giant raffia floral handbag. "Follow me."

Her fast-stepping spiked heels make it hard to argue with her. But I'm not sure how I feel about this cemetery visit. Mia and Shankdaddy aren't exactly dead to me. I've never visited Bilki's grave because she's not dead to me, either. Still, I know this visit is important to Del.

We pass an abandoned brick garment factory, a burned-out tire warehouse that still reeks of melted rubber, and a condemned elementary school that looks suspiciously like Colt High. Only our school will never deteriorate like this one because it's scheduled for demolition soon. It will simply disappear in a rumbling puff of smoke, later this fall, which is probably best, considering its history.

This lengthy walk leaves us dripping with sweat. It's been a hot September. Celine distracts us from the heat by telling family stories, not skipping the parts most people edit out, saying things like, "Do you know my fadda, Shankdaddy, mixed bourbon with his cereal on Sunday mornings before church?" and "My sister, Mia, used to make up the funniest rhymes that no lady could repeat." She slaps her knee. "Oh how Principal Millicent Dibble hated her rebellious behavior. She thought that Cricket girl was a saint. I wonder what she thinks of her perfect little Cricket now?"

Celine shares some wholesome family stuff, too. "Whenever Shankdaddy sold a new CD, he played Santa Claus to the neighborhood kids, filling new athletic socks with gift certificates for video games and hanging them on their doorknobs."

At the end of each story, Celine tosses back her head full of sapphire braids and wails with a laugh as big and bold as the crystal blue Jamaican sky.

Her well-told stories keep us from noticing exactly when the street crowds vanish and the music dies away. We've arrived at a place so far down Manburn Street that nothing is familiar. In fact, I wonder if we're even on the same street. The pavement is eroded down to potholes and pebbles, exploding with hairy weeds. We keep going until there is no more pavement. We cross an open field of tall yellow grass, filled with glistening granite headstones. A cool breeze blows welcome relief. The wind whistles through the headstones like the open prairie, or some western ghost town. This place doesn't feel like Hartford. I'm disoriented but fortunately not dizzy. I see no blue fingernails, no bluesy straw hats. I wonder if my dead friends are gone, now that Cricket is in jail. If they are, I may miss them.

Celine strolls past row after row of granite headstones labeled with names like Trevor, Desmond, and Paulette. These names hail from Jamaica, that warm Caribbean island bursting with emerald grottos, cerulean mountains, and ruby red ackee fruit. It's odd to think of these vibrant islanders taking their eternal rest in a dull New England straw field, strewn with crooked gray stones jutting from the land like bad British teeth. Celine's hibiscus flower dress swishes by their headstones, and they lean her way. She halts with breathless recognition beside two small markers set close together, taking up only one plot.

"I got stones in my passway, and my road seem dark as night," quotes Celine.

I recognize those Robert Johnson lyrics and instinctively reach for Rosalita.

Del reads the names on the headstones. "Mia Mendoza Delaney and Dauntay 'Shankdaddy' Delaney." A full bourbon bottle rests beside Shankdaddy's grave.

Del asks, "Dauntay? That's a Jamaican name, right?"

"Yes." Celine sits by the grave and spreads her skirt around her like a tropical flowerbed. She slips into island speak. "Your grandfadda's people were Irish and Jamaican. He met my mudda when they were both schoolchildren in Kingston. They weren't much more than children when I was born there. They moved here a few years later. Shankdaddy was a wandering man. He left my mudda for some woman who played with his band. Then he replaced her with Anna Mendoza, a fan he met while touring with the Hoodoo Chickens in Mexico. Anna was Mia's mother. She disappeared before Mia's first birthday. Nobody knows where she went or why. That's another mystery for you two detectives to solve, one day. My own mudda stayed in Hartford until I turned eighteen. Then she returned to Jamaica. Thanks to her, I was better off than Mia, growing up. She had only her fadda, and he couldn't get her to behave, any more than he could get himself to behave. Shankdaddy and Mia lived up to their Irish namesake, 'Delaney,' which means 'disobedient child. There now, you know your family story.'"

Del touches his mother's name, engraved in the stone above the short years of her life:

Mia Mendoza Delaney
1976–1994

My mind floods with the power of Mia's name: how Grumps and Del tried not to mention it to me in order to protect Will Pyne from wrongful imprisonment, and how hearing it made Worthy and Cricket flee their dining room, and eventually, fall apart completely.

Celine pats Angel's gray wings and takes the guitar. "I don't mean to offend, Nephew, but I must tell you: your mudda was no angel. She softly picks the opening notes of Bob Marley's "Redemption Song." "I knew she had a secret baby, but she never told me where you were. She was afraid my fadda would pry the information out of me if he ever heard about it. Lord knows what he would have done to Will. After Mia died, I tried to find you and failed. I know now that Lila couldn't tell me where you were because your fadda, Will, asked her to keep your location secret, for his sake. He was sure he'd go to prison, if anyone discovered his whereabouts. When I heard on the news that you were in New Hampshire, the stars told me you would find me. The star beings know everything that happens on our planet. Earth and sky are connected."

Celine notices Del's heaving chest and stops playing the guitar. "It's over now, Nephew. Your mudda's killer is found." She pats his heart. "We must let her go."

She opens her enormous raffia purse and removes a familiar straw hat and an earring with the word "LOVE" carved across it. I can hardly breathe as she places these funerary items on the ground. Del's face softens. Mine tenses up. These things are the property of my otherworldly friends. The thought of anyone else touching them feels like an invasion of their personal property.

Celine stiffens and eyes me flatly, which tells me she is about to lecture me on something. "Mona Lisa, in the old Jamaican way, the belongings of the restless dead must be broken to free them from their torment. You must be the one to sever their connection to this earth because you are the one who serves as their connection; for you have seen their ghosts."

Del squeezes my arm apologetically, "Mona, I'm sorry I didn't believe you about seeing Mom."

"It's okay," I say, trying to focus on my final task for Mia and ignore the fire ants crawling between Del and me.

Celine hands me a pair of heavy wire cutters from her bottomless purse. "Here you go."

They remind me of the day I found out Grumps had died and cut up my bed sheets, the day Mom cut her hair. The wind blows hard, tousling my hair. That's enough of a sign from my dead friends for me to continue. I waste no time, cutting Shankdaddy's straw hat in two and snapping Mia's earring in the middle of the word, "LOVE." Maybe this action will allow Will to move on.

I wince, recalling the pain of cutting my bangs after Grumps died. Only, this time, I don't feel any pain.

Celine raises her arms, signaling we should stand.

"Now we sing, " she says. "Mona, you play your Rosalita. Nephew, you play your Angel. I'm sure you play better than Mona's band partner, Beetle-boy. He misses every B chord."

Celine pokes Del with her well-manicured finger and they both laugh. I can't laugh. I'm realizing for the first time that I've lost my band and Beetle. Soon Del will be gone, too. Solving Mia's case has taken a lot from me.

Celine turns to Del dreamily, "You know, your mudda could really sing the blues." She fluffs her dress. "I ain't such a bad singer, myself. On occasion, I sang with the Hoodoo Chickens. Today, we three will sing Mona's song, 'Skinny Bones.'" She winks at me with a wide rum-ball eye. "I know Shankdaddy likes that one. I will begin."

I open with an E7 chord—arpeggiated—and Celine's harrowing set of pipes explodes onto the first line.

I walked into her room, wasn't nobody there…

Del and I pat our guitars signaling we'll both stick to instrumental accompaniment after hearing Celine's otherworldly voice. Her dynamite rendition of "Skinny Bones" confirms Shankdaddy's heavy hand in writing it. This is the tale of a stolen daughter, a murdered baby sister, a lost mother, and a woman frozen in time as a teenager. *Just a child all her days.* Celine's voice whistles through the yellow grass and between the headstones, until the ground itself sings, calling down to Mia's long gone skinny bones.

We head back to Celine's place, sweaty, worn out and taking it all in. Del bends to tighten the laces on one of his heavy black boots. He's been limping badly, so badly I'm wondering if he'll make it the last few blocks.

Celine declares, "I have special presents for you when we return!"

This news gives us both a much-needed energy boost. When we reach the golden stairs of her stoop, he's wincing but makes it to the top. Celine rifles through her closet and emerges wearing a gratified expression. She's carrying a tombstone gray jacket and a pale green jazz hat.

"Here you go!" She holds the jacket up to me and it falls full length on my frame. "My father wore this jacket on a dinner date with a zombie woman, and lived to tell the tale. You cavort with restless spirits, which is almost the same thing. So you need its protection." She hands the hat to Del. "This is for you. It was Shankdaddy's good luck hat. It matches your eyes."

My cell phone rings, startling us. It's Officer Mealy, asking me if I can come downtown to sign a statement. The spell of our enchanted afternoon is broken. We say our good-byes, knowing it's time for my blue-fingered friend and Del's blue-haired aunt to fade away. I must return to the real world, where my band partner's mom is headed for jail, and the stardust from Del Pyne's lips remains on mine, as he heads for the altar.

Part III

Twenty

Silent Fall

It's the first week of October, two weeks since Cricket's arrest. I should be playing a concert in Boston this weekend. But my band blew up with a bang before our first concert date. Mom and I are both curled up on the stained navy futon she has cherished since college. She is bathing her sorrows in a steaming cup of Jamaican coffee, courtesy of Celine. The vapor rises and whirls upward, into two long steamy legs. She hops to her feet, reaching for that steam like it's an old friend come to visit. But the vapor quickly vanishes, and she curls into a ball again.

We all see our "ghosts" in different ways. Mine breeze by with a feathery touch, stop by to jam the blues, emerge from the blue smoke of a dream, or appear as another teenager wearing a band tee shirt. I don't know how to tell Mom that neither of us will be seeing her old friend, Mia, anymore, not in any form, solid or steamy. Cricket's capture has allowed Mia's spirit to fade into a field of yellow grass that lies somewhere between Manburn Street and forever. I thought Mom would be happier after Del and I caught Mia's killer and got Will off the hook. But she has a new excuse for her depression: Dad told her that he wants a divorce. I have trouble sympathizing as I've lost both men who matter to me, having sent the mother of one to prison, and having refused to tell the other how I feel about him. At least I have plenty of material for blues songs. Plus, Mom and I are not alone in our despair; everyone in New England is depressed right now. A true catastrophe has hit our region. Our autumn leaves have failed to produce their usual radiant color.

I sit slumped beside Mom on the futon, watching a Sunday morning news feature on this problem called "Silent Fall." The television blares gothic organ music, making Mom curl up tighter and me slump lower. The camera captures an aerial view of the banks of the Connecticut River, awash with dull beige leaves. The image looks more like a historic sepia photo than a live October foliage shot. A reporter stands in front of the Connecticut Science Center, dabbing her hollow eyes. The camera pans back and forth, from the building's winding façade—designed to echo the form of the river—to the unnaturally bland landscape along its banks.

The camera lens closes in on the reporter's tense face. She speaks somberly. "I stand beside the Connecticut River, a waterway that runs the length of New England, with its source in the four lakes of Indian Stream, New Hampshire."

I stop nibbling my peanut butter, banana, and honey sandwich. I've never heard anyone in Hartford mention Indian Stream before.

The commentator's mascara streams down her cheeks like war paint. "Today, this is our river of sorrow, as the leaves along its banks remain colorless. Dendrologists are baffled as to why New England boasts no colorful leaves this fall. Innkeepers, restaurateurs, and shop owners are devastated by the lack of autumn tourist reservations."

Celine raises the volume of a perky reggae song to drown out the television. She bogles around the room as if there's some reason to celebrate. It's times like these that remind me why I love the blues.

She stops in front of the television, wagging a finger back and forth. "Sistas, men are like a splash of hot sauce. They flava things up, but you can easily do without them. It's time to stop wallowing. Put on your Jam Doung colors. We're going to Jamaica." She resumes dancing to an upbeat island two-step.

Mom pretends not to hear her. Celine turns off the television. "Lila, your husband is gone. Maybe he'll come back. Maybe he won't. What's the difference? You never loved him. Now you can find true love. It's never too late."

Mom raises her hands in surrender. "Fine, I'll go to Jamaica."

Celine turns to me, reading my face like it's an astrological chart. "You must come too, Guitar Girl."

I squint, warily. "I'll pass on the island fun. Enjoy yourselves."

I know Celine is only including me in their vacation because she's worried I'll head to my cabin up north to wallow over Del's upcoming nuptials, or more pathetic, that I'll make some last-ditch effort to stop his wedding.

Her rum-ball eyes peer into my soul. "We both know Delaney Pyne is engaged to be married to another woman. Be careful not to set yourself up for a disastrous fall."

"Don't worry," I assure her. "No hot sauce or moldy bologna for me."

As soon as I hear them leave, I hop in my pickup and speed north on I-91, following the dreary Connecticut River foliage all the way to my cabin in Indian Stream.

Somehow, I hoped Indian Stream was far enough removed from Hartford to have avoided our tree trouble. I imagined that the oak, sugar maple, and white birch of the Great North Woods would glow with at least a hint of fall color. But none of these trees radiate their former light. Even the conifers have browned. I'm greeted by a beige woodland and a peaceless hush. It's not the curious silence I heard when I came here a few months ago, or even the respectful quiet I sensed after Grumps died. This is a rigid, aching stillness, like a red-cheeked kid slapped by a drunken parent and told to shut up. This silence trembles.

Listless leaves droop off the high oaks like dirty tears. There isn't a gold or crimson rebel in the bunch. Fallen pine needles heap in scorched stacks beside faded bundles of bittersweet, ivy, and bracken ferns. A mourning warbler stumbles through these crestfallen woods like a refugee wondering where her true home has gone.

Grumps' cabin appears cold and unresponsive, like a stillborn child. All that's left of the fall maple leaves painted on his door is a peeling crimson smear. Only an artist of Bilki's caliber could repaint that.

A scruffy crow hops around on the mismatched blue hood of my truck. I'm grateful to see a moving creature even if it doesn't bother to caw. A bald eagle breaks the eerie silence with a screech as it lands on my cabin roof, preferring it to the needle-less pines. Bilki speaks inside my head, "Eagles stand for high ideals." I examine the eagle charm on my bracelet, its silver eyes stern and unwavering.

I wonder: Does this eagle screech serve as a blessing to reward me for putting Mia's killer behind bars? Or, is it scolding me because her son is getting married in two weeks, and I appear to be stalking him?"

The predator's wide wings expand and break the dead air with a thwomp, pushing hard toward the sun, till it fades into October's bright blue sky, its high ideals vanished.

I find the cabin shockingly sunlit inside. I realize it's because all the window-covering vines lay in sickly heaps on the ground. Sunlight streams onto the Skittles-colored glassware on the kitchen shelves, creating a welcome rainbow in the midst of this cursed and colorless land. I can't believe how clean the place is. Someone has dusted and mopped the floor. A loaf of whole grain bread, a bunch of ripe bananas, a jar of crunchy peanut butter and a plastic bottle of local honey, shaped like a bear, sit on the countertop. A perfect pile of chopped hardwood rests beside the stove. These logs weren't here when I left the place and neither was the food. The woods may be uninviting but the inside of this cabin feels homey, a little too homey.

A thud out back draws my attention to the kitchen window. I peer out, presuming it's Del, the person I know is responsible for maintaining and stocking everything. But through the window, I see it's Marilynn makng the noise by knocking her backside against a dead and hollow tree. She's trying to bash a beehive off a low limb. There's another larger bear, behind her, with gray flabby haunches, a cracked bulbous nose, rows of loose, sloppy flesh that droop beneath his eyes and yellowed claws. This is the same bear I saw at Del's house the day of his band practice, the same bear from the mural in my room. I guess I didn't imagine The Great Bear, after all. But I blink, and he's gone. Did I really see him, this time, either?

A spiky-haired head pops up from behind Marilynn. It's Del! He must have been leaning down, probably smashing bananas, feeding the bears. I scan the nearby trees and spot a Harley sticking out from behind a weary maple. It has green flames on it. Finally I get to see the famous vehicle from Cricket's story! This is more than a bike. Its story has been told so many times it's become a Pegasus or Thunderbird to me, a magical beast that could soar from the earth to the stars above.

"Welcome home, Mona Lisa," Del says.

Marilynn's copper penny eyes flash. She bares her teeth at me, before disappearing into the sparsely clothed trees.

I lean out the window. "Del, I can't believe you cleaned and stocked my cabin. How did you know I'd be coming here today?"

He leans on my windowsill. "Aunt Celine texted me that you were on your way."

"She is a psychic, after all." I quip, before reminding myself not to flirt with a guy who is about to be married. "You didn't have to do all this work on the cabin."

"I wanted to do it. I'd be lying if I said I didn't miss you."

There's no good response to this—unless I want to set myself up for heartbreak. But I won't push him away again, like I did the night of the Farewell Dance, and after we forced a confession out of Cricket.

I realize it's early October and ask, "Why aren't you at school?"

"I'm still doing an Independent Study on the woods."

I would like the sound of this if I didn't think he'd planned it so he could be up here for his wedding. I feel my thoughts slipping downhill.

Bilki whispers, "Good deeds merit thanks."

Hearing her voice lifts my spirits, and I heed her words. "How about a cup of coffee? It's the least I can do to thank you for all the work you've done."

Del follows me inside. I brew fresh coffee grounds in Grumps' old kettle, while he puts another log in the wood-stove. Smoking wood and smoky coffee create a blissful smell

I'd almost forgotten. Grumps knew how to make coffee and damn it if mine doesn't smell as good. Still, I stiffly await Del's reaction to my first-ever homemade pot of coffee.

He sips and grins. "Delicious. This tastes exactly like the stuff your grandfather used to make."

"Thanks," I say, wondering if Scales brews decent coffee. I glance out the window and recoil at the sight of so many beige leaves. "What's up with the foliage, Del?"

"I don't know. The forestry school has been inundated with people demanding answers. Up here things are usually past full color by now. This leaf problem is the only thing anybody at the general store is talking about."

It occurs to me that he is incorrect, that a good portion of this dinky town is probably talking about his upcoming wedding on Halloween. But I force myself to stay on target. "Did Grumps ever tell you any old Indian stories about why the autumn leaves change color?"

"There was one about a hunter and a bear. But I'm fuzzy on the details." Del heaves a sigh before continuing, like he hates to say what he's about to. "Your great aunt definitely knows it. You could ask her."

"Black Racer Woman?" I croak. "I have no idea where she lives or how to get in touch with her. I'm not even sure I want to, after what she did to your leg. Besides, we're not exactly close. The fact is, I never even knew I had a great aunt until the Winnipesaukee Powwow."

He spills coffee on the floor. "Ha! I remember that powwow. I wanted to stick around to talk to you, privately, to straighten things out between us, but Scales needed a ride back to school and you were busy yapping with Captain America."

Captain America. So that's how he sees Beetle. I want to say that, at least, Captain America is a good guy while Scales is a sour cheating lemon who visited Black Racer Woman's booth to purchase a love charm to lure him away from me. But I don't say that because the jealousy raging through me is the same dark emotion that was responsible for ending his mother's life.

I allow myself one probing question. "Del, why did Scales need to rush off on the day of the powwow?"

He counts on his fingers, as though he is trying to remember the details of that day. His face falls flat. "Mona Lisa, I honestly don't remember why she was in such a hurry."

I know what happened: he was hexed. I've seen enough weirdness in the world to know that a thing like this can really happen. But there's no point in telling him that.

"Too bad you didn't stick around. You missed the verbal fireworks between Grumps and my great aunt. He called her a wicked witch."

He shrugs. "That is how she's generally perceived. Your grandfather had argued with her since forever. I don't know the particulars, other than they heavily disagree on some tribal obligation related to bears." He makes that furry teepee shape with his eyebrows; only he does it more fiercely than I've seen before. "Take it from me: obligation is a bitch. I can't believe I'm supposed to get married in a few weeks." He eyes me greedily, as if I'm a fading Polaroid picture that's about to vanish.

I try a straight question. "Where is your bride?"

His eyes fall on my lips in an expression that could be interpreted as regret. "She's performing in a musical on Cape Cod."

"Seriously? We both know the Cape shuts down after Labor Day. They must have finished their run weeks ago. Where is she, right now?"

"Shopping for wedding stuff in Boston, I guess. I haven't heard from her much. I'm afraid she knows how I feel about you."

My heart flutters at his words. "It's ridiculous for Scales to be jealous of me. You and I were only working together to clear your father's name."

"Really? Is that all we were doing?" Del picks up Rosalita and plays the chorus to our song, "Sometimes you laugh. Sometimes you lie…" His eyes glue shut. I know he is remembering our amazing kiss. If he won't speak plainly, I will.

"Damn it Del. You're getting married. You don't talk to your bride, and you told me you loved me."

Those words quaver but I'm proud of myself for getting them out. His eyes turn woodsy green, as though he wants to fade into the forest with the bears. "The trouble is, I hate broken promises, Mona Lisa. I made a promise to Scales, like my dad promised my mom he'd pick her up on the last day of school." His words crack. "Dad failed Mom. He didn't trust her and he believed a lie. She died because of it. If he'd looked for her and kept his promise, she'd still be alive. So I'm going to keep my promise. Everybody has a code they live by. Mine is keeping promises."

I finally understand his perspective. To him, a broken promise can kill. I think of how betrayed Will felt when he heard Mia had chosen Worthy over him. But if he'd searched for her to confront her and kept his promise to pick her up, she'd still be alive. Del is right about that. Still, his reasoning is flawed. I'm about to remind Del that Cricket Dill was more to blame for his parents' mishap than any broken promises, when a high-pitched voice tinkles through the air like shattered crystal.

"You don't have to break your promise to me, Delsy. I'll do it for you."

It's Scales. She's standing in my doorway, wearing a pink and green flannel shirt and carrying a stylish shopping bag from someplace far, far away from Indian Stream.

"As of this moment, we are officially unengaged," she says, throwing the shopping bag at me. "As for you Mona Lisa LaPierre, I came here to bring you a thank you gift for helping Will —you know, the guy who is supposed to become my father-in-law. But please, keep the shirt." She kicks the bag my way. "The color suits you perfectly. It's yellow."

I recall I was wearing a yellow George Harrison "Here Comes the Sun" shirt when Scales and I first met. She may think it's my favorite color. Only, I doubt that's what she means by her remark.

Her eyes flare at Del. "Speaking of colors, for these last few months I've tried to tell myself I liked to wear white. But just so you know, I hate white. Thanks to what I just overheard, I don't have to worry about that anymore. Our wedding is off. I'm breaking your promise for you, and I'm leaving this dump of a hick town for good."

Del starts to speak and then snaps his jaw shut, like a bear with a mouthful of mashed bananas that he doesn't want to lose.

Scales holds out her hand like a traffic cop. "Please refrain from jumping for joy, Delaney Pyne. In the interest of full disclosure I want you to know I met a Native American musician of my own. He's a Mashpee Wampanoag jazz singer from the Cape named Cliff. I planned on telling him today that it was over because I was getting married. But you have offered me and Cliff a second chance." She turns to me. "Who knows, Mona. Maybe Cliff and I will start a duo. It seems anybody can do that successfully nowadays."

I step between the would-be bride and groom. "Scales, I want you to know I didn't come here to stalk your fiancé. I came here because the fall leaves look so bad."

Her skin flares the fuchsia color of Celine's hibiscus dress. "Mona, do you hear yourself?" She mimics me in a whiny voice, tossing her lemony head from side to side, "'I came here to help the leaves.' What kind of Native American Earth Mother bullshit is that? You're a phony, just like your great aunt! Her love potions are fake. I know that for a fact. I also know she is insane, the way she cackles like a fairy tale villain. Ha! Ha! Ha! You two are both psychotic. I mean, you never crack a smile. I must be a total loser to have admired you." She raises a finger as if to correct herself. "Although, I must admit you do not suck as a musician."

She slaps the air. "Good luck, you two. Have fun protecting your stupid trees and your stupid bears. I am relieved to know I will not be stuck here for the rest of my life, living with a bear magnet. They're always prowling around you, Del, and I don't understand why that doesn't bother you. They're dangerous as hell, regardless of what Mona's Looney Tunes grandfather told you. Good-bye, Del Pyne." She stretches her arms as if liberated, "And good-bye, Indian Stream!"

Twenty-one

Finding Indian Stream

Early October nights in northern New Hampshire bring the kind of cool that normally prompts New England leaves to blush scarlet, or shine like golden flint corn, or erupt into fiery squash blossoms. But those colors are only memories. Autumn in New England appears to have vanished.

The Yale Forestry School sent Del and other students on a road trip to research the leaf problem. I'm happy for the space. I've got to figure out where my musical career is going. Del also needs to think about where he is going, after his big breakup with Scales.

Bilki would appreciate his work with the trees. I think of how much she loved to paint vibrant foliage, how much she loved color, period. She used to sign her holiday cards with the phrase, "May the colors of your world be many."

I ask her, "Bilki, what can be done to bring color to these leaves?"

She replies, "Not every door is locked."

I cringe, but only briefly. I'm learning to process her cryptic remarks as helpful advice, rather than perturbing provocation.

Maybe there are some unlocked doors built into the floors or walls or cabin furniture that she wants me to uncover. I start with my room, knocking my knuckles on the blue leaf floor mural, then the dresser painted with azure cornflowers, and then the bedposts covered with teal ivy. I hit the headboard, which is bolted to the wall, and voilà! I hear a hollow clunk on the left side. I hit it harder with my palm and a door pops open. Inside, I discover a long narrow wooden compartment, containing a handmade map that looks like something from a Disney pirate movie. It shows a "Snapping Turtle Rock" linked with a dotted line to a stream marked "Yellow Clay," on to a "Tipping Rock," and beyond in the direction of a rising sun, to a place called "White Woods," which is marked with a skull and crossbones over the initials "BRW."

I flip it over and it says:

Dear Lila,
Here's a map, so you can always find me.
Your loving aunt,
BRW

Black Racer Woman. I don't think of her as anyone's loving aunt. But Del said she knew a story about autumn leaves, so I need to visit her right now, loving or not.

I head out for the first landmark on the map. It's the "Snapping Turtle Rock" I saw on the first day I arrived in Indian Stream. With all the woodland greenery oddly withered, I follow a clear dirt path to the stream marked "Yellow Clay." It runs across ten different logging trails rutted with tire treads from heavy machinery. This must be the real Indian Stream. I can imagine the beautiful golden clay pottery it once produced.

A tipping rock looms ahead. I've seen similar rocks in Mohegan territory—a large boulder balanced on a smaller one that can be jiggled to make a thunderous sound. This boulder is twice as big as the ones in Connecticut. In a rare cultural communique, my mother once told me that old-time Indians used these tipping rocks to send messages over long distances. I wonder if Black Racer Woman shared any messages by rocking this giant boulder, and with whom.

Over the next rise, I spot what appears to be an autumn blizzard. I move closer and realize it's a white birch forest, with feathery strips of snowy bark peeling off the tree trunks like ancient pages, hinting at some long-forgotten story. I step into these white woods and discover a faint trail of smoke. I follow it to an old-time birch bark wigwam that reminds me a little of my toy wigwam, back home. Mom always insisted wigwams were passé, that eastern Indians today all live in regular apartments, mobile homes, or modern houses. Now, I know of at least one exception.

Black Racer Woman emerges from the bark house wrapped in a musty moth-eaten wool blanket. She smells of rotting woods, much like The Great Bear.

"Welcome, Great Niece! I see you found the map." She extends her arms invitingly. "You are just in time for lunch. Come inside and get warm." She pulls back a stiff mildewed deerskin door flap at the entrance of her white birch bark home and points to a cot made from crossed sticks, lashed together with twine and covered with a bearskin. "Please, have a seat here with your guitar."

I eye the formless, eyeless, lifeless bear draped across the cot and say, "No thanks."

"Suit yourself." She stirs a steaming black kettle of some orange mixture over a crackling fire. A sweet earthy smell wafts my way, not like any stew I know of, more like an intoxicating mix of stars and autumn dreams.

The shelves inside her wigwam are made of split logs, separated by bricks, lined with Mason jars filled with stewed tomatoes, pickled squash, dried wolf beans, and ground flint corn. A battered fishing pole, a well-polished hunting rifle, a pistol, and plenty of ammo boxes lean against the wall. On the floor lay various wooden utensils—bowls, spoons, and dippers, all carved with woodland Indian trails and floral designs.

Black Racer Woman scoops some of her kettle concoction into a maple bowl and hands me a wooden spoon. I'm starving and about to chomp down a heaping spoonful of what appears to be orange pineo mushroom stew but could just as easily be made from deadly orange jack o'lantern mushrooms. I think of how Bear, Grumps, and Bilki distrust my great aunt and how easy it would be for her to poison this food. I need to figure out if she is trustworthy before I can accept her hospitality.

I put the spoon down. "People say you caused the accident in which Mom hit a bear because of some crazy old Indian myth."

"Nothing of the sort. The day of her accident was chaotic. Will was on a bender. He needed someone to babysit Del, but your grandparents were sick with the flu. He asked your mom to do it because he knew she was up here visiting me. She'd come for the same reason you're here, right now; she wanted to find out why the fall leaves weren't changing their usual colors. When I told her it was because we needed a bear sacrifice, she got upset. She drove to Will's in such a hurry she didn't watch where she was going and crashed into that poor old bear. Her truck was a mess but her face looked worse. You're lucky to be alive because she was newly pregnant with you when it happened."

"What? Why couldn't Mom tell me this, herself?"

"That would require her to face reality, and that accident shook her up so badly that she lost touch with everything, permanently. She claimed it was Mia Delaney who saved her life and yours. Of course, Mia was already dead. But Lila didn't accept that. She saw Mia's ghost all the time after she died, especially when she was in Hartford.

I don't mention to my great aunt that I see the dead. I'm afraid she'll think I'm as crazy as my mom. But I'm grateful to her for helping me understand how my spirit became entwined with Mia's long ago, and why Mia chose to haunt me. It would seem Mom wasn't getting the job done of finding her killer. So Mia enlisted me.

I realize I'm off-topic and refocus. "Aunty. I appreciate all of this critical family information. But none of it explains why Grumps blames you for Mom's accident."

Black Racer Woman grabs me with an arm that's much stronger than I imagined. "He blames me because he is an illogical fool! As I said, your Mom and I had been discussing the need for a bear sacrifice to save these woods when the call came and she rushed off and hit that bear. That's what you call a bad coincidence. Grumps assumed the death of that bear was somehow my doing because your mother had been with me, beforehand." She slaps her hands on her hips. "How could I have caused her accident when I was sitting right here when it happened?"

"Do you believe in animal sacrifice or not?"

"I've been known to snare a rabbit or shoot a turkey when I'm hungry. I killed a pineo mushroom to make this stew. There are many forms of sacrifice."

"That's not an answer."

"All right. Yes, I believe in sacrifice! I have stayed here to protect this place, all my life. As you can see, living here is my sacrifice." She points to the surrounding white birch trees. "The beauty of these woods makes it all worthwhile. Once upon a time, they were crawling with black racer snakes. They were beautiful creatures that didn't bother anybody. But the newcomers confused them with rattlesnakes and put bounties on them. My family gave me my name so I would represent the interest of those snakes. Your Indian name is quite the opposite. I chose it so you could represent those who sacrifice animals. The universe is about balance. Our people have lived in this magnificent forest for thousands of years because we maintained that balance."

I try not to think about the fact that she chose my Indian name because I hate it. Nobody but Mom and I knows it, and I want to keep it that way. "Couldn't you perform your sacrifice in these woods just as well living in a cabin?"

"No. Living this way helps me see things the old way. Every tree is precious to me. That old mindset helps me stand in the way of what some people call progress. The lumber companies want to log these woods so they spread rumors about me. If they can have me convicted of a serious crime—like murder—they can steal my trees. They've tried to evict my family from here for centuries. Some man even wrote a book once, claiming our tribe was extinct, in order to steal our land." She pulls a glowing stick from the fire and waves it like a wand. "That's when my great grandmother took action and turned the author into a toad."

My feet shift, ready to run, but she blocks the door. I jiggle my bracelet. It's become a habit when I'm scared. I think of it as dialing spiritual 911.

Black Racer Woman flips her braid off her shoulder and lets loose a flock-of-crows laugh. "I'm kidding about the toad, Mona Lisa. I'm no witch—as some would have you believe."

I detect a slight serpentine hiss in her words. "Besides, there is someone else more worthy of that description.

"Who are you talking about?"

"I heard at the general store that Cricket Dill's sentence may be reduced because of mitigating circumstances. Your principal testified that Mia bullied Cricket as a teenager. She claimed the poor fragile thing had been seeing a school psychologist for her depression and suicidal tendencies, due to Mia's abuse. I guess Cricket tried to jump off the roof of some high-rise in Hartford called City Place. I believe you know the building." Her eyes do that solar flare thing again.

I swallow the lump in my throat. "This makes no sense. The school janitor told me that Mia's murder inquiry made Principal Dibble's life a living hell. Why would she be so quick to forgive Cricket?"

"Perhaps you should go to Hartford and ask her yourself."

"But you and I need to talk more about the leaves."

"The leaves can wait. Right now you need to find out why Mia Delaney's murderer is going to skate—before Del or Will Pyne overreact to that news."

Twenty-two

The Janitor's Closet

I toss on Shankdaddy's zombie-woman jacket and hop in my truck. I think of how awesome it would have been to wear this on our defunct Haunted Bonepile concert tour. But the dead had other plans for me. Mia pushed me to spend time with Beetle and Del so I could solve her murder.

The corpse-gray Connecticut River lined with sepia leaves leads me to my apartment. I yell for Mom. She's supposed to be back from sunny Jamaica, but I hear no reply. No matter. Even when she's here, she's not fully present. Dad's autumn tweed professor blazers, plaid scarves, and nubby fall sweaters lay colorfully scattered across the living room—an homage to the missing autumn leaves. Mom must be preparing to send his stuff to Russia. The mess in here reminds me of the way Grumps' cabin in Indian Stream looked when I first arrived. I slump, remembering that Grumps is gone.

The fridge contains a half-empty box of chardonnay, a head of browning iceberg lettuce, and a frozen Tupperware container full of orange Jamaican beef patties. I open it and their sharp turmeric smell makes my stomach growl, even though I know that actually eating meat would make me wretch. I break open a couple but discover no vegetarian ones. I rummage though the cupboards and find no bananas, honey, peanut butter, or even bread.

My stomach growls as I carry Rosalita on the short walk to my high school. I hope to grill Millicent Dibble about why she changed her attitude toward Cricket. The feel of my guitar bouncing against my back on this familiar street is comforting. A high chain-link fence wraps around the school. The sign on it says "Scheduled for Demolition 10/31." That's Halloween, less than four weeks away. It's also the anniversary of the day that I considered jumping off City Place. I can't believe Cricket Dill considered the same stunt because of Mia's taunts.

I snort at the classic green Coupe de Ville sedan parked near the school with the familiar license plate, MILLY. Stepping through the unlocked gate, recollections of high school flood in. I picture the first time I saw Beetle walk up these crumbling front steps two at a time, his butterscotch bangs blowing in the wind, his sparkling licorice eyes checking out every girl but me. That was Freshman year, when Lizzy and I began our obsessive habit of texting Beatles lyrics in order to secretly gossip about him. It was entertaining until junior year when she abandoned me and moved to Toronto, right after the City Place incident. I miss her. Maybe I can get a gig in Toronto and we can hang out together. I loved her most recent text, when her new stepdad took the family to Europe. It said, "Standing in the dock at Southampton, Trying to get to Holland or France." That was one of her better ones; our texts grew up with us. My very first text about Beetle said, "I wanna hold your hand." How childish is that? How ironic? The first time I held what I thought was Beetle's hand, it was actually the hand of Del's mom.

My relationship with Beetle was forgettable until my very last day of high school when my cupcake-pink Dead Kittens tee shirt caught his eye. I feel warm inside at the thought of how great we both looked at the Farewell Dance. I shake away that smug thought, remembering how mean I was to Beetle that night and how jealous I was of whatever happened between him and Rasima. Jealousy is lethal. It pushed Cricket Dill to lock Mia Delaney in a basement closet, which in turn ruined the lives of Will and Del, not to mention how it had traumatized Millicent Dibble. That's why I don't understand her push for leniency toward Cricket. She found a dead student in her school basement. I would think she'd hate Cricket for creating that nightmare. Then again, there's her compulsive need to champion the innocent, like B.B., and perhaps to some warped extent, Cricket.

All the desks, chairs, and tables in the building are gone. The bare walls are rife with shadows. I imagine seeing a girl with curly dark hair but know she's imaginary because Mia's spirit is contentedly laid to rest, now that her killer has been found.

I assume Millicent Dibble is here to gather the last of her things before the demolition. I step onto the tumbledown chessboard of the main hallway and shout her name. It echoes in the empty halls, like a group of long lost students is calling for her. I head down to her basement office, past a blueprint taped to the stairwell that says "Demolition Plan." Red and green X's made from strips of electrical tape cover sections of the walls, marking the locations for the explosives. Thank God Rosalita is with me. I pass the music room and instinctively pull her around and finger the first notes to "You are My Lightning." I can't resurrect the warm feelings this room used to generate. It's not the same without all the sheet music stands, clarinets, guitars, keyboards, drums, and music geeks.

At the end of the hall, I smell cigarette smoke. "Hello!"

"Hello, yourself," rasps a familiar voice. "I'm down here. Is that you, Mona LaPierre?"

"Yes, Principal Dibble." I'm shocked at how childish my voice sounds.

"Come on down!"

I consider what I'll say to her carefully because I owe Millicent Dibble a good deal. Her cat helped launch my band's success. I also sympathize with her loss of her music career to rheumatism. My own fingers drift onto Rosalita's strings. I pick a few notes, just to be sure they still work.

I follow the scent of smoke. The once-flickering fluorescent lights are completely out. I have to feel my way down, pressing my palms into the cold, lumpy cinderblock wall. Something squeaks near my foot and I swear I'll die if I've stepped on a mouse. At the bottom, the door to her old basement office is cracked open, and a beam of light shoots out. Millicent Dibble is hunched over her infamous card table desk with a flashlight sitting on top that illuminates a wild river of yellowed locks, flowing over a pile of paperwork.

"Mona!" She sets her glowing cigarette on the edge of the card table desk and thrusts out a gnarled, rheumatoid hand for me to shake. "I haven't had the chance to properly thank you for solving Mia Delaney's murder. It is so fitting that the resolution of her case coincides with the closing of our school. Your investigative work has completed the circle, as you Native Americans say."

I let that comment slide. She shoves the last of her things into a cardboard box—the framed picture of her with her hot man, her monogrammed pad of paper that says, "M.A.D" (I still wonder what that middle initial stands for), and a brass plaque with the Confucian quote: "A true teacher is one who, keeping the past alive, is also able to understand the present." Grotesque as it seems, I suppose working in this janitor's closet is one way for Dibble to keep the past alive.

Millicent Dibble stares at the boxed remains of her career. "I can't believe this is the last of my things." She shakes her head, disbelieving. "I've finally retired."

"Congratulations." I say, trying to sound upbeat.

The flashlight beam on her desk highlights the deep pencil lines on her face, lines that write the history of the last two decades of Colt High, including the tale of Mia Delaney's disappearance, murder, and the decades-long investigation into her death.

"Principal Dibble, why did you tell the police you would speak on behalf of Cricket Dill?"

A feline gleam fills her usually lightless eyes. "I couldn't let her serve a sentence she didn't deserve. Little Cricket locked up a fellow student to keep her away from a boy she liked, not to commit homicide. She was a troubled, innocent girl. She thought it would buy her a bit of time to win a boy's heart, not end a girl's life." She grunts with loathing, "Besides, you didn't know Mia Delaney. She probably locked Cricket up a dozen times. Everything was a game to her. She toyed with people. Mia was cruel. She came from a terrible family."

Her flashlight goes out. The only light comes from the sizzling ash of her cigarette, hanging off the end of the card table desk. Millicent Dibble whacks her flashlight and the beam returns, falling on the photo in her box of belongings. I recognize the man with her now. It's Shankdaddy! My mind races. Celine said he was a notorious ladies' man. Irving Stone said Dibble once played guitar. Maybe, they were in a band together. Maybe Dibble lost her innocence to him. Maybe he jilted her, like Celine's mom. I remember Shankdaddy telling me how people who kill for love turn into ugly fiery angels.

Millicent Dibble notices me scrutinizing the picture and takes a drag of her cigarette. I stare into it, watching it burn. She waves her flashlight at the corner of the room, "I suppose you're looking for your band mascot, Mr. B.B. King."

Truthfully, I hadn't thought of her cat. But I'm not about to admit that. "Absolutely," I say, bending down, pretending to try and locate B.B. The flashlight blacks out again. I think nothing of it, until the door slams behind me. I hear the sound of a metal lock, rattling to a close. If this is Millicent Dibble's idea of a joke, it's not funny. She is elderly. She may be suffering from dementia and not realize what she's doing. I vigorously push away that thought.

She coughs and rasps through the door. "Poor B.B. passed away last month. Not that you would care." She snivels.

Unbelievable. Dibble has locked me in here because she's grieving over her dead cat, and she wants to take it out on me. I wish I'd never worn that Dead Kittens tee shirt to school. Then she would have never labeled me a cat-hater and locked me in this closet on the last day of my senior year. Then Mom wouldn't have sent me to Indian Stream for the summer. Then I wouldn't have met Del, and I wouldn't have linked Cricket to Mia's death. Then Cricket would not have been jailed, and now up for early release. Then I wouldn't be here. Millicent Dibble is right: things have come full circle. She has locked me inside the janitor's closet, again.

I try the door, to see if the lock is damaged like everything else at Colt High. No such luck. My mind floods with images of Will's locked doors, covered with swirling painted vortexes. I wish one of his vortexes would appear for me on this door.

I attempt to speak endearingly. "Please unlock the door."

Her voice shifts down an octave. "I saw you eyeing that picture of me with that wicked, wicked man. He took everything from me, even my music. My fingers failed to play guitar when he left me."

"Do you mean Shankdaddy?"

She groans, as if in pain, upon hearing his name. I recall the lure of his smoky gray eyes, his face and body made of carved granite, his big mocking white teeth. Like so many heavenly bodies, Shankdaddy had a dark side. But I'm also aware of his other side, the side that stuffed gift certificates for video games into kids' athletic socks, and I've witnessed the way he made unearthly blues that scraped the bottom of your soul. He lived life by his own rules. But perhaps he should have been a tad more careful of the people he crushed like bugs along the way, people like Celine's mom and Millicent Dibble. Now look what he's left behind—an ugly fiery angel.

I hug my guitar tight, sympathizing. "I'm truly sorry about your hands. I can't imagine life without Rosalita." My eyes water, my feet and palms moisten. I know how the steers in my slaughterhouse apartment felt when they were corralled before killing.

"Nice try, Mona. But you're no innocent. You're a careless musician like Shankdaddy, and you're mean like Mia. I know what you did to Rasima's foot on the last day of school. I heard how you cheated on poor Beetle at the Farewell Dance. I've seen the foul band tee shirts you wear. Cricket would never wear anything like that. She's sweet. Mia ridiculed her for being skinny and plain. Poor Cricket only wanted to contain that wild girl, ever so briefly. That rotten groupie didn't deserve any happiness and neither did her pedophile musician-biker boyfriend. They both preyed on innocents.

I can hear Shankdaddy telling me how ugly fiery angels burn everything in their path, especially those who make beautiful music.

"Little Carrie Arquette wouldn't hurt anyone, intentionally," she went on.

Carrie Arquette—Cricket. Her nickname is ridiculous, and she's certainly not innocent, no matter what Millicent Dibble says. I think back on Dibble's words the first time she locked me in here. *People who hurt innocents are criminals.* What a hypocrite. She eats meat. Of course, even I eat plants and fish, and they're living beings, too. Everyone hurts someone or something in order to survive. By Dibble's estimation, everyone would be a criminal.

Millicent Dibble inhales words with her cigarette. "When I came to work the week after Mia went missing, I heard a noise in the school basement. It sounded like a caged bear, snarling, growling, simply vile. I thought perhaps it might be Mia. But, as it happened, I couldn't find my keys that day. So there was no way to check. Someone had pinched them, and I guessed who that might be. Coincidentally, our janitor lost his keys. I figured I'd wait till he found his keys before calling a locksmith. I hoped this delay might give Shankdaddy time to show up in search of his daughter.

"It's only right you should want closure and felt the need to speak to the man. He owed you at least that much. But I sense something went wrong."

I hear a foot grind a cigarette butt into the floor and a lighter flick. Millicent Dibble sighs. "Yes, something went wrong all right. That Sunday, the newspaper featured an article about the Hoodoo Chickens' Mexican tour. It turned out Shankdaddy had already left the country for the summer. He wasn't coming to look for his daughter. I went home and downed a few bourbons to console myself. When I returned to my office, I no longer heard any noise in the basement, so I wrote that earlier noise off to my imagination. I needed a vacation and took off for Lake Winnipesaukee for the rest of the summer.

She coughs through her words. "You see, Mona Lisa, what happened to Mia was an accident. It was simply the universe's way of wiping away the wicked."

"I agree," I lie, desperately. "Please let me go."

She clears her throat with determination. "No! You came here to try and persuade me not to testify for Cricket. But she is innocent and doesn't deserve to go to prison! You don't care about who you hurt. You're just like Mia—selfish.

Dibble traipses back up the stairs, humming "As The Years Go Passing By," by Gary Moore, stopping occasionally to hack out a cough.

I whip out my cell phone. No service. I wish I'd left Mom a note telling her where I was going, even though our relationship lately has been more about me keeping an eye on her. So here I am, locked inside four mortuary gray cinderblock walls, moonbeams streaming through a lunchbox-sized window, illuminating a waterless sink. I miss the old dripping sound in here, that tortuous, life-saving sound of falling water. I sniff and find the scent of mouse is definitely stronger than the last time I was inside this closet. B.B. must have been a decent mouser. I also detect an underlying fruity aroma that's probably demolition dynamite.

I've got to get out of here.

I listen for someone else's step—a delivery person, a demolition expert, a nostalgic student or teacher who forgot something or wants one last stroll through their old haunt. What I want is anyone who might hear me scream. I'm saving my lungs to make that final scream count. Of course, Mia probably had these same thoughts.

I jangle my bracelet, hoping Bilki will hear it. Yet, she remains mum. I can't imagine why she would remain silent during this crisis, of all crises, unless of course she's only a figment of my delusionary mind.

A glimmer of light slides across my feet like the reflection of a shooting star. I look up and see a familiar silhouette. It's Mia. She's wearing her Rush band tee shirt with the rabbit coming out of the hat and one LOVE earring. Breaking the other one didn't release her spirit because her real killer remained free. I'm overcome with the urge to do something for Mia, to give her a gift, or do her a favor to make up for thinking I'd caught her killer when I hadn't. I've let her down by not setting the record straight about how she died. I search for paper and pen and see that Millicent Dibble has removed everything. I have only one option, the same option Mia had. I drag my arm across the jagged piece of broken cinderblock and cut open a gash. Blood trickles down, soaking the side of my Bonepile tee shirt. Normally this amount of blood would make me faint. Not now. I know it's my only ink. I use it to scribble a crucial message on the wall. My words are painfully neat and explicit.

Dibble did this to me and Mia.

Mia nods, gratefully. She dips a finger in my still-wet blood and draws a crimson bear on the wall. An icy chill runs down my spine. What does this mean? Am I some kind of sacrifice, like the bear Mom killed?

Day passes into frigid night. Thank God I have this zombie woman jacket. I keep my fingers warm by playing Rosalita. I try to stay upbeat by sticking to early Beatles songs. But eventually I slip into the melancholy section of the Lennon and McCartney songbook. Then I give up on the Fab Four, altogether, and nosedive into pitch-black 32-20 blues. I have to keep playing to distract myself from the cold. It's October, after all, and the building's heat is off. I dream about the warm bearskin on the cot in Black Racer Woman's cabin. I don't care if my PETA mom would hate me dreaming about bearskin. It would feel fantastic wrapped around me right now. She probably hasn't even noticed that my pickup truck is outside her apartment, or that I'm missing.

The sun rises and falls. Thirsty days blur into desert dry nightmares. I haven't heard Millicent Dibble's footsteps in a while. I hear every street vehicle as music. At night, the police cars and ambulances screech the evening's overture with a medley of piercing sirens. At dawn the trucks play the opening number, choking their diesel engines to life, until the steady hum of cars sounds like a swarm of killer bees. I wonder why vehicles are the only things I hear? Are they all I want to hear? Is it because they represent the hope of escape?

I play the title line to the Beatles' "When I Get Home," over and over, emphasizing the "when."

When?

Millicent Dibble must have left by now. I slam a fist into the wall and let loose an amp-blowing scream. Footsteps shuffle down the stairs.

"Help me!" I shout to my unknown liberator.

The pesticide canister outside the janitor's closet door clinks on the handle. This sounds ominous. I wrap my jacket around me and fail to suppress a dry-throated cough with my sandpaper tongue. It sticks to the roof of my mouth.

"Keep the noise down," rasps Millicent Dibble, clanking the canister harder.

I know what's in that canister. She'll melt my lungs with that pesticide if I make any more noise.

Millicent Dibble sings B.B. King's "Why I Sing the Blues." Even with her cigarette-scorched throat, she's got a good voice. Her raspiness works with the blues. She should have continued with vocals after her fingers failed. It might have saved her mental health. Her tune sticks in my head. But I won't play anything on Rosalita that's rolled off her filthy tongue. I think about my truck sitting outside Mom's apartment. She definitely won't come looking for me. She and Shankdaddy have something in common: expecting them to act responsibly is hopeless. I play a few lines from "Your Mother Should Know." My fingers cramp and quit.

I survey the charms on my bracelet. The paintbrushes, palette, and easel. My mind enlarges them, growing them to full size. My mind paints a wall mural with a swirling portal on the wall. What's on the other side of that portal? Is it safe? I stare at my eagle charm and it grows into a full-size bird, my protector-companion. Rosalita and I step through the portal, trailed by our winged friend. We emerge on the other side to find a blue bear playing a guitar under a maple tree that's literally on fire. In the sky overhead, the stars are shaped like musical notes. The bear hands me a skeleton key, also shaped like a musical note, and tells me to unlock the stars. I ask him which star fits the key, and he says, "All of them. You hold the key to the universe." I reach up and turn the key in a random star and a powwow drum falls from the sky. The blue bear grabs it and beats an ancient drum song. I sing along, my heart pounding, pounding, pounding, the eagle thwomping its wings to the beat.

I squeeze my head, trying to make the pounding stop. My lips feel crunchy. My throat burns. I blink at the sight of the shriveled mottled purple and orange skin on my hands. What I wouldn't give for a cup of water. I could drink the entire Connecticut River. It was different for Mia when she was trapped here, because she had water. I want to cry but my dry eyes can't manufacture anything but hard salt crystals; they lack the moisture to flow. My eyelids are as crusty as my lips. They're sore and raw. I have to pry them open or they stick shut, ripping off eyelashes each and every time I try.

This is it. I can't sing anymore. Neither can I recall exactly where I am. I know I'm not in Indian Stream. I stumble madly into a hard wall, with something smeared on it. Perhaps these are words. Did I write them? Yes, of course I did. But I can't read them now because my vision is blurred. The memory of my strange reality returns. I remember I'm locked in the janitor's closet. Hallucination and vision impairment must be symptoms of dehydration. Forgetfulness could be another. Outside, I hear a car engine start and tires squeal away. I'm wild with elation. Millicent Dibble has departed.

But my voice is nearly gone. I need to scream for help one last time before I have no voice left. Someone on the street might hear. Before considering the consequences, I let loose a jagged scream like crushed ice. Instantly, furious feet scurry my way.

What have I done? I've committed suicide! Millicent Dibble will gas me with that pesticide canister. I'm done. All I can do now is rage. *Rage to survive.* That's what Etta James said. I can do that. I hear her footsteps, and I don't care anymore. I won't give up. I rasp the words to Etta's song "At Last," as the canister bangs against the door. I've become Millicent Dibble, desperate, lovelorn, suffering, wailing the blues. I want this to be over. I want to hear the hissing of the open canister, to see the hose slide under the door, to taste the burning chemicals and feel myself melt away.

The canister bangs harder, as if it's smashing the door lock. "What, not enough room for a hose under the door?" I ask, nearly voiceless. "Did the executioner forget her key?" I think of B.B. King's song "Somebody done changed the lock on my door," and I start playing it, squeaking out the lyrics like a mouse. *'Cause I done changed, I done changed that lock on my door.* With what little voice and time I have left, I sing the blues. It's my last protest against Millicent Dibble before she sprays her deadly pesticide. I'm glad she'll hear me singing about jealousy because I know it will hurt her. It will conjure the pain of her unrequited love and send her weltering in the blues.

A weary voice says, "Mona Lisa? Is that you?"

This isn't Millicent Dibble. It almost sounds like Del. I'm hallucinating.

The voice calls again, "Are you in there, Mona Lisa?"

It is Del. "Yes. Help me. Dibble did this to me." I speak quickly, in case I lose consciousness.

I hear the canister clank again; this time it smashes off the door lock. There's a whirl of motion. Del swoops me and Rosalita up the dark basement stairs, holding a flashlight ahead of us like it's my final tunnel of white light. I shouldn't have sung that last song because now I'm having trouble swallowing. My throat is so dry I can barely breathe. How stupid is it for me to die, here and now, in Del's arms? He rushes me down the main school hallway. I know I'm leaving Colt High for the last time. I feel the wind, the deliciously moist New England wind. I never realized how wonderful dampness could feel. There are patches of light overhead, giant nighttime starbursts. No, they're streetlamps. I've been in a dark place for too long to see light correctly. Del leans me against one of the lamp poles and presses a water bottle to my lips. The water splatters and sputters down the dry insides of my throat like rain on

Death Valley. I cherish this elixir of life. I can feel things start to work again inside me, like oiled gears, repairing themselves. For the first time in days, I think I might survive.

Something green gleams beneath one of the streetlights. It's Del's dad's bike. He sets me gently on that Harley with the green flames, jabbering that I need to hold on because he won't wait for the police. It's too risky to stay put another minute in case Dibble should return.

"I can hold on," I assure him, barely audibly.

While we ride, I feel someone holding my back, supporting me. I look down and see deathly blue fingernails gripping my waist.

Del careens into my apartment driveway where Mom and Celine are pacing, shaking their cell phones at the sky. They shout relief as we pull in. Del relays my story and carries me inside. Mom phones the police. I lay on the couch while Celine feeds me sips of water. She offers me a small piece of a Jamaican beef patty. In my delirium, I see the dead cattle from my slaughterhouse apartment circle me, hanging their droopy heads, blinking their bloodshot eyes. I push away the beef patty and accept a cracker. I drink a gallon of water and pass out.

I wake to the smell of rubbing alcohol, the glare of fluorescent lights, the feel of tubes pulling on my arms, and the sound of Mom raging at a baby-faced police officer, saying, "That monstrous woman must not make bail."

A woman with a stethoscope around her neck hovers over me. Mom and Celine sit at the foot of my bed. Del's arm is wrapped around my shoulder. I don't feel fire ants this time, just the warmth of a million stars.

"How'd you know I was in danger?" I ask him, feebly.

Celine overhears my question. She puts a hand on her hip, and cocks her head. "Yes, Nephew, how did you know?"

The doctor folds her arms, also awaiting his reply.

Del's eyes shift down and to the left, surreptitiously. "It was the weirdest thing. When I went to Mona's cabin and found it empty, I was afraid she'd gone back to Beetle. I went to bed early, depressed, and I had a dream about my mom. I don't know why but I decided to ride that old Harley to Hartford., as if I was rescuing my mother from high school. As I pulled in, I heard Mona Lisa scream."

Del keeps rattling his head back and forth as if he's shuffling and reshuffling the images inside it. "I know this sounds ridiculous but when I saw Mom in that dream, she looked so real." His eyes won't meet mine.

The doctor rolls her eyes and leaves the room.

Celine clucks her tongue. "Is that so?"

Twenty-three

The Hunter

I prod the fire, hoping to see a powerful vision in the bursting flames, a vision that will tell me what my future holds. The embers gleam like celestial nebulae, erupting into molten crimson and gold—the very colors that remain missing from this autumn landscape. Yet no extraordinary image appears. There will be no visions for me today.

I lean back and return to Del's arms. Firelight flickers against the shadowy dusk. He hands me half a peanut butter, banana, and honey sandwich and munches his half, eagerly. I barely nibble mine. He pulls the pot of coffee from the cooking rack he's set over the fire and fills my blue speckled cup. It tastes smoky wonderful. But two sips is more than enough. My stomach gets full on next to nothing, these days. The doctors say it should feel normal again by Halloween. They also say I'm suffering from post-traumatic stress and shouldn't make any big decisions for a while. Del insists that this fire and the fresh New Hampshire air will heal me. Lying together beside this campfire feels a little too comfortable, like when we were lying together on the floor of that white floral room at the back of his garage. I'm torn between the allure of this deep coziness and my future career in Stadt and St. Louis and all of the other musical places I want to be.

The sun drops below the mountains, turning the sky a grizzly gray. I lay back on the soft moss, tucking the scratchy blueberry wool blanket I brought outside up to my chin, staring into the darkening sky, considering the endless possibilities overhead. The Great Bear, Ursa Major, has yet to rise. That constellation always reminds me of the old bear I saw when I was confused in the woods behind Del's house, that bear in the mural in my bedroom, that bear who appeared with Del and Marilynn a few weeks ago. The Great Bear. Real or imagined, I'm tired of bears. I picture the red bear Mia painted in blood on the wall of the janitor's closet. What did it mean? I hope she wasn't suggesting I carry out some weird bear sacrifice, like my great aunt was trying to do when Del stopped her. Del would hate it if I killed a bear. He cares so deeply for them; he's practically one of them.

Del's eyes continue to gleam in the firelight. He misunderstands my riveted gaze for distance and pulls me to him, filling my mouth with fiery kisses that taste like newborn stars.

I stop him. "I don't know where I'm going anymore." The words fall from my lips, like blues' notes fall from my fingertips—light, bent, and slightly dissonant.

He pulls me close. "You're not yourself."

"We all had roles to play," I say, letting more careless words tumble.

Del leaps to his feet. "Why did you just recite John Lennon's quote from when the Beatles broke up? Are you breaking up with me?"

He circles the fire. I get up and wrap my arms around his waist from behind, warming him and myself, remembering how it felt when I almost lost him. "What I meant is that we all had a part to play in solving your mom's murder."

"Ah, my mother. Now that I feel like I finally know her, I don't think I know you."

He turns and kisses me again, this time until it hurts. I break away, babbling concerns about what will happen to Cricket Dill, now that she is free. Del asks me if I have lingering feelings for Beetle. I scoff and do not mention that I returned Beetle's locket in the mail only this morning. If I tell him that, he'll ask why I kept it so long. The truth is, I don't know.

Del picks up Angel and plays the tune we wrote the first time I visited his house. He tries adding a new verse:

No longer young, no longer free
We've both seen more than we should see
Past ghostly shadows, and endless lies…

He tilts his guitar handle my way, prompting me to add the concluding line. But I shrug, at a loss for lyrics. What can follow *endless lies*?

A line jumps into my head: *Now grown so loveless, we break all our ties.* But I don't dare utter that. It sounds as bad as it feels.

How about, "*Into the bluest October skies?*" he asks.

"Nice," I say, not meaning it. "That lyric is definitely you, Del—forever hopeful. You see beyond darkness into light, just like Bilki. I'm more like my Great Aunt Black Racer Woman, murky and dangerous."

I can't tell him what I really think of his lyrics: that they lack magic. Something has changed. I hear John Lennon repeat in my head, *We all had roles to play.* I squeeze my head with my hands.

Del pulls me back to him by my belt, which is loose from all the weight I've lost since getting trapped in the janitor's closet. I don't resist. "You're right about your aunt being dark and dangerous," he says. "Just hearing her name creeps me out. How does somebody get a name like that?" He lifts his furry teepee eyebrows, as if something strange just occurred to him. "You know, I never asked, do you have a traditional Indian name?"

Something clicks inside of me. I consider my Indian name and its peculiar connotations. "It's *Nadialwinno*," I say. "Bilki gave it to me. It means 'Hunter.'"

"You, a hunter?" he stifles a nervous laugh. "You're a vegetarian."

My eyes twinkle. "Not exactly, I eat fried fish. I'm Abenaki, after all. But, yeah, essentially I don't eat things people hunt. I always figured it was a sarcastic zinger. Mom got into a fight with Bilki over the name. But Bilki insisted it was the only proper name for me."

There is an awkward pause in the conversation, as we both remember Bilki, and stare up into the uncertain night, where The Great Bear sits newly in the northern sky.

Earth and sky are connected, you know. I remember that's what Black Racer Woman said. She also talked about balance and how all bears have their hunters. I scan the sky. The Hunter constellation has not appeared yet.

Headlights glare through the woods and a van grumbles toward us, bumping along the rocky dirt all the way up to our fire. I'm grateful for the distraction until I realize it's Will.

He hops out and kicks the edge of our blanket. "Well look who's here. If it isn't sonny boy and Little Lila all cozied up together by the fire. Son, I don't know why you had to wait till the last minute to call off that wedding. The whole planet knew lemonhead had to go."

"You're hysterical, Pops." Del eyes him, suspiciously. "What are you doing here?"

Will raises a finger to indicate he is about to reveal his motive. He opens the back of the van and hauls out a four-foot high, three-foot wide rectangular brown paper package, shuffling his feet as he pulls it, trying to keep it from hitting the ground.

"Is that what I think it is?" asks Del.

Will's bile-green eyes catch the firelight. They are bulging more than usual. Del limps over to help him with the cumbersome package. Will yanks it away like he's a little kid with a new toy he refuses to share.

"This ain't for you, Delaney Pyne. It's something I promised your friend, Little Lila —though I kind of figured you'd be here at her cabin when I arrived." Will clears his throat suggestively. "Celine predicted I'd find you two together when I saw her and Big Lila at my new gallery yesterday." He licks his gray teeth. "Ten points for the pretty psychic with the sapphire braids!"

I clench my own teeth at his mention of Celine. "You met Mom and Celine in Hartford?"

Will examines his watch. "Sure, they stopped by my gallery. Lots of people visit me now. I'm a local hero. *The Hartford News* calls me "Mia Delaney's faithful lover and avenger.' Women adore me. As soon as Del helps me move the rest of my paintings to Hartford, I'm out of Indian Stream for good." He rubs his hands together, "Good riddance to this hick town. I'm looking forward to spending time with your mom and Celine." He pinches up his eyes, tenderly. "Celine is a wise woman. She says these dull leaves are a dark sign. I believe her. I could listen to that woman talk for hours. Damn, she's great. I had one hell of a time with her and your mom, and I didn't drink a single drop."

He leans a dreamy elbow on Del's shoulder. "Son, I've been clean and sober for a month now. When you sent Cricket Dill to jail for your mom's murder, I gave up drinking, as my thank you to the universe." He leans another elbow on me. "Then after what happened with Mona and Millicent Dibble, I gave up even thinking about drinking. I hope the judge throws away the key on that monster principal bitch."

He shakes a cocktail napkin that has a telephone number written on it in hibiscus-colored ink and grins like a wildcat. "Guess whose number this is?"

A hot acid rush infuses my chest. So much for Celine and her "I hate moldy bologna and hot sauce" routine. I ask Will, "You think it's okay to date Mia's sister?" I fold my arms protectively.

"Yes I do. She's the first woman who has made me laugh since Mia died." He lowers his pitch. "By the way, Big Lila said to tell you that Beetle is asking for you, now that his crazy mother is free." He shoots Del a worried glance.

I struggle to maintain a blank expression.

Del breaks the tension by reaching for his father's brown paper package again. Will pushes him away.

Del's bad leg gives out, and I reach for him before he topples over.

"Whoa," he says, catching himself before I do.

"Sorry, Son, this present is for Little Lila and only Little Lila." Will shoves the package, face front, in my direction. "Let 'er rip m'lady."

Something makes me hesitate to tear off the brown paper wrapping.

Will shakes his gift at me eagerly. "C'mon! Open it! It won't bite!"

I give in and rip the paper. Anything is better than listening to him say another word about Beetle or his new obsession with Celine. Will holds the package to his chest from behind, so it faces the firelight and me. I step back a few yards to examine what Will brought me. It's a huge painted photo of my loathsome face. My imperfections are blown up several feet high, enhanced by Will's incisive slashes of paint, creating a swirling vortex around my fingers. He's made them my portal, my means of escape from here and Hartford and this entire planet; they can take me anywhere I want to go. I love that. Each element of this work is perfectly executed: the muddy eyes, the shaggy tree bark hair. Except, my hair and eyes aren't their usual colorless selves. Thanks to Will's artistry, they're streaked with red, blue and yellow, like the flames in the fire. At first I don't understand. I think he's gone overboard with color. Then I realize he's used the hues that naturally make up brown. There is so much more color in this world than most people see. All painters know that. All humans should.

Still, I'm slightly miffed over how Will has altered my mouth, painting it with a wry, strawberry, Mona Lisa smile, just like Bilki's. A log slips in the fire, making the flames blossom into a plume that stretches toward the stars, lighting Will's portrait like a glowing *chiaroscuro*, momentarily transforming it into the style of Leonardo da Vinci's *Mona Lisa* masterpiece.

"Not bad, eh, Little Lila?" Will nervously reaches for the hip pocket on his pants that used to hold his flask and slaps his pants leg. "I hope you don't mind me adding that smile. Since you never smile, I wanted to see what you looked like with one." He jingles the change in his pockets and shifts his hips back and forth, anticipating my verdict.

I consider the surprising details of the portrait: the iconic smile, the eye-glint of a blues musician's tortured soul. Will nailed that; he knows torture. The hair shows texture, reflecting its bark-like quality. Yes, this is a true likeness and artfully done. I have to admit, Will is a virtuoso.

"I love it, Will," I tell him.

"May the colors of your world be many," he says, evoking Bilki's favorite saying. "May the colors of your world be many," I repeat, somewhat melancholy, thinking of the dull autumn leaves. I give the world's scariest man a hug to make sure he hasn't been lying to me about being sober. Tropical men's cologne with a hint of hibiscus has replaced his whiskey scent, and he appears to have showered. Will continues to hold the painting in front of him while I admire it.

Del sneers at my portrait, his lichen-green eyes bulging enough to be mistaken for his dad's. He hasn't said a word since viewing the painting. He clearly hates it. At least he hasn't voiced that opinion. I don't think it's wise of him to be overly critical, due to his dad's fragile state of early recovery from alcohol addiction.

Will sags over his son's negative reaction. "What's wrong, Son? You liked it well enough when you saw it before."

I don't want Del to respond. I try and keep things upbeat, pointing out what I perceive to be the painting's true element of genius. "Will, I love your decision to blend colorful fall leaves into the background. Those leaves pick up the colors in my hair, and they seem so hopeful right now." I tug at the maple leaf charm on my bracelet.

"What leaves?" mumbles Will. His monster gumball eyes widen like never before. He swings the canvas around to face him, so he can inspect it. He has not actually viewed the uncovered painting, till now. After examining the front of his work, he teeter-totters. Del rushes over to steady him.

I hear a rustle in the beige woods and quickly turn my head. I've learned to be wary of bears. But it's not a bear. Out of the dreary trees steps a woman made of stars with a strawberry smile, carrying a paintbrush and palette in her twinkling hand. I can't believe it. This is the first time I've actually seen Bilki.

"I put those leaves in Will's painting to remind you that you can save these dreary woods," she says. "The Hunter and The Bear must both make sacrifices to make that happen."

Del calls out, "Mona Lisa, I can't believe it."

Will slaps both hands on his head, in awe. "Me, either."

"I know!" I say. But when I look their way, I realize they're not looking at the woman made of stars. They can't see her. She is not the miracle they're acknowledging. They're staring at my face.

"You're smiling, Little Lila. You look just like my painting!"

"He's right, Mona Lisa. You have an amazing smile." Del eyes his father suspiciously. "Dad, when did you add the colored leaves to your painting?"

"I didn't paint those leaves, Son. I swear. I don't know who did."

"Bilki painted them," I explain, flush with newfound wisdom. "And she told me what I need to do…"

Twenty-four

The Charms of Wabanaki

It's Halloween, when the bounds between the living and the dead are as lacey as a spider's web. This is the night when monsters come out to play. I picture all the little vampires and Frankensteins hitting the streets of Hartford, taking a break from their trick-or-treating to watch the demolition of my school. That event was scheduled for sundown. It's well past that now. I wonder if Del and his dad took time off from moving paintings into his new gallery to watch the big blowup. I'm sure the Hartford Police hooted and hollered when the place came tumbling down. Not every unsolved teen murder case leads to such an embarrassing conclusion: the school principal did it. Ha! It's almost a cliché. Deep down, doesn't every high school student suspect her principal of being wicked?

Good riddance, Colt High, home of the homicidal Millicent Dibble. I lift my wrist, looking to kiss the bumblebee charm on my bracelet that Dad sent me as a graduation gift, albeit belatedly. I twirl the charms on my wrist around, searching for the bee mascot, but it's gone! I drop to my knees and comb the cold pine floorboards, filling my hands and knees with splinters. I spot it under the picture of Bilki and hook it back on with a sigh. I want to remember Colt High, for better or for worse, not to mention my absent dad. All of the charms on this bracelet help me hold those memories and make me who I am. Losing one is like losing a part of myself.

From this low angle, I notice a new keyhole in the wall. After finding that secret compartment in my room, I know this cabin holds endless secrets. The potential of opening this new locked door sends me frantically hunting down Grumps' skeleton keys. I flip through them until I'm down to the ones that haven't fit anything yet. The first one is far too big for the hole. The second one turns in the lock but jams, as if the tumbler hasn't been used in decades. I force it, even though I'm worried the key will snap. My charm bracelet jangles and jangles, as I twist and turn the key. Finally, it gives. I pull open this stubborn door to find a locked iron box inside. The box contains a much tinier keyhole, the size used to lock diaries. This is absurd. Grumps doesn't have any keys this small.

Then I remember something and examine the charms on my bracelet. There's a paintbrush, palette, easel, wolf, history book, guitar, musical note, log cabin, woodstove, bear, eagle, star, maple leaf, powwow drum, arrowhead, moccasin, robin, trout, spider's web, and a key…Yes, a key! I recall my dream about the blue bear that handed me a key, shaped like a musical note, and how he told me to go outside and unlock the stars. Grumps treated his keys with reverence, as though they held some special magic."

I pinch the key charm between my thumb and forefinger to try it in the locked box. I insert it into the keyhole and hear a gentle click. I open it and find a single sheet of handmade yellow parchment paper inside, its edges wax-pressed with fragments of fall leaves. My heart plummets when I see these leafy remnants of autumn's former glory, now inexplicably missing from the landscape. Painted in the center is the image of a hunter chasing a bear through a forest. Swirling paintbrush strokes inveigle the eye into the vortex at the center of the scene; it looks like a portal into another world.

"Thanks, Bilki," I say. This is clearly her work.

I stand up and touch Bilki's cheek in the picture on the wall. It feels warm. I flip the paper over and it says, "The Story of The Great Bear." Grumps wasn't kidding! This must be the Secret of Wabanaki he was talking about. This is what Mom was searching for and failed to find, right after he died. Funny that she would be scrambling around for something Bilki painted, especially when it turns out, it's a mere story.

I hear Bilki scolding, "A mere story! Remember: stories are what human beings hold most sacred."

I feel humbled and solemn.

Scribbled in the corner of this parchment are the words, "Read this in autumn by firelight." I grab the scratchy wool blanket from the foot of my bed along with a couple of logs and head out to face this chilly late October night. The fire pit remains filled with charcoal from where Del and I shared our fire. I pile some fresh kindling and new logs on top of the charred remains. Overhead, the New Hampshire sky sparkles with a bold galactic majesty, offering all the infinite possibilities of a glittering, newborn universe. The golden rays of Grandmother Moon sear through a wispy cloud, bathing the woods in the healing white light of a loving cosmos.

I start a fire, sending sparks hopping and swirling into the night, like waltzing stars. A winding trail of smoke climbs through the clouds toward the Milky Way, sending my wishes to the heavens. A log falls and flames flare, illuminating the edge of the woods. A twig crackling in the distance makes me mindful of the animals cloistered in the shadows. A gentle west wind blows dry beige leaves along the ground, and they clatter like ghostly applause, hastening me to begin.

I wrap my blanket tight and read:

"This story takes place in a time when the autumn leaves were not as colorful as they are now. In those days, the people harvested and prepared their crops, game, fish, and foragings in a despondent way, as the fading summer greenery signaled that the first snowfall was not far ahead. The animals shared in this gloom, especially the bears, which wearily filled up on bark, berries, and bugs, preparing for their great hibernation. Indeed, the bears were most disturbed by this bleak time, as it offered them a poor send-off for their long winter's nap. The humans also wished for something to cheer them, knowing how hard it would be to survive the coming season of darkness and cold.

"An old black bear wanted to alleviate this melancholia. The creature lifted its head to the sky and told the Great Spirit it wanted to help its fellow creatures during this trying time. At the same moment, a hunter offered a pinch of tobacco to a fire and made the same proposition to the Great Spirit.

"The Great Spirit lifted both creatures to the sky and explained that making this season less grim would require a sacrifice from both of them. The Great Spirit asked the bear to lay down its life for the hunter, and for the hunter to take the life of The Great Bear.

"The hunter begged to switch roles with the bear, saying that the animal was too great to sacrifice. The bear argued that its tremendous size and medicine made its sacrifice more powerful.

"The Great Spirit agreed with the bear, instructing the hunter to kill the animal that very night, there among the stars. With a sore heart, the hunter shot an arrow into the bear's chest and slit the animal's throat with a knife. The Great Spirit told the hunter to set the lifeless creature's remains afire, there atop the burning stars.

"A great flaming pyre licked the sky, and the bear's blood and fat rained down from the heavens, upon the dreary woodlands, transforming the once dull fall leaves to vibrant shades of crimson and gold. When the earthly creatures saw this rapturous sight, their own life-blood was renewed.

"Forever after, the constellations of The Great Bear and The Hunter remained among the stars to remind us that every fall a sacrifice must take place to renew autumn's glory. The Hunter must take the Bear's life, to repaint the leaves and bring color into our world."

This is the story that so vexed Black Racer Woman. I see how her strict interpretation of it caused conflict with Grumps. He thought the tale of the hunter and the bear was an allegory for sacrifice, urging his family to make personal concessions to protect these woodlands. She viewed it as a rigid mandate to kill a bear. That's why she tried to kill one, herself, but failed when Del stepped in front of it and took her bullet in his leg. This story also explains why Mom hates fall. Black Racer Woman definitely made her hit that bear with her truck. I'm sure of it, now, regardless of her claims to the contrary.

I throw another log on the fire. The flames erupt, illuminating the woods. I swallow hard at the sight of the dry leaves catching the firelight. An icy wind slaps my cheek, drawing me closer to the fire's warmth. My mind feels as crisp as the late October air. I survey the stars, knowing my grandparents are up there, shining down on me, along with the Hunter and The Great Bear. I wave to them all, and a shooting star falls from the sky, signaling change. The wispy cloud-cover thins like fading faces. I wouldn't mind seeing my dead friends right now. But for their sake, I hope they've found their rest.

A shadowy silhouette passes over the flames. A woman's face glows orange in the firelight. The long rope of her snake-like braid shines silver. This is no spirit from the other side. It's Black Racer Woman. I know what she wants me to do, and I won't do it. I edge backwards on my hands, piercing them with bull briars, bruising them on stones. I consider a sprint but lack the strength.

She points to the parchment paper beside me that is catching the firelight. "These trees have waited long enough. It's time for you to do your duty. This paper is what your grandfather refused to give me in his will. He left me a copy, which is worthless. Only the real thing can activate the ancient magic of the deed that must be done."

I snatch the paper to my chest.

She shakes her head. "Oh, yes, that story belongs to you, Mona Lisa. You have claimed it, along with the responsibility it entails. I couldn't save you from that responsibility, although I tried. I had to try, after I saw how it affected your mother. But there's nothing I can do to help you now. *Nadialwinno*, Hunter, you know what you must do. We Wabanaki are the keepers of these woodlands. You have been chosen to perform the ritual that is required to bring color to our world."

"*Nadialwinno*! That's why you named me Hunter! You plotted this all along!"

There is no hint of humanity on her face. Hers is the stone cold countenance of a prescient messenger from the stars.

"My sister Bilki and I both knew the truth about our family's cosmic responsibility," she says. "Your mother learned it. Your grandfather didn't like it. But none of that matters now. What matters is that you are the one who must act. You are the hunter. You must kill the bear." She fades back into the beige woods.

Musky honey infuses my nose. I know that smell. I bolt for the cabin but I'm too late. Marilynn has already blocked my path, standing up on two legs, like a giant wall of fur, rolling her huge shoulders and head, swatting her paws in my direction, mist flying off her rippling coffee-colored back. Clearly, Marilynn is not herself. She must be sick or injured. I dart sideways toward the pickup. She charges me but I make it into the driver's seat and slam the door. Her copper-penny eyes flash metallically through the truck window. She leans into the door, pushing, tilting the pickup onto two wheels, clicking her curled yellow claws against the window, flicking her ears upright and alert. The shock of blond fur atop her head surges straight up like a warrior's headdress. Her snout quivers back, exposing pink gums, baring a full range of sharp teeth that glisten like gold in the firelight.

She pulls back an arm for momentum to swat at my window again. This time, the glass cracks on impact. I turn on the ignition in the truck and hit the gas—hard. She leaps in front of me, shaking the earth. I spin the wheel away, closing my eyes. She falls backwards, nicked by my fender, but able to rise. I keep driving, turning back briefly to make sure I really didn't hurt her.

I bounce along the dirt road past the cluster of four birch trees, thumping over nasty frost heaves and potholes I can't dodge in the dark. Energy surges through me like a thousand stabbing knives. Grumps and Del were crazy to feed the bears. I scan frantically but don't see any other bears around. I cringe at the thought of the monster that Marilynn has become. I fear Black Racer Woman may be right. Perhaps I am the hunter. Perhaps I do need to sacrifice this horrible bear to make these woods colorful again. Still, I'm not prepared to do it. My gas pedal remains pressed to the rubber mat, as I whizz toward the road that follows the great Connecticut River south, far away from here.

A sliver of sun crests the rippling skyline. I must have stayed up later than I thought. Everything begins to look clearer in the rising light. I wonder if the whole scene with my great aunt and the bear was a bad dream.

I hit a serious pothole with a bang and my adrenaline surges. Maybe it's the reality check I need because somehow it's suddenly morning. I reach for the phone in my jeans pocket and find it dead, so I plug it into its charger. Dawn gleams brightly over the horizon, reminding me that it's a new day, filled with hope. I think about what Orpheus said about getting me a gig in St. Louis.

ST. LOUIS. Now there's an idea.

I jerk the truck away from the blinding sunrise, and turn onto an even bumpier dirt road that heads due west. I romp over boulder after boulder, wondering if my tires will survive another mile, never mind another twelve hundred. My tires aren't my only worry. This lousy dirt road will slug me up and down endless mountains and valleys and give me far too much time to change my mind about my destination. Still, I'm pointed west, and that's a start. It's the kind of hopeful start that Mia and Will yearned for on her last day of school and never enjoyed. I picture them driving off together into the sunset on his Harley with green flames, the way they'd hoped, the way Cricket told everyone they did. If all had gone according to plan, they might have lived happily ever after.

I can't picture me enjoying that sort of blissfully coupled existence with Del. I'm a dedicated blues musician. I'm destined for somebody to do me wrong on another rocky river shore. Otherwise, what will I sing about? The secret of making great music is not just finding your harmony with someone else; it's mastering the discordant tones of human existence, tones manufactured through hours of blood, sweat, and tears. Shankdaddy taught me that, and I'm grateful for it, regardless of whatever else he did wrong.

I rev the engine faster, clouding the air with grit from the unpaved road. Bang! I hit a wicked boulder, the worst so far. It's so dusty I couldn't even see it. This isn't a hot Harley I'm driving; it's a beat up pickup. It's kicking up clunky stones and dust, bumping and banging me forward, as long as these tires hold out. Sunbeams trickle through the settling dust like falling stars, as that burning fireball in the eastern sky continues to rise, its rays crowning the New Hampshire hilltops.

My phone rings, startling me. I guess it's finally charged.

I hit the speaker, "Hello."

"Hey, It's Del. Where are you, Mona Lisa? I just got back here from Hartford. Can you believe what's happened?"

My pickup veers to the right, even though I didn't turn the wheel. I wonder if I've got a flat tire or a broken axle. That last boulder may have done me in.

"Hold on, Del. I've got to find a place to pull over and check the truck."

I step out, blinking, rubbing my faulty eyes. I must be overtired because I'm seeing things. The doctor warned me about not getting enough sleep after what I went through in that basement closet. I try to shake away what's before me because it can't be true. The rising sunbeams have illuminated something unimaginable. The valley below me is full of lustrous crimson and gold trees. It is the first day of November, far too late in the season for colorful fall foliage to first emerge this far north. Yet, these woods have suddenly transformed into a spectral palette, as if a cosmic miracle just rained down from the stars.

I hear Del calling out from the phone in my hand, "Are you there, Mona?"

"I'm here," I whisper, returning the phone to my ear.

"You are seeing this, aren't you? Can you believe it? It's awesome. Isn't it?"

I think quickly, groping for an answer that gets me off the hook. "You did this, Delaney Pyne. You made this miracle. You saved these woods by sacrificing and devoting yourself to the bears and to this place. New Hampshire is where you belong."

On the other end of the line, a chair shuffles, "Where exactly are you, Mona Lisa?"

"I'm on the road."

"Are you on your way home to the cabin?"

"No."

I hear a guitar string twang and hold its vibration. "I thought we were forever, Mona, like the stars."

"You're like the stars, Del, dependable and luminous. You're the one everyone was talking about when they said somebody had to make a sacrifice for these woods, not me. And you succeeded. You'll have your forestry degree soon and settle down in Indian Stream, for good. You gave yourself to these woods and this is the result. You're like The Great Bear from the old Wabanaki story. But that story has nothing to do with me. I'm destined for someplace else, someplace far from here, someplace bigger and duskier."

His voice falters, skipping pieces of words. "But you said you were The Hunter. If I'm The Great Bear, that means we're connected. Don't break our connection, Mona Lisa."

My throat dries and I fail to swallow. I wasn't ready to have this conversation. But I think of Shankdaddy leaving Dibble without a word and realize I owe Del something.

"Yes, we are connected," I say. "But I'm only eighteen. You're only twenty. We have plenty of roads we need to travel before we get *too* connected. We've both lived with parents who were trapped by youthful entanglements. I won't wind up like them. I need to get away from New England for a while, to leave my family weirdness behind me and perform a true reality check."

The pitch of his voice rises. "Before you go anywhere, my mechanic Dad should perform a reality check on that relic of a truck of yours."

"Oh man, the truck! I got so distracted by the leaves that I forgot to check the tires. Hold on."

I lay the phone down on the hood and inspect the front and back wheels. They appear fine. But the dust on the road has settled, and I see something behind the truck. I walk toward it, for a closer look. I know I'm overtired because I'm definitely seeing things. I shut my eyes, hoping to improve my vision, hoping more than I've hoped for anything in my entire life. When I reopen them, the faulty image remains. Before me lies a fallen creature with chestnut brown eyes, a cracked bulbous nose, and a balding head, soaked in a pool of blood that shimmers in the broken dawn like a puddle of stars.

I yank on my hair—like Beetle does when he is confused. I'm picturing the blood red bear that Mia painted on the wall of the janitor's closet. It was a sign, a sign I should have heeded. I've suffered a star-crossed accident, like Mom. I've killed the ancient bear.

I tremble as the east wind calls my name, "*Nadialwinno.*" Hunter.

"That's not my name!" I protest.

The ocean blue sky swallows the last morning star. Rounded and full, the newborn sun tops the prickly pines. My knees fall to the frosty earth, and my back bows to the blooming dawn. I am older now, not eighteen, nor even eight hundred. I am forever, like the stars and the seasons, like The Great Bear and the blues song that repeats and circles back again. I grind my heels into the earth and force myself to stand and take my first timeless step. I no longer walk a finite woman's trail. I am one with the circle, one with the universe. I am in step with it all. Toe heel, toe heel. I soar into the cosmos and cross a chain of stars, in gold, crimson, and stellar blue. I ride an icy comet to The Hunter constellation and call it home. I wave to a million starry ancestors and their light shines through me. Toe heel, toe heel, toe heel…

Author's Note

This book is a work of fiction inspired by the ancient Mohegan connection to the Wabanaki, passed on to me through Oral Tradition by Mohegan Elder Gladys Tantaquidgeon and Abenaki Elder Elie Joubert, stating that the Mohegan were affiliated with that confederacy which famously includes the Abenaki, Maliseet, Passamaquoddy, Mi'kmaq, and Penobscot. The word Wabanaki means "people of the dawnland" in the Algonquin language.

To learn more about the traditions of the Wabanaki, Abenaki, Mohegan, and The Great Bear reflected in this story, visit tribal websites and the following sources:

Brooks, Lisa Tanya. *The Common Pot: The Recovery of Native Space in the Northeast*. Vol. 7. U of Minnesota Press, 2008.

Bruchac, Joseph, and Ka-Hon-Hes. *The Faithful Hunter: Abenaki Stories*. Greenfield Review Press, 1988.

Bruchac, Margaret. *Dreaming Again: Algonkian Poetry*. lulu. com, 2012.

Calloway, Colin G., ed. *Dawnland Encounters: Indians and Europeans in Northern New England.* UPNE, 2000.

Dana, Carol. *When No One is Looking.* lulu.com, 2014.

Fawcett, Melissa Jayne, and Melissa Tantaquidgeon Zobel. *Medicine Trail: The life and lessons of Gladys Tantaquidgeon.* University of Arizona Press, 2000.

Nicolar, Joseph, *The Life and Traditions of the Red Man.* C.H. Glass, 1893.

Savageau, Cheryl. *Mother/land.* Salt Publishing, 2006.

Soctomah, Donald. *Remember Me, Mikwid Hamin: Tomah Joseph's Gift to Franklin Roosevelt.* Tilbury House, 2010.

Senier, Siobhan, ed. *Dawnland Voices: An Anthology of Indigenous Writing from New England.* U of Nebraska Press, 2014.

Speck, Frank G., and Jesse Moses. "The Celestial Bear Comes Down to Earth." *Reading Publ. Mus. Art. Gall. Scient. Publ* 7 (1945)

To download a teacher's guide to this book visit: www.melissatantaquidgeonzobel.com/#!teachers-guide/cr7q

To receive a free catalog of Poisoned Pen Press titles, please provide your name and address through one of the following ways:

Phone: 1-800-421-3976
Facsimile: 1-480-949-1707
Email: info@poisonedpenpress.com
Website: www.poisonedpenpress.com

Poisoned Pen Press / The Poisoned Pencil
6962 E. First Ave. Ste 103
Scottsdale, AZ 85251

Young Adult
PAP
Z

CPSIA information can be obtained at www.ICGtesting.com
Printed in the USA
BVOW08s2314111015

421941BV00003B/65/P

9 781929 345120